AN OUNCE OF PREVENTION . . .

Madeline Hammond's beautiful eyes were flashing angrily as she demanded, "You're my foreman, Stewart. I insist you tell me the special orders you gave your top three hands."

Stewart shifted uneasily before saying, "My orders were that at least one of them must be on guard near you day and night."

"For heaven's sake, why?"

"Miss Hammond, you've been having such a good time entertaining guests that you forget Don Carlos and his guerrillas."

"You mean, you still think Don Carlos may try to make off with me?" she exclaimed.

"I don't think. I know."

Books by Zane Grey

Published by POCKET BOOKS

ZANE GREY

THE LIGHT OF WESTERN STARS

PUBLISHED BY POCKET BOOKS NEW YORK

Cover art by Murray Tinkleman

POCKET BOOKS, a Simon & Schuster division of
GULF & WESTERN CORPORATION
1230 Avenue of the Americas, New York, N.Y. 10020

ISBN: 0-671-83498-3

First Pocket Books printing March, 1962

20 19 18 17 16 15 14 13 12

POCKET and colophon are trademarks of Simon & Schuster.

Printed in the U.S.A.

CONTENTS

THE LIGHT OF WESTERN STARS

A Gentleman of the Range

When Madeline Hammond stepped from the train at El Cajon, New Mexico, it was nearly midnight, and her first impression was of a huge dark space of cool, windy emptiness, strange and silent, stretching away under great blinking white stars.

"Miss, there's no one to meet you," said the conductor, rather anxiously.

"I wired my brother," she replied. "The train being so late —perhaps he grew tired of waiting. He will be here presently. But, if he should not come—surely I can find a hotel?"

"There's lodgings to be had. Get the station agent to show you. If you'll excuse me—this is no place for a lady like you to be alone at night. It's a rough little town—mostly Mexicans, miners, cowboys. And they carouse a lot. Besides, the revolution across the border has stirred up some excitement along the line. Miss, I guess it's safe enough, if you—"

"Thank you. I am not in the least afraid."

As the train started to glide away Miss Hammond walked toward the dimly lighted station. As she was about to enter she encountered a Mexican with sombrero hiding his features and a blanket mantling his shoulders.

"Is there any one here to meet Miss Hammond?" she asked.

"*No sabe,* Señora," he replied from under the muffling blanket, and he shuffled away into the shadow.

She entered the empty waiting-room. An oil-lamp gave out a thick yellow light. The ticket window was open, and through it she saw there was neither agent nor operator in the little compartment. A telegraph instrument clicked faintly.

Madeline Hammond stood tapping a shapely foot on the floor, and with some amusement contrasted her reception in

El Cajon with what it was when she left a train at the Grand Central. The only time she could remember ever having been alone like this was once when she had missed her maid and her train at a place outside of Versailles—an adventure that had been a novel and delightful break in the prescribed routine of her much-chaperoned life. She crossed the waiting-room to a window and, holding aside her veil, looked out. At first she could descry only a few dim lights, and these blurred in her sight. As her eyes grew accustomed to the darkness she saw a superbly built horse standing near the window. Beyond was a bare square. Or, if it was a street, it was the widest one Madeline had ever seen. The dim lights shone from low, flat buildings. She made out the dark shapes of many horses, all standing motionless with drooping heads. Through a hole in the window glass came a cool breeze, and on it breathed a sound that struck coarsely upon her ear—a discordant mingling of laughter and shout, and the tramp of boots to the hard music of a phonograph.

"Western revelry," mused Miss Hammond, as she left the window. "Now, what to do? I'll wait here. Perhaps the station agent will return soon, or Alfred will come for me."

As she sat down to wait she reviewed the causes which accounted for the remarkable situation in which she found herself. That Madeline Hammond should be alone, at a late hour, in a dingy little Western railroad station, was indeed extraordinary.

The close of her débutante year had been marred by the only unhappy experience of her life—the disgrace of her brother and his leaving home. She dated the beginning of a certain thoughtful habit of mind from that time, and a dissatisfaction with the brilliant life society offered her. The change had been so gradual that it was permanent before she realized it. For a while an active outdoor life—golf, tennis, yachting—kept this realization from becoming morbid introspection. There came a time when even these lost charm for her, and then she believed she was indeed ill in mind. Travel did not help her.

There had been months of unrest, of curiously painful wonderment that her position, her wealth, her popularity no longer sufficed. She believed she had lived through the dreams and fancies of a girl to become a woman of the world. And she had gone on as before, a part of the glittering show, but

2

no longer blind to the truth—that there was nothing in her luxurious life to make it significant.

Sometimes from the depths of her there flashed up at odd moments intimations of a future revolt. She remembered one evening at the opera when the curtain had risen upon a particularly well-done piece of stage scenery—a broad space of deep desolateness, reaching away under an infinitude of night sky, illumined by stars. The suggestion it brought of vast wastes of lonely, rugged earth, of a great, blue-arched vault of starry sky, pervaded her soul with a strange, sweet peace.

When the scene was changed she lost this vague new sense of peace, and she turned away from the stage in irritation. She looked at the long, curved tier of glittering boxes that represented her world. It was a distinguished and splendid world—the wealth, fashion, culture, beauty, and blood of a nation, She, Madeline Hammond, was a part of it. She smiled, she listened, she talked to the men who from time to time strolled into the Hammond box, and she felt that there was not a moment when she was natural, true to herself. She wondered why these people could not somehow, some way be different; but she could not tell what she wanted them to be. If they had been different they would not have fitted the place; indeed, they would not have been there at all. Yet she thought wistfully that they lacked something for her.

And suddenly realizing she would marry one of these men if she did not revolt, she had been assailed by a great weariness, an icy-sickening sense that life had palled upon her. She was tired of fashionable society. She was tired of polished, imperturbable men who sought only to please her. She was tired of being fêted, admired, loved, followed, and importuned; tired of people; tired of houses, noise, ostentation, luxury. She was so tired of herself!

In the lonely distances and the passionless stars of boldly painted stage scenery she had caught a glimpse of something that stirred her soul. The feeling did not last. She could not call it back. She imagined that the very boldness of the scene had appealed to her; she divined that the man who painted it had found inspiration, joy, strength, serenity in rugged nature. And at last she knew what she needed—to be alone, to brood for long hours, to gaze out on lonely, silent, darkening stretches, to watch the stars, to face her soul, to find her real self.

3

Then it was she had first thought of visiting the brother who had gone West to cast his fortune with the cattlemen. As it happened, she had friends who were on the eve of starting for California, and she made a quick decision to travel with them. When she calmly announced her intention of going out West her mother had exclaimed in consternation; and her father, surprised into pathetic memory of the black sheep of the family, had stared at her with glistening eyes. "Why, Madeline! You want to see that wild boy!" Then he had reverted to the anger he still felt for his wayward son, and he had forbidden Madeline to go. Her mother forgot her haughty poise and dignity. Madeline, however, had exhibited a will she had never before been known to possess. She stood her ground even to reminding them that she was twenty-four and her own mistress. In the end she had prevailed, and that without betraying the real state of her mind.

Her decision to visit her brother had been too hurriedly made and acted upon for her to write him about it, and so she had telegraphed him from New York, and also, a day later, from Chicago, where her traveling friends had been delayed by illness. Nothing could have turned her back then. Madeline had planned to arrive in El Cajon on October 3rd, her brother's birthday, and she had succeeded, though her arrival occurred at the twenty-fourth hour. Her train had been several hours late. Whether or not the message had reached Alfred's hands she had no means of telling, and the thing which concerned her now was the fact that she had arrived and he was not there to meet her.

It did not take long for thought of the past to give way wholly to the reality of the present.

"I hope nothing has happened to Alfred," she said to herself. "He was well, doing splendidly, the last time he wrote. To be sure, that was a good while ago; but, then he never wrote often. He's all right. Pretty soon he'll come, and how glad I'll be! I wonder if he has changed."

As Madeline sat waiting in the yellow gloom she heard the faint, intermittent click of the telegraph instrument, the low hum of wires, the occasional stamp of an iron-shod hoof, and a distant vacant laugh rising above the sounds of the dance. These commonplace things were new to her. She became conscious of a slight quickening of her pulse. Madeline had only a limited knowledge of the West. Like all of her class, she had

4

traveled Europe and had neglected America. A few letters from her brother had confused her already vague ideas of plains and mountains, as well as of cowboys and cattle. She had been astounded at the interminable distance she had traveled, and if there had been anything attractive to look at in all that journey she had passed it in the night. And here she sat in a dingy little station, with telegraph wires moaning a lonely song in the wind.

A faint sound like the rattling of thin chains diverted Madeline's attention. At first she imagined it was made by the telegraph wires. Then she heard a step. The door swung wide; a tall man entered, and with him came the clinking rattle. She realized then that the sound came from his spurs. The man was a cowboy, and his entrance recalled vividly to her that of Dustin Farnum in the first act of "The Virginian."

"Will you please direct me to a hotel?" asked Madeline, rising.

The cowboy removed his sombrero, and the sweep he made with it and the accompanying bow, despite their exaggeration, had a kind of rude grace. He took two long strides toward her.

"Lady, are you married?"

In the past Miss Hammond's sense of humor had often helped her to overlook critical exactions natural to her breeding. She kept silence, and she imagined it was just as well that her veil hid her face at the moment. She had been prepared to find cowboys rather striking, and she had been warned not to laugh at them.

This gentleman of the range deliberately reached down and took up her left hand. Before she recovered from her start of amaze he had stripped off her glove.

"Fine spark, but no wedding ring," he drawled. "Lady, I'm glad to see you're not married."

He released her hand and returned the glove.

"You see, the only ho-tel in this here town is against boarding married women."

"Indeed?" said Madeline, trying to adjust her wits to the situation.

"It sure is," he went on. "Bad business for ho-tels to have married women. Keeps the boys away. You see, this isn't Reno."

Then he laughed rather boyishly, and from that, and the

5

way he slouched on his sombrero, Madeline realized he was half drunk. As she instinctively recoiled she not only gave him a keener glance, but stepped into a position where a better light shone on his face. It was like red bronze, bold, raw, sharp. He laughed again, as if goodnaturedly amused with himself, and the laugh scarcely changed the hard set of his features. Like that of all women whose beauty and charm had brought them much before the world, Miss Hammond's intuition had been developed until she had a delicate and exquisitely sensitive perception of the nature of men and of her effect upon them. This crude cowboy, under the influence of drink, had affronted her; nevertheless, whatever was in his mind, he meant no insult.

"I shall be greatly obliged if you will show me to the hotel," she said.

"Lady, you wait here," he replied, slowly, as if his thought did not come swiftly. "I'll go fetch the porter."

She thanked him, and as he went out, closing the door, she sat down in considerable relief. It occurred to her that she should have mentioned her brother's name. Then she fell to wondering what living with such uncouth cowboys had done to Alfred. He had been wild enough in college, and she doubted that any cowboy could have taught him much. She alone of her family had ever believed in any latent good in Alfred Hammond, and her faith had scarcely survived the two years of silence.

Waiting there, she again found herself listening to the moan of the wind through the wires. The horse outside began to pound with heavy hoofs, and once he whinnied. Then Madeline heard a rapid pattering, low at first and growing louder, which presently she recognized as the galloping of horses. She went to the window, thinking, hoping her brother had arrived. But as the clatter increased to a roar, shadows sped by—lean horses, flying manes and tails, sombreroed riders, all strange and wild in her sight. Recalling what the conductor had said, she was at some pains to quell her uneasiness. Dust clouds shrouded the dim lights in the windows. Then out of the gloom two figures appeared, one tall, the other slight. The cowboy was returning with a porter.

Heavy footsteps sounded without, and lighter ones dragging along, and then suddenly the door rasped open, jarring the whole room. The cowboy entered, pulling a disheveled figure

6

—that of a priest, a padre, whose mantle had manifestly been disarranged by the rude grasp of his captor. Plain it was that the padre was extremely terrified.

Madeline Hammond gazed in bewilderment at the little man, so pale and shaken, and a protest trembled upon her lips; but it was never uttered, for this half-drunken cowboy now appeared to be a cool, grim-smiling devil; and stretching out a long arm, he grasped her and swung her back to the bench.

"You stay there!" he ordered.

His voice, though neither brutal nor harsh nor cruel, had the unaccountable effect of making her feel powerless to move. No man had ever before addressed her in such a tone. It was the woman in her that obeyed—not the personality of proud Madeline Hammond.

The padre lifted his clasped hands as if supplicating for his life, and began to speak hurriedly in Spanish. Madeline did not understand the language. The cowboy pulled out a huge gun and brandished it in the priest's face. Then he lowered it, apparently to point it at the priest's feet. There was a red flash, and then a thundering report that stunned Madeline. The room filled with smoke and the smell of powder. Madeline did not faint or even shut her eyes, but she felt as if she were fast in a cold vise. When she could see distinctly through the smoke she experienced a sensation of immeasurable relief that the cowboy had not shot the padre. But he was still waving the gun, and now appeared to be dragging his victim toward her. What possibly could be the drunken fool's intention? This must be, this surely was a cowboy trick. She had a vague, swiftly flashing recollection of Alfred's first letters descriptive of the extravagant fun of cowboys. Then she vividly remembered a moving picture she had seen—cowboys playing a monstrous joke on a lone school-teacher. Madeline no sooner thought of it than she made certain her brother was introducing her to a little wild West amusement. She could scarcely believe it, yet it must be true. Alfred's old love of teasing her might have extended even to this outrage. Probably he stood just outside the door or window laughing at her embarrassment.

Anger checked her panic. She straightened up with what composure this surprise had left her and started for the door. But the cowboy barred her passage—grasped her arms. Then

Madeline divined that her brother could not have any knowledge of this indignity. It was no trick. It was something that was happening, that was real, that threatened she knew not what. She tried to wrench free, feeling hot all over at being handled by this drunken brute. Poise, dignity, culture—all the acquired habits of character—fled before the instinct to fight. She was athletic. She fought, She struggled desperately. But he forced her back with hands of iron. She had never known a man could be so strong. And then it was the man's coolly smiling face, the paralyzing strangeness of his manner, more than his strength, that weakened Madeline until she sank trembling against the bench.

"What—do you—mean?" she panted.

"Dearie, ease up a little on the bridle," he replied, gaily.

Madeline thought she must be dreaming. She could not think clearly. It had all been too swift, too terrible for her to grasp. Yet she not only saw this man, but also felt his powerful presence. And the shaking priest, the haze of blue smoke, the smell of powder—these were not unreal.

Then close before her eyes burst another blinding red flash, and close at her ears bellowed another report. Unable to stand, Madeline slipped down onto the bench. Her drifting faculties refused clearly to record what transpired during the next few moments; presently, however, as her mind steadied somewhat, she heard, though as in a dream, the voice of the padre hurrying over strange words. It ceased, and then the cowboy's voice stirred her.

"Lady, say *Si—Si*. Say it—quick! Say it—*Si!*"

From sheer suggestion, a force irresistible at this moment when her will was clamped by panic, she spoke the word.

"And now, lady—so we can finish this properly—what's your name?"

Still obeying mechanically, she told him.

He stared for a while, as if the name had awakened associations in a mind somewhat befogged. He leaned back unsteadily. Madeline heard the expulsion of his breath, a kind of hard puff, not unusual in drunken men.

"What name?" he demanded.

"Madeline Hammond. I am Alfred Hammond's sister."

He put his hand up and brushed at an imaginary something before his eyes. Then he loomed over her, and that hand, now shaking a little, reached out for her veil. Before he could touch it, however, she swept it back, revealing her face.

"You're—not—*Majesty* Hammond?"

How strange—stranger than anything that had ever happened to her before—was it to hear that name on the lips of this cowboy! It was a name by which she was familiarly known, though only those nearest and dearest to her had the privilege of using it. And now it revived her dulled faculties, and by an effort she regained control of herself.

"You are *Majesty* Hammond," he replied; and this time he affirmed wonderingly rather than questioned.

Madeline rose and faced him.

"Yes, I am."

He slammed his gun back into its holster.

"Well, I reckon we won't go on with it, then."

"With what, sir? And why did you force me to say *Si* to this priest?"

"I reckon that was a way I took to show him you'd be willing to get married."

"Oh! . . . You—you! . . ." Words failed her.

This appeared to galvanize the cowboy into action. He grasped the padre and led him toward the door, cursing and threatening, no doubt enjoining secrecy. Then he pushed him across the threshold and stood there breathing hard and wrestling with himself.

"Here—wait—wait a minute, Miss—Miss Hammond," he said, huskily. "You could fall into worse company than mine —though I reckon you sure think not. I'm pretty drunk, but I'm—all right otherwise. Just wait—a minute."

She stood quivering and blazing with wrath, and watched this savage fight his drunkenness. He acted like a man who had been suddenly shocked into a rational state of mind, and he was now battling with himself to hold on to it. Madeline saw the dark, damp hair lift from his brows as he held it up to the cool wind. Above him she saw the white stars in the deep-blue sky, and they seemed as unreal to her as any other thing in this strange night. They were cold, brilliant, aloof, distant; and looking at them, she felt her wrath lessen and die and leave her calm.

The cowboy turned and began to talk.

"You see—I was pretty drunk," he labored. "There was a *fiesta*—and a wedding. I do fool things when I'm drunk. I

9

made a fool bet I'd marry the first girl who came to town. . . .
If you hadn't worn that veil—the fellows were joshing
me—and Ed Linton was getting married—and everybody always wants to gamble. . . . I must have been pretty drunk."

After the one look at her when she had first put aside her
veil he had not raised his eyes to her face. The cool audacity
had vanished in what was either excessive emotion or the
maudlin condition peculiar to some men when drunk. He
could not stand still; perspiration collected in beads upon his
forehead; he kept wiping his face with his scarf, and he
breathed like a man after violent exertions.

"You see—I was pretty—" he began.

"Explanations are not necessary," she interrupted. "I am
very tired—distressed. The hour is late. Have you the slightest
idea what it means to be a gentleman?"

His bronzed face burned to a flaming crimson.

"Is my brother here—in town tonight?" Madeline went on.

"No. He's at his ranch."

"But I wired him."

"Like as not the message is over at his box at the P.O. He'll
be in town tomorrow. He's shipping cattle for Stillwell."

"Meanwhile I must go to a hotel. Will you please—"

If he heard her last words he showed no evidence of it. A
noise outside had attracted his attention. Madeline listened.
Low voices of men, the softer liquid tones of a woman, drifted in through the open door. Evidently the speakers were approaching the station. Footsteps crunching in gravel attested
to this, and quicker steps, coming with deep tones of men in
anger, told of a quarrel. Then the woman's voice, hurried and
broken, rising higher, was eloquent of vain appeal.

The cowboy's demeanor startled Madeline into anticipation
of something dreadful. She was not deceived. From outside
came the sound of a scuffle, a muffled shot, a groan, the thud
of a falling body, a woman's low cry, and footsteps padding
away in rapid retreat.

Madeline Hammond leaned weakly back in her seat, cold
and sick, and for a moment her ears throbbed to the tramp of
the dancers across the way and the rhythm of the cheap
music. Then into the open door-place flashed a girl's tragic
face, lighted by dark eyes and framed by dusky hair. The girl
reached a slim brown hand round the side of the door and

10

held on as if to support herself. A long black scarf accentuated her gaudy attire.

"Señor—Gene!" she exclaimed; and breathless glad recognition made a sudden break in her terror.

"Bonita!" The cowboy leaped to her. "Girl! Are you hurt?"

"No, Señor."

He took hold of her. "I heard—somebody got shot. Was it Danny?"

"No, Señor."

"Did Danny do the shooting? Tell me, girl."

"No, Señor."

"I'm sure glad. I thought Danny was mixed up in that. He had Stillwell's money for the boys—I was afraid. . . . Say, Bonita, but *you'll* get in trouble. Who was with you! What did you do?"

"Señor Gene—they Don Carlos *vaqueros*—they quarrel over me. I only dance a leetle, smile a leetle and they quarrel. I beg they be good—watch out for Sheriff Hawe . . . and now Sheriff Hawe put me in jail. I so frighten; he try make leetle love to Bonita once, and now he hate me like he hate Señor Gene."

"Pat Hawe won't put you in jail. Take my horse and hit the Peloncillo trail. Bonita, promise to stay away from El Cajon."

"*Si*, Señor."

He led her outside. Madeline heard the horse snort and champ his bit. The cowboy spoke low; only a few words were intelligible—"stirrups . . . wait . . . out of town . . . mountain . . . trail . . . now ride!"

A moment's silence ensued, and was broken by a pounding of hoofs, a pattering of gravel. Then Madeline saw a big, dark horse run into the wide space. She caught a glimpse of windswept scarf and hair, a little form low down in the saddle. The horse was outlined in black against the line of dim lights. There was something wild and splendid in his flight.

Directly the cowboy appeared again in the doorway.

"Miss Hammond, I reckon we want to rustle out of here. Been bad goings-on. And there's a train due."

She hurried into the open air, not daring to look back or to either side. Her guide strode swiftly. She had almost to run to keep up with him. Many conflicting emotions confused her. She had a strange sense of this stalking giant beside her, silent except for his jangling spurs. She had a strange feeling of the

11

cool, sweet wind and the white stars. Was it only her disordered fancy, or did these wonderful stars open and shut? She had a queer, disembodied thought that somewhere in ages back, in another life, she had seen these stars. The night seemed dark, yet there was a pale, luminous light—a light from the stars—and she fancied it would always haunt her.

Suddenly aware that she had been led beyond the line of houses, she spoke:

"Where are you taking me?"

"To Florence Kingsley," he replied.

"Who is she?"

"I reckon she's your brother's best friend out here."

Madeline kept pace with the cowboy for a few moments longer, and then she stopped. It was as much from necessity to catch her breath as it was from recurring fear. All at once she realized what little use her training had been for such an experience as this. The cowboy, missing her, came back the few intervening steps. Then he waited, still silent, looming beside her.

"It's so dark, so lonely," she faltered. "How do I know . . . what warrant can you give me that you—that no harm will befall me if I go farther?"

"None, Miss Hammond, except that I've seen your face."

2

A Secret Kept

Because of that singular reply Madeline found faith to go farther with the cowboy. But at the moment she really did not think about what he had said. Any answer to her would have served if it had been kind. His silence had augmented her nervousness, compelling her to voice her fear. Still, even if he had not replied at all she would have gone on with him. She shuddered at the idea of returning to the station, where she believed there had been murder; she could hardly have forced herself to go back to those dim lights of the street; she did not want to wander around alone in the dark.

And as she walked on into the windy darkness, much relieved that he had answered as he had, reflecting that he had yet to prove his words true, she began to grasp the deeper significance of them. There was a revival of pride that made her feel that she ought to scorn to think at all about such a man. But Madeline Hammond discovered that thought was involuntary, that there were feelings in her never dreamed of before this night.

Presently Madeline's guide turned off the walk and rapped at a door of a low-roofed house.

"Hullo—who's there?" a deep voice answered.

"Gene Stewart," said the cowboy. "Call Florence—quick!"

Thump of footsteps followed, a tap on a door, and voices. Madeline heard a woman exclaim: "Gene! here when there's a dance in town! Something wrong out on the range." A light flared up and shone bright through a window. In another moment there came a patter of soft steps, and the door opened to disclose a woman holding a lamp.

"Gene! Al's not—"

"Al is all right," interrupted the cowboy.

Madeline had two sensations then—one of wonder at the note of alarm and love in the woman's voice, and the other of unutterable relief to be safe with a friend of her brother's.

"It's Al's sister—came on tonight's train," the cowboy was saying. "I happened to be at the station, and I've fetched her up to you."

Madeline came forward out of the shadow.

"Not—not really *Majesty* Hammond!" exclaimed Florence Kingsley. She nearly dropped the lamp, and she looked and looked, astounded beyond belief.

"Yes, I am really she," replied Madeline. "My train was late, and for some reaon Alfred did not meet me. Mr.—Mr. Stewart saw fit to bring me to you instead of taking me to a hotel."

"Oh, I'm so glad to meet you," replied Florence, warmly. "Do come in. I'm so surprised, I forgot my manners. Why, Al never mentioned your coming."

"He surely could not have received my messages," said Madeline, as she entered.

The cowboy, who came in with her satchel, had to stoop to

enter the door, and, once in, he seemed to fill the room. Florence set the lamp down upon the table. Madeline saw a young woman with a smiling, friendly face, and a profusion of fair hair hanging down over her dressing-gown.

"Oh, but Al will be glad!" cried Florence. "Why, you are white as a sheet. You must be tired. What a long wait you had at the station! I heard the train come in hours ago as I was going to bed. That station is lonely at night. If I had known you were coming! Indeed, you are very pale. Are you ill?"

"No. Only I am very tired. Traveling so far by rail is harder than I imagined. I did have rather a long wait after arriving at the station, but I can't say that it was lonely."

Florence Kingsley searched Madeline's face with keen eyes, and then took a long, significant look at the silent Stewart. With that she deliberately and quietly closed a door leading into another room.

"Miss Hammond, what has happened?" She had lowered her voice.

"I do not wish to recall all that has happened," replied Madeline. "I shall tell Alfred, however, that I would rather have met a hostile Apache than a cowboy."

"Please don't tell Al that!" cried Florence. Then she grasped Stewart and pulled him close to the light. "Gene, you're drunk!"

"I was pretty drunk," he replied, hanging his head.

"Oh, what have you done?"

"Now, see here, Flo, I only—"

"I don't want to know. I'd tell it. Gene, aren't you ever going to learn decency? Aren't you ever going to stop drinking! You'll lose all your friends. Stillwell has stuck to you. Al's been your best friend. Molly and I have pleaded with you, and now you've gone and done—God knows what!"

"What do women want to wear veils for?" he growled. "I'd have known her but for that veil."

"And you wouldn't have insulted *her*. But you would the next girl who came along. Gene, you are hopeless. Now, you get out of here and don't ever come back."

"Flo!" he entreated.

"I mean it."

"I reckon then I'll come back tomorrow and take my medicine," he replied.

"Don't you dare!" she cried.

14

Stewart went out and closed the door.

"Miss Hammond, you—you don't know how this hurts me," said Florence. "What you must think of us! It's so unlucky that you should have had this happen right at first. Now, maybe you won't have the heart to stay. Oh, I've known more than one Eastern girl to go home without ever learning what we really are out here. Miss Hammond, Gene Stewart is a fiend when he's drunk. All the same I *know,* whatever he did, he meant no shame to you. Come now, don't think about it again tonight." She took up the lamp and led Madeline into a little room. "This is out West," she went on, smiling, as she indicated the few furnishings; "but you can rest. You're perfectly safe. Won't you let me help you undress—can't I do anything for you?"

"You are very kind, thank you, but I can manage," replied Madeline.

"Well, then, good night. The sooner I go the sooner you'll rest. Just forget what happened and think how fine a surprise you're to give your brother tomorrow."

With that she slipped out and softly shut the door.

As Madeline laid her watch on the bureau she noticed that the time was past two o'clock. It seemed long since she had gotten off the train. When she had turned out the lamp and crept wearily into bed she knew what it was to be utterly spent. She was too tired to move a finger. But her brain whirled.

She had at first no control over it, and a thousand thronging sensations came and went and recurred with little logical relation. There were the roar of the train; the feeling of being lost, the sound of pounding hoofs; a picture of her brother's face as she had last seen it five years before; a long, dim line of lights; the jingle of silver spurs; night, wind, darkness, stars. Then the gloomy station, the shadowy blanketed Mexican, the empty room, the dim lights across the square, the tramp of the dancers and vacant laughs and discordant music, the door flung wide and the entrance of the cowboy. She did not recall how he had looked or what he had done. And the next instant she saw him cool, smiling, devilish—saw him in violence; the next his bigness, his apparel, his physical being were vague as outlines in a dream. The white face of the padre flashed along in the train of thought, and it brought the same dull, half-blind, indefinable state of mind subsequent to

15

that last nerve-breaking pistol-shot. That passed, and then clear and vivid rose memories of the rest that had happened —strange voices betraying fury of men, a deadened report, a moan of mortal pain, a woman's poignant cry. And Madeline saw the girl's great tragic eyes and the wild flight of the big horse into the blackness, and the dark, stalking figure of the silent cowboy, and the white stars that seemed to look down remorselessly.

This tide of memory rolled over Madeline again and again, and gradually lost its power and faded. All distress left her, and she felt herself drifting. How black the room was—as black with her eyes open as it was when they were shut! And the silence—it was like a cloak. There was absolutely no sound. She was in another world from that which she knew. She thought of this fair-haired Florence and of Alfred; and, wondering about them, she dropped to sleep.

When she awakened the room was bright with sunlight. A cool wind blowing across the bed caused her to put her hands under the blanket. She was lazily and dreamily contemplating the mud walls of this little room when she remembered where she was and how she had come there.

How great a shock she had been subjected to was manifest in a sensation of disgust that overwhelmed her. She even shut her eyes to try and blot out the recollection. She felt that she had been contaminated.

Presently Madeline Hammond again awoke to the fact she had learned the preceding night—that there were emotions to which she had heretofore been a stranger. She did not try to analyze them, but she exercised her self-control to such good purpose that by the time she had dressed she was outwardly her usual self. She scarcely remembered when she had found it necessary to control her emotions. There had been no trouble, no excitement, no unpleasantness in her life. It had been ordered for her—tranquil, luxurious, brilliant, varied, yet always the same.

She was not surprised to find the hour late, and was going to make inquiry about her brother when a voice arrested her. She recognized Miss Kingsley's voice addressing some one outside, and it had a sharpness she had not noted before.

"So you came back, did you? Well, you don't look very proud of yourself this mawnin'. Gene Stewart, you look like a coyote."

16

"Say, Flo, if I am a coyote I'm not going to sneak," he said.

"What 'd you come for?" she demanded.

"I said I was coming round to take my medicine."

"Meaning you'll not run from Al Hammond? Gene, your skull is as thick as an old cow's. Al will never know anything about what you did to his sister unless you tell him. And if you do that he'll shoot you. *She* won't give you away. She's a thoroughbred. Why, she was so white last night I thought she'd drop at my feet, but she never blinked an eyelash. I'm a woman, Gene Stewart, and if I could feel like Miss Hammond I know how awful an ordeal she must have had. Why, she's one of the most beautiful, most sought after, the most exclusive women in New York City. There's a crowd of millionaires and lords and dukes after her. How terrible it'd be for a woman like her to be kissed by a drunken cowpuncher! I say it—"

"Flo, I never insulted her that way," broke out Stewart.

"It was worse, then?" she queried, sharply.

"I made a bet that I'd marry the first girl who came to town. I was on the watch and pretty drunk. When she came—well, I got Padre Marcos and tried to bully her into marrying me."

"Oh, Lord!" Florence gasped. "It's worse than I feared. . . . Gene, Al will kill you."

"That'll be a good thing," replied the cowboy, dejectedly.

"Gene Stewart, it certainly would, unless you turn over a new leaf," retorted Florence. "But don't be a fool." And here she became earnest and appealing. "Go away, Gene. Go join the rebels across the border—you're always threatening that. Anyhow, don't stay here and run any chance of stirring Al up. He'd kill you just the same as you would kill another man for insulting your sister. Don't make trouble for Al. That'd only make sorrow for *her*, Gene."

The subtle import was not lost upon Madeline. She was distressed because she could not avoid hearing what was not meant for her ears. She made an effort not to listen, and it was futile.

"Flo, you can't see this a man's way," he replied, quietly. "I'll stay and take my medicine."

"Gene, I could sure swear at you or any other pighead of a cowboy. Listen. My brother-in-law, Jack, heard something of what I said to you last night. He doesn't like you. I'm afraid

17

he'll tell Al. For Heaven's sake, man, go downtown and shut him up and yourself, too."

Then Madeline heard her come into the house and presently rap on the door and call softly:

"Miss Hammond. Are you awake?"

"Awake and dressed, Miss Kingsley. Come in."

"Oh! You've rested. You look so—so different. I'm sure glad. Come out now. We'll have breakfast, and then you may expect to meet your brother any moment."

"Wait, please. I heard you speaking to Mr. Stewart. It was unavoidable. But I am glad. I must see him. Will you please ask him to come into the parlor a moment?"

"Yes," replied Florence, quickly; and as she turned at the door she flashed at Madeline a woman's meaning glance. "Make him keep his mouth shut!"

Presently there were slow, reluctant steps ouside the front door, then a pause, and the door opened. Stewart stood bareheaded in the sunlight. Madeline remembered with a kind of shudder the tall form, the embroidered buckskin vest, the red scarf, the bright leather wristbands, the wide silver-buckled belt and chaps. Her glance seemed to run over him swift as lightning. But as she saw his face now she did not recognize it. The man's presence roused in her a revolt. Yet something in her, the incomprehensible side of her nature, thrilled in the look of this splendid dark-faced barbarian.

"Mr. Stewart, will you please come in?" she asked, after that long pause.

"I reckon not," he said. The hopelessness of his tone meant that he knew he was not fit to enter a room with her, and did not care or cared too much.

Madeline went to the door. The man's face was hard, yet it was sad, too. And it touched her.

"I shall not tell my brother of your—your rudeness to me," she began. It was impossible for her to keep the chill out of her voice, to speak with other than the pride and aloofness of her class. Nevertheless, despite her loathing, when she had spoken so far it seemed that kindness and pity followed involuntarily. "I choose to overlook what you did because you were not wholly accountable, and because there must be no trouble between Alfred and you. May I rely on you to keep silence and to seal the lips of that priest? And you know there

18

was a man killed or injured there last night. I want to forget that dreadful thing. I don't want it known that I heard—"

"The Greaser didn't die," interrupted Stewart.

"Ah! then that's not so bad, after all. I am glad for the sake of your friend—the little Mexican girl."

A slow scarlet wave overspread his face, and his shame was painful to see. That fixed in Madeline's mind a conviction that if he was a heathen he was not wholly bad. And it made so much difference that she smiled down at him.

"You will spare me further distress, will you not, please?"

His hoarse reply was incoherent, but she needed only to see his working face to know his remorse and gratitude.

Madeline went back to her room; and presently Florence came for her, and directly they were sitting at breakfast. Madeline Hammond's impression of her brother's friend had to be reconstructed in the morning light. She felt a wholesome, frank, sweet nature. She liked the slow Southern drawl. And she was puzzled to know whether Florence Kingsley was pretty or striking or unusual. She had a youthful glow and flush, the clear tan of outdoors, a face that lacked the soft curves and lines of Eastern women, and her eyes were light gray, like crystal, steady, almost piercing, and her hair was a beautiful bright, waving mass.

Florence's sister was the elder of the two, a stout woman with a strong face and quiet eyes. It was a simple fare and service they gave to their guest; but they made no apologies for that. Indeed, Madeline felt their simplicity to be restful. She was sated with respect, sick of admiration, tired of adulation; and it was good to see that these Western women treated her as very likely they would have treated any other visitor. They were sweet, kind; and what Madeline had at first thought was a lack of expression or vitality she soon discovered to be the natural reserve of women who did not live superficial lives. Florence was breezy and frank, her sister quaint and not given much to speech. Madeline thought she would like to have these women near her if she were ill or in trouble. And she reproached herself for a fastidiousness, a hypercritical sense of refinement that could not help distinguishing what these women lacked.

"Can you ride?" Florence was asking. "That's what a Westerner always asks any one from the East. Can you ride like a man—astride, I mean? Oh, that's fine. You look strong

19

enough to hold a horse. We have some fine horses out here. I reckon when Al comes we'll go out to Bill Stillwell's ranch. We'll have to go, whether we want to or not, for when Bill learns you are here he'll just pack us all off. You'll love old Bill. His ranch is run down, but the range and the rides up in the mountains—they are beautiful. We'll hunt and climb, and most of all we'll ride. I love a horse—I love the wind in my face, and a wide stretch with the mountains beckoning. You must have the best horse on the ranges. And that means a scrap between Al and Bill and all the cowboys. We don't all agree about horses, except in case of Gene Stewart's iron-gray."

"Does Mr. Stewart own the best horse in the country?" asked Madeline. Again she had an inexplicable thrill as she remembered the wild flight of Stewart's big dark steed and rider.

"Yes, and that's all he does own," replied Florence. "Gene can't keep even a quirt. But he sure loves that horse and calls him—"

At this juncture a sharp knock on the parlor door interrupted the conversation. Florence's sister went to open it. She returned presently and said:

"It's Gene. He's been dawdlin' out there on the front porch and he knocked to let us know Miss Hammond's brother is comin'."

Florence hurried into the parlor, followed by Madeline. The door stood open, and disclosed Stewart sitting on the porch steps. From down the road came a clatter of hoofs. Madeline looked out over Florence's shoulder and saw a cloud of dust approaching, and in it she distinguished outlines of horses and riders. A warmth spread over her, a little tingle of gladness, and the feeling recalled her girlish love for her brother. What would he be like after long years?

"Gene, has Jack kept his mouth shut?" queried Florence; and again Madeline was aware of a sharp ring in the girl's voice.

"No," replied Stewart.

"Gene! You won't let it come to a fight? Al can be managed. But Jack hates you and he'll have his friends with him."

"There won't be any fight."

"Use your brains now," added Florence; and then she turned to push Madeline gently back into the parlor.

20

Madeline's glow of warmth changed to a blank dismay. Was she to see her brother act with the violence she now associated with cowboys? The clatter of hoofs stopped before the door. Looking out, Madeline saw a bunch of dusty, wiry horses pawing the gravel and tossing lean heads. Her swift glance ran over the lithe horsemen, trying to pick out the one who was her brother. But she could not. Her glance, however, caught the same rough dress and hard aspect that characterized the cowboy Stewart. Then one rider threw his bridle, leaped from the saddle, and came bounding up the porch steps. Florence met him at the door.

"Hello, Flo. Where is she?" he called, eagerly. With that he looked over her shoulder to espy Madeline. He actually jumped at her. She hardly knew the tall form and the bronzed face, but the warm flash of blue eyes was familiar. As for him, he had no doubt of his sister, it appeared, for with broken welcome he threw his arms around her, then held her off and looked searchingly at her.

"Well, sister," he began, when Florence turned hurriedly from the door and interrupted him.

"Al, I think you'd better stop the wrangling out there."

He stared at her, appeared suddenly to hear the loud voices from the street, and then, releasing Madeline, he said:

"By George! I forgot, Flo. There is a little business to see to. Keep my sister in here, please, and don't be fussed up now."

He went out on the porch and called to his men:

"Shut off your wind, Jack! And you, too, Blaze! I didn't want you fellows to come here. But as you would come, you've got to shut up. This is my business."

Whereupon he turned to Stewart, who was sitting on the fence.

"Hello, Stewart!" he said.

It was a greeting; but there was that in the voice which alarmed Madeline.

Stewart leisurely got up and leisurely advanced to the porch.

"Hello, Hammond!" he drawled.

"Drunk again last night?"

"Well, if you want to know, and if it's any of your mix, yes, I was—pretty drunk," replied Stewart.

It was a kind of cool speech that showed the cowboy in

control of himself and master of the situation—not an easy speech to follow up with undue inquisitiveness. There was a short silence.

"Damn it, Stewart," said the speaker, presently, "here's the situation: It's all over town that you met my sister last night at the station and—and insulted her. Jack's got it in for you, so have these other boys. But it's my affair. Understand, I didn't fetch them here. They can see you square yourself, or else—Gene, you've been on the wrong trail for some time, drinking and all that. You're going to the bad. But Bill thinks, and I think, you're still a man. We never knew you to lie. Now what have you to say for yourself?"

"Nobody is insinuating that I *am* a liar?" drawled Stewart.

"No."

"Well, I'm glad to hear that. You see, Al, I was pretty drunk last night, but not drunk enough to forget the least thing I did. I told Pat Hawe so this morning when he was curious. And that's polite for me to be to Pat. Well, I found Miss Hammond waiting alone at the station. She wore a veil, but I knew she was a lady, of course. I imagine, now that I think of it, that Miss Hammond found my gallantry rather startling, and—"

At this point Madeline, answering to unconsidered impulse, eluded Florence and walked out upon the porch.

Sombreros flashed down and the lean horses jumped.

"Gentlemen," said Madeline, rather breathlessly; and it did not add to her calmness to feel a hot flush in her cheeks, "I am very new to Western ways, but I think you are laboring under a mistake, which, in justice to Mr. Stewart, I want to correct. Indeed, he was rather—rather abrupt and strange when he came up to me last night; but as I understand him now, I can attribute that to his gallantry. He was somewhat wild and sudden and—sentimental in his demand to protect me—and it was not clear whether he meant his protection for last night or forever; but I am happy to say he offered me no word that was not honorable. And he saw me safely here to Miss Kingsley's home."

3

Sister and Brother

Then Madeline returned to the little parlor with the brother whom she had hardly recognized.

"Majesty!" he exclaimed. "To think of your being here!"

The warmth stole back along her veins. She remembered how that pet name had sounded from the lips of this brother who had given it to her.

"Alfred!"

Then his words of gladness at the sight of her, his chagrin at not being at the train to welcome her, were not so memorable of him as the way he clasped her, for he had held her that way the day he left home, and she had not forgotten. But now he was so much taller and bigger, so dusty and strange and different and forceful, that she could scarcely think him the same man. She even had a humorous thought that here was another cowboy bullying her, and this time it was her brother.

"Dear old girl," he said, more calmly, as he let her go, "you haven't changed at all, except to grow lovelier. Only you're a woman now, and you've fulfilled the name I gave you. God! how sight of you brings back home! It seems a hundred years since I left. I missed you more than all the rest."

Madeline seemed to feel with his every word that she was remembering him. She was so amazed at the change in him that she could not believe her eyes. She saw a bronzed, strong-jawed, eagle-eyed man, stalwart, superb of height, and, like the cowboys, belted, booted, spurred. And there was something hard as iron in his face that quivered with his words. It seemed that only in those moments when the hard lines broke and softened could she see resemblance to the face she remembered. It was his manner, the tone of his voice, and the tricks of speech that proved to her he was really Alfred.

She had bidden goodby to a disgraced, disinherited, dissolute boy. Well she remembered the handsome pale face with its weakness and shadows and careless smile, with the ever-present cigarette hanging between the lips. The years had passed, and now she saw him a man—the West had made him a man. And Madeline Hammond felt a strong, passionate gladness and gratefulness, and a direct check to her suddenly inspired hatred of the West.

"Majesty, it was good of you to come. I'm all broken up. How did you ever do it? But never mind that now. Tell me about that brother of mine."

And Madeline told him, and then about her sister Helen. Question after question he fired at her; and she told him of her mother; of Aunt Grace, who had died a year ago; of his old friends, married, scattered, vanished. But she did not tell him of his father, for he did not ask.

Quite suddenly the rapid-fire questioning ceased; he choked, was silent a moment, and then burst into tears. It seemed to her that a long, stored-up bitterness was flooding away. It hurt her to see him—hurt her more to hear him. And in the succeeding few moments she grew closer to him than she had ever been in the past. Had her father and mother done right by him? Her pulse stirred with unwonted quickness. She did not speak, but she kissed him, which, for her, was an indication of unusual feeling. And when he recovered command over his emotions he made no reference to his breakdown, nor did she. But that scene struck deep into Madeline Hammond's heart. Through it she saw what he had lost and gained.

"Alfred, why did you not answer my last letters?" asked Madeline. "I had not heard from you for two years."

"So long? How time flies! Well, things went bad with me about the last time I heard from you. I always intended to write some day, but I never did."

"Things went wrong? Tell me."

"Majesty, you mustn't worry yourself with my troubles. I want you to enjoy your stay and not be bothered with my difficulties."

"Please tell me. I suspected something had gone wrong. That is partly why I decided to come out."

"All right; if you must know," he began; and it seemed to Madeline that there was a gladness in his decision to unburden himself. "You remember all about my little ranch, and that for a while I did well raising stock? I wrote you all that. Majesty, a man makes enemies anywhere. Perhaps an Eastern man in the West can make, if not so many, certainly more bitter ones. At any rate, I made several. There was a cattleman, Ward by name—he's gone now—and he and I had trouble over cattle. That gave me a back-set. Pat Hawe, the sheriff here, has been instrumental in hurting my business. He's not so much of a rancher, but he has influence at Santa Fé and El Paso and Douglas. I made an enemy of him. I never did anything to him. He hates Gene Stewart, and upon one occasion I spoiled a little plot of his to get Gene in his clutches. The real reason for his animosity toward me is that he loves Florence, and Florence is going to marry me."

"Alfred!"

"What's the matter, Majesty? Didn't Florence impress you favorably?" he asked, with a keen glance.

"Why—yes, indeed. I like her. But I did not think of her in relation to you—that way. I am greatly surprised. Alfred, is she well born? What connections?"

"Florence is just a girl of ordinary people. She was born in Kentucky, was brought up in Texas. My aristocratic and wealthy family would scorn—"

"Alfred, you are still a Hammond," said Madeline, with uplifted head.

Alfred laughed. "We won't quarrel, Majesty. I remember you, and in spite of your pride you've got a heart. If you stay here a month you'll love Florence Kingsley. I want you to know she's had a great deal to do with straightening me up. . . . Well, to go on with my story. There's Don Carlos, a Mexican rancher, and he's my worst enemy. For that matter, he's as bad an enemy of Bill Stillwell and other ranchers. Stillwell, by the way, is my friend and one of the finest men on earth. I got in debt to Don Carlos before I knew he was so mean. In the first place I lost money at faro—I gambled some when I came West—and then I made unwise cattle deals. Don Carlos is a wily Greaser, he knows the ranges, he has the water, and he is dishonest. So he outfigured me. And now I am practically ruined. He has not gotten possession of my ranch, but that's only a matter of time, pending lawsuits at Santa Fé. At present I have a few hundred cattle running on Stillwell's range, and I am his foreman."

"Foreman?" queried Madeline.

"I am simply boss of Stillwell's cowboys, and right glad of my job."

Madeline was conscious of an inward burning. It required an effort to retain her outward tranquillity. Annoying consciousness she had also of the returning sense of new disturbing emotions. She began to see just how walled in from unusual thought-provoking incident and sensation had been her exclusive life.

"Cannot your property be reclaimed?" she asked. "How much do you owe?"

"Ten thousand dollars would clear me and give me another start. But, Majesty, in this country that's a good deal of money, and I haven't been able to raise it. Stillwell's in worse shape than I am."

Madeline went over to Alfred and put her hands on his shoulders.

"We must not be in debt."

He stared at her as if her words had recalled something long forgotten. Then he smiled.

"How imperious you are! I'd forgotten just who my beautiful sister really is. Majesty, you're not going to ask me to take money from you?"

"I am."

"Well, I'll not do it. I never did, even when I was in college, and then there wasn't much beyond me."

"Listen, Alfred," she went on, earnestly, "this is entirely different. I had only an allowance then. You had no way to know that since I last wrote you I had come into my inheritance from Aunt Grace. It was—well, that doesn't matter. Only, I haven't been able to spend half the income. It's mine. It's not father's money. You will make me very happy if you'll consent. Alfred, I'm so—so amazed at the change in you. I'm so happy. You must never take a backward step from now on. What is ten thousand dollars to me? Sometimes I spend that in a month. I throw money away. If you let me help you it will be doing me good as well as you. Please, Alfred."

He kissed her, evidently surprised at her earnestness. And indeed Madeline was surprised herself. Once started, her speech had flowed.

"You always were the best of fellows, Majesty. And if you really care—if you really want to help me I'll be only too glad to accept. It will be fine. Florence will go wild. And that Greaser won't harass me any more. Majesty, pretty soon some titled fellow will be spending your money; I may as well take a little before he gets it all," he finished, jokingly.

"What do you know about me?" she asked, lightly.

"More than you think. Even if we are lost out here in the woolly West we get news. Everybody knows about Anglesbury. And that Dago duke who chased you all over Europe, that Lord Castleton has the running now and seems about to win. How about it, Majesty?"

Madeline detected a hint that suggested scorn in his gay speech. And deep in his searching glance she saw a flame. She became thoughtful. She had forgotten Castleton, New York society.

"Alfred," she began, seriously, "I don't believe any titled gentleman will ever spend my money, as you elegantly express it."

"I don't care for that. It's you!" he cried, passionately, and he grasped her with a violence that startled her. He was white; his eyes were now like fire. "You are so splendid—so wonderful. People called you the American Beauty, but you're more than that. You're the American Girl! Majesty, marry no man unless you love him, and love an *American*. Stay away from Europe long enough to learn to know the men—the real men of your own country."

"Alfred, I'm afraid there are not always real men and real love for American girls in international marriages. But Helen knows this. It'll be her choice. She'll be miserable if she marries Anglesbury."

"It'll serve her just right," declared her brother. "Helen was always crazy for glitter, adulation, fame. I'll gamble she never saw more of Anglesbury than the gold and ribbons on his breast."

"I am sorry. Anglesbury is a gentleman; but it is the money he wanted, I think. Alfred, tell me how you came to know about me, 'way out here? You may be assured I was astonished to find that Miss Kingsley knew me as Majesty Hammond."

"I imagine it was a surprise," he replied, with a laugh. "I told Florence about you—gave her a picture of you. And, of course, being a woman, she showed the picture and talked. She's in love with you. Then, my dear sister, we do get New

27

York papers out here occasionally, and we can see and read. You may not be aware that you and your society friends are objects of intense interest in the U.S. in general, and the West in particular. The papers are full of you, and perhaps a lot of things you never did."

"That Mr. Stewart knew, too. He said, 'You're not *Majesty* Hammond?' "

"Never mind his impudence!" exclaimed Alfred; and then again he laughed. "Gene is all right, only you've got to know him. I'll tell you what he did. He got hold of one of those newspaper pictures of you—the one in the *Times;* he took it away from here, and in spite of Florence he wouldn't fetch it back. It was a picture of you in riding-habit with your blue-ribbon horse, White Stockings—remember? It was taken at Newport. Well, Stewart tacked the picture up in his bunk-house and named his beautiful horse Majesty. All the cow-boys knew it. They would see the picture and tease him un-mercifully. But he didn't care. One day I happened to drop in on him and found him just recovering from a carouse. I saw the picture, too, and I said to him, 'Gene, if my sister knew you were a drunkard she'd not be proud of having her picture stuck up in your room.' Majesty, he did not touch a drop for a month, and when he did drink again he took the picture down, and he has never put it back."

Madeline smiled at her brother's amusement, but she did not reply. She simply could not adjust herself to these queer free Western ways. Her brother had eloquently pleaded for her to keep herself above a sordid and brilliant marriage, yet he not only allowed a cowboy to keep her picture in his room, but actually spoke of her and used her name in a temperance lecture. Madeline just escaped feeling disgust. She was saved from this, however, by nothing less than her brother's naïve gladness that through subtle suggestion Stewart had been per-suaded to be good for a month. Something made up of Stew-art's effrontery to her; of Florence Kingsley meeting her, frankly as it were, as an equal; of the elder sister's slow, quiet acceptance of this visitor who had been honored at the courts of royalty; of that faint hint of scorn in Alfred's voice, and his amused statement in regard to her picture and the name Maj-esty—something made up of all these stung Madeline Ham-mond's pride, alienated her for an instant, and then stimulated

28

her intelligence, excited her interest, and made her resolve to learn a little about this incomprehensible West.

"Majesty, I must run down to the siding," he said, consulting his watch. "We're loading a shipment of cattle. I'll be back by supper-time and bring Stillwell with me. You'll like him. Give me the check for your trunk."

She went into the little bedroom and, taking up her bag, she got out a number of checks.

"Six! Six trunks!" he exclaimed. "Well, I'm very glad you intend to stay awhile. Say, Majesty, it will take me as long to realize who you really are as it'll take to break you of being a tenderfoot. I hope you packed a riding-suit. If not you'll have to wear trousers! You'll have to do that, anyway, when we go up in the mountains."

"No!"

"You sure will, as Florence says."

"We shall see about that. I don't know what's in the trunks. I never pack anything. My dear brother, what do I have maids for?"

"How did it come that you didn't travel with a maid?"

"I wanted to be alone. But don't you worry. I shall be able to look after myself. I dare say it will be good for me."

She went to the gate with him.

"What a shaggy, dusty horse! He's wild, too. Do you let him stand that way without being haltered? I should think he would run off."

"Tenderfoot! You'll be great fun, Majesty, especially for the cowboys."

"Oh, will I?" she asked, constrainedly.

"Yes, and in three days they will be fighting one another over you. That's going to worry me. Cowboys fall in love with a plain woman, an ugly woman, any woman, so long as she's young. And you! Good Lord! They'll go out of their heads."

"You are pleased to be facetious, Alfred. I think I have had quite enough of cowboys, and I haven't been here twenty-four hours."

"Don't think too much of first impressions. That was my mistake when I arrived here. Good-by. I'll go now. Better rest awhile. You look tired."

The horse started as Alfred put his foot in the stirrup and was running when the rider slipped his leg over the saddle.

Madeline watched him in admiration. He seemed to be loosely fitted to the saddle, moving with the horse.

"I suppose that's a cowboy's style. It pleases me," she said. "How different from the seat of Eastern riders!"

Then Madeline sat upon the porch and fell to interested observation of her surrounding. Near at hand it was decidedly not prepossessing. The street was deep in dust, and the cool wind whipped up little puffs. The houses along this street were all low, square, flat-roofed structures made of some kind of red cement. It occurred to her suddenly that this building-material must be the adobe she had read about. There was no person in sight. The long street appeared to have no end, though the line of houses did not extend far. Once she heard a horse trotting at some distance, and several times the ringing of a locomotive bell. Where were the mountains, wondered Madeline. Soon low over the house-roofs she saw a dim, dark-blue, rugged outline. It seemed to charm her eyes and fix her gaze. She knew the Adirondacks, she had seen the Alps from the summit of Mont Blanc, and had stood under the great black, white-tipped shadow of the Himalayas. But they had not drawn her as these remote Rockies. This dim horizon line boldly cutting the blue sky fascinated her. Florence Kingsley's expression "beckoning mountains" returned to Madeline. She could not see or feel so much as that. Her impression was rather that these mountains were aloof, unattainable, that if approached they would recede or vanish like the desert mirage.

Madeline went to her room, intending to rest awhile, and she fell asleep. She was aroused by Florence's knock and call.

"Miss Hammond, your brother has come back with Stillwell."

"Why, how I have slept!" exclaimed Madeline. "It's nearly six o'clock."

"I'm sure glad. You were tired. And the air here makes strangers sleepy. Come, we want you to meet old Bill. He calls himself the last of the cattlemen. He has lived in Texas and here all his life."

Madeline accompanied Florence to the porch. Her brother, who was sitting near the door, jumped up and said:

"Hello, Majesty!" And as he put his arm around her he turned toward a massive man whose broad, craggy face began to ripple and wrinkle. "I want to introduce my friend Stillwell to you. Bill, this is my sister, the sister I've so often told you about—Majesty."

"Wal, wal, Al, this 's the proudest meetin' of my life," replied Stillwell, in a booming voice. He extended a huge hand. "Miss—Miss Majesty, sight of you is as welcome as the rain an' flowers to an old desert cattleman."

Madeline greeted him, and it was all she could do to repress a cry at the way he crunched her hand in a grasp of iron. He was old, white-haired, weather-beaten, with long furrows down his cheeks and with gray eyes almost hidden in wrinkles. If he was smiling she fancied it a most extraordinary smile. The next instant she realized that it had been a smile, for his face appeared to stop rippling, the light died, and suddenly it was like rudely chiseled stone. The quality of hardness she had seen in Stewart was immeasurably intensified in this old man's face.

"Miss Majesty, it's plumb humiliatin' to all of us thet we wasn't on hand to meet you," Stillwell said. "Me an' Al stepped into the P. O. an' said a few mild an' cheerful things. Them messages ought to hev been sent out to the ranch. I'm sure afraid it was a bit unpleasant fer you last night at the station."

"I was rather anxious at first and perhaps frightened," replied Madeline.

"Wal, I'm some glad to tell you thet there's no man in these parts except your brother thet I'd as lief hev met you as Gene Stewart."

"Indeed?"

"Yes, an' thet's takin into consideration Gene's weakness, too. I'm allus fond of sayin' of myself thet I'm the last of the old cattlemen. Wal, Stewart's not a native Westerner, but he's my pick of the last of the cowboys. Sure, he's young, but he's the last of the old style—the picturesque—an' chivalrous, too, I make bold to say, Miss Majesty, as well as the old hard-ridin' kind. Folks are down on Stewart. An' I'm only sayin' a good word for him because he is down, an' mebbe last night he might hev scared you, you bein' fresh from the East."

Madeline liked the old fellow for his loyalty to the cowboy he evidently cared for; but as there did not seem anything for her to say, she remained silent.

"Miss Majesty, the day of the cattleman is about over. An' the day of the cowboy, such as Gene Stewart, *is* over. There's

31

no place for Gene. If these weren't modern days he'd come near bein' a gun-man, same as we had in Texas, when I ranched there in the 'seventies. But he can't fit nowhere now; he can't hold a job, an' he's goin' down."

"I am sorry to hear it," murmured Madeline. "But, Mr. Stillwell, aren't these modern days out here just a little wild— yet? The conductor on my train told me of rebels, bandits, raiders. Then I have had other impressions of—well, that were wild enough for me."

"Wal, its some more pleasant an' excitin' these days than for many years," replied Stillwell. "The boys hev took to packin' guns again. But thet's owin' to the revolution in Mexico. There's goin' to be trouble along the border. I reckon people in the East don't know there *is* a revolution. Wal, Madero will oust Diaz, an' then some other rebel will oust Madero. It means trouble on the border an' across the border, too. I wouldn't wonder if Uncle Sam had to get a hand in the game. There's already been holdups on the railroads an' raids along the Rio Grande Valley. An' these little towns are full of Greasers, all disturbed by the fightin' down in Mexico. We've been hevin' shootin'-scrapes an' knifin'-scrapes, an some cattle-raidin'. I hev been losin' a few cattle right along. Reminds me of old times; an' pretty soon, if it doesn't stop, I'll take the old-time way to stop it."

"Yes, indeed, Majesty," put in Alfred, "you have hit upon an interesting time to visit us."

"Wal, thet sure 'pears to be so," rejoined Stillwell. "Stewart got in trouble down heah today, an' I'm more than sorry to hev to tell you thet your name figgered in it. But I couldn't blame him, fer I sure would hev done the same myself."

"That so?" queried Alfred, laughing. "Well, tell us about it."

Madeline simply gazed at her brother, and, though he seemed amused at her consternation, there was mortification in his face.

It required no great perspicuity, Madeline thought, to see that Stillwell loved to talk, and the way he squared himself and spread his huge hands over his knees suggested that he meant to do his opportunity justice.

"Miss Majesty, I reckon, bein' as you're in the West now, thet you must take things as they come, an' mind each thing a little less than the one before. If we old fellers hedn't been thet way we'd never hev lasted.

"Last night wasn't particular bad, ratin' with some other nights lately. There wasn't much doin'. But I had a hard knock. Yesterday when we started in with a bunch of cattle I sent one of my cowboys, Danny Mains, along ahead, carryin' money to get in town before dark. Wal, Danny was held up. I don't distrust the lad. There's been strange Greasers in town lately, an' mebbe they knew about the money comin'.

"Wal, when I arrived with the cattle I was some put to it to make ends meet. An' today I wasn't in no angelic humor. When I hed my business all done I went around pokin' my nose heah an' there, tryin' to get scent of thet money. An' I happened in at a hall we hev thet does duty fer jail an' hospital an' election-post an' what not. Wal, just then it was doin' duty as a hospital. Last night was *fiesta* night—these Greasers hev a *fiesta* every week or so—an' one Greaser who hed been hurt was layin' in the hall, where he had been fetched from the station. Somebody hed sent off to Douglas fer a doctor, but he hedn't come yet. I've hed some experience with gunshot wounds, an' I looked this feller over. He wasn't shot up much, but I thought there was danger of blood-poisonin'. Anyway, I did all I could.

"The hall was full of cowboys, ranchers, Greasers, miners, an' town folks, along with some strangers. I was about to get started up this way when Pat Hawe come in.

"Pat he's the sheriff. I reckon, Miss Majesty, thet sheriffs are new to you, an' fer sake of the West I'll explain to you thet we don't hev many of the real thing any more. Garrett, who killed Billy the Kid an' was killed himself near a year or so ago—he was the kind of sheriff thet helps to make a self-respectin' country. But this Pat Hawe—wal, I reckon there's no good in my sayin' what I think of him. He come into the hall, an' he was roarin' about things. He was goin' to arrest Danny Mains on sight. Wal, I just polite-like told Pat thet the money was mine an' he needn't get riled about it. An' if I wanted to trail the thief I reckon I could do it as well as anybody. Pat howled thet law was law, an' he was goin' to lay down the law. Sure it 'peared to me thet Pat was daid set to arrest the first man he could find excuse to.

"Then he cooled down a bit an' was askin' questions about the wounded Greaser when Gene Stewart come in. Whenever

Pat an' Gene come together it reminds me of the early days back in the 'seventies. Jest naturally everybody shut up. Fer Pat hates Gene, an' I reckon Gene ain't very sweet on Pat. They're jest natural foes in the first place, an' then the course of events here in El Cajon has been aggravatin'.

" 'Hello, Stewart! You're the feller I'm lookin' fer,' said Pat.

"Stewart eyed him an' said, mighty cool an' sarcastic, 'Hawe, you look a good deal fer me when I'm hittin' up the dust the other way.'

"Pat went red at thet, but he held in. 'Say, Stewart, you-all think a lot of thet roan horse of yourn, with the aristocratic name?'

" 'I reckon I do,' replied Gene, shortly.

" 'Wal, where is he?'

" 'Thet's none of your business, Hawe.'

" 'Oho! it ain't, hey? Wal, I guess I can make it my business. Stewart, there was some queer goings-on last night thet you know somethin' about. Danny Mains robbed—Stillwell's money gone—your roan horse gone—thet little hussy Bonita gone—an' this Greaser near gone, too. Now, seein' thet you was up late an' prowlin' round the station where this Greaser was found, it ain't onreasonabe to think you might know how he got plugged—is it?'

"Stewart laughed kind of cold, an' he rolled a cigarette, all the time eyin' Pat, an' then he said if he'd plugged the Greaser it'd never hev been sich a bunglin' job.

" 'I can arrest you on suspicion, Stewart, but before I go thet far I want some evidence. I want to round up Danny Mains an' thet little Greaser girl. I want to find out what's become of your hoss. You've never lent him since you hed him, an' there ain't enough raiders across the border to steal him from you. It's got a queer look—thet hoss bein' gone.'

" 'You sure are a swell detective, Hawe, an' I wish you a heap of luck,' replied Stewart.

"Thet 'peared to nettle Pat beyond bounds, an' he stamped around an' swore. Then he had an idea. It jest stuck out all over him, an' he shook his finger in Stewart's face.

" 'You was drunk last night?'

"Stewart never batted an eye.

" 'You met some woman on Number Eight, didn't you?' shouted Hawe.

34

" 'I met a lady,' replied Stewart, quiet an' menacin' like.

" 'You met Al Hammond's sister, an' you took her up to Kingsley's. An' cinch this, my cowboy cavalier, I'm goin' up there an' ask this grand dame some questions, an' if she's as close-mouthed as you are *I'll arrest her!*'

"Gene Stewart turned white. I fer one expected to see him jump like lightning, as he does when he's riled sudden. But he was calm an' he was thinkin' hard. Presently he said:

" 'Pat, thet's a fool idee, an' if you do the trick it'll hurt you all the rest of your life. There's absolutely no reason to frighten Miss Hammond. An' tryin' to arrest her would be such a damned outrage as won't be stood fer in El Cajon. If you're sore on me send me to jail. I'll go. If you want to hurt Al Hammond, go an' do it some man kind of way. Don't take your spite out on us by insultin' a lady who has come hyar to hev a little visit. We're bad enough without bein' low-down as Greasers.'

"It was a long talk for Gene, an' I was as surprised as the rest of the fellers. Think of Gene Stewart talkin' soft an' sweet to thet red-eyed coyote of a sheriff! An' Pat, he looked so devilishly gleeful thet if somethin' about Gene hadn't held me tight I'd hev got in the game myself. It was plain to me an' others who spoke of it afterwards thet Pat Hawe hed forgotten the law an' the officer in the man an' his hate.

" 'I'm a-goin', an' I'm a-goin' right now!' he shouted.

"An' after thet any one could hev heerd a clock tick a mile off. Stewart seemed kind of chokin', an' he seemed to hev been bewildered by the idee of Hawe's confrontin' you.

"An' finally he burst out: 'But, man, think who it is! It's Miss Hammond! If you seen her, even if you was locoed or drunk, you—you couldn't do it.'

" 'Couldn't I? Wal, I'll show you damn quick. What do I care who she is? Them swell Eastern women—I've heerd of them. They're not so much. This Hammond woman—'

"Suddenly Hawe shut up, an' with his red mug turnin' green he went for his gun."

Stillwell paused in his narrative to get breath, and he wiped his moist brow. And now his face began to lose its cragginess. It changed, it softened, it rippled and wrinkled, and all that strange mobility focused and shone in a wonderful smile.

"An' then, Miss Majesty, then there was somethin' happened. Stewart took Pat's gun away from him and throwed it

35

on the floor. An' what followed was beautiful. Sure it was the beautifulest sight I ever seen. Only it was over so soon! A little while after, when the doctor came, he hed another patient beside the wounded Greaser, an' he said thet this new one would require about four months to be up an' around cheerful-like again. An' Gene Stewart hed hit the trail for the border."

4

A Ride from Sunrise to Sunset

Next morning, when Madeline was aroused by her brother, it was not yet daybreak; the air chilled her, and in the gray gloom she had to feel around for matches and lamp. Her usual languid manner vanished at a touch of the cold water. Presently, when Alfred knocked on her door and said he was leaving a pitcher of hot water outside, she replied, with chattering teeth, "Th-thank y-you, b-but I d-don't ne-need any now." She found it necessary, however to warm her numb fingers before she could fasten hooks and buttons. And when she was dressed she marked in the dim mirror that there were tinges of red in her cheeks.

"Well, if I haven't some color!" she exclaimed.

Breakfast waited for her in the dining-room. The sisters ate with her. Madeline quickly caught the feeling of brisk action that seemed to be in the air. From the back of the house sounded the tramp of boots and voices of men, and from outside came a dull thump of hoofs, the rattle of harness, and creak of wheels. Then Alfred came stamping in.

"Majesty, here's where you get the real thing," he announced, merrily. "We're rushing you off, I'm sorry to say; but we must hustle back to the ranch. The fall round-up begins tomorrow. You will ride in the buckboard with Florence and Stillwell. I'll ride on ahead with the boys and fix up a little for you at the ranch. Your baggage will follow, but won't get there till tomorrow sometime. It's a long ride out—nearly fifty miles by wagon-road. Flo, don't forget a couple of robes. Wrap her up well. And hustle getting ready. We're waiting."

A little later, when Madeline went out with Florence, the gray gloom was lightening. Horses were champing bits and pounding gravel.

"Mawnin', Miss Majesty," said Stillwell, gruffly, from the front seat of a high vehicle.

Alfred bundled her up into the back seat, and Florence after her, and wrapped them with robes. Then he mounted his horse and started off. "Gid-eb!" growled Stillwell, and with a crack of his whip the team jumped into a trot. Florence whispered into Madeline's ear:

"Bill's grouchy early in the mawnin'. He'll thaw out soon as it gets warm."

It was still so gray that Madeline could not distinguish objects at any considerable distance, and she left El Cajon without knowing what the town really looked like. She did know that she was glad to get out of it, and found an easier task of dispelling persistent haunting memory.

"Here come the cowboys," said Florence.

A line of horsemen appeared coming from the right and fell in behind Alfred, and gradually they drew ahead, to disappear from sight. While Madeline watched them the gray gloom lightened into dawn. All about her was bare and dark; the horizon seemed close; not a hill nor a tree broke the monotony. The ground appeared to be flat, but the road went up and down over little ridges. Madeline glanced backward in the direction of El Cajon and the mountains she had seen the day before, and she saw only bare and dark ground, like that which rolled before.

A puff of cold wind struck her face and she shivered. Florence noticed her and pulled up the second robe and tucked it closely round her up to her chin.

"If we have a little wind you'll sure feel it," said the Western girl.

Madeline replied that she already felt it. The wind appeared to penetrate the robes. It was cold, pure, nipping. It was so thin she had to breathe as fast as if she were under ordinary exertion. It hurt her nose and made her lungs ache.

"Aren't you co-cold?" asked Madeline.

"I?" Florence laughed. "I'm used to it. I never get cold."

The Western girl sat with ungloved hands on the outside of

the robe she evidently did not need to draw up around her. Madeline thought she had never seen such a clear-eyed, healthy, splendid girl.

"Do you like to see the sun rise?" asked Florence.

"Yes, I think I do," replied Madeline, thoughtfully. "Frankly, I have not seen it for years."

"We have beautiful sunrises, and sunsets from the ranch are glorious."

Long lines of pink fire ran level with the eastern horizon, which appeared to recede as day brightened. A bank of thin, fleecy clouds was turning rose. To the south and west the sky was dark; but every moment it changed, the blue turning bluer. The eastern sky was opalescent. Then in one place gathered a golden light, and slowly concentrated till it was like fire. The rosy bank of cloud turned to silver and pearl, and behind it shot up a great circle of gold. Above the dark horizon gleamed an intensely bright disk. It was the sun. It rose swiftly, blazing out the darkness between the ridges and giving color and distance to the sweep of land.

"Wal, wal," drawled Stillwell, and stretched his huge arm as if he had just awakened, "thet's somethin' like."

Florence nudged Madeline and winked at her.

"Fine mawnin', girl," went on old Bill, cracking his whip. "Miss Majesty, it'll be some oninterestin' ride all mawnin'. But when we get up a bit you'll sure like it. There! Look to the southwest, jest over thet farthest ridge."

Madeline swept her gaze along the gray, sloping horizon-line to where dark-blue spires rose far beyond the ridge.

"Peloncillo Mountains," said Stillwell. "Thet's home, when we get there. We won't see no more of them till afternoon, when they rise up sudden-like."

Peloncillo! Madeline murmured the melodious name. Where had she heard it? Then she remembered. The cowboy Stewart had told the little Mexican girl Bonita to "hit the Peloncillo trail." Probably the girl had ridden the big, dark horse over this very road at night, alone. Madeline had a little shiver that was not occasioned by the cold wind.

"There's a jack!" cried Florence, suddenly.

Madeline saw her first jack-rabbit. It was as large as a dog, and its ears were enormous. It appeared to be impudently tame, and the horses kicked dust over it as they trotted by. From then on old Bill and Florence vied with each other in calling Madeline's attention to many things along the way. Coyotes stealing away into the brush; buzzards flapping over the carcass of a cow that had been mired in a wash; queer little lizards running swiftly across the road; cattle grazing in the hollows; adobe huts of Mexican herders; wild, shaggy horses, with heads high, watching from the gray ridges—all these things Madeline looked at, indifferently at first, because indifference had become habitual with her, and then with an interest that flourished up and insensibly grew as she rode on. It grew until sight of a little ragged Mexican boy astride the most diminutive burro she had ever seen awakened her to the truth. She became conscious of faint, unmistakable awakening of long-dead feelings—enthusiasm and delight. When she realized that, she breathed deep of the cold, sharp air and experienced an inward joy. And she divined then, though she did not know why, that henceforth there was to be something new in her life, something she had never felt before, something good for her soul in the homely, the commonplace, the natural, and the wild.

Meanwhile, as Madeline gazed about her and listened to her companions, the sun rose higher and grew warm and soared and grew hot; the horses held tirelessly to their steady trot, and mile after mile of rolling land slipped by.

From the top of a ridge Madeline saw down into a hollow where a few of the cowboys had stopped and were sitting round a fire, evidently busy at the noonday meal. Their horses were feeding on the long, gray grass.

"Wal, smell of thet burnin' greasewood makes my mouth water," said Stillwell. "I'm sure hungry. We'll noon hyar an' let the hosses rest. It's a long pull to the ranch."

He halted near the camp-fire, and, clambering down, began to unharness the team. Florence leaped out and turned to help Madeline.

"Walk round a little," she said. "You must be cramped from sitting still so long. I'll get lunch ready."

Madeline got down, glad to stretch her limbs, and began to stroll about. She heard Stillwell throw the harness on the ground and slap his horses. "Roll, you sons-of-guns!" he said. Both horses bent their fore legs, heaved down on their sides, and tried to roll over. One horse succeeded on the fourth try, and then heaved up with a satisfied snort and shook off the

39

dust and gravel. The other one failed to roll over, and gave it up, half rose to his feet, and then lay down on the other side.

"He's sure going to feel the ground," said Florence, smiling at Madeline. "Miss Hammond, I suppose that prize horse of yours—White Stockings—would spoil his coat if he were heah to roll in this greasewood and cactus."

During lunch-time Madeline observed that she was an object of manifestly great interest to the three cowboys. She returned the compliment, and was amused to see that a glance their way caused them painful embarrassment. They were grown men—one of whom had white hair—yet they acted like boys caught in the act of stealing a forbidden look at a pretty girl.

"Cowboys are sure all flirts," said Florence, as if stating an uninteresting fact. But Madeline detected a merry twinkle in her clear eyes. The cowboys heard, and the effect upon them was magical. They fell to shamed confusion and to hurried useless tasks. Madeline found it difficult to see where they had been bold, though evidently they were stricken with conscious guilt. She recalled appraising looks of critical English eyes, impudent French stares, burning Spanish glances—gantlets which any American girl had to run abroad. Compared with foreign eyes the eyes of these cowboys were those of smiling, eager babies.

"Haw, haw!" roared Stillwell. "Florence, you just hit the nail on the haid. Cowboys are all plumb flirts. I was wonderin' why them boys nooned hyar. This ain't no place to noon. Ain't no grazin' or wood wuth burnin' or nuthin.' Them boys jest held up, throwed the packs, an' waited fer us. It ain't so surprisin' for Booly an' Ned—they're young an' coltish—but Nels there, why, he's old enough to be the paw of both you girls. It sure is amazin' strange."

A silence ensued. The white-haired cowboy, Nels, fussed aimlessly over the camp-fire, and then straightened up with a very red face.

"Bill, you're a dog-gone liar," he said. "I reckon I won't stand to be classed with Booly an' Ned. There ain't no cowboy on this range thet's more appreciatin' of the ladies than me, but I shore ain't ridin' out of my way. I reckon I hev enough ridin' to do. Now, Bill, if you've sich dog-gone good eyes mebbe you seen somethin' on the way out?"

"Nels, I hevn't seen nothin'," he replied, bluntly. His levity disappeared, and the red wrinkles narrowed around his searching eyes.

"Jest take a squint at these hoss tracks," said Nels, and he drew Stillwell a few paces aside and pointed to large hoof-prints in the dust. "I reckon you know the hoss thet made them?"

"Gene Stewart's roan, or I'm a son-of-a-gun!" exclaimed Stillwell, and he dropped heavily to his knees and began to scrutinize the tracks. "My eyes are sure pore; but, Nels, they ain't fresh."

"I reckon them tracks was made early yesterday mornin'."

"Wal, what if they was?" Stillwell looked at his cowboy. "It's sure as thet red nose of yourn Gene wasn't ridin' the roan."

"Who's sayin' he was? Bill, it's more'n your eyes thet's gettin' old. Just foller them tracks. Come on."

Stillwell walked slowly, with his head bent, muttering to himself. Some thirty paces or more from the camp-fire he stopped short and again flopped to his knees. Then he crawled about, evidently examining horse tracks,

"Nels, whoever was straddlin' Stewart's hoss met somebody. An' they hauled up a bit, but didn't git down."

"Tolerable good for you, Bill, thet reasonin'," replied the cowboy.

Stillwell presently got up and walked swiftly to the left for some rods, halted, and faced toward the southwest, then retraced his steps. He looked at the imperturbable cowboy.

"Nels, I don't like this a little," he growled. "Them tracks make straight fer the Peloncillo trail."

"Shore," replied Nels.

"Wal?" went on Stillwell, impatiently.

"I reckon you know what hoss made the other tracks?"

"I'm thinkin' hard, but I ain't sure."

"It was Danny Mains's bronc."

"How do you know thet?" demanded Stillwell, sharply.

"Bill, the left front foot of thet little hoss always wears a shoe thet sets crooked. Any of the boys can tell you I'd know thet track if I was blind."

Stillwell's ruddy face clouded and he kicked at a cactus plant.

"Was Danny comin' or goin'?" he asked.

"I reckon he was hittin' across country fer the Peloncillo

41

trail. But I ain't shore of thet without back-trailin' him a ways. I was jest waitin' fer you to come up."

"Nels, you don't think the boy's sloped with thet little hussy, Bonita?"

"Bill, he shore was sweet on Bonita, same as Gene was, an' Ed Linton before he got engaged, an' all the boys. She's shore chain-lightin', thet little black-eyed devil. Danny might hev sloped with her all right. Danny was held up on the way to town, an' then in the shame of it he got drunk. But he'll show up soon."

"Wal, mebbe you an' the boys are right. I believe you are. Nels, there ain't no doubt on earth about who was ridin' Stewart's hoss?"

"Thet's as plain as the hoss's tracks."

"Wal, it's all amazin' strange. It beats me. I wish the boys would ease up on drinkin'. I was pretty fond of Danny an' Gene. I'm afraid Gene's done fer, sure. If he crosses the border where he can fight it won't take long fer him to get plugged. I guess I'm gettin' old. I don't stand things like I used to."

"Bill, I reckon I'd better hit the Peloncillo trail. Mebbe I can find Danny."

"I reckon you had, Nels," replied Stillwell. "But don't take more'n a couple of days. We can't do much on the roundup without you. I'm short of boys."

That ended the conversation. Stillwell immediately began to hitch up his team, and the cowboys went out to fetch their stray horses. Madeline had been curiously interested, and she saw that Florence knew it.

"Things happen, Miss Hammond," she said, soberly, almost sadly.

Madeline thought. And then straightway Florence began brightly to hum a tune and to busy herself repacking what was left of the lunch. Madeline suddenly conceived a strong liking and respect for this Western girl. She admired the consideration or delicacy or wisdom—whatever it was—which kept Florence from asking her what she knew or thought or felt about the events that had taken place.

Soon they were once more bowling along the road down a gradual incline, and then they began to climb a long ridge that had for hours hidden what lay beyond. That climb was rather tiresome, owing to the sun and the dust and the restricted view.

When they reached the summit Madeline gave a little gasp of pleasure. A deep, gray, smooth valley opened below and sloped up on the other side in little ridges like waves, and these led to the foothills, dotted with clumps of brush or trees, and beyond rose dark mountains, pine-fringed and crag-spired.

"Wal, Miss Majesty, now we're gettin' somewhere," said Stillwell, cracking his whip. "Ten miles across this valley an' we'll be in the foothills where the Apaches used to run."

"Ten miles!" exclaimed Madeline. "It looks no more than half a mile to me."

"Wal, young woman, before you go to ridin' off alone you want to get your eyes corrected to Western distance. Now, what'd you call them black things off there on the slope?"

"Horsemen. No, cattle," replied Madeline, doubtfully.

"Nope. Jest plain, everyday cactus. An' over hyar—look down the valley. Somethin' of a pretty forest, ain't thet?" he asked, pointing.

Madeline saw a beautiful forest in the center of the valley toward the south.

"Wal, Miss Majesty, thet's jest this deceivin' air. There's no forest. It's a mirage."

"Indeed! How beautiful it is!" Madeline strained her gaze on the dark blot, and it seemed to float in the atmosphere, to have clearly defined margins, to waver and shimmer, and then it faded and vanished.

The mountains dropped down again behind the horizon, and presently the road began once more to slope up. The horses slowed to a walk. There was a mile of rolling ridge, and then came the foothills. The road ascended through winding valleys. Trees and brush and rocks began to appear in the dry ravines. There was no water, yet all along the sandy washes were indications of floods at some periods. The heat and the dust stifled Madeline, and she had already become tired. Still she looked with all her eyes and saw birds, and beautiful quail with crests, and rabbits, and once she saw a deer.

"Miss Majesty," said Stillwell, "in the early days the Indians made this country a bad one to live in. I reckon you never heerd much about them times. Surely you was hardly born

43

then. I'll hev to tell you some day how I fought Comanches in the Panhandle—thet was northern Texas—an' I had some mighty hair-raisin' scares in this country with Apaches."

He told her about Cochise, chief of the Chiricahua Apaches, the most savage and bloodthirsty tribe that ever made life a horror for the pioneer. Cochise befriended the whites once; but he was the victim of that friendliness, and he became the most implacable of foes. Then Geronimo, another Apache chief, had, as late as 1885, gone on the war-path, and had left a bloody trail down the New Mexico and Arizona line almost to the border. Lone ranchmen and cowboys had been killed, and mothers had shot their children and then themselves at the approach of the Apache. The name Apache curdled the blood of any woman of the Southwest in those days.

Madeline shuddered, and was glad when the old frontiersman changed the subject and began to talk of the settling of that country by the Spaniards, the legends of lost gold-mines handed down to the Mexicans, and strange stories of heroism and mystery and religion. The Mexicans had not advanced much in spite of the spread of civilization to the Southwest. They were still superstitious, and believed the legends of treasures hidden in the walls of their missions, and that unseen hands rolled rocks down the gullies upon the heads of prospectors who dared to hunt for the lost mines of the padres.

"Up in the mountains back of my ranch there's a lost mine," said Stillwell. "Mebbe it's only a legend. But somehow I believe it's there. Other lost mines hev been found. An' as fer the rollin' stones, I sure know thet's true, as any one can find out if he goes trailin' up the gulch. Mebbe thet's only the weatherin' of the cliffs. It's a sleepy, strange country, this Southwest, an', Miss Majesty, you're a-goin' to love it. You'll call it ro-mantic. Wal, I reckon ro-mantic is correct. A feller gets lazy out hyar an' dreamy, an' he wants to put off work till tomorrow. Thet's the Mexican of it.

"But I like best to think of what a lady said to me onct—an eddicated lady like you, Miss Majesty. Wal, she said it's a land where it's always afternoon. I liked thet. I always get up sore in the mawnin's, an' don't feel like things. An' sunset is my time. I reckon I don't want nothin' any finer than sunset from my ranch. You look out over a valley that spreads wide between Guadalupe Mountains an' the Chiricahuas, down

44

across the red Arizona desert clear to the Sierra Madres in Mexico. Two hundred miles, Miss Majesty! An' all as clear as print! An' the sun sets behind all thet! When my time comes to die I'd like it to be on my porch smokin' my pipe an' facin' the west."

So the old cattleman talked on while Madeline listened, and Florence dozed in her seat, and the sun began to wane, and the horses climbed steadily. Presently, at the foot of the steep ascent, Stillwell got out and walked, leading the team. During this long climb fatigue claimed Madeline, and she drowsily closed her eyes, to find when she opened them again that the glaring white sky had changed to a steel-blue. The sun had sunk behind the foothills and the air was growing chilly. Stillwell had returned to the driving-seat and was chuckling to the horses. Shadows crept up out of the hollows.

"Wal, Flo," said Stillwell, "I reckon we'd better hev the rest of thet lunch before dark."

"You didn't leave much of it," laughed Florence, as she produced the basket from under the seat.

While they ate, the short twilight shaded and gloom filled the hollows. Madeline saw the first star, a faint, winking point of light. The sky had now changed to a hazy gray. Madeline saw it gradually clear and darken, to show other faint stars. After that there was perceptible deepening of the gray and an enlarging of the stars and a brightening of newborn ones. Night seemed to come on the cold wind. Madeline was glad to have the robes close around her and to lean against Florence. The hollows were now black, but the tops of the foothills gleamed pale in a soft light. The steady tramp of the horses went on, and the creak of wheels and crunching of gravel. Madeline grew so sleepy that she could not keep her weary eyelids from falling. There were drowsier spells in which she lost a feeling of where she was, and these were disturbed by the jolt of wheels over a rough place. Then came a blank interval, short or long, which ended in a more violent lurch of the buckboard. Madeline awoke to find her head on Florence's shoulder. She sat up laughing and apologizing for her laziness. Florence assured her they would soon reach the ranch.

Madeline observed then that the horses were once more trotting. The wind was colder, the night darker, the foothills flatter. And the sky was now a wonderful deep velvet-blue blazing wilh millions of stars. Some of them were magnificent. How strangely white and alive! Again Madeline felt the insistence of familiar yet baffling associations. These whit/ stars called strangely to her or haunted her.

5

The Round-up

It was a crackling and roaring fire that awakened Madeline next morning, and the first thing she saw was a huge stone fireplace in which lay a bundle of blazing sticks. Someone had kindled a fire while she slept. For a moment the curious sensation of being lost returned to her. She just dimly remembered reaching the ranch and being taken into a huge house and a huge, dimly lighted room. And it seemed to her that she had gone to sleep at once, and had awakened without remembering how she had gotten to bed.

But she was wide awake in an instant. The bed stood near one end of an enormous chamber. The adobe walls resembled a hall in an ancient feudal castle, stone-floored, stone-walled, with great darkened rafters running across the ceiling. The few articles of furniture were worn out and sadly dilapidated. Light flooded into the room from two windows on the right of the fireplace and two on the left, and another large window near the bedstead. Looking out from where she lay, Madeline saw a dark, slow up-sweep of mountain. Her eyes returned to the cheery, snapping fire, and she watched it while gathering courage to get up. The room was cold. When she did slip her bare feet out upon the stone floor she very quickly put them back under the warm blankets. And she was still in bed trying to pluck up her courage when, with a knock on the door and a cheerful greeting, Florence entered, carrying steaming hot water.

"Good mawnin', Miss Hammond. Hope you slept well. You sure were tired last night. I imagine you'll find this old rancho house as cold as a barn. It'll warm up directly. Al's gone with the boys and Bill. We're to ride down on the range after a while when your baggage comes."

Florence wore a woolen blouse with a scarf round her neck, a short corduroy divided skirt, and boots; and while she talked she energetically heaped up the burning wood in the fireplace, and laid Madeline's clothes at the foot of the bed, and heated a rug and put that on the floor by the bedside. And lastly, with a sweet, direct smile, she said:

"Al told me—and I sure saw myself—that you weren't used to being without your maid. Will you let me help you?"

"Thank you, I am going to be my own maid for a while. I expect I do appear a very helpless individual, but really I do not feel so. Perhaps I have had just a little too much waiting on."

"All right. Breakfast will be ready soon, and after that we'll look about the place."

Madeline was charmed with the old Spanish house, and the more she saw of it the more she thought what a delightful home it could be made. All the doors opened into a courtyard, or patio, as Florence called it. The house was low, in the shape of a rectangle, and so immense in size that Madeline wondered if it had been a Spanish barracks. Many of the rooms were dark, without windows, and they were empty. Others were full of ranchers' implements and sacks of grain and bales of hay. Florence called these last alfalfa. The house itself appeared strong and well preserved, and it was very picturesque. But in the living-rooms were only the barest necessities, and these were worn out and comfortless.

However, when Madeline went outdoors she forgot the cheerless, bare interior. Florence led the way out on a porch and waved a hand at a vast, colored void. "That's what Bill likes," she said.

At first Madeline could not tell what was sky and what was land. The immensity of the scene stunned her faculties of conception. She sat down in one of the old rocking chairs and looked and looked, and knew that she was not grasping the reality of what stretched wondrously before her.

"We're up at the edge of the foothills," Florence said. "You remember we rode around the northern end of the mountain range? Well, that's behind us now, and you look down across the line into Arizona and Mexico. That long slope of gray is the head of the San Bernardino Valley. Straight across you see

47

the black Chiricahua Mountains, and away down to the south the Guadalupe Mountains. That awful red gulf between is the desert, and far, far beyond the dim, blue peaks are the Sierra Madres in Mexico."

Madeline listened and gazed with straining eyes, and wondered if this was only a stupendous mirage, and why it seemed so different from all else that she had seen, and so endless, so baffling, so grand.

"It'll sure take you a little while to get used to being up high and seeing so much," explained Florence. "That's the secret—we're up high, the air is clear, and there's the whole bare world beneath us. Don't it somehow rest you? Well, it will. Now see those specks in the valley. They are stations, little towns. The railroad goes down that way. The largest speck is Chiricahua. It's over forty miles by trail. Here round to the north you can see Don Carlos's rancho. He's fifteen miles off, and I sure wish he were a thousand. That little green square about half-way between here and Don Carlos—that's Al's ranch. Just below us are the adobe houses of the Mexicans. There's a church, too. And here to the left you see Stillwell's corrals and bunkhouses and his stables all falling to pieces. The ranch has gone to ruin. All the ranches are going to ruin. But most of them are little one-horse affairs—see that cloud of dust down in the valley? It's the round-up. The boys are there, and the cattle. Wait, I'll get the glasses."

By their aid Madeline saw in the foreground a great, dense herd of cattle with dark, thick streams and dotted lines of cattle leading in every direction. She saw streaks and clouds of dust, running horses, and a band of horses grazing; and she descried horsemen standing still like sentinels, and others in action.

"The round-up! I want to know all about it—to see it," declared Madeline. "Please tell me what it means, what it's for, and then take me down there."

"It's sure a sight, Miss Hammond. I'll be glad to take you down, but I fancy you'll not want to go close. Few Eastern people who regularly eat their choice cuts of roast beef and porterhouse have any idea of the open range and the struggle cattle have to live and the hard life of cowboys. It'll sure open your eyes, Miss Hammond. I'm glad you care to know. Your brother would have made a big success in this cattle business if it hadn't been for crooked work by rival ranchers. He'll make it yet, in spite of them."

"Indeed he shall," replied Madeline. "But tell me, please, all about the round-up."

"Well, in the first place, every cattleman has to have a brand to identify his stock. Without it no cattleman, nor half a hundred cowboys, if he had so many, could ever recognize all the cattle in a big herd. There are no fences on our ranges. They are all open to everybody. Some day I hope we'll be rich enough to fence a range. The different herds graze together. Every calf has to be caught, if possible, and branded with the mark of its mother. That's no easy job. A maverick is an unbranded calf that has been weaned and shifts for itself. The maverick then belongs to the man who finds it and brands it. These little calves that lose their mothers sure have a cruel time of it. Many of them die. Then the coyotes and wolves and lions prey on them. Every year we have two big round-ups, but the boys do some branding all the year. A calf should be branded as soon as it's found. This is a safeguard against cattle-thieves. We don't have the rustling of herds and bunches of cattle like we used to. But there's always the calf-thief, and always will be as long as there's cattle-raising. The thieves have a good many cunning tricks. They kill the calf's mother or slit the calf's tongue so it can't suck and so loses its mother. They steal and hide a calf and watch it till it's big enough to fare for itself, and then brand it. They make imperfect brands and finish them at a later time.

"We have our big round-up in the fall, when there's plenty of grass and water, and all the riding-stock as well as the cattle are in fine shape. The cattlemen in the valley meet with their cowboys and drive in all the cattle they can find. Then they brand and cut out each man's herd and drive it toward home. Then they go on up or down the valley, make another camp, and drive in more cattle. It takes weeks. There are so many Greasers with little bands of stock, and they are crafty and greedy. Bill says he knows Greaser cowboys, *vaqueros,* who never owned a steer or a cow, and now they've got growing herds. The same might be said of more than one white cowboy. But there's not as much of that as there used to be."

"And the horses? I want to know about them," said Madeline, when Florence paused.

"Oh, the cow-ponies! Well, they sure are interesting. Broncos, the boys call them. Wild! They're wilder than the steers they have to chase. Bill's got broncos heah that never have been broken and never will be. And not every boy can ride them, either. The *vaqueros* have the finest horses. Don Carlos has a black that I'd give anything to own. And he has other fine stock. Gene Stewart's big roan is a Mexican horse, the swiftest and proudest I ever saw. I was up on him once and—oh, he can run! He likes a woman, too, and that's sure something I want in a horse. I heard Al and Bill talking at breakfast about a horse for you. They were wrangling. Bill wanted you to have one, and Al another. It was funny to hear them. Finally they left the choice to me until the round-up is over. Then I suppose every cowboy on the range will offer his best mount. Come, let's go out to the corrals and look over the few horses left."

For Madeline the morning hours flew by, with a goodly part of the time spent on the porch gazing out over that ever-changing vista. At noon a teamster drove up with her trunks. Then while Florence helped the Mexican woman get lunch Madeline unpacked part of her effects and got out things for which she would have immediate need. After lunch she changed her dress for a riding-habit and, going outside, found Florence waiting with the horses.

The Western girl's clear eyes seemed to take stock of Madeline's appearance in one swift, inquisitive glance and then shone with pleasure.

"You sure look—you're a picture, Miss Hammond. That riding-outfit is a new one. What it'd look like on me or another woman I can't imagine, but on you it's—it's stunning. Bill won't let you go within a mile of the cowboys. If they see you that'll be the finish of the round-up."

While they rode down the slope Florence talked about the open ranges of New Mexico and Arizona.

"Water is scarce," she said. "If Bill could afford to pipe water down from the mountains he'd have the finest ranch in the valley."

She went on to tell that the climate was mild in winter and hot in summer. Warm, sunshiny days prevailed nearly all the year round. Some summers it rained, and occasionally there would be a dry year, the dreaded *año seco* of the Mexicans. Rain was always expected and prayed for in the mid-summer months, and when it came the grama-grass sprang up, making the valleys green from mountain to mountain. The intersecting valleys, ranging between the long slope of foothills, afforded the best pasture for cattle, and these were jealously sought by the Mexicans who had only small herds to look after. Stillwell's cowboys were always chasing *vaqueros* off land that belonged to Stillwell. He owned twenty thousand acres of unfenced land adjoining the open range. Don Carlos possessed more acreage than that, and his cattle were always mingling with Stillwell's. And in turn Don Carlos's *vaqueros* were always chasing Stillwell's cattle away from the Mexican's watering-place. Bad feeling had been manifested for years, and now relations were strained to the breaking-point.

As Madeline rode along she made good use of her eyes. The soil was sandy and porous, and she understood why the rain and water from the few springs disappeared so quickly. At a little distance the grama-grass appeared thick, but near at hand it was seen to be sparse. Bunches of greasewood and cactus plants were interspersed here and there in the grass. What surprised Madeline was the fact that, though she and Florence had seemed to be riding quite awhile, they had apparently not drawn any closer to the round-up. The slope of the valley was noticeable only after some miles had been traversed. Looking forward, Madeline imagined the valley only a few miles wide. She would have been sure she could walk the horse across it in an hour. Yet that black, bold range of Chiricahua Mountains was distant a long day's journey for even a hard-riding cowboy. It was only by looking back that Madeline could grasp the true relation of things; she could not be deceived by distance she had covered.

Gradually the black dots enlarged and assumed shape of cattle and horses moving round a great dusty patch. In another half-hour Madeline rode behind Florence to the outskirts of the scene of action. They drew rein near a huge wagon in the neighborhood of which were more than a hundred horses grazing and whistling and trotting about and lifting heads to watch the new-comers. Four cowboys stood mounted guard over this drove of horses. Perhaps a quarter of a mile farther out was a dusty mêlée. A roar of tramping hoofs filled Madeline's ears. The lines of marching cattle had merged into a great, moving herd half obscured by dust.

"I can make little of what is going on," said Madeline. "I want to go closer."

They trotted across half the intervening distance, and when Florence halted again Madeline was still not satisfied and asked to be taken nearer. This time, before they reined in again, Al Hammond saw them and wheeled his horse in their direction. He yelled something which Madeline did not understand, and then halted them.

"Close enough," he called; and in the din his voice was not very clear. "It's not safe. Wild steers! I'm glad you came, girls. Majesty, what do you think of that bunch of cattle?"

Madeline could scarcely reply what she thought, for the noise and dust and ceaseless action confused her.

"They're milling, Al," said Florence.

"We just rounded them up. They're milling, and that's bad. The *vaqueros* are hard drivers. They beat us all hollow, and we drove some, too." He was wet with sweat, black with dust, and out of breath. "I'm off now. Flo, my sister will have enough of this in about two minutes. Take her back to the wagon. I'll tell Bill you're here, and run in whenever I get a minute."

The bawling and bellowing, the crackling of horns and pounding of hoofs, the dusty whirl of cattle, and the flying cowboys disconcerted Madeline and frightened her a little; but she was intensely interested and meant to stay there until she saw for herself what that strife of sound and action meant. When she tried to take in the whole scene she did not make out anything clearly and she determined to see it little by little.

"Will you stay longer?" asked Florence; and, receiving an affirmative reply, she warned Madeline: "If a runaway steer or angry cow comes this way let your horse go. He'll get out of the way."

That lent the situation excitement, and Madeline became absorbed. The great mass of cattle seemed to be eddying like a whirlpool, and from that Madeline understood the significance of the range word "milling." But when Madeline looked at one end of the herd she saw cattle standing still, facing outward, and calves cringing close in fear. The motion of the cattle slowed from the inside of the herd to the outside and gradually ceased. The roar and tramp of hoofs and crack of horns and thump of heads also ceased in degree, but the bawling and bellowing continued. While she watched, the herd spread, grew less dense, and stragglers appeared to be about to bolt through the line of mounted cowboys.

From that moment so many things happened, and so swiftly, that Madeline could not see a tenth of what was going on within eyesight. It seemed horsemen darted into the herd and drove out cattle. Madeline pinned her gaze on one cowboy who rode a white horse and was chasing a steer. He whirled a lasso around his head and threw it; the rope streaked out and the loop caught the leg of the steer. The white horse stopped with wonderful suddenness, and the steer slid in the dust. Quick as a flash the cowboy was out of the saddle, and, grasping the legs of the steer before it could rise, he tied them with a rope. It had all been done almost as quickly as thought. Another man came with what Madeline divined was a branding-iron. He applied it to the flank of the steer. Then it seemed the steer was up with a jump, wildly looking for some way to run, and the cowboy was circling his lasso. Madeline saw fires in the background, with a man in charge, evidently heating the irons. Then this same cowboy roped a heifer which bawled lustily when the hot iron seared its hide. Madeline saw the smoke rising from the touch of the iron, and the sight made her shrink and want to turn away, but she resolutely fought her sensitiveness. She had never been able to bear the sight of any animal suffering. The rough work in men's lives was as a sealed book to her; and now, for some reason beyond her knowledge, she wanted to see and hear and learn some of the everyday duties that made up those lives.

"Look, Miss Hammond, there's Don Carlos!" said Florence. "Look at that black horse!"

Madeline saw a dark-faced Mexican riding by. He was too far away for her to distinguish his features, but he reminded her of an Italian brigand. He bestrode a magnificent horse.

Stillwell rode up to the girls then and greeted them in his big voice.

"Right in the thick of it, hey? Wal, thet's sure fine. I'm glad to see, Miss Majesty, thet you ain't afraid of a little dust or smell of burnin' hide an' hair."

"Couldn't you brand the calves without hurting them?" asked Madeline.

"Haw, haw! Why, they ain't hurt none. They jest bawl for their mammas. Sometimes, though, we hev to hurt one jest to find which is his mamma."

"I want to know how you tell what brand to put on those calves that are separated from their mothers," asked Madeline.

"Thet's decided by the round-up bosses. I've one boss an' Don Carlos has one. They decide everything, an' they hev to be obeyed. There's Nick Steele, my boss. Watch him! He's ridin' a bay in among the cattle there. He orders the calves an' steers to be cut out. Then the cowboys do the cuttin' out an' the brandin'. We try to divide up the mavericks as near as possible."

At this juncture Madeline's brother joined the group evidently in search of Stillwell.

"Bill, Nels just rode in," he said.

"Good! We sure need him. Any news of Danny Mains?"

"No. Nels said he lost the trail when he got on hard ground."

"Wal, wal. Say, Al, your sister is sure takin' to the roundup. An' the boys are gettin' wise. See thet son-of-a-gun Ambrose cuttin' capers all around. He'll sure do his prettiest. Ambrose is a ladies' man, he thinks."

The two men and Florence joined in a little pleasant teasing of Madeline, and drew her attention to what appeared to be really unnecessary feats of horsemanship all made in her vicinity. The cowboys evinced their interest in covert glances while recoiling a lasso or while passing to and fro. It was all too serious for Madeline to be amused at that moment. She did not care to talk. She sat her horse and watched.

The lithe, dark *vaqueros* fascinated her. They were here, there, everywhere, with lariats flying, horses plunging back, jerking calves and yearlings to the grass. They were cruel to their mounts, cruel to their cattle. Madeline winced as the great silver rowels of the spurs went plowing into the flanks of their horses. She saw these spurs stained with blood, choked with hair. She saw the *vaqueros* break the legs of calves and let them lie till a white cowboy came along and shot them. Calves were jerked down and dragged many yards; steers were pulled by one leg. These *vaqueros* were the most superb horsemen Madeline had ever seen, and she had seen the Cossacks and Tatars of the Russian steppes. They were swift, graceful, daring; they never failed to catch a running steer and the lassoes always went true. What sharp dashes the horses made, and wheelings here and there, and sudden stops, and how they braced themselves to withstand the shock!

The cowboys, likewise, showed wonderful horsemanship, and, reckless as they were, Madeline imagined she saw consideration for steed and cattle that was wanting in the *vaqueros*. They changed mounts oftener than the Mexican riders, and the horses they unsaddled for fresh ones were not so spent, so wet, so covered with lather. It was only after an hour or more of observation that Madeline began to realize the exceedingly toilsome and dangerous work cowboys had to perform. There was little or no rest for them. They were continually among wild and vicious and wide-horned steers. In many instances they owed their lives to their horses. The danger came mostly when the cowboy leaped off to tie and brand a calf he had thrown. Some of the cows charged with lowered, twisting horns. Time and again Madeline's heart leaped to her throat for fear a man would be gored. One cowboy roped a calf that bawled loudly. Its mother dashed in and just missed the kneeling cowboy as he rolled over. Then he had to run, and he could not run very fast. He was bow-legged and appeared awkward. Madeline saw another cowboy thrown and nearly run over by a plunging steer. His horse bolted as if it intended to leave the range. Then close by Madeline a big steer went down at the end of a lasso. The cowboy who had thrown it nimbly jumped down, and at that moment, his horse began to rear and prance and suddenly to lower his head close to the ground and kick high. He ran round in a circle, the fallen steer on the taut lasso acting as a pivot. The cowboy loosed the rope from the steer, and then was dragged about on the grass. It was almost frightful for Madeline to see that cowboy go at his horse. But she recognized the mastery and skill. Then two horses came into collision on the run. One horse went down; the rider of the other was unseated and was kicked before he could get up. This fellow limped to his mount and struck at him, while the horse showed his teeth in a vicious attempt to bite.

All the while this ceaseless activity was going on there was a strange uproar—bawl and bellow, the shock of heavy bodies meeting and falling, the shrill jabbering of the *vaqueros,* and the shouts and banterings of the cowboys. They took sharp orders and replied in jest. They went about this stern toil as if it were a game to be played in good humor. One sang a rollicking song, another whistled, another smoked a cigarette. The sun was hot, and they, like their horses, were dripping with sweat. The characteristic red faces had taken on so much dust that cowboys could not be distinguished from *vaqueros* except by the difference in dress. Blood was not wanting on tireless hands. The air was thick, oppressive, rank with the smell of cattle and of burning hide.

Madeline began to sicken. She choked with dust, was almost stifled by the odor. But that made her all the more determined to stay there. Florence urged her to come away, or at least move back out of the worst of it. Stillwell seconded Florence. Madeline, however, smilingly refused. Then her brother said: "Here, this is making you sick. You're pale." And she replied that she intended to stay until the day's work ended. Al gave her a strange look, and made no more comment. The kindly Stillwell then began to talk.

"Miss Majesty, you're seein' the life of the cattleman an' cowboy—the real thing—same as it was in the early days. The ranchers in Texas an' some in Arizona hev took on style, new-fangled idees thet are good, an' I wish we could follow them. But we've got to stick to the old-fashioned, open-range round-up. It looks cruel to you, I can see thet. Wal, mebbe so, mebbe so. Them Greasers are cruel, thet's certain. Fer thet matter, I never seen a Greaser who wasn't cruel. But I reckon all the strenuous work you've seen today ain't any tougher than most any day of a cowboy's life. Long hours on hossback, poor grub, sleepin' on the ground, lonesome watches, dust an' sun an' wind an' thirst, day in an' day out all the year round—thet's what a cowboy has.

"Look at Nels there. See, what little hair he has is snow-white. He's red an' thin an' hard—burned up. You notice thet hump of his shoulders. An' his hands, when he gets close— jest take a peep at his hands. Nels can't pick up a pin. He can't hardly button his shirt or untie a knot in his rope. He looks sixty years—an old man. Wal, Nels ain't seen forty. He's a young man, but he's seen a lifetime fer every year. Miss Majesty, it was Arizona thet made Nels what he is, the Arizona desert an' the work of a cowman. He's seen ridin' at Cañon Diablo an' the Verdi an' Tonto Basin. He knows every mile of Aravaipa Valley an' the Pinaleno country. He's ranged from Tombstone to Douglas. He hed shot bad white men an' bad Greasers before he was twenty-one. He's seen some life, Nels has. My sixty years ain't nothin'; my early days in the Staked Plains an' on the border with Apaches ain't nothin' to what Nels has seen an' lived through. He's just come to be part of the desert; you might say he's stone an' fire an' silence an' cactus an' force. He's a man, Miss Majesty, a wonderful man. Rough he'll seem to you. Wal, I'll show you pieces of quartz from the mountains back of my ranch an' they're thet rough they'd cut your hands. But there's pure gold in them. An' so it is with Nels an' many of these cowboys.

"An' there's Price—Monty Price. Monty stands fer Montana, where he hails from. Take a good look at him, Miss Majesty. He's been hurt, I reckon. Thet accounts fer him bein' without hoss or rope; an' thet limp. Wal, he's been ripped a little. It's sure rare an' seldom thet a cowboy gets foul of one of them thousands of sharp horns; but it does happen."

Madeline saw a very short, wizened little man, ludicrously bow-legged, with a face the color and hardness of a burned-out cinder. He was hobbling by toward the wagon, and one of his short, crooked legs dragged.

"Not much to look at, is he?" went on Stillwell. "Wal, I know it's natural thet we're all best pleased by good looks in any one, even a man. It hedn't ought to be thet way. Monty Price looks like hell. But appearances are sure deceivin'. Monty saw years of ridin' along the Missouri bottoms, the big prairies, where there's high grass an' sometimes fires. In Montana they have blizzards that freeze cattle standin' in their tracks. An' hosses freeze to death. They tell me thet a drivin' sleet in the face with the mercury forty below is somethin' to ride against. You can't get Monty to say much about cold. All you hev to do is watch him, how he hunts the sun. It never gets too hot fer Monty. Wal, I reckon he was a little more prepossessin' once. The story thet come to us about Monty is this: He got caught out in a prairie fire an' could hev saved himself easy, but there was a lone ranch right in the line of fire, an' Monty knowed the rancher was away, an' his wife an' baby was home. He knowed, too, the way the wind was, thet the ranch-house would burn. It was a long chance he was takin'. But he went over, put the woman up behind him, wrapped the baby an' his hoss's haid in a wet blanket, an' rode away. Thet was sure some ride, I've heerd. But the fire ketched Monty at last. The woman fell an' was lost, an' then his hoss. An' Monty ran an' walked an' crawled through the

57

fire with thet baby, an' he saved it. Monty was never much good as a cowboy after thet. He couldn't hold no jobs. Wal, he'll have one with me as long as I have a steer left."

6

A Gift and a Purchase

For a week the scene of the round-up lay within riding distance of the ranch-house, and Madeline passed most of this time in the saddle, watching the strenuous labors of the *vaqueros* and cowboys. She overestimated her strength and more than once had to be lifted from her horse. Stillwell's pleasure in her attendance gave place to concern. He tried to persuade her to stay away from the round-up, and Florence grew even more solicitous.

Madeline, however, was not moved by their entreaties.

She grasped only dimly the truth of what it was she was learning—something infinitely more than the rounding up of cattle by cowboys, and she was loath to lose an hour of her opportunity.

Her brother looked out for her as much as his duties permitted; but for several days he never once mentioned her growing fatigue and the strain of excitement, or suggested that she had better go back to the house with Florence. Many times she felt the drawing power of his keen blue eyes on her face. And at these moments she sensed more than brotherly regard. He was watching her, studying her, weighing her, and the conviction was vaguely disturbing. It was disquieting for Madeline to think that Alfred might have guessed her trouble. From time to time he brought cowboys to her and introduced them, and laughed and jested, trying to make the ordeal less embarrassing for these men so little used to women.

Before the week was out, however, Alfred found occasion to tell her that it would be wiser for her to let the round-up go on without gracing it further with her presence. He said it laughingly; nevertheless, he was serious. And when Madeline turned to him in surprise he said, bluntly:

"I don't like the way Don Carlos follows you around. Bill's afraid that Nels or Ambrose or one of the cowboys will take a fall out of the Mexican. They're itching for the chance. Of course, dear, it's absurd to you, but it's true."

Absurd it certainly was, yet it served to show Madeline how intensely occupied she had been with her own feelings, roused by the tumult and toil of the round-up. She recalled that Don Carlos had been presented to her, and that she had not liked his dark, striking face with its bold, prominent, glittering eyes and sinister lines; and she had not liked his suave, sweet, insinuating voice or his subtle manner, with its slow bows and gestures. She had thought he looked handsome and dashing on the magnificent black horse. However, now that Alfred's words made her think, she recalled that wherever she had been in the field the noble horse, with his silver-mounted saddle and his dark rider, had been always in her vicinity.

"Don Carlos has been after Florence for a long time," said Alfred. "He's not a young man by any means. He's fifty, Bill says; but you can seldom tell a Mexican's age from his looks. Don Carlos is well educated and a man we know very little about. Mexicans of his stamp don't regard women as we white men do. Now, my dear, beautiful sister from New York, I haven't much use for Don Carlos; but I don't want Nels or Ambrose to make a wild throw with a rope and pull the Don off his horse. So you had better ride up to the house and stay there."

"Alfred, you are joking, teasing me," said Madeline.

"Indeed not," replied Alfred. "How about it, Flo?"

Florence replied that the cowboys would upon the slightest provocation treat Don Carlos with less ceremony and gentleness than a roped steer. Old Bill Stillwell came up to be importuned by Alfred regarding the conduct of cowboys on occasion, and he not only corroborated the assertion, but added emphasis and evidence of his own.

"An', Miss Majesty," he concluded, "I reckon if Gene Stewart was ridin' fer me, thet grinnin' Greaser would hev hed a bump in the dust before now."

Madeline had been wavering between sobriety and laughter until Stillwell's mention of his ideal of cowboy chivalry decided in favor of the laughter.

"I am not convinced, but I surrender," she said. "You have only some occult motive for driving me away. I am sure that handsome Don Carlos is being unjustly suspected. But as I have seen a little of cowboys' singular imagination and gallantry, I am rather inclined to fear their possibilities. So goodby."

Then she rode with Florence up the long, gray slope to the ranch-house. That night she suffered from excessive weariness, which she attributed more to the strange working of her mind than to riding and sitting her horse. Morning, however, found her in no disposition to rest. It was not activity that she craved, or excitement, or pleasure. An unerring instinct, rising clear from the thronging sensations of the last few days, told her that she had missed something in life. It could not have been love, for she loved brother, sister, parents, friends; it could not have been consideration for the poor, the unfortunate, the helpless; she had expressed her sympathy for these by giving freely; it could not have been pleasure, culture, travel, society, wealth, position, fame, for these had been hers all her life. Whatever this something was, she had baffling intimations of it, hopes that faded on the verge of realizations, haunting promises that were unfulfilled. Whatever it was, it had remained hidden and unknown at home and here in the West it began to allure and drive her to discovery. Therefore she could not rest; she wanted to go and see; she was no longer chasing phantoms; it was a hunt for treasure that held aloof, as intangible as the substance of dreams.

That morning she spoke a desire to visit the Mexican quarters lying at the base of the foothills. Florence protested that this was no place to take Madeline. But Madeline insisted, and it required only a few words and a persuading smile to win Florence over.

From the porch the cluster of adobe houses added a picturesque touch of color and contrast to the waste of gray valley. Near at hand they proved the enchantment lent by distance. They were old, crumbling, broken down, squalid. A few goats climbed around upon them; a few mangy dogs barked announcement of visitors; and then a troop of half-naked, dirty, ragged children ran out. They were very shy, and at first retreated in affright. But kind words and smiles gained their confidence, and then they followed in a body, gathering a quota of new children at each house. Madeline at once conceived the idea of doing something to better the condition of these poor Mexicans, and with this in mind she decided to have a look indoors. She fancied she might have been an apparition, judging from the effect her presence had upon the first woman she encountered. While Florence exercised what little Spanish she had command of, trying to get women to talk, Madeline looked about the miserable little rooms. And there grew upon her a feeling of sickness, which increased as she passed from one house to another. She had not believed such squalor could exist anywhere in America. The huts reeked with filth; vermin crawled over the dirt floors. There was absolutely no evidence of water, and she believed what Florence told her—that these people never bathed. There was little evidence of labor. Idle men and women smoking cigarettes lolled about, some silent, others jabbering. They did not resent the visit of the American women, nor did they show hospitality. They appeared stupid. Disease was rampant in these houses; when the doors were shut there was no ventilation, and even with the doors open Madeline felt choked and stifled. A powerful penetrating odor pervaded the rooms that were less stifling than others, and this odor Florence explained came from a liquor the Mexicans distilled from a cactus plant. Here drunkenness was manifest, a terrible inert drunkenness that made its victims deathlike.

Madeline could not extend her visit to the little mission-house. She saw a padre, a starved, sad-faced man who, she instinctively felt, was good. She managed to mount her horse and ride up to the house; but, once there, she weakened and Florence had almost to carry her indoors. She fought off a faintness, only to succumb to it when alone in her room. Still, she did not entirely lose consciousness, and soon recovered to the extent that she did not require assistance.

Upon the morning after the end of the round-up, when she went out on the porch, her brother and Stillwell appeared to be arguing about the identity of a horse.

"Wal, I reckon it's my old roan," said Stillwell, shading his eyes with his hand.

"Bill, if that isn't Stewart's horse my eyes are going back on me," replied Al. "It's not the color or shape—the distance is too far to judge by that. It's the motion—the swing."

"Al, mebbe you're right. But they ain't no rider up on thet hoss. Flo, fetch my glass."

Florence went into the house, while Madeline tried to discover the object of attention. Presently far up the gray hollow along a foothill she saw dust, and then the dark, moving figure of a horse. She was watching when Florence returned with the glass. Bill took a long look, adjusted the glasses carefully, and tried again.

"Wal, I hate to admit my eyes are gettin' pore. But I guess I'll hev to. Thet's Gene Stewart's hoss, saddled, an' comin' at a fast clip without a rider. It's amazin' strange, an' some in keepin' with other things concernin' Gene."

"Give me the glass," said Al. "Yes, I was right. Bill, the horse is not frightened. He's coming steadily, he's got something on his mind."

"Thet's a trained hoss, Al. He has more sense than some men I know. Take a look with the glasses up the hollow. See anybody?"

"No."

"Swing up over the foothills—where the trail leads. Higher —along thet ridge where the rocks begin. See anybody?"

"By Jove! Bill—two horses! But I can't make out much for dust. They are climbing fast. One horse gone among the rocks. There—the other's gone. What do you make of that?"

"Wal, I can't make no more 'n you. But I'll bet we know somethin' soon, fer Gene's hoss is comin' faster as he nears the ranch."

The wide hollow sloping up into the foothills lay open to unobstructed view, and less than half a mile distant Madeline saw the riderless horse coming along the white trail at a rapid canter. She watched him, recalling the circumstances under which she had first seen him, and then his wild flight through the dimly lighted streets of El Cajon out into the black night. She thrilled again and believed she would never think of that starry night's adventure without a thrill. She watched the horse and felt more than curiosity. A shrill, piercing whistle pealed in.

"Wal, he's seen us, thet's sure," said Bill.

The horse neared the corrals, disappeared into a lane and then, breaking his gait again, thundered into the inclosure and pounded to a halt some twenty yards from where Stillwell waited for him.

One look at him at close range in the clear light of day was enough for Madeline to award him a blue ribbon over all horses, even her prize-winning White Stockings. The cowboy's great steed was no lithe, slender-bodied mustang. He was a charger, almost tremendous of build, with a black coat faintly mottled in gray, and it shone like polished glass in the sun. Evidently he had been carefully dressed down for this occasion, for there was no dust on him, nor a kink in his beautiful mane, nor a mark on his glossy hide.

"Come hyar, you son-of-a-gun," said Stillwell.

The horse dropped his head, snorted, and came obediently up. He was neither shy nor wild. He poked a friendly nose at Stillwell, and then looked at Al and the women. Unhooking the stirrups from the pommel, Stillwell let them fall and began to search the saddle for something which he evidently expected to find. Presently from somewhere among the trappings he produced a folded bit of paper, and after scrutinizing it handed it to Al.

"Addressed to you; and I'll bet you two bits I know what's in it," he said.

Alfred unfolded the letter, read it, and then looked at Stillwell.

"Bill, you're a pretty good guesser. Gene's made for the border. He sent the horse by somebody, no names mentioned, and wants my sister to have him if she will accept."

"Any mention of Danny Mains?" asked the rancher.

"Not a word."

"Thet's bad. Gene'd know about Danny if anybody did. But he's a close-mouthed cuss. So he's sure hittin' for Mexico. Wonder if Danny's goin', too? Wal, there's two of the best cowmen I ever seen gone to hell, an' I'm sorry."

With that he bowed his head and, grumbling to himself, went into the house. Alfred lifted the reins over the head of the horse and, leading him to Madeline, slipped the knot over her arm and placed the letter in her hand.

"Majesty, I'd accept the horse," he said. "Stewart is only a cowboy now, and tough as any I've known. But he comes of a good family. He was a college man and a gentleman once. He went to the bad out here, like so many fellows go, like I nearly did. Then he had told me about his sister and mother. He cared a good deal for them. I think he has been a source of unhappiness to them. It was mostly when he was reminded of this in some way that he'd get drunk. I have always stuck to him, and I would do so yet if I had the chance. You can see

63

Bill is heartbroken about Danny Mains and Stewart. I think he rather hoped to get good news. There's not much chance of them coming back now, at least not in the case of Stewart. This giving up his horse means he's going to join the rebel forces across the border. What wouldn't I give to see that cowboy break loose on a bunch of Greasers! Oh, damn the luck! I beg your pardon, Majesty. But I'm upset, too. I'm sorry about Stewart. I liked him pretty well before he thrashed that coyote of a sheriff, Pat Hawe, and afterward I guess I liked him more. You read the letter, sister, and accept the horse."

In silence Madeline bent her gaze from her brother's face to the letter:

FRIEND AL: I'm sending my horse down to you because I'm going away and haven't the nerve to take him where he'd get hurt or fall into strange hands.

If you think it's all right, why, give him to your sister with my respects. But if you don't like the idea, Al, or if she won't have him, then he's for you. I'm not forgetting your kindness to me, even if I never showed it. And, Al, my horse has never felt a quirt or a spur, and I'd like to think you'd never hurt him. I'm hoping your sister will take him. She'll be good to him, and she can afford to take care of him. And, while I'm waiting to be plugged by a Greaser bullet, if I happen to have a picture in mind of how she'll look upon my horse, why, man, it's not going to make any difference to you. She needn't ever know it.

Between you and me, Al, don't let her or Flo ride alone over Don Carlos's way. If I had time I could tell you something about that slick Greaser. And tell your sister, if there's ever any reason for her to run away from anybody when she's up on that roan, just let her lean over and yell in his ear. She'll find herself riding the wind. So long.

GENE STEWART

Madeline thoughtfully folded the letter and murmured, "How he must love his horse!"

"Well, I should say so," replied Alfred. "Flo will tell you. She's the only person Gene ever let ride that horse, unless, as

Bill thinks, the little Mexican girl, Bonita, rode him out of El Cajon the other night. Well, sister mine, how about it—will you accept the horse?"

"Assuredly. And very happy indeed am I to get him. Al, you said, I think, that Mr. Stewart named him after me—saw my nickname in the New York paper?"

"Yes."

"Well, I will not change his name. But, Al, how shall I ever climb up on him? He's taller than I am. What a giant of a horse! Oh, look at him—he's nosing my hand. I really believe he understood what I said. Al, did you ever see such a splendid head and such beautiful eyes? They are so large and dark and soft—and human. Oh, I am a fickle woman, for I am forgetting White Stockings."

"I'll gamble he'll make you forget any other horse," said Alfred. "You'll have to get on him from the porch."

As Madeline was not dressed for the saddle, she did not attempt to mount.

"Come, Majesty—how strange that sounds!—we must get acquainted. You have now a new owner, a very severe young woman who will demand loyalty from you and obedience, and some day, after a decent period, she will expect love."

Madeline led the horse to and fro, and was delighted with his gentleness. She discovered that he did not need to be led. He came at her call, followed her like a pet dog, rubbed his black muzzle against her. Sometimes, at the turns in their walk, he lifted his head and with ears forward looked up the trail by which he had come, and beyond the foothills. He was looking over the range. Some one was calling to him, perhaps, from beyond the mountains. Madeline liked him the better for that memory, and pitied the wayward cowboy who had parted with his only possession for very love of it.

That afternoon when Alfred lifted Madeline to the back of the big roan she felt high in the air.

"We'll have a run out to the mesa," said her brother, as he mounted. "Keep a tight rein on him, and ease up when you want him to go faster. But don't yell in his ear unless you want Florence and me to see you disappear on the horizon."

He trotted out of the yard, down by the corrals, to come out on the edge of a gray, open flat that stretched several miles to the slope of a mesa. Florence led, and Madeline saw that she rode like a cowboy. Alfred drew on to her side, leaving Madeline in the rear. Then the leading horses broke into a gallop. They wanted to run, and Madeline felt with a thrill that she would hardly be able to keep Majesty from running, even if she wanted to. He sawed on the tight bridle as the others drew away and broke from pace to gallop. Then Florence put her horse into a run. Alfred turned and called to Madeline to come along.

"This will never do. They are running away from us," said Madeline, and she eased up her hold on the bridle. Something happened beneath her just then; she did not know at first exactly what. As much as she had been on horseback she had never ridden at a running gait. In New York it was not decorous or safe. So when Majesty lowered and stretched and changed the stiff, jolting gallop for a wonderful, smooth, gliding run it required Madeline some moments to realize what was happening. It did not take long for her to see the distance diminishing between her and her companions. Still they had gotten a goodly start and were far advanced. She felt the steady even rush of the wind. It amazed her to find how easily, comfortably she kept to the saddle. The experience was new. The one fault she had heretofore found with riding was the violent shaking-up. In this instance she experienced nothing of that kind, no strain, no necessity to hold on with a desperate awareness of work. She had never felt the wind in her face, the whip of a horse's mane, the buoyant, level spring of a running gait. It thrilled her, exhilarated her, fired her blood. Suddenly she found herself alive, throbbing; and, inspired by she knew not what, she loosened the bridle and, leaning far forward, she cried, "Oh, you splendid fellow, run!"

She heard from under her a sudden quick clattering roar of hoofs, and she swayed back with the wonderfully swift increase in Majesty's speed. The wind stung her face, howled in her ears, tore at her hair. The gray plain swept by on each side, and in front seemed to be waving toward her. In her blurred sight Florence and Albert appeared to be coming back. But she saw presently, upon nearer view, that Majesty was overhauling the other horses, was going to pass them. Indeed, he did pass them, shooting by so as almost to make them appear standing still. And he ran on, not breaking his gait till he reached the steep side of the mesa, where he slowed down and stopped.

"Glorious!" exclaimed Madeline. She was all in a blaze and

every muscle and nerve of her body tingled and quivered. Her hands, as she endeavored to put up the loosened strands of hair, trembled and failed of their accustomed dexterity. Then she faced about and waited for her companions.

Alfred reached her first, laughing, delighted, yet also a little anxious.

"Holy smoke! But can't he run? Did he bolt on you?"

"No, I called in his ear," replied Madeline.

"So that was it. That's the woman of you, and forbidden fruit. Flo said she'd do it the minute she was on him. Majesty, you can ride. See if Flo doesn't say so."

The Western girl came up then with her pleasure bright in her face.

"It was just great to see you. How your hair burned in the wind! Al, she sure can ride. Oh, I'm so glad! I was a little afraid. And that horse! Isn't he grand? Can't he run?"

Alfred led the way up the steep zigzag trail to the top of the mesa. Madeline saw a beautiful flat surface of short grass, level as a floor. She uttered a little cry of wonder and enthusiasm.

"Al, what a place for golf! This would be the finest links in the world."

"Well, I've thought of that myself," he replied. "The only trouble would be—could anybody stop looking at the scenery long enough to hit a ball? Majesty, look!"

And then it seemed that Madeline was confronted by a spectacle too sublime and terrible for her gaze. The immensity of this red-ridged, deep-gulfed world descending by incalculable distances refused to be grasped, and awed her, shocked her.

"Once, Majesty, when I first came out West, I was down and out—determined to end it all," said Alfred. "And I happened to climb up here looking for a lonely place to die. When I saw that I changed my mind."

Madeline was silent. She remained so during the ride around the rim of the mesa and down the steep trail. This time Alfred and Florence failed to tempt her into a race. She had been awe-struck; she had been exalted; she had been confounded; and she recovered slowly without divining exactly what had come to her.

She reached the ranch-house far behind her companions, and at supper-time was unusually thoughtful. Later, when they assembled on the porch to watch the sunset, Stillwell's humorous complainings inspired the inception of an idea which flashed up in her mind swift as lightning. And then by listening sympathetically she encouraged him to recite the troubles of a poor cattleman. They were many and long and interesting, and rather numbing to the life of her inspired idea.

"Mr. Stillwell, could ranching here on a large scale, with up-to-date methods, be made—well, not profitable, exactly, but to pay—to run without loss?" she asked, determined to kill her new-born idea at birth or else give it breath and hope of life.

"Wal, I reckon it could," he replied, with a short laugh. "It'd sure be a money-maker. Why, with all my bad luck an' equipment I've lived pretty well an' paid my debts an' haven't really lost any money except the original outlay. I reckon thet's sunk fer good."

"Would you sell—if someone would pay your price?"

"Miss Majesty, I'd jump at the chance. Yet somehow I'd hate to leave hyar. I'd jest be fool enough to go sink the money in another ranch."

"Would Don Carlos and these other Mexicans sell?"

"They sure would. The Don has been after me fer years, wantin' to sell thet old rancho of his; an' these herders in the valley with their stray cattle, they'd fall daid at sight of a little money."

"Please tell me, Mr. Stillwell, exactly what you would do here if you had unlimited means?" went on Madeline.

"Good Lud!" ejaculated the rancher, and stared so he dropped his pipe. Then with his clumsy huge fingers he re-filled it, relighted it, took a few long pulls, puffed great clouds of smoke, and, squaring round, hands on his knees, he looked at Madeline with piercing intentness. His hard face began to relax and soften and wrinkle into a smile.

"Wal, Miss Majesty, it jest makes my old heart warm up to think of sich a thing. I dreamed a lot when I first come hyar. What would I do if I hed unlimited money? Listen. I'd buy out Don Carlos an' the Greasers. I'd give a job to every good cowman in this country. I'd make them prosper as I prospered myself. I'd buy all the good horses on the ranges. I'd fence twenty thousand acres of the best grazin'. I'd drill fer water in the valley. I'd pipe water down from the mountains. I'd dam

68

up that draw out there. A mile-long dam from hill to hill would give me a big lake, an' hevin' an eye fer beauty, I'd plant cottonwoods around it. I'd fill that lake full of fish. I'd put in the biggest field of alfalfa in the Southwest. I'd plant fruit trees an' garden. I'd tear down them old corrals an' barns an' bunk-houses to build new ones. I'd put in grass an' flowers all around an' bring young pine trees down from the mountains. An' when all thet was done I'd sit in my chair an' smoke an' watch the cattle stringin' in fer water an' stragglin' back into the valley. An' I see the cowboys ridin' easy an' heah them singin' in their bunks. An' thet red sun out there wouldn't set on a happier man in the world than Bill Stillwell, last of the old cattlemen."

Madeline thanked the rancher, and then rather abruptly retired to her room, where she felt no restraint to hide the force of that wonderful idea, now full-grown and tenacious and alluring.

Upon the next day, late in the afternoon, she asked Alfred if it would be safe for her to ride out to the mesa.

"I'll go with you," he said, gaily.

"Dear fellow, I want to go alone," she replied.

"Ah!" Alfred exclaimed, suddenly serious. He gave her just a quick glance, then turned away. "Go ahead. I think it's safe. I'll make it safe by sitting here with my glass and keeping an eye on you. Be careful coming down the trail. Let the horse pick his way. That's all."

She rode Majesty across the wide flat, up the zigzag trail across the beautiful grassy level to the far rim of the mesa, and not till then did she lift her eyes to face the southwest.

Madeline looked from the gray valley at her feet to the blue Sierra Madres, gold-tipped in the setting sun. Her vision embraced in that glance distance and depth and glory hitherto unrevealed to her. The gray valley sloped and widened to the black sentinel Chiricahuas, and beyond was lost in a vast corrugated sweep of earth, reddening down to the west, where a golden blaze lifted the dark, rugged mountains into bold relief. The scene had infinite beauty. But after Madeline's first swift, all-embracing flash of enraptured eyes, thought of beauty passed away. In that darkening desert there was something illimitable. Madeline saw the hollow of a stupendous hand; she felt a mighty hold upon her heart. Out of the endless space, out of silence and desolation and mystery and age,

69

came slow-changing colored shadows, phantoms of peace, and they whispered to Madeline. They whispered that it was a great, grim, immutable earth; that time was eternity; that life was fleeting. They whispered for her to be a woman; to love someone before it was too late; to love anyone, everyone; to realize the need of work, and in doing it to find happiness.

She rode back across the mesa and down the trail, and, once more upon the flat, she called to the horse and made him run. His spirit seemed to race with hers. The wind of his speed blew her hair from its fastenings. When he thundered to a halt at the porch steps Madeline, breathless and disheveled, alighted with the mass of her hair tumbling around her.

Alfred met her, and his exclamation, and Florence's rapt eyes shining on her face, and Stillwell's speechlessness made her self-conscious. Laughing, she tried to put up the mass of hair.

"I must look a fright," she panted.

"Wal, you can say what you like," replied the old cattleman, "but I know what I think."

Madeline strove to attain calmness.

"My hat—and my combs—went on the wind. I thought—my hair would go, too. . . . There is the evening star. . . . I think I am very hungry."

And then she gave up trying to be calm, and likewise to fasten up her hair, which fell again in a golden mass.

"Mr. Stillwell," she began, and paused, strangely aware of a hurried note, a deeper ring in her voice. "Mr. Stillwell, I want to buy your ranch—to engage you as my superintendent. I want to buy Don Carlos's ranch and other property to the extent, say, of fifty thousand acres. I want you to buy horses and cattle—in short, to make all those improvements which you said you had so long dreamed of. Then I have ideas of my own, in the development of which I must have your advice and Alfred's. I intend to better the condition of those poor Mexicans in the valley. I intend to make life a little more worth living for them and for the cowboys of this range. Tomorrow we shall talk it all over, plan all the business details."

Madeline turned from the huge, ever-widening smile that beamed down upon her and held out her hands to her brother.

"Alfred, strange, is it not, my coming out to you? Nay, don't smile. I hope I have found myself—my work, my happiness—here under the light of that western star."

7

Her Majesty's Rancho

Five months brought all that Stillwell had dreamed of, and so
many more changes and improvements and innovations that it
was as if a magic touch had transformed the old ranch. Madeline and Alfred and Florence had talked over a fitting name,
and had decided on one chosen by Madeline. But this instance
was the only one in the course of developments in which
Madeline's wishes were not complied with. The cowboys
named the new ranch "Her Majesty's Rancho." Stillwell said
the names cowboys bestowed were felicitous, and as unchangeable as the everlasting hills; Florence went over to the
enemy; and Alfred, laughing at Madeline's protest, declared
the cowboys had elected her queen of the ranges, and that
there was no help for it. So the name stood "Her Majesty's
Rancho."

The April sun shone down upon a slow-rising green knoll
that nestled in the lee of the foothills, and seemed to center
bright rays upon the long ranch-house, which gleamed snow-
white from the level summit. The grounds around the house
bore no semblance to Eastern lawns or parks; there had been
no landscape-gardening; Stillwell had just brought water and
grass and flowers and plants to the knoll-top, and there had
left them, as it were, to follow nature. His idea may have been
crude, but the result was beautiful. Under that hot sun and
balmy air, with cool water daily soaking into rich soil, a green
covering sprang into life, and everywhere upon it, as if by
magic, many colored flowers rose in the sweet air. Pale wild
flowers, lavender daisies, fragile bluebells, white four-petaled
lilies, like Eastern mayflowers, and golden poppies, deep sunset gold, color of the West, bloomed in happy confusion. California roses, crimson as blood, nodded heavy heads and

trembled with the weight of bees. Low down in bare places, isolated, open to the full power of the sun, blazed the vermilion and magenta blossoms of cactus plants.

Green slopes led all the way down to where new adobe barns and sheds had been erected, and wide corrals stretched high-barred fences down to the great squares of alfalfa gently inclining to the gray of the valley. The bottom of a dammed-up hollow shone brightly with its slowly increasing acreage of water, upon which thousands of migratory wild-fowl whirred and splashed and squawked, as if reluctant to leave this cool, wet surprise so new in the long desert journey to the northland. Quarters for the cowboys—comfortable, roomy adobe houses that not even the lamest cowboy dared designate as crampy bunks—stood in a row upon a long bench of ground above the lake. And down to the edge of the valley the cluster of Mexican habitations and the little church showed the touch of the same renewing hand.

All that had been left of the old Spanish house which had been Stillwell's home for so long was the bare, massive structure, and some of this had been cut away for new doors and windows. Every modern convenience, even to hot and cold running water and acetylene light, had been installed; and the whole interior painted and carpentered and furnished. The ideal sought had not been luxury, but comfort. Every door into the patio looked out upon dark, rich grass and sweet-faced flowers, and every window looked down the green slopes.

Madeline's rooms occupied the west end of the building and comprised four in number, all opening out upon the long porch. There was a small room for her maid, another which she used as an office, then her sleeping-apartment; and, lastly, the great light chamber which she had liked so well upon first sight, and which now, simply yet beautifully furnished and containing her favorite books and pictures, she had come to love as she had never loved any room at home. In the morning the fragrant, balmy air blew the white curtains of the open windows; at noon the drowsy, sultry quiet seemed to creep in for the siesta that was characteristic of the country; in the afternoon the westering sun peeped under the porch roof and painted the walls with gold bars that slowly changed to red.

Madeline Hammond cherished a fancy that the transformation she had wrought in the old Spanish house and in the people with whom she had surrounded herself, great as that transformation had been, was as nothing compared to the one wrought in herself. She had found an object in life. She was busy, she worked with her hands as well as mind, yet she seemed to have more time to read and think and study and idle and dream than ever before. She had seen her brother through his difficulties, on the road to all the success and prosperity that he cared for. Madeline had been a conscientious student of ranching and an apt pupil of Stillwell. The old cattleman, in his simplicity, gave her the place in his heart that was meant for the daughter he had never had. His pride in her, Madeline thought, was beyond reason or belief or words to tell. Under his guidance, sometimes accompanied by Alfred and Florence, Madeline had ridden the ranges and had studied the life and work of the cowboys. She had camped on the open range, slept under the blinking stars, ridden forty miles a day in the face of dust and wind. She had taken two wonderful trips down into the desert—one trip to Chiricahua, and from there across the waste of sand and rock and alkali and cactus to the Mexican borderline; and the other through the Aravaipa Valley, with its deep, red-walled cañons and wild fastnesses.

This breaking-in, this training into Western ways though she had been a so-called outdoor girl, had required great effort and severe pain; but the education, now past its primary grades, had become a labor of love. She had perfect health, abounding spirits. She was so active that she had to train herself into taking the midday siesta, a custom of the country and imperative during the hot summer months. Sometimes she looked in her mirror and laughed with sheer joy at sight of the lithe, audacious, brown-faced flashing-eyed creature reflected there. It was not so much joy in her beauty as sheer joy of life. Eastern critics had been wont to call her beautiful in those days when she had been pale and slender and proud and cold. She laughed. If they could only see her now! From the tip of her golden head to her feet she was alive, pulsating, on fire.

Sometimes she thought of her parents, sister, friends, of how they had persistently refused to believe she could or would stay in the West. They were always asking her to come home. And when she wrote, which was dutifully often, the

73

last thing under the sun that she was likely to mention was the change in her. She wrote that she would return to her old home some time, of course, for a visit; and letters such as this brought returns that amused Madeline, sometimes saddened her. She meant to go back East for a while, and after that once or twice every year. But the initiative was a difficult step from which she shrank. Once home, she would have to make explanations, and these would not be understood. Her father's business had been such that he could not leave it for the time required for a Western trip, or else, according to his letter, he would have come for her. Mrs. Hammond could not have been driven to cross the Hudson River; her un-American idea of the wilderness westward was that Indians still chased buffalo on the outskirts of Chicago. Madeline's sister Helen had long been eager to come, as much from curiosity, Madeline thought, as from sisterly regard. And at length Madeline concluded that the proof of her breaking permanent ties might better be seen by visiting relatives and friends before she went back East. With that in mind she invited Helen to visit her during the summer, and bring as many friends as she liked.

No slight task indeed was it to oversee the many business details of Her Majesty's Rancho and to keep a record of them. Madeline found the course of business training upon which her father had insisted to be invaluable to her now. It helped her to assimilate and arrange the practical details of cattle-raising as put forth by the blunt Stillwell. She split up the great stock of cattle into different herds, and when any of these were out running upon the open range she had them closely watched. Part of the time each herd was kept in an inclosed range, fed and watered, and carefully handled by a big force of cowboys. She employed three cowboy scouts whose sole duty was to ride the ranges searching for stray, sick, or crippled cattle or motherless calves, and to bring these in to be treated and nursed. There were two cowboys whose business was to master a pack of Russian stag-hounds and to hunt down the coyotes, wolves, and lions that preyed upon the herds. The better and tamer milch cows were separated from the ranging herds and kept in a pasture adjoining the dairy. All branding was done in corrals, and calves were weaned from mother-cows at the proper time to benefit both. The old method of branding and classing, that had so shocked Madeline, had been abandoned, and one had been inaugurated whereby cattle and cowboys and horses were spared brutality and injury.

Madeline established an extensive vegetable farm, and she planted orchards. The climate was superior to that of California, and, with abundant water, trees and plants and gardens flourished and bloomed in a way wonderful to behold. It was with ever-increasing pleasure that Madeline walked through acres of ground once bare, now green and bright and fragrant. There were poultry yards and pig pens and marshy quarters for ducks and geese. Here in the farming section of the ranch Madeline found employment for the little colony of Mexicans. Their lives had been as hard and barren as the dry valley where they had lived. But as the valley had been transformed by the soft, rich touch of water, so their lives had been transformed by help and sympathy and work. The children were wretched no more, and many that had been blind could now see, and Madeline had become to them a new and blessed virgin.

Madeline looked abroad over these lands and likened the change in them and those who lived by them to the change in her heart. It may have been fancy, but the sun seemed to be brighter, the sky bluer, the wind sweeter. Certain it was that the deep green of grass and garden was not fancy, nor the white and pink of blossom, nor the blaze and perfume of flower, nor the sheen of lake and the fluttering of new-born leaves. Where there had been monotonous gray there was now vivid and changing color. Formerly there had been silence both day and night; now during the sunny hours there was music. The whistle of prancing stallions pealed in from the grassy ridges. Innumerable birds had come and, like the northward-journeying ducks, they had tarried to stay. The song of meadow-lark and blackbird and robin, familiar to Madeline from childhood, mingled with the new and strange heart-throbbing song of mockingbird and the piercing blast of the desert eagle and the melancholy moan of turtledove.

One April morning Madeline sat in her office wrestling with a problem. She had problems to solve every day. The majority of these were concerned with the management of twenty-seven incomprehensible cowboys. This particular problem involved Ambrose Mills, who had eloped with her French maid, Christine.

Stillwell faced Madeline with a smile almost as huge as his bulk.

"Wal, Miss Majesty, we ketched them; but not before Padre Marcos had married them. All thet speedin' in the autoomoobile was jest a-scarin' of me to death fer nothin'. I tell you Link Stevens is crazy about runnin' thet car. Link never hed no sense even with a hoss. He ain't afraid of the devil hisself. If my hair hedn't been white it'd be white now. No more rides in thet thing fer me! Wal, we ketched Ambrose an' the girl too late. But we fetched them back, an' they're out there now, spoonin', sure oblivious to their shameless conduct."

"Stillwell, what shall I say to Ambrose? How shall I punish him? He has done wrong to deceive me. I never was so surprised in my life. Christine did not seem to care any more for Ambrose than any of the other cowboys. What does my authority amount to? I must do something. Stillwell, you must help me."

Whenever Madeline fell into a quandary she had to call upon the old cattleman. No man ever held a position with greater pride than Stillwell, but he had been put to tests that steeped him in humility. Here he scratched his head in great perplexity.

"Doggone the luck! What's this elopin' bizness to do with cattle-raisin'? I don't know nothin' but cattle. Miss Majesty, it's amazin' strange what these cowboys hev come to. I never seen no cowboys like these we've got hyar now. I don't know them any more. They dress swell an' read books, an' some of them hev actooly stopped cussin' an' drinkin'. I ain't sayin' all this is against them. Why, now, they're jest the finest bunch of cow-punchers I ever seen or dreamed of. But managin' them now is beyond me. When cowboys begin to play thet game gol-lof an' run off with French maids I reckon Bill Stillwell has got to resign."

"Stillwell! Oh, you will not leave me? What in the world would I do?" exclaimed Madeline, in great anxiety.

"Wal, I sure won't leave you, Miss Majesty. No. I never'll do thet. I'll run the cattle bizness fer you an' see after the hosses an' other stock. But I've got to hev a foreman who can handle this amazin' strange bunch of cowboys."

"You've tried half a dozen foremen. Try more until you find the man who meets your requirements," said Madeline. "Never mind that now. Tell me how to impress Ambrose—to make him an example, so to speak. I must have another maid. And I do not want a new one carried off in this summary manner."

"Wal, if you fetch pretty maids out hyar you can't expect nothin' else. Why, thet black-eyed little French girl, with her white skin an' pretty airs an' smiles an' shrugs, she had the cowboys crazy. It'll be wuss with the next one."

"Oh dear!" sighed Madeline.

"An' as fer impressin' Ambrose, I reckon I can tell you how to do thet. Jest give it to him good an' say you're goin' to fire him. That'll fix Ambrose, an' mebbe scare the other boys fer a spell."

"Very well, Stillwell, bring Ambrose in to see me, and tell Christine to wait in my room."

It was a handsome, debonair, bright-eyed cowboy that came tramping into Madeline's presence. His accustomed shyness and awkwardness had disappeared in an excited manner. He was a happy boy. He looked straight into Madeline's face as if he expected her to wish him joy. And Madeline actually found that expression trembling to her lips. She held it back until she could be severe. But Madeline feared she would fail of much severity. Something warm and sweet, like a fragrance, had entered the room with Ambrose.

"Ambrose, what have you done?" she asked.

"Miss Hammond, I've been and gone and got married," replied Ambrose, his words tumbling over one another. His eyes snapped, and there was a kind of glow upon his clean-shaven brown cheek. "I've stole a march on the other boys. There was Frank Slade pushin' me close, and I was havin' some runnin' to keep Jim Bell back in my dust. Even old man Nels made eyes at Christine! So I wasn't goin' to take any chances. I just packed her off to El Cajon and married her."

"Oh, so I heard," said Madeline, slowly, as she watched him. "Ambrose, do you—love her?"

He reddened under her clear gaze, dropped his head, and fumbled with his new sombrero, and there was a catch in his breath. Madeline saw his powerful brown hand tremble. It affected her strangely that this stalwart cowboy, who could rope and throw and tie a wild steer in less than one minute, should tremble at a mere question. Suddenly he raised his head, and at the beautiful blaze of his eyes Madeline turned her own away.

"Yes, Miss Hammond, I love her," he said. "I think I love her in the way you're askin' about. I know the first time I saw her I thought how wonderful it'd be to have a girl like that for my wife. It's all been so strange—her comin' an' how she made me feel. Sure I never knew many girls, and I haven't seen any girls at all for years. But when she came! A girl makes a wonderful difference in a man's feelin's and thoughts. I guess I never had any before. Leastways, none like I have now. My—it—well, I guess I have a little understandin' now of Padre Marcos's blessin'."

"Ambrose, have you nothing to say to me?" asked Madeline.

"I'm sure sorry I didn't have time to tell you. But I was in some hurry."

"What did you intend to do? Where were you going when Stillwell found you?"

"We'd just been married. I hadn't thought of anything after that. Suppose I'd have rustled back to my job. I'll sure have to work now and save my money."

"Oh, well, Ambrose, I am glad you realize your responsibilities. Do you earn enough—is your pay sufficient to keep a wife?"

"Sure it is! Why, Miss Hammond, I never before earned half the salary I'm gettin' now. It's some fine to work for you. I'm goin' to fire the boys out of my bunk-house and fix it up for Christine and me. Say, won't they be jealous?"

"Ambrose, I—I congratulate you. I wish you joy," said Madeline. "I—I shall make Christine a little wedding-present. I want to talk to her for a few moments. You may go now."

It would have been impossible for Madeline to say one severe word to that happy cowboy. She experienced difficulty in hiding her own happiness at the turn of events. Curiosity and interest mingled with her pleasure when she called to Christine.

"Mrs. Ambrose Mills, please come in."

No sound came from the other room.

"I should like very much to see the bride," went on Madeline.

Still there was no stir or reply.

"Christine!" called Madeline.

Then it was as if a little whirlwind of flying feet and entreating hands and beseeching eyes blew in upon Madeline.

Christine was small, graceful, plump, with very white skin and very dark hair. She had been Madeline's favorite maid for years and there was sincere affection between the two. Whatever had been the blissful ignorance of Ambrose, it was manifestly certain that Christine knew how she had transgressed. Her fear and remorse and appeal for forgiveness were poured out in an incoherent storm. Plain it was that the little French maid had been overwhelmed. It was only after Madeline had taken the emotional girl in her arms and had forgiven and soothed her that her part in the elopement became clear. Christine was in a maze. But gradually, as she talked and saw that she was forgiven, calmness came in some degree, and with it a story which amused yet shocked Madeline. The unmistakable, shy, marveling love, scarcely realized by Christine, gave Madeline relief and joy. If Christine loved Ambrose there was no harm done. Watching the girl's eyes, wonderful with their changes of thought, listening to her attempts to explain what it was evident she did not understand, Madeline gathered that if ever a caveman had taken unto himself a wife, if ever a barbarian had carried off a Sabine woman, then Ambrose Mills had acted with the violence of such ancient forebears. Just how it all happened seemed to be beyond Christine.

"He say he love me," repeated the girl, in a kind of rapt awe. "He ask me to marry him—he kees me—he hug me—he lift me on ze horse—he ride with me all night—he marry me."

And she exhibited a ring on the third finger of her left hand. Madeline saw that, whatever had been the state of Christine's feeling for Ambrose before this marriage, she loved him now. She had been taken forcibly, but she was won.

After Christine had gone, comforted and betraying her shy eagerness to get back to Ambrose, Madeline was haunted by the look in the girl's eyes, and her words. Assuredly the spell of romance was on this sunny land. For Madeline there was a nameless charm, a nameless thrill combating her sense of the violence and unfitness of Ambrose's wooing. Something, she knew not what, took arms against her intellectual arraignment of the cowboy's method of getting himself a wife. He had said straight out that he loved the girl—he had asked her to marry him—he kissed her—he hugged her—he lifted her upon his horse—he rode away with her through the night—and he

79

married her. In whatever light Madeline reviewed this thing she always came back to her first natural impression; it thrilled her, charmed her. It went against all the precepts of her training; nevertheless, it was somehow splendid and beautiful. She imagined it stripped another artificial scale from her over-sophisticated eyes.

Scarcely had she settled again to the task on her desk when Stillwell's heavy tread across the porch interrupted her. This time when he entered he wore a look that bordered upon the hysterical; it was difficult to tell whether he was trying to suppress grief or glee.

"Miss Majesty, there's another amazin' strange thing sprung on me. Hyars Jim Bell come to see you, an', when I taxed him, sayin' you was tolerable busy, he up an' says he was hungry an' he ain't a-goin' to eat any more bread made in a washbasin! Says he'll starve first. Says Nels hed the gang over to his bunk an' feasted them on bread you taught him how to make in some newfangled bucket-machine with a crank. Jim says thet bread beat any cake he ever eat, an' he wants you to show him how to make some. Now, Miss Majesty, as superintendent of this ranch I ought to know what's goin' on. Mebbe Jim is jest a-joshin' me. Mebbe he's gone clear dotty. Mebbe I hev. An' beggin' your pardon, I want to know if there's any truth in what Jim says Nels says."

Whereupon it became necessary for Madeline to stifle her mirth and to inform the sadly perplexed old cattleman that she had received from the East a patent breadmixer, and in view of the fact that her household women had taken fright at the contrivance, she had essayed to operate it herself. This had turned out to be so simple, so saving of time, energy and flour, so much more cleanly than the old method of mixing dough with the hands, and particularly it had resulted in such good bread, that Madeline had been pleased. Immediately she ordered more of the breadmixers. One day she had happened upon Nels making biscuit dough in his washbasin, and she had delicately and considerately introduced to him the idea of her new method. Nels, it appeared, had a great reputation as a breadmaker, and he was proud of it. Moreover, he was skeptical of any claptrap thing with wheels and cranks. He consented, however, to let her show how the thing worked and to sample some of the bread. To that end she had him come up to the house, where she won him over. Stillwell laughed loud and long.

"Wal, wal, wal!" he exclaimed, at length. "Thet's fine, an' it's powerful funny. Mebbe you don't see how funny? Wal, Nels has just been lordin' it over the boys about how you showed *him*, an' now you'll hev to show every last cowboy on the place the same thing. Cowboys are the jealousest kind of fellers. They're all crazy about you anyway. Take Jim out hyar. Why, thet lazy cow-puncher jest never would make bread. He's notorious fer shirkin' his share of the grub deal. I've knowed Jim to trade off washin' the pots an' pans fer a lonely watch on a rainy night. All he wants is to see you show him the same as Nels is crowin' over. Then he'll crow over his bunkie, Frank Slade, an' then Frank'll get lonely to know all about this wonderful breadmachine. Cowboys are amazin' critters, Miss Majesty. An' now thet you've begun with them this way, you'll hev to keep it up. I will say I never seen such a bunch to work. You've sure put heart in them."

"Indeed, Stillwell, I am glad to hear that," replied Madeline. "And I shall be pleased to teach them all. But may I not have them all up here at once—at least those off duty?"

"Wal, I reckon you can't onless you want to hev them scrappin'," rejoined Stillwell, dryly. "What you've got on your hands now, Miss Majesty, is to let 'em come one by one, an' make each cowboy think you're takin' more especial pleasure in showin' him than the feller who came before him. Then mebbe we can go on with the cattle-raisin'."

Madeline protested, and Stillwell held inexorably to what he said was wisdom. Several times Madeline had gone against his advice, to her utter discomfiture and rout. She dared not risk it again, and resigned herself gracefully and with subdued merriment to her task. Jim Bell was ushered into the great, light, spotless kitchen, where presently Madeline appeared to put on an apron and roll up her sleeves. She explained the use of the several pieces of aluminum that made up the breadmixer and fastened the bucket to the table shelf. Jim's life might have depended upon this lesson, judging from his absorbed manner and his desire to have things explained over and over, especially the turning of the crank. When Madeline had to take Jim's hand three times to show him the simple mechanism and then he did not understand she began to have faint misgivings as to his absolute sincerity. She guessed that as long as she touched Jim's hand he never would understand. Then as she began to measure out flour and milk and lard and salt and yeast she saw with despair that Jim was not looking at the ingredients, was not paying the slightest attention to them. His eyes were covertly upon her.

"Jim, I am not sure about you,' said Madeline, severely. "How can you learn to make bread if you do not watch me mix it?"

"I am a-watchin' you," replied Jim, innocently.

Finally Madeline sent the cowboy on his way rejoicing with the breadmixer under his arm. Next morning, true to Still-well's prophecy, Frank Slade, Jim's bunkmate, presented himself cheerfully to Madeline and unbosomed himself of a long-deferred and persistent desire to relieve his overworked comrade of some of the housekeeping in their bunk.

"Miss Hammond," said Frank, "Jim's orful kind wantin' to do it all hisself. But he ain't very bright, an' I didn't believe him. You see, I'm from Missouri, an' you'll *have* to show me."

For a whole week Madeline held clinics where she expounded the scientific method of modern breadmaking. She got a good deal of enjoyment out of her lectures. What boys these great hulking fellows were! She saw through their simple ruses. Some of them were grave as deacons; others wore expressions important enough to have fitted the faces of statesmen signing government treaties. These cowboys were children; they needed to be governed; but in order to govern them they had to be humored. A more lighthearted, fun-loving crowd of boys could not have been found. And they were grown men. Stillwell explained that the exuberance of spirits lay in the difference in their fortunes. Twenty-seven cowboys, in relays of nine, worked eight hours a day. That had never been heard of before in the West. Stillwell declared that cowboys from all points of the compass would head their horses toward Her Majesty's Rancho.

8

El Capitan

Stillwell's interest in the revolution across the Mexican line had manifestly increased with the news that Gene Stewart had achieved distinction with the rebel forces. Thereafter the old cattleman sent for El Paso and Douglas newspapers, wrote to ranchmen he knew on the big bend of the Rio Grande, and he would talk indefinitely to any one who would listen to him. There was not any possibility of Stillwell's friends at the ranch forgetting his favorite cowboy. Stillwell always prefaced his eulogy with an apologetic statement that Stewart had gone to the bad. Madeline liked to listen to him, though she was not always sure which news was authentic and which imagination.

There appeared to be no doubt, however, that the cowboy had performed some daring feats for the rebels. Madeline found his name mentioned in several of the border papers. When the rebels under Madero stormed and captured the city of Juarez, Stewart did fighting that won him the name of El Capitan. This battle apparently ended the revolution. The capitulation of President Diaz followed shortly, and there was a feeling of relief among ranchers on the border from Texas to California. Nothing more was heard of Gene Stewart until April, when a report reached Stillwell that the cowboy had arrived in El Cajon, evidently hunting trouble. The old cattleman saddled a horse and started post-haste for town. In two days he returned, depressed in spirit. Madeline happened to be present when Stillwell talked to Alfred.

"I got there too late, Al," said the cattleman. "Gene was gone. An' what do you think of this? Danny Mains hed jest left with a couple of burros packed. I couldn't find what way he went, but I'm bettin' he hit the Peloncillo trail."

"Danny will show up some day," replied Alfred. "What did you learn about Stewart? Maybe he left with Danny."

"Not much," said Stillwell, shortly. "Gene's hell-bent fer election! No mountains fer him."

"Well, tell us about him."

Stillwell wiped his sweaty brow and squared himself to talk.

"Wal, it's sure amazin' strange about Gene. It's got me lo-coed. He arrived in El Cajon a week ago. He was trained down like as if he'd been ridin' the range all winter. He hed plenty of money—Mex, they said. An' all the Greasers was crazy about him. Called him El Capitan. He got drunk an' went roarin' round fer Pat Hawe. You remember that Greaser who was plugged last October—the night Miss Majesty arrived? Wal, he's daid. He's daid, an' people says thet Pat is a-goin' to lay thet killin' onto Gene. I reckon thet's jest talk, though Pat is mean enough to do it, if he hed the nerve. Any-way, if he was in El Cajon he kept mighty much to hisself. Gene walked up an' down, up an' down, all day an night, look-in' fer Pat. But he didn't find him. An', of course, he kept gettin' drunker. He jest got plumb bad. He made lots of trou-ble, but there wasn't no gun-play. Mebbe thet made him sore, so he went an' licked Flo's brother-in-law. Thet wasn't so bad. Jack sure needed a lickin'. Wal, then Gene met Danny an' tried to get Danny drunk. An' he couldn't! What do you think of that? Danny hedn't been drinkin'—wouldn't touch a drop. I'm sure glad of thet, but it's so amazin' strange. Why, Danny was a fish fer red liquor. I guess he an' Gene had some pretty hard words, though I'm not sure about thet. Anyway, Gene went down to the railroad an' got on an engine, an' he was in the engine when it pulled out. Lord, I hope he doesn't hold up the train! If he gets gay over in Arizona he'll go to the pen at Yuma. An' thet pen is a graveyard fer cowboys. I wired to agents along the railroad to look out for Stewart, an' to wire back to me if he's located."

"Suppose you do find him, Stillwell, what can you do?" in-quired Alfred.

The old man nodded gloomily.

"I straightened him up once. Mebbe I can do it again." Then, brightening somewhat, he turned to Madeline. "I jest hed an idee, Miss Majesty. If I can get him, Gene Stewart is the cowboy I want fer my foreman. *He* can manage this bunch of cow-punchers thet are drivin' me dotty. What's more, since he's fought fer the rebels an' got that name El Capitan, all the Greasers in the country will kneel to him. Now, Miss Majesty, we hevn't got rid of Don Carlos an' his *vaqueros* yet. To be sure, he sold you his house an' ranch an' stock. But you remember nothin' was put in black and white about when he should get out. An' Don Carlos ain't gettin' out. I don't like the looks of things a little bit. I'll tell you now thet Don Carlos knows somethin' about the cattle I lost, an' thet you've been losin' right along. Thet Greaser is hand an' glove with the rebels. I'm willin' to gamble thet when he does get out he an' his *vaqueros* will make another one of the bands of guerrillas thet are harassin' the border. This revolution ain't over yet. It's jest commenced. An' all these gangs of outlaws are goin' to take advantage of it. We'll see some old times, mebbe. Wal, I need Gene Stewart. I need him bad. Will you let me hire him, Miss Majesty, if I can get him straightened up?"

The old cattleman ended huskily.

"Stillwell, by all means find Stewart, and do not wait to straighten him up. Bring him to the ranch," replied Madeline.

Thanking her, Stillwell led his horse away.

"Strange how he loves that cowboy!" murmured Madeline.

"Not so strange Majesty," replied her brother. "Not when you know. Stewart has been with Stillwell on some hard trips into the desert alone. There's no middle course of feeling between men facing death in the desert. Either they hate each other or love each other. I don't know, but I imagine Stewart did something for Stillwell—saved his life, perhaps. Besides, Stewart's a lovable chap when he's going straight. I hope Stillwell brings him back. We do need him, Majesty. He's a born leader. Once I saw him ride into a bunch of Mexicans whom we suspected of rustling. It was fine to see him. Well, I'm sorry to tell you that we are worried about Don Carlos. Some of his *vaqueros* came into my yard the other day when I had left Flo alone. She had a bad scare. These *vaqueros* have been different since Don Carlos sold the ranch. For that matter, I never would have trusted a white woman alone with them. But they are bolder now. Something's in the wind. They've got assurance. They can ride off any night and cross the border."

During the succeeding week Madeline discovered that a good deal of her sympathy for Stillwell in his hunt for the reckless Stewart had insensibly grown to be sympathy for the cowboy. It was rather a paradox, she thought, that opposed to the continual reports of Stewart's wildness as he caroused from town to town were the continual expressions of good will and faith and hope universally given out by those near her at the ranch. Stillwell loved the cowboy; Florence was fond of him; Alfred liked and admired him, pitied him; the cowboys swore their regard for him the more he disgraced himself. The Mexicans called him *El Gran Capitan*. Madeline's personal opinion of Stewart had not changed in the least since the night it had been formed. But certain attributes of his, not clearly defined in her mind, and the gift of his beautiful horse, his valor with the fighting rebels, and all this strange regard for him, especially that of her brother, made her exceedingly regret the cowboy's present behavior.

Meanwhile Stillwell was so earnest and zealous that one not familiar with the situation would have believed he was trying to find and reclaim his own son. He made several trips to little stations in the valley, and from these he returned with a gloomy face. Madeline got the details from Alfred. Stewart was going from bad to worse—drunk, disorderly, savage, sure to land in the penitentiary. Then came a report that hurried Stillwell off to Rodeo. He returned on the third day, a crushed man. He had been so bitterly hurt that no one, not even Madeline, could get out of him what had happened. He admitted finding Stewart, failing to influence him; and when the old cattleman got so far he turned purple in the face and talked to himself, as if dazed: "But Gene was drunk. He was *drunk*, or he couldn't hev treated old Bill like thet!"

Madeline was stirred with an anger toward the brutal cowboy that was as strong as her sorrow for the loyal old cattleman. And it was when Stillwell gave up that she resolved to take a hand. The persistent faith of Stillwell, his pathetic excuses in the face of what must have been Stewart's violence, perhaps baseness, actuated her powerfully, gave her new insight into human nature. She honored a faith that remained unshaken. And the strange thought came to her that Stewart must somehow be worthy of such a faith, or he never could have inspired it. Madeline discovered that she wanted to believe that somewhere deep down in the most depraved and sinful wretch upon earth there was some grain of good. She yearned to have the faith in human nature that Stillwell had in Stewart.

She sent Nels, mounted upon his own horse, and leading Majesty, to Rodeo in search of Stewart. Nels had instructions to bring Stewart back to the ranch. In due time Nels returned, leading the roan without a rider.

"Yep, I shore found him," replied Nels, when questioned. "Found him half sobered up. He'd been in a scrap an' somebody hed put him to sleep, I guess. Wal, when he seen thet roan hoss he let out a yell an' grabbed him round the neck. The hoss knowed him, all right. Then Gene hugged the hoss an' cried—cried like—I never seen no one who cried like he did. I waited awhile, an' was jest goin' to say somethin' to him when he turned on me red-eyed, mad as fire. 'Nels,' he said, 'I care a hell of a lot fer thet hoss, an' I liked you pretty well, but if you don't take him away quick I'll shoot you both.' Wal, I lit out. I didn't even git to say howdy to him."

"Nels, you think it useless—any attempt to see him—persuade him?" asked Madeline.

"I shore do, Miss Hammond," replied Nels, gravely. "I've seen a few sun-blinded an' locoed an' snake-poisoned an' skunk-bitten cow-punchers in my day, but Gene Stewart beats em' all. He's shore runnin' wild fer the divide."

Madeline dismissed Nels, but before he got out of earshot she heard him speak to Stillwell, who awaited him on the porch.

"Bill, put this in your pipe an' smoke it—none of them scraps Gene has hed was over a woman! It used to be thet when he was drunk he'd scrap over every pretty Greaser girl he'd run across. Thet's why Pat Hawe thinks Gene plugged the strange *vaquero* who was with little Bonita thet night last fall. Wal, Gene's scrappin' now jest to git shot up hisself, for some reason thet only God Almighty knows."

Nel's story of how Stewart wept over his horse influenced Madeline powerfully. Her next move was to persuade Alfred to see if he could do better with this doggedly bent cowboy. Alfred needed only a word of persuasion, for he said he had considered going to Rodeo of his own accord. He went, and returned alone.

"Majesty, I can't explain Stewart's singular actions," said Alfred. "I saw him, talked with him. He knew me, but nothing I said appeared to get to him. He has changed terribly. I fancy his once magnificent strength is breaking. It—it actually hurt me to look at him. I couldn't have fetched him back here

—not as he is now. I heard all about him, and if he isn't downright out of his mind he's hell-bent, as Bill says, on getting killed. Some of his escapades are—are not for your ears. Bill did all any man could do for another. We've all done our best for Stewart. If you'd been given a chance perhaps you could have saved him. But it's too late. Put it out of mind now, dear."

Madeline, however, did not forget nor give it up. If she had forgotten or surrendered, she felt that she would have been relinquishing infinitely more than hope to aid one ruined man. But she was at a loss to know what further steps to take. Days passed, and each one brought additional gossip of Stewart's headlong career toward the Yuma penitentiary. For he had crossed the line into Cochise County, Arizona, where sheriffs kept a stricter observance of law. Finally a letter came from a friend of Nels's in Chiricahua saying that Stewart had been hurt in a brawl there. His hurt was not serious, but it would probably keep him quiet long enough to get sober, and this opportunity, Nels's informant said, would be a good one for Stewart's friends to take him home before he got locked up. This epistle inclosed a letter to Stewart from his sister. Evidently, it had been found upon him. It told a story of illness and made an appeal for aid. Nels's friend forwarded this letter without Stewart's knowledge, thinking Stillwell might care to help Stewart's family. Stewart had no money, he said.

The sister's letter found its way to Madeline. She read it, tears in her eyes. It told Madeline much more than its brief story of illness and poverty and wonder why Gene had not written home for so long. It told of motherly love, sisterly love, brotherly love—dear family ties that had been broken. It spoke of pride in this El Capitan brother who had become famous. It was signed "your loving sister Letty."

Not improbably, Madeline revolved in mind, this letter was one reason for Stewart's headstrong, long-continued abasement. It had been received too late—after he had squandered the money that would have meant so much to mother and sister. Be that as it might, Madeline immediately sent a bank draft to Stewart's sister with a letter explaining that the money was drawn in advance on Stewart's salary. This done, she impulsively determined to go to Chiricahua herself.

The horseback rides Madeline had taken to this little Arizona hamlet had tried her endurance to the utmost; but the journey by automobile, except for some rocky bits of road and sandy stretches, was comfortable, and a matter of only a few hours. The big touring car was still a kind of seventh wonder to the Mexicans and cowboys; not that automobiles were very new and strange, but because this one was such an enormous machine and capable of greater speed than an express train. The chauffeur who had arrived with the car found his situation among the jealous cowboys somewhat far removed from a bed of roses. He had been induced to remain long enough to teach the operating and mechanical technique of the car. And choice fell upon Link Stevens, for the simple reason that of all the cowboys he was the only one with any knack for mechanics. Now Link had been a hard-riding, hard-driving cowboy, and that winter he had sustained an injury to his leg, caused by a bad fall, and was unable to sit his horse. This had been gall and wormwood to him. But when the big white automobile came and he was elected to drive it, life was once more worth living for him. But all the other cowboys regarded Link and his machine as some correlated species of demon. They were deathly afraid of both.

It was for this reason that Nels, when Madeline asked him to accompany her to Chiricahua, replied, reluctantly, that he would rather follow on his horse. However, she prevailed over his hesitancy, and with Florence also in the car they set out. For miles and miles the valley road was smooth, hard-packed, and slightly downhill. And when speeding was perfectly safe, Madeline was not averse to it. The grassy plain sailed backward in gray sheets, and the little dot in the valley grew larger and larger. From time to time Link glanced round at unhappy Nels, whose eyes were wild and whose hands clutched his seat. While the car was crossing the sandy and rocky places, going slowly, Nels appeared to breathe easier. And when it stopped in the wide, dusty street of Chiricahua Nels gladly tumbled out.

"Nels, we shall wait here in the car while you find Stewart," said Madeline.

"Miss Hammond, I reckon Gene'll run when he sees us, if he's able to run," replied Nels. "Wal, I'll go find him an' make up my mind then what we'd better do."

Nels crossed the railroad track and disappeared behind the low, flat houses. After a little time he reappeared and hurried up to the car. Madeline felt his gray gaze searching her face.

"Miss Hammond, I found him," said Nels. "He was sleepin'. I woke him. He's sober an' not bad hurt; but I don't believe you ought to see him. Mebbe Florence—"

"Nels, I want to see him myself. Why not? What did he say when you told him I was here?"

"Shore I didn't tell him that. I jest says, 'Hullo, Gene!' an' he says, 'My Gawd! Nels! Mebbe I ain't glad to see a human bein'.' He asked me who was with me, an' I told him Link an' some friends. I said I'd fetch them in. He hollered at thet. But I went, anyway. Now, if you really *will* see him, Miss Hammond, it's a good chance. But shore it's a touchy matter, an' you'll be some sick at sight of him. He's layin' in a Greaser hole over here. Likely the Greasers hev been kind to him. But they're shore a poor lot."

Madeline did not hesitate a moment.

"Thank you, Nels. Take me at once. Come, Florence."

They left the car, now surrounded by gaping-eyed Mexican children, and crossed the dusty space to a narrow lane between red adobe walls. Passing by several houses, Nels stopped at the door of what appeared to be an alleyway leading back. It was filthy.

"He's in there, around thet first corner. It's a patio, open an' sunny. An', Miss Hammond, if you don't mind, I'll wait here for you. I reckon Gene wouldn't like any fellers around when he sees you girls."

It was that which made Madeline hesitate then and go forward slowly. She had given no thought at all to what Stewart might feel when suddenly surprised by her presence.

"Florence, you wait also," said Madeline, at the doorway, and turned in alone.

And she had stepped into a brokendown patio littered with alfalfa straw and debris, all clear in the sunlight. Upon a bench, back toward her, sat a man looking out through the rents in the broken wall. He had not heard her. The place was not quite so filthy and stifling as the passages Madeline had come through to get there. Then she saw that it had been used as a corral. A rat ran boldly across the dirt floor. The air swarmed with flies, which the man brushed at with weary hand. Madeline did not recognize Stewart. The side of his face exposed to her gaze was black, bruised, bearded. His clothes were ragged and soiled. There were bits of alfafa in his hair. His shoulders sagged. He made a wretched and hope-

90

less figure sitting there. Madeline divined something of why Nels shrank from being present.

"Mr. Stewart. It is I, Miss Hammond, come to see you," she said.

He grew suddenly perfectly motionless, as if he had been changed to stone. She repeated her greeting.

His body jerked. He moved violently as if instinctively to turn and face this intruder; but a more violent movement checked him.

Madeline waited. How singular that this ruined cowboy had pride which kept him from showing his face! And was it not shame more than pride?

"Mr. Stewart, I have come to talk with you, if you will let me."

"Go away," he muttered.

"Mr. Stewart!" she began, with involuntary hauteur. But instantly she corrected herself, became deliberate and cool, for she saw that she might fail to be even heard by this man. "I have come to help you. Will you let me?"

"For God's sake! You—you—" he choked over the words. "Go away!"

"Stewart, perhaps it was for God's sake that I came," said Madeline, gently. "Surely it was for yours—and your sister's —" Madeline bit her tongue, for she had not meant to betray her knowledge of Letty.

He groaned, and, staggering up to the broken wall, he leaned there with his face hidden. Madeline reflected that perhaps the slip of speech had been well.

"Stewart, please let me say what I have to say?"

He was silent. And she gathered courage and inspiration.

"Stillwell is deeply hurt, deeply grieved that he could not turn you back from this—this fatal course. My brother is also. They wanted to help you. And so do I. I have come, thinking somehow I might succeed where they have failed. Nels brought your sister's letter. I—I read it. I was only the more determined to try to help you, and indirectly help your mother and Letty. Stewart, we want you to come to the ranch. Stillwell needs you for his foreman. The position is open to you, and you can name your salary. Both Al and Stillwell are worried about Don Carlos, the *vaqueros*, and the raids down along the border. My cowboys are without a capable leader. Will you come?"

"No," he answered.

"But Stillwell wants you so badly."

"No."

"Stewart, I want you to come."

"No."

His replies had been hoarse, loud, furious. They disconcerted Madeline, and she paused, trying to think of a way to proceed. Stewart staggered away from the wall, and, falling upon the bench, he hid his face in his hands. All his motions, like his speech, had been violent.

"Will you please go away?" he asked.

"Stewart, certainly I cannot remain here longer if you insist upon my going. But why not listen to me when I want so much to help you? Why?"

"I'm a damned blackguard," he burst out. "But I was a gentleman once, and I'm not so low that I can stand for you seeing me here."

"When I made up my mind to help you I made it up to see you wherever you were. Stewart, come away, come back with us to the ranch. You are in a bad condition now. Everything looks black to you. But that will pass. When you are among friends again you will get well. You will be your old self. The very fact that you were once a gentleman, that you came of good family, makes you owe so much more to yourself. Why, Stewart, think how young you are! It is a shame to waste your life. Come back with me."

"Miss Hammond, this was my last plunge," he replied, despondently. "It's too late."

"Oh no, it is not so bad as that."

"It's too late."

"At least make an effort, Stewart. Try!"

"No. There's no use. I'm done for. Please leave me—thank you for—"

He had been savage, then sullen, and now he was grim. Madeline all but lost power to resist his strange, deadly, cold finality. No doubt he knew he was doomed. Yet something halted her—held her even as she took a backward step. And she became conscious of a subtle change in her own feeling. She had come into that squalid hole, Madeline Hammond, earnest enough, kind enough in her own intentions; but she had been almost imperious—a woman habitually, proudly used to being obeyed. She divined that all the pride, blue blood, wealth, culture, distinction, all the impersonal condescending persuasion, all the fatuous philanthropy on earth would not avail to turn this man a single hair's-breadth from his downward career to destruction. Her coming had terribly augmented his bitter hate of himself. She was going to fail to help him. She experienced a sensation of impotence that amounted almost to distress. The situation assumed a tragic keenness. She had set forth to reverse the tide of a wild cowboy's fortunes; she faced the swift wasting of his life, the damnation of his soul. The subtle consciousness of change in her was the birth of that faith she had reversed in Stillwell. And all at once she became merely a woman, brave and sweet and indomitable.

"Stewart, look at me," she said.

He shuddered. She advanced and laid a hand on his bent shoulder. Under the light touch he appeared to sink.

"Look at me," she repeated.

But he could not lift his head. He was abject, crushed. He dared not show his swollen, blackened face. His fierce, cramped posture revealed more than his features might have shown; it betrayed the torturing shame of a man of pride and passion, a man who had been confronted in his degradation by the woman he had dared to enshrine in his heart. It betrayed his love.

"Listen, then," went on Madeline, and her voice was unsteady. "Listen to me, Stewart. The greatest men are those who have fallen deepest into the mire, sinned most, suffered most, and then have fought their evil natures and conquered. I think you can shake off this desperate mood and be a man."

"No!" he cried.

"Listen to me again. Somehow I know you're worthy of Stillwell's love. Will you come back with us—for his sake?"

"No. It's too late, I tell you."

"Stewart, the best thing in life is faith in human nature. I have faith in you. I believe you are worth it."

"You're only kind and good—saying that. You can't mean it."

"I mean it with all my heart," she replied, a sudden rich warmth suffusing her body as she saw the first sign of his softening. "Will you come back—if not for your own sake or Stillwell's—then for mine?"

"What am I to such a woman as you?"

"A man in trouble, Stewart. But I have come to help you, to show my faith in you."

"If I believed that I might try," he said.

"Listen," she began, softly, hurriedly. "My word is not lightly given. Let it prove my faith in you. Look at me now and say you will come."

He heaved up his big frame as if trying to cast off a giant's burden, and then slowly he turned toward her. His face was a blotched and terrible thing. The physical brutalizing marks were there, and at that instant all that appeared human to Madeline was the dawning in dead, furnace-like eyes of a beautiful light.

"I'll come," he whispered, huskily. "Give me a few days to straighten up, then I'll come."

9

The New Foreman

Toward the end of the week Stillwell informed Madeline that Stewart had arrived at the ranch and had taken up quarters with Nels.

"Gene's sick. He looks bad," said the old cattleman. "He's so weak an' shaky he can't lift a cup. Nels says that Gene has hed some bad spells. A little liquor would straighten him up now. But Nels can't force him to drink a drop, an' has hed to sneak some liquor in his coffee. Wal, I think we'll pull Gene through. He's forgotten a lot. I was goin' to tell him what he did to me up at Rodeo. But I know if he'd believe it he'd be sicker than he is. Gene's losin' his mind, or he's got somethin' powerful strange on it."

From that time Stillwell, who evidently found Madeline his most sympathetic listener, unburdened himself daily of his hopes and fears and conjectures.

Stewart was really ill. It became necessary to send Link Stevens for a physician. Then Stewart began slowly to mend and presently was able to get up and about. Stillwell said the cowboy lacked interest and seemed to be a broken man. This statement, however, the old cattleman modified as Stewart continued to improve. Then presently it was a good augury of Stewart's progress that the cowboys once more took up the teasing relation which had been characteristic of them before his illness. A cowboy was indeed out of sorts when he could not vent his peculiar humor on somebody or something. Stewart had evidently become a broad target for their badinage.

"Wal, the boys are sure after Gene," said Stillwell, with his huge smile. "Joshin' him all the time about how he sits around an' hangs around an' loafs around jest to get a glimpse of you, Miss Majesty. Sure all the boys hev a pretty bad case over their pretty boss, but none of them is a marker to Gene. He's got it so bad, Miss Majesty, thet he actoolly don't know they are joshin' him. It's the amazin'est strange thing I ever seen. Why, Gene was always a feller thet you could josh. An' he'd laugh an' get back at you. But he was never before deaf to talk, an' there was a certain limit no feller cared to cross with him. Now he takes every word an' smiles dreamy like, an' jest looks an' looks. Why, he's beginnin' to make me tired. He'll never run thet bunch of cowboys if he doesn't wake up quick."

Madeline smiled her amusement and expressed a belief that Stillwell wanted too much in such short time from a man who had done body and mind a grievous injury.

It had been impossible for Madeline to fail to observe Stewart's singular behavior. She never went out to take her customary walks and rides without seeing him somewhere in the distance. She was aware that he watched for her and avoided meeting her. When she sat on the porch during the afternoon or at sunset Stewart could always be descried at some point near. He idled listlessly in the sun, lounged on the porch of his bunk-house, sat whittling the top bar of the corral fence, and always it seemed to Madeline he was watching her. Once, while going the rounds with her gardener, she encountered Stewart and greeted him kindly. He said little, but he was not embarrassed. She did not recognize in his face any feature that she remembered. In fact, on each of the few occasions when she had met Stewart he had looked so different that she had no consistent idea of his facial appearance. He was now pale, haggard, drawn. His eyes held a shadow through which shone, a soft, subdued light; and, once having observed this,

Madeline fancied it was like the light in Majesty's eyes, in the dumb, worshiping eyes of her favorite stag-hound. She told Stewart that she hoped he would soon be in the saddle again, and passed on her way.

That Stewart loved her Madeline could not help but see. She endeavored to think of him as one of the many who, she was glad to know, liked her. But she could not regulate her thoughts to fit the order her intelligence prescribed. Thought of Stewart dissociated itself from thought of the other cowboys. When she discovered this she felt a little surprise and annoyance. Then she interrogated herself, and concluded that it was not that Stewart was so different from his comrades, but that circumstances made him stand out from them. She recalled her meeting with him that night when he had tried to force her to marry him. This was unforgettable in itself. She recalled subsequent mention of him, and found it had been peculiarly memorable. The man and his actions seemed to hinge on events. Lastly, the fact standing clear of all others in its relation to her interest was that he had been almost ruined, almost lost, and she had saved him. That alone was sufficient to explain why she thought of him differently. She had befriended, uplifted the other cowboys; she had saved Stewart's life. To be sure, he had been a ruffian, but a woman could not save the life of even a ruffian without remembering it with gladness. Madeline at length decided her interest in Stewart was natural, and that her deeper feeling was pity. Perhaps the interest had been forced from her; however, she gave the pity as she gave everything.

Stewart recovered his strength, though not in time to ride at the spring round-up; and Stillwell discussed with Madeline the advisability of making the cowboy his foreman.

"Wal, Gene seems to be gettin' along," said Stillwell. "But he ain't like his old self. I think more of him at thet. But where's his spirit? The boys'd ride roughshod all over him. Mebbe I'd do best to wait longer now, as the slack season is on. All the same, if those *vaqueros* of Don Carlos's don't lay low I'll send Gene over there. Thet'll wake him up."

A few days afterward Stillwell came to Madeline, rubbing his big hands in satisfaction and wearing a grin that was enormous.

"Miss Majesty, I reckon before this I've said things was amazin' strange. But *now* Gene Stewart has gone an' done it!

96

Listen to me. Them Greasers down on our slope hev been gettin' prosperous. They're growin' like bad weeds. And they got a new padre—the little old feller from El Cajon, Padre Marcos. Wal, this was all right, all the boys thought, except Gene. An' he got blacker'n thunder an' roared round like a dehorned bull. I was sure glad to see he could get mad again. Then Gene haids down the slope fer the church. Nels an' me follered him, thinkin' he might hev been took sudden with a crazy spell or somethin'. He hasn't never been just right yet since he left off drinkin'. Wal, we run into him comin' out of the church. We never was so dumfounded in our lives. Gene was crazy, all right—he sure hed a spell. But it was the *kind* of spell he hed thet paralyzed us. He ran past us like a streak, an' we follered. We couldn't ketch him. We heerd him laugh —the strangest laugh I ever heerd! You'd thought the feller was suddenly made a king. He was like thet feller who was tied in a buryin'-sack an' throwed into the sea, an' cut his way out, an' swam to the island where the treasures was, an' stood up yellin', 'The world is mine!' Wal, when we got up to his bunk-house he was gone. He didn't come back all day an' all night. Frankie Slade, who has a sharp tongue, says Gene hed gone crazy fer liquor an' thet was his finish. Nels was some worried. An' I was sick.

"Wal, this mawnin' I went over to Nels's bunk. Some of the fellers was there, all speculatin' about Gene. Then big as life Gene struts round the corner. He wasn't the same Gene. His face was pale an' his eyes burned like fire. He had thet old mockin', cool smile, an' somethin' besides thet I couldn't understand. Frankie Slade up an' made a remark—no wuss than he'd been makin' fer days—an' Gene tumbled him out of his chair, punched him good, walked all over him. Frankie wasn't hurt so much as he was bewildered. 'Gene,' he says, 'what the hell struck you?' An' Gene says, kind of sweet like, 'Frankie, you may be a nice feller when you're alone, but your talk's offensive to a gentleman.'

"After thet what was said to Gene was with a nice smile. Now, Miss Majesty, it's beyond me what to allow for Gene's sudden change. First off, I thought Padre Marcos had converted him. I actoly thought thet. But I reckon it's only Gene Stewart come back—the old Gene Stewart *an'* some. Thet's all I care about. I'm rememberin' how I once told you thet Gene was the last of the cowboys. Perhaps I should hev said he's the last of my *kind* of cowboys. Wal, Miss Majesty, you'll be appreciatin' of what I meant from now on."

It was also beyond Madeline to account for Gene Stewart's antics, and, making allowances for the old cattleman's fancy, she did not weigh his remarks very heavily. She guessed why Stewart might have been angry at the presence of Padre Marcos. Madeline supposed that it was rather an unusual circumstance for a cowboy to be converted to religious belief. But it was possible. And she knew that religious fervor often manifested itself in extremes of feeling and action. Most likely, in Stewart's case, his real manner had been both misunderstood and exaggerated. However, Madeline had a curious desire, which she did not wholly admit to herself, to see the cowboy and make her own deductions.

The opportunity did not present itself for nearly two weeks. Stewart had taken up his duties as foreman, and his activities were ceaseless. He was absent most of the time, ranging down toward the Mexican line. When he returned Stillwell sent for him.

This was late in the afternoon of a day in the middle of April. Alfred and Florence were with Madeline on the porch. They saw the cowboy turn his horse over to one of the Mexican boys at the corral and then come with weary step up to the house, beating the dust out of his gauntlets. Little streams of gray sand trickled from his sombrero as he removed it and bowed to the women.

Madeline saw the man she remembered, but with a singularly different aspect. His skin was brown; his eyes were piercing and dark and steady; he carried himself erect; he seemed preoccupied, and there was not a trace of embarrassment in his manner.

"Wal, Gene, I'm sure glad to see you," Stillwell was saying. "Where do you hail from?"

"Guadalupe Cañon," replied the cowboy.

Stillwell whistled.

"Way down there! You don't mean you followed them hoss tracks thet far?"

"All the way from Don Carlos's rancho across the Mexican line. I took Nick Steele with me. Nick is the best tracker in the outfit. This trail we were on led along the foothill valleys. First we thought whoever made it was hunting for water. But they passed two ranches without watering. At Seaton's Wash

98

they dug for water. Here they met a pack-train of burros that came down the mountain trail. The burros were heavily loaded. Horse and burro tracks struck south from Seaton's to the old California emigrant road. We followed the trail through Guadalupe Cañon and across the border. On the way back we stopped at Slaughter's ranch, where the United States cavalry are camping. There we met foresters from the Peloncillo forest reserve. If these fellows knew anything they kept it to themselves. So we hit the trail home."

"Wal, I reckon you know enough?" inquired Stillwell, slowly.

"I reckon," replied Stewart.

"Wal, out with it, then," said Stillwell, gruffly. "Miss Hammond can't be kept in the dark much longer. Make your report to her."

The cowboy shifted his gaze to Madeline. He was cool and slow.

"We're losing a few cattle on the open range. Night drives by *vaqueros*. Some of these cattle are driven across the valley, others up into the foothills. So far as I can find out no cattle are being driven south. So this raiding is a blind to fool the cowboys. Don Carlos is a Mexican rebel. He located his rancho here a few years ago and pretended to raise cattle. All the time he has been smuggling arms and ammunition across the border. He was for Madero against Diaz. Now he is against Madero because he and all the rebels think Madero failed to keep his promises. There will be another revolution. And all the arms go from the States across the border. Those burros I told about were packed with contraband goods."

"That's a matter for the United States cavalry. They are patrolling the border," said Alfred.

"They can't stop the smuggling of arms, not down in that wild corner." replied Stewart.

"What is my—my duty? What has it to do with me?" inquired Madeline, somewhat perturbed.

"Wal, Miss Majesty, I reckon it hasn't nothing to do with you," put in Stillwell. "Thet's my business an' Stewart's. But I jest wanted you to know. There might be some trouble follerin' my orders."

"Your orders?"

"I want to send Stewart over to fire Don Carlos an' his *vaqueros* off the range. They've got to go. Don Carlos is break-

99

in' the law of the United States an' doin' it on our property and with our horses. Hev I your permission, Miss Hammond?"

"Why, assuredly you have! Stillwell, you know what to do. Alfred, what do you think best?"

"It'll make trouble, Majesty, but it's got to be done," replied Alfred. "Here you have a crowd of Eastern friends due next month. We want the range to ourselves then. But, Stillwell, if you drive those *vaqueros* off, won't they hang around in the foothills? I declare they are a bad lot."

Stillwell's mind was not at ease. He paced the porch with a frown clouding his brow.

"Gene, I reckon you got this Greaser deal figgered better'n me," said Stillwell. "Now what do you say?"

"He'll have to be forced off," replied Stewart, quietly. "The Don's pretty slick, but his *vaqueros* are bad actors. It's just this way. Nels said the other day to me, 'Gene, I haven't packed a gun for years until lately, and it feels good whenever I meet any of those strange Greasers.' You see, Stillwell, Don Carlos has *vaqueros* coming and going all the time. They're guerrilla bands, that's all. And they're getting uglier. There have been several shooting scrapes lately. A rancher named White, who lives up the valley, was badly hurt. It's only a matter of time till something stirs up the boys here. Stillwell, you know Nels and Monty and Nick."

"Sure I know 'em. And you're not mentionin' one more particular cowboy in my outfit," said Stillwell, with a dry chuckle and a glance at Stewart.

Madeline divined the covert meaning, and a slight thrill passed over her, as if a cold wind had blown in from the hills.

"Stewart, I see you carry a gun," she said, pointing to a black handle protruding from a sheath swinging low along his leather chaps.

"Yes, ma'am."

"Why do you carry it?" she asked.

"Well," he said, "it's not a pretty gun—and it's heavy."

She caught the inference. The gun was not an ornament. His keen, steady, dark gaze caused her vague alarm. What had once seemed cool and audacious about this cowboy was now cold and powerful and mystical. Both her instinct and her intelligence realized the steel fiber of the man's nature. As she was his employer, she had the right to demand that he should not do what was so chillingly manifest that he might do. But Madeline could not demand. She felt curiously young and weak, and the five months of Western life were as if they had never been. She now had to do with a question involving human life. And the value she placed upon human life and its spiritual significance was a matter far from her cowboy's thoughts. A strange idea flashed up. Did she place too much value upon all human life? She checked that, wondering, almost horrified at herself. And then her intuition told her that she possessed a far stronger power to move these primitive men than any woman's stern rule or order.

"Stewart, I do not fully understand what you hint that Nels and his comrades might do. Please be frank with me. Do you mean Nels would shoot upon little provocation?"

"Miss Hammond, as far as Nels is concerned, shooting is now just a matter of his meeting Don Carlos's *vaqueros*. It's wonderful what Nels has stood from them, considering the Mexicans he's already killed."

"Already killed! Stewart, you are not in earnest?" cried Madeline shocked.

"I am. Nels has seen hard life along the Arizona border. He likes peace as well as any man. But a few years of that doesn't change what the early days made of him. As for Nick Steele and Monty, they're just bad men, and looking for trouble."

"How about yourself, Stewart? Stillwell's remark was not lost upon me," said Madeline, prompted by curiosity.

Stewart did not reply. He looked at her in respectful silence. In her keen earnestness Madeline saw beneath his cool exterior and was all the more baffled. Was there a slight, inscrutable, mocking light in his eyes, or was it only her imagination? However, the cowboy's face was as hard as flint.

"Stewart, I have come to love my ranch," said Madeline, slowly, "and I care a great deal for my—my cowboys. It would be dreadful if they were to kill anybody, or especially if one of them should be killed."

"Miss Hammond, you've changed things considerable out here, but you can't change these men. All that's needed to start them is a little trouble. And this Mexican revolution is bound to make rough times along some of the wilder passes across the border. We're in line, that's all. And the boys are stirred up."

"Very well, then, I must accept the inevitable. I am facing a rough time. And some of my cowboys cannot be checked much longer. But, Stewart, whatever you have been in the past, you have changed." She smiled at him, and her voice was singularly sweet and rich. "Stillwell has so often referred to you as the last of his kind of cowboy. I have just a faint idea of what a wild life you have led. Perhaps that fits you to be a leader of such rough men. I am no judge of what a leader should do in this crisis. My cowboys are entailing risk in my employ; my property is not safe; perhaps my life even might be endangered. I want to rely upon you, since Stillwell believes, and I, too, that you are the man for this place. I shall give you no orders. But is it too much to ask that you be *my* kind of a cowboy?"

Madeline remembered Stewart's former brutality and shame and abject worship, and she measured the great change in him by the contrast afforded now in his dark, changeless, intent face.

"Miss Hammond, what kind of a cowboy is that?" he asked.

"I—I don't exactly know. It is that kind which I feel you *might* be. But I do know that in the problem at hand I want your actions to be governed by reason, not passion. Human life is not for any man to sacrifice unless in self-defense or in protecting those dependent upon him. What Stillwell and you hinted makes me afraid of Nels and Nick Steele and Monty. Cannot they be controlled? I want to feel that they will not go gunning for Don Carlos's men. I want to avoid all violence. And yet when my guests come I want to feel that they will be safe from danger or fright or even annoyance. May I not rely wholly upon you, Stewart? Just trust you to manage these obstreperous cowboys and protect my property and Alfred's, and take care of us—of me, until this revolution is ended? I have never had a day's worry since I bought the ranch. It is not that I want to shirk my responsibilities; it is that I like being happy. May I put so much faith in you?"

"I hope so, Miss Hammond," replied Stewart. It was an instant response, but none the less fraught with consciousness of responsibility. He waited a moment, and then, as neither Stillwell nor Madeline offered further speech, he bowed and turned down the path, his long spurs clinking in the gravel.

"Wal, wal," exclaimed Stillwell, "thet's no little job you give him, Miss Majesty."

"It was a woman's cunning, Stillwell," said Alfred. "My sister used to be a wonder at getting her own way when we were kids. Just a smile or two, a few sweet words or turns of thought, and she had what she wanted."

"Al, what a character to give me!" protested Madeline. "Indeed, I was deeply in earnest with Stewart. I do not understand just why, but I trust him. He seems like iron and steel. Then I was a little frightened at the prospect of trouble with the *vaqueros*. Both you and Stillwell have influenced me to look upon Stewart as invaluable. I thought it best to confess my utter helplessness and to look to him for support."

"Majesty, whatever actuated you, it was a stroke of diplomacy," replied her brother. "Stewart has got good stuff in him. He was down and out. Well, he's made a game fight, and it looks as if he'd win. Trusting him, giving him responsibility, relying upon him, was the surest way to strengthen his hold upon himself. Then that little touch of sentiment about being your kind of cowboy and protecting you—well, if Gene Stewart doesn't develop into an Argus-eyed knight I'll say I don't know cowboys. But, Majesty, remember, he's a composite of tiger breed and forked lightning, and don't imagine he has failed you if he gets into a fight."

"I'll sure tell you what Gene Stewart will do," said Florence. "Don't I know cowboys? Why, they used to take me up on their horses when I was a baby. Gene Stewart will be the kind of cowboy your sister said he *might* be, whatever that is. She may not know and we may not guess, but he knows."

"Wal, Flo, there you hit plumb center," replied the old cattleman. "An' I couldn't be gladder if he was my own son."

10

Don Carlos's *Vaqueros*

Early the following morning Stewart, with a company of cowboys, departed for Don Carlos's rancho. As the day wore on without any report from him, Stillwell appeared to grow more at ease; and at nightfall he told Madeline that he guessed there was now no reason for concern.

"Wal, though it's sure amazin' strange," he continued, "I've been worryin' some about how we was goin' to fire Don Carlos. But Gene has a way of doin' things."

Next day Stillwell and Alfred decided to ride over to Don Carlos's place, taking Madeline and Florence with them, and upon the return trip to stop at Alfred's ranch. They started in the cool, gray dawn, and after three hours' riding, as the sun began to get bright, they entered a mesquite grove, surrounding corrals and barns, and a number of low, squat buildings and a huge, rambling structure, all built of adobe and mostly crumbling to ruin. Only one green spot relieved the bald red of grounds and walls; and this evidently was made by the spring which had given both value and fame to Don Carlos's range. The approach to the house was through a wide courtyard, bare, stony, hard packed, with hitching rails and watering troughs in front of a long porch. Several dusty, tired horses stood with drooping heads and bridles down, their wet flanks attesting to travel just ended.

"Wal, doggone it, Al, if there ain't Pat Hawe's hoss I'll eat it," exclaimed Stillwell.

"What's Pat want here, anyhow?" growled Alfred.

No one was in sight; but Madeline heard loud voices coming from the house. Stillwell dismounted at the porch and stalked in at the door. Alfred leaped off his horse, helped Florence and Madeline down, and, bidding them rest and wait on the porch, he followed Stillwell.

"I hate these Greaser places," said Florence, with a grimace. "They're so mysterious and creepy. Just watch now. They'll be dark-skinned, beady-eyed, soft-footed Greasers slip right up out of the ground! There'll be an ugly face in every door and window and crack."

"It's like a huge barn with its characteristic odor permeated by tobacco smoke," replied Madeline, sitting down beside Florence. "I don't think very much of this end of my purchase. Florence, isn't that Don Carlos's black horse over there in the corral?"

"It sure is. Then the Don's heah yet. I wish we hadn't been in such a hurry to come over. There! That doesn't sound encouraging."

From the corridor came the rattling of spurs, tramping of

boots, and loud voices. Madeline detected Alfred's quick notes when he was annoyed: "We'll rustle back home, then." he said. The answer came, "No!" Madeline recognized Stewart's voice, and she quickly straightened up. "I won't have them in here," went on Alfred.

"Outdoors or in, they've got to be with us!" replied Stewart, sharply. "Listen, Al," came the boom of Stillwell's big voice, "now that we've butted in over hyar with the girls, you let Stewart run things."

Then a crowd of men tramped pell-mell out upon the porch. Stewart, dark-browed and somber, was in the lead. Nels hung close to him, and Madeline's quick glance saw that Nels had undergone some indescribable change. The grinning, brilliant-eyed Don Carlos came jostling out beside a gaunt, sharp-featured man wearing a silver shield. This, no doubt, was Pat Hawe. In the background behind Stillwell and Alfred stood Nick Steele, head and shoulders over a number of *vaqueros* and cowboys.

"Miss Hammond, I'm sorry you came," said Stewart, bluntly. "We're in a muddle here. I've insisted that you and Flo be kept close to us. I'll explain later. If you can't stop your ears I beg you to overlook rough talk."

With that he turned to the men behind him: "Nick, take Booly, go back to Monty and the boys. Fetch out that stuff. All of it. Rustle, now!"

Stillwell and Alfred disengaged themselves from the crowd to take up positions in front of Madeline and Florence. Pat Hawe leaned against a post and insolently ogled Madeline and then Florence. Don Carlos pressed forward. His whole figure filled Madeline's reluctant but fascinated eyes. He wore tight velveteen breeches, with a heavy fold down the outside seam, which was ornamented with silver buttons. Round his waist was a sash, and a belt with fringed holster, from which protruded a pearl-handled gun. A vest or waistcoat, richly embroidered, partly concealed a blouse of silk and wholly revealed a silken scarf round his neck. His swarthy face showed dark lines, like cords, under the surface. His little eyes were exceedingly prominent and glittering. To Madeline his face seemed to be a bold, handsome mask through which his eyes piercingly betrayed the evil nature of the man.

He bowed low with elaborate and sinuous grace. His smile

revealed brilliant teeth, enhanced the brilliance of his eyes. He slowly spread deprecatory hands.

"Señoritas, I beg a thousand pardons," he said. How strange it was for Madeline to hear English spoken in a soft, whiningly sweet accent! "The gracious hospitality of Don Carlos has passed with his house."

Stewart stepped forward and, thrusting Don Carlos aside, he called, "Make way, there!"

The crowd fell back to the tramp of heavy boots. Cowboys appeared staggering out of the corridor with long boxes. These they placed side by side upon the floor of the porch.

"Now, Hawe, we'll proceed with our business," said Stewart. "You see the boxes, don't you?"

"I reckon I see a good many things round hyar," replied Hawe, meaningly.

"Well, do you intend to open these boxes upon my say-so?"

"No!" retorted Hawe. "It's not my place to meddle with property as come by express an' all accounted fer regular."

"You call yourself a sheriff!" exclaimed Stewart, scornfully.

"Mebbe you'll think so before long," rejoined Hawe, sullenly.

"I'll open them. Here, one of you boys, knock the tops off these boxes," ordered Stewart. "No, not you, Monty. You use your eyes. Let Booly handle the ax. Rustle, now!"

Monty Price had jumped out of the crowd into the middle of the porch. The manner in which he gave way to Booly and faced the *vaqueros* was not significant of friendliness or trust.

"Stewart, you're dead wrong to bust open them boxes. Thet's ag'in' the law," protested Hawe, trying to interfere.

Stewart pushed him back. Then Don Carlos, who had been stunned by the appearance of the boxes, suddenly became active in speech and person. Stewart thrust him back also. The Mexican's excitement increased. He wildly gesticulated; he exclaimed shrilly in Spanish. When, however, the lids were wrenched open and an inside packing torn away he grew rigid and silent. Madeline raised herself behind Stillwell to see that the boxes were full of rifles and ammunition.

"There, Hawe! What did I tell you?" demanded Stewart. "I came over here to take charge of this ranch. I found these boxes hidden in an unused room. I suspected what they were. Contraband goods!"

"Wal, supposin' they are? I don't see any call fer such all-

106

fired fuss as you're makin', Stewart. I calkilate you're some stuck on your new job an' want to make a big show before—"

"Hawe, stop slinging that kind of talk," interrupted Stewart. "You got too free with your mouth once before! Now here, I'm supposed to be consulting an officer of the law. Will you take charge of these contraband goods?"

"Say, you're holdin' on high an' mighty," replied Hawe, in astonishment that was plainly pretended. "What're you drivin' at?"

Stewart muttered an imprecation. He took several swift strides across the porch; he held out his hands to Stillwell as if to indicate the hopelessness of intelligent and reasonable arbitration; he looked at Madeline with a glance eloquent of his regret that he could not handle the situation to please her. Then as he wheeled he came face to face with Nels, who had slipped forward out of the crowd.

Madeline gathered serious import from the steel-blue meaning flash of eyes whereby Nels communicated something to Stewart. Whatever that something was, it dispelled Stewart's impatience. A slight movement of his hand brought Monty Price forward with a jump. In these sudden jumps of Monty's there was a suggestion of restrained ferocity. Then Nels and Monty lined up behind Stewart. It was a deliberate action, even to Madeline, unmistakably formidable. Pat Hawe's face took on an ugly look; his eyes had a reddish gleam. Don Carlos added a pale face and extreme nervousness to his former expressions of agitation. The cowboys edged away from the *vaqueros* and the bronzed, bearded horsemen who were evidently Hawe's assistants.

"I'm driving at this," spoke up Stewart, presently; and now he was slow and caustic. "Here's contraband of war! Hawe, do you get that? Arms and ammunition for the rebels across the border! I charge you as an officer to confiscate these goods and to arrest the smuggler—Don Carlos."

These words of Stewart's precipitated a riot among Don Carlos and his followers, and they surged wildly around the sheriff. There was an upflinging of brown, clenching hands, a shrill, jabbering babel of Mexican voices. The crowd around Don Carlos grew louder and denser with the addition of armed *vaqueros* and barefooted stable-boys and dusty-booted herdsmen and blanketed Mexicans the last of whom suddenly slipped from doors and windows and round corners. It was a motley assemblage. The laced, fringed, ornamented *vaqueros* presented a sharp contrast to the bare-legged, sandal-footed boys and the ragged herders. Shrill cries, evidently from Don Carlos, somewhat quieted the commotion. Then Don Carlos could be heard addressing Sheriff Hawe in an exhortation of mingled English and Spanish. He denied, he avowed, he proclaimed, and all in rapid, passionate utterance. He tossed his black hair in his vehemence; he waved his fists and stamped the floor; he rolled his glittering eyes; he twisted his thin lips into a hundred different shapes, and like a cornered wolf showed snarling white teeth.

It seemed to Madeline that Don Carlos denied knowledge of the boxes of contraband goods, then knowledge of their real contents, then knowledge of their destination, and, finally, everything except that they were there in sight, damning witnesses to somebody's complicity in the breaking of neutrality laws. Passionate as had been his denial of all this, it was as nothing compared to his denunciation of Stewart.

"Señor Stewart, he keel my *vaquero!*" shouted Don Carlos, as, sweating and spent, he concluded his arraignment of the cowboy. "Him you must arrest! Señor Stewart a bad man! He keel my *vaquero!*"

"Do you hear thet?" yelled Hawe. "The Don's got you figgered fer thet little job at El Cajon last fall."

The clamor burst into a roar. Hawe began shaking his finger in Stewart's face and hoarsely shouting. Then a lithe young *vaquero*, swift as an Indian, glided under Hawe's uplifted arm. Whatever the action he intended, he was too late for its execution. Stewart lunged out, struck the *vaquero*, and knocked him off the porch. As he fell a dagger glittered in the sunlight and rolled clinking over the stones. The man went down hard and did not move. With the same abrupt violence, and a manner of contempt, Stewart threw Hawe off the porch, then Don Carlos, who, being less supple, fell heavily. Then the mob backed before Stewart's rush until all were down in the courtyard.

The shuffling of feet ceased, the clanking of spurs, and the shouting. Nels and Monty, now reinforced by Nick Steele, were as shadows of Stewart, so closely did they follow him. Stewart waved them back and stepped down into the yard. He was absolutely fearless; but what struck Madeline so keenly was his magnificent disdain. Manifestly, he knew the nature

108

of the men with whom he was dealing. From the look of him it was natural for Madeline to expect them to give way before him, which they did, even Hawe and his attendants sullenly retreating.

Don Carlos got up to confront Stewart. The prostrate *vaquero* stirred and moaned, but did not rise.

"You needn't jibber Spanish to me," said Stewart. "You can talk American, and you can understand American. If you start a rough-house here you and your Greasers will be cleaned up. You've got to leave this ranch. You can have the stock, the packs and traps in the second corral. There's grub, too. Saddle up and hit the trail. Don Carlos, I'm dealing more than square with you. You're lying about these boxes of guns and cartridges. You're breaking the laws of my country, and you're doing it on property in my charge. If I let smuggling go on here I'd be implicated myself. Now you get off the range. If you don't I'll have the United States cavalry here in six hours, and you can gamble they'll get what my cowboys leave of you."

Don Carlos was either a capital actor and gratefully relieved at Stewart's leniency or else he was thoroughly cowed by references to the troops."

"*Si Señor! Gracias, Señor!*" he exclaimed; and then, turning away, he called to his men. They hurried after him, while the fallen *vaquero* got to his feet with Stewart's help and staggered across the courtyard. In a moment they were gone, leaving Hawe and his several comrades behind.

Hawe was spitefully ejecting a wad of tobacco from his mouth and swearing in an undertone about "white-livered Greasers." He cocked his eye speculatively at Stewart.

"Wal, I reckon as you're so hell-bent on doin' it up brown that you'll try to fire me off'n the range, too?"

"If I ever do, Pat, you'll need to be carried off," replied Stewart. "Just now I'm politely inviting you and your deputy sheriffs to leave."

"We'll go; but we're coming' back one of these days, an' when we do we'll put you in irons."

"Hawe, if you've got it in that bad for me, come over here in the corral and let's fight it out."

"I'm an officer, and I don't fight outlaws an' sich except when I hev to make arrests."

"Officer! You're a disgrace to the county. If you ever did

get irons on me you'd take me some place out of sight, shoot me, and then swear you killed me in self-defense. It wouldn't be the first time you pulled that trick, Pat Hawe."

"Ho, ho!" laughed Hawe, derisively. Then he started toward the horses.

Stewart's long arm shot out, his hand clapped on Hawe's shoulder, spinning him round like a top.

"You're leaving, Pat, but before you leave you'll come out with your play or you'll crawl," said Stewart. "You've got it in for me, man to man. Speak up now and prove you're not the cowardly skunk I've always thought you. I've called your hand."

Pat Hawe's face turned a blackish-purple hue.

"You can jest bet thet I've got it in fer you," he shouted, hoarsely. "You're only a low-down cow-puncher. You never hed a dollar or a decent job till you was mixed up with thet Hammond woman—"

Stewart's hand flashed out and hit Hawe's face in a ringing slap. The sheriff's head jerked back, his sombrero fell to the ground. As he bent over to reach it his hand shook, his arm shook, his whole body shook.

Monty Price jumped straight forward and crouched down with a strange, low cry.

Stewart seemed all at once rigid, bending a little.

"Say *Miss Hammond,* if there's occasion to use her name," said Stewart, in a voice that seemed coolly pleasant, yet had a deadly undernote.

Hawe did a moment's battle with strangling fury, which he conquered in some measure.

"I said you was a low-down, drunken cow-puncher, a tough as damn near a desperado as we ever hed on the border," went on Hawe, deliberately. His speech appeared to be addressed to Stewart. although his flame-pointed eyes were rivited upon Monty Price. "I know you plugged that *vaquero* last fall, an' when I git my proof I'm comin' after you."

"That's all right. Hawe. You can call me what you like, and you can come after me when you like," replied Stewart. "But you're going to get in bad with me. You're in bad now with Monty and Nels. Pretty soon you'll queer yourself with all the cowboys and the ranchers, too. If that don't put sense into you— Here, listen to this. You knew what these boxes contained. You know Don Carlos has been smuggling arms and

110

ammunition across the border. You know he is hand and glove with rebels. You've been wearing blinders, and it has been to your interest. Take a hunch from me. That's all. Light out now, and the less we see of your handsome mug the better we'll like you."

Muttering, cursing, pallid of face, Hawe climbed astride his horse. His comrades followed suit. Certain it appeared that the sheriff was contending with more than fear and wrath. He must have had an irresistible impulse to fling more invective and threat upon Stewart, but he was speechless. Savagely he spurred his horse, and as it snorted and leaped he turned in his saddle, shaking his fist. His comrades led the way, with their horses clattering into a canter. They disappeared through the gate.

When, later in the day, Madeline and Florence, accompanied by Alfred and Stillwell, left Don Carlos's ranch it was not any too soon for Madeline. The inside of the Mexican's home was more unprepossessing and uncomfortable than the outside. The halls were dark, the rooms huge, empty, and musty; and there was an air of silence and secrecy and mystery about them most fitting to the character Florence had bestowed upon the place.

On the other hand, Alfred's ranch-house, where the party halted to spend the night, was picturesquely located, small and cozy, camplike in its arrangement, and altogether agreeable to Madeline.

The day's long rides and the exciting events had wearied her. She rested while Florence and the two men got supper. During the meal Stillwell expressed satisfaction over the good riddance of the *vaqueros*, and with his usual optimism trusted he had seen the last of them. Alfred, too, took a decidedly favorable view of the day's proceedings. However, it was not lost upon Madeline that Florence appeared unusually quiet and thoughtful. Madeline wondered a little at the cause. She remembered that Stewart had wanted to come with them, or detail a few cowboys to accompany them, but Alfred had laughed at the idea and would have none of it.

After supper Alfred monopolized the conversation by describing what he wanted to do to improve his home before he and Florence were married.

Then at an early hour they all retired.

Madeline's deep slumbers were disturbed by a pounding upon the wall, and then by Florence's crying out in answer to a call:

"Get up! Throw some clothes on and come out!"

It was Alfred's voice.

"What's the matter?" asked Florence, as she slipped out of bed.

"Alfred, is there anything wrong?" added Madeline, sitting up.

The room was dark as pitch, but a faint glow seemed to mark the position of the window.

"Oh, nothing much," replied Alfred. "Only Don Carlos's rancho going up in smoke."

"Fire!" cried Florence, sharply.

"You'll think so when you see it. Hurry out. Majesty, old girl, now you won't have to tear down that heap of adobe, as you threatened. I don't believe a wall will stand after that fire."

"Well, I'm glad of it," said Madeline. "A good healthy fire will purify the atmosphere over there and save me expense. Ugh! that haunted rancho got on my nerves! Florence, I do believe you've appropriated part of my riding-habit. Doesn't Alfred have lights in this house?"

Florence laughingly helped Madeline to dress. Then they hurriedly stumbled over chairs, and, passing through the dining-room, went out upon the porch.

Away to the westward, low down along the horizon, she saw leaping red flames and wind-swept columns of smoke.

Stillwell appeared greatly perturbed.

"Al, I'm lookin' fer that ammunition to blow up," he said. "There was enough of it to blow the roof off the rancho."

"Bill, surely the cowboys would get that stuff out the first thing," replied Alfred, anxiously.

"I reckon so. But all the same, I'm worryin'. Mebbe there wasn't time. Supposin' thet powder went off as the boys was goin' fer it or carryin' it out! We'll know soon. If the explosion doesn't come quick now we can figger the boys got the boxes out."

For the next few moments there was a silence of sustained and painful suspense. Florence gripped Madeline's arm. Madeline felt a fullness in her throat and a rapid beating of her heart. Presently she was relieved with the others when Stillwell declared the danger of an explosion needed to be feared no longer.

"Sure you can gamble on Gene Stewart," he added.

The night happened to be partly cloudy, with broken rifts showing the moon, and the wind blew unusually strong. The brightness of the fire seemed subdued. It was like a huge bonfire smothered by some great covering, penetrated by different, widely separated points of flame. These corners of flame flew up, curling in the wind, and then died down. Thus the scene was constantly changing from dull light to dark. There came a moment when a blacker shade overspread the wide area of flickering gleams and then obliterated them. Night enfolded the scene. The moon peeped a curved yellow rim from under broken clouds. To all appearances the fire had burned itself out. But suddenly a pinpoint of light showed where all had been dense black. It grew and became long and sharp. It moved. It had life. It leaped up. Its color warmed from white to red. Then from all about it burst flame on flame, to leap into a great changing pillar of fire that climbed high and higher. Huge funnels of smoke, yellow, black, white, all tinged with the color of fire, slanted skyward, drifting away on the wind.

"Wal, I reckon we won't hev the good of them two thousand tons of alfalfa we was figgerin' on," remarked Stillwell.

"Ah! Then that last outbreak of fire was burning hay," said Madeline. "I do not regret the rancho. But it's too bad to lose such a quantity of good feed for the stock."

"It's lost, an' no mistake. The fire's dyin' as quick as she flared up. Wal, I hope none of the boys got risky to save a saddle or blanket. Monty—he's hell on runnin' the gantlet of fire. He's like a hoss that's jest been dragged out of a burnin' stable an' runs back sure locoed. There! She's smolderin' down now. Reckon we-all might jest as well turn in again. It's only three o'clock."

"I wonder how the fire originated?" remarked Alfred. "Some careless cowboy's cigarette, I'll bet."

Stillwell rolled out his laugh.

"Al, you sure are a free-hearted, trustin' feller. I'm some doubtin' the cigarette idee; but you can gamble if it was a cigarette it belonged to a cunnin' *vaquero,* an' wasn't dropped accident-like."

113

"Now, Bill, you don't mean Don Carlos burned the rancho?" ejaculated Alfred, in mingled amaze and anger.

Again the old cattleman laughed.

"Powerful strange to say, my friend, ole Bill means jest thet."

"Of course Don Carlos set that fire," put in Florence, with spirit. "Al, if you live out heah a hundred years you'll never learn that Greasers are *treacherous*. I know Gene Stewart suspected something underhand. That's why he wanted us to hurry away. That's why he put me on the black horse of Don Carlos's. He wants that horse for himself, and feared the Don would steal or shoot him. And you, Bill Stillwell, you're as bad as Al. You never distrust anybody till it's too late. You've been singing ever since Stewart ordered the *vaqueros* off the range. But you sure haven't been thinking."

"Wal, now, Flo, you needn't pitch into me jest because I hev a natural Christian spirit," replied Stillwell, much aggrieved. "I reckon I've hed enough trouble in my life so's not to go lookin' fer more. Wal, I'm sorry about the hay burnin'. But mebbe the boys saved the stock. An' as fer that ole adobe house of dark holes an' underground passages, so long's Miss Majesty doesn't mind, I'm darn glad it burned. Come, let's all turn in again. Somebody'll ride over early an' tell us what's what."

Madeline awakened early, but not so early as the others, who were up and had breakfast ready when she went into the dining room. Stillwell was not in an amiable frame of mind. The furrows of worry lined his broad brow and he continually glanced at his watch, and growled because the cowboys were so late in riding over with the news. He gulped his breakfast, and while Madeline and the others ate theirs he tramped up and down the porch. Madeline noted that Alfred grew nervous and restless. Presently he left the table to join Stillwell outside.

"They'll slope off to Don Carlos's rancho and leave us to ride home alone," observed Florence.

"Do you mind?" questioned Madeline.

"No, I don't exactly mind; we've got the fastest horses in this county. I'd like to run that big black devil off his legs. No, I don't mind; but I've no hankering for a situation Gene Stewart thinks—"

Florence began disconnectedly, and she ended evasively.

Madeline did not press the point, although she had some sense of misgiving. Stillwell tramped in, shaking the floor with his huge boots; Alfred followed him, carrying a field-glass.

"Not a hoss in sight," complained Stillwell. "Somethin' wrong over Don Carlos's way. Miss Majesty, it'll be jest as well fer you an' Flo to hit the home trail. We can telephone over an' see that the boys know you're comin'."

Alfred, standing in the door, swept the gray valley with his field-glass.

"Bill, I see running stock-horses or cattle; I can't make out which. I guess we'd better rustle over there."

Both men hurried out, and while the horses were being brought up and saddled Madeline and Florence put away the breakfast dishes, then speedily donned spurs, sombreros, and gauntlets.

"Here are the horses ready," called Alfred. "Flo, that black Mexican horse is a prince."

The girls went out in time to hear Stillwell's good-by as he mounted and spurred away. Alfred went through the motions of assisting Madeline and Florence to mount, which assistance they always flouted, and then he, too, swung up astride.

"I guess it's all right," he said, rather dubiously. "You really must not go over toward Don Carlos's. It's only a few miles home."

"Sure it's all right. We can ride, can't we?" retorted Florence. "Better have a care for yourself, going off over there to mix in goodness knows what."

Alfred said good-by, spurred his horse, and rode away.

"If Bill didn't forget to telephone!" exclaimed Florence. "I declare he and Al were sure rattled."

Florence dismounted and went into the house. She left the door open. Madeline had some difficulty in holding Majesty. It struck Madeline that Florence stayed rather long indoors. Presently she came out with sober face and rather tight lips.

"I couldn't get anybody on the 'phone. No answer. I tried a dozen times."

"Why, Florence!" Madeline was more concerned by the girl's looks than by the information she imparted.

"The wire's been cut," said Florence. Her gray glance swept swiftly after Alfred, who was now far out of earshot. "I don't like this a little bit. Heah's where I've got to 'figger,' as Bill says."

She pondered a moment, then hurried into the house, to return presently with the field-glass that Alfred had used. With this she took a survey of the valley, particularly in the direction of Madeline's ranch-house. This was hidden by low, rolling ridges which were quite close by.

"Anyway, nobody in that direction can see us leave heah," she mused. "There's mesquite on the ridges. We've got cover long enough to save us till we can see what's ahead."

"Florence, what—what do you expect?" asked Madeline, nervously.

"I don't know. There's never any telling about Greasers. I wish Bill and Al hadn't left us. Still, come to think of that, they couldn't help us much in case of a chase. We'd run right away from them. Besides, they'd shoot. I guess I'm as well as satisfied that we've got the job of getting home on our own hands. We don't dare follow Al toward Don Carlos's ranch. We know there's trouble over there. So all that's left is to hit the trail for home. Come, let's ride. You stick like a Spanish needle to me."

A heavy growth of mesquite covered the top of the first ridge, and the trail went through it. Florence took the lead, proceeding cautiously, and as soon as she could see over the summit she used the field-glass. Then she went on. Madeline, following closely, saw down the slope of the ridge to a bare, wide, grassy hollow, and onward to more rolling land, thick with cactus and mesquite. Florence appeared cautious, deliberate, yet she lost no time. She was ominously silent. Madeline's misgivings took definite shape in the fear of *vaqueros* in ambush.

Upon the ascent of the third ridge, which Madeline remembered was the last uneven ground between the point she had reached and home, Florence exercised even more guarded care in advancing. Before she reached the top of this ridge she dismounted, looped her bridal round a dead snag, and, motioning Madeline to wait, she slipped ahead through the mesquite out of sight. Madeline waited, anxiously listening and watching. Certain it was that she could not see or hear anything alarming. The sun began to have a touch of heat; the morning breeze rustled the thin mesquite foliage; the deep magenta of a cactus flower caught her eye; a long-tailed, cruel-beaked, brown bird sailed so close to her she could have touched it with her whip. But she was only vaguely aware of these things. She was watching for Florence, listening for some sound fraught with untoward meaning. All of a sudden she saw Majesty's ears were held straight up. Then Florence's face, now strangely white, showed round the turn of the trail.

" 'S-s-s-sh!" whispered Florence, holding up a warning finger. She reached the black horse and petted him, evidently to still an uneasiness he manifested. "We're in for it," she went on. "A whole bunch of *vaqueros* hiding among the mesquite over the ridge! They've not seen or heard us yet. We'd better risk riding ahead, cut off the trail, and beat them to the ranch. Madeline, you're white as death! Don't faint *now!*"

"I shall not faint. But you frighten me. Is there danger? What shall we do?"

"There's danger. I wouldn't deceive you," went on Florence, in an earnest whisper. "Things have turned out just as Gene Stewart hinted. Ah, we should—Al should have listened to Gene! I believe—I'm afraid Gene *knew!*"

"Knew what?" asked Madeline.

"Never mind now. Listen. We daren't take the back trail. We'll go on. I've a scheme to fool that grinning Don Carlos. Get down, Madeline—hurry."

Madeline dismounted.

"Give me your white sweater. Take it off— And that white hat! Hurry, Madeline."

"Florence, what on earth do you mean?" cried Madeline.

"Not so loud," whispered the other. Her gray eyes snapped. She had divested herself of sombrero and jacket, which she held out to Madeline. "Heah. Take these. Give me yours. Then get up on the black. I'll ride Majesty. Rustle now, Madeline. This is no time to talk."

"But, dear, why—why do you want—? Ah! You're going to make the *vaqueros* take you for me!"

"You guessed it. Will you—"

"I shall not allow you to do anything of the kind," returned Madeline.

It was then that Florence's face, changing, took on the hard, stern sharpness so typical of a cowboy's. Madeline had caught glimpses of that expression in Alfred's face, and on Stewart's when he was silent, and on Stillwell's always. It was a look of iron and fire—unchangeable, unquenchable will. There was even much of violence in the swift action whereby Florence compelled Madeline to the change of apparel.

117

"It'd been my idea, anyhow, if Stewart hadn't told me to do it," said Florence, her words as swift as her hands. "Don Carlos is after you—*you, Miss Madeline Hammond!* He wouldn't ambush a trail for any one else. He's not killing cowboys these days. He wants you for some reason. So Gene thought, and now I believe him. Well, we'll know for sure in five minutes. You ride the black; I'll ride Majesty. We'll slip round through the brush, out of sight and sound, till we can break out into the open. Then we'll split. You make straight for the ranch. I'll cut loose for the valley where Gene said positively the cowboys were with the cattle. The *vaqueros* will take me for you. They all know those striking white things you wear. They'll chase me. They'll never get anywhere near me. And you'll be on a fast horse. He can take you home ahead of any *vaqueros*. But you won't be chased. I'm staking all on that. Trust me, Madeline. If it were only my calculation, maybe I'd— It's because I remember Stewart. That cowboy knows things. Come, this heah's the safest and smartest way to fool Don Carlos." Madeline felt herself more forced than persuaded into acquiescence. She mounted the black and took up the bridle. In another moment she was gliding her horse off the trail in the tracks of Majesty. Florence led off at right angles, threading a slow passage through the mesquite. She favored sandy patches and open aisles between the trees, and was careful not to break a branch. Often she stopped to listen. This detour of perhaps half a mile brought Madeline to where she could see open ground, the ranch-house only a few miles off, and the cattle dotting the valley. She had not lost her courage, but it was certain that these familiar sights somewhat lightened the pressure upon her breast. Excitement gripped her. The shrill whistle of a horse made both the black and Majesty jump. Florence quickened the gait down the slope. Soon Madeline saw the edge of the brush, the gray-bleached grass and level ground.

Florence waited at the opening between the low trees. She gave Madeline a quick, bright glance.

"All over but the ride! That'll sure be easy. Bolt now an keep your nerve!"

When Florence wheeled the fiery roan and screamed in his ear Madeline seemed suddenly to grow lax and helpless. The big horse leaped into thundering action. This was memorable of Bonita of the flying hair and the wild night ride. Florence's hair streamed on the wind and shone gold in the sunlight. Yet Madeline saw her with the same thrill with which she had seen the wild-riding Bonita. Then hoarse shouts unclamped Madeline's power of movement, and she spurred the black into the open.

He wanted to run and he was swift. Madeline loosened the reins—laid them loose upon his neck. His action was strange to her. He was hard to ride. But he was fast, and she cared for nothing else. Madeline knew horses well enough to realize that the black had found he was free and carrying a light weight. A few times she took up the bridle and pulled to right or left, trying to guide him. He kept a straight course, however, and crashed through small patches of mesquite and jumped the cracks and washes. Uneven ground offered no perceptible obstacle to his running. To Madeline there was now a thrilling difference in the lash of wind and the flash of the gray ground underneath. She was running away from something; what that was she did not know. But she remembered Florence, and she wanted to look back, yet hated to do so for fear of the nameless danger Florence had mentioned.

Madeline listened for the pounding of pursuing hoofs in her rear. Involuntarily she glanced back. On the mile or more of gray level between her and the ridge there was not a horse, a man, or anything living. She wheeled to look back on the other side, down the valley slope.

The sight of Florence riding Majesty in zigzag flight before a whole troop of *vaqueros* blanched Madeline's cheek and made her grip the pommel of her saddle in terror. That strange gait of her roan was not his wonderful stride. Could Majesty be running wild? Madeline saw one *vaquero* draw closer, whirling his lasso round his head, but he did not get near enough to throw. So it seemed to Madeline. Another *vaquero* swept across in front of the first one. Then, when Madeline gasped in breathless expectancy, the roan swerved to elude the attack. It flashed over Madeline that Florence was putting the horse to some such awkward flight as might have been expected of an Eastern girl frightened out of her wits. Madeline made sure of this when, after looking again, she saw that Florence, in spite of the horse's breaking gait and the irregular course, was drawing slowly and surely down the valley.

Madeline had not lost her head to the extent of forgetting her own mount and the nature of the ground in front. When, presently, she turned again to watch Florence, uncertainty ceased in her mind. The strange features of that race between girl and *vaqueros* were no longer in evidence. Majesty was in his beautiful, wonderful stride, low down along the ground, stretching, with his nose level and straight for the valley. Between him and the lean horses in pursuit lay an ever-increasing space. He was running away from the *vaqueros*. Florence was indeed "riding the wind," as Stewart had aptly expressed his idea of flight upon the fleet roan.

A dimness came over Madeline's eyes, and it was not all owing to the sting of the wind. She rubbed it away, seeing Florence as a flying dot in a strange blur. What a daring, intrepid girl! This kind of strength—and aye, splendid thought for a weaker sister—was what the West inculcated in a woman.

The next time Madeline looked back Florence was far ahead of her pursuers and going out of sight behind a low knoll. Assured of Florence's safety, Madeline put her mind to her own ride and the possibilities awaiting at the ranch. She remembered the failure to get any of her servants or cowboys on the telephone. To be sure, a windstorm had once broken the wire. But she had little real hope of such being the case in this instance. She rode on, pulling the black as she neared the ranch. Her approach was from the south and off the usual trail, so that she went up the long slope of the knoll toward the back of the house. Under these circumstances she could not consider it out of the ordinary that she did not see any one about the grounds.

It was perhaps fortunate for her, she thought, that the climb up the slope cut the black's speed so she could manage him. He was not very hard to stop. The moment she dismounted, however, he jumped and trotted off. At the edge of the slope, facing the corrals, he halted to lift his head and shoot up his ears. Then he let out a piercing whistle and dashed down the lane.

Madeline, prepared by that warning whistle, tried to fortify herself for a new and unexpected situation; but as she espied an unfamiliar company of horsemen rapidly riding down a hollow leading from the foothills she felt the return of fears gripping at her like cold hands, and she fled precipitously into the house.

11

A Band of Guerrillas

Madeline bolted the door, and, flying into the kitchen, she told the scared servants to shut themselves in. Then she ran to her own rooms. It was only a matter of a few moments for her to close and bar the heavy shutters, yet even as she was fastening the last one in the room she used as an office a clattering roar of hoofs seemed to swell up to the front of the house. She caught a glimpse of wild, shaggy horses and ragged, dusty men. She had never seen any *vaqueros* that resembled these horsemen. *Vaqueros* had grace and style; they were fond of lace and glitter and fringe; they dressed their horses in silvered trappings. But, the riders now tramping into the driveway were uncouth, lean, savage. They were guerrillas, a band of the raiders who had been harassing the border since the beginning of the revolution. A second glimpse assured Madeline that they were not all Mexicans.

The presence of outlaws in that band brought home to Madeline her real danger. She remembered what Stillwell had told her about recent outlaw raids along the Rio Grande. These flying bands, operating under the excitement of the revolution, appeared here and there, everywhere, in remote places, and were gone as quickly as they came. Mostly they wanted money and arms, but they would steal anything, and unprotected women had suffered at their hands.

Madeline, hurriedly collecting her securities and the considerable money she had in her desk, ran out, closed and locked the door, crossed the patio to the opposite side of the house, and, entering again, went down a long corridor, trying to decide which of the many unused rooms would be best to hide in. And before she made up her mind she came to the last room. Just then a battering on door or window in the direction of the kitchen and shrill screams from the servant women increased Madeline's alarm.

She entered the last room. There was no lock or bar upon the door. But the room was large and dark, and it was half full of bales of alfalfa hay. Probably it was the safest place in the house; at least time would be necessary to find any one hidden there. She dropped her valuables in a dark corner and covered them with loose hay. That done, she felt her way down a narrow aisle between the piled-up bales and presently crouched in a niche.

With the necessity of action over for the immediate present, Madeline became conscious that she was quivering and almost breathless. Her skin felt tight and cold. There was a weight on her chest; her mouth was dry, and she had a strange tendency to swallow. Her listening faculty seemed most acute. Dull sounds came from parts of the house remote from her. In the intervals of silence between these sounds she heard the squeaking and rustling of mice in the hay. A mouse ran over her hand.

She listened, waiting, hoping yet dreading to hear the clattering approach of her cowboys. There would be fighting—blood—men injured, perhaps killed. Even the thought of violence of any kind hurt her. But perhaps the guerrillas would run in time to avoid a clash with her men. She hoped for that, prayed for it. Through her mind flitted what she knew of Nels, of Monty, of Nick Steele; and she experienced a sensation that left her somewhat chilled and sick. Then she thought of the dark-brown, fire-eyed Stewart. She felt a thrill drive away the cold nausea. And her excitement augmented.

Waiting, listening increased all her emotions. Nothing appeared to be happening. Yet hours seemed to pass while she crouched there. Had Florence been overtaken? Could any of those lean horses outrun Majesty? She doubted it; she knew it could not be true. Nevertheless, the strain of uncertainty was torturing.

Suddenly the bang of the corridor door pierced her through and through with the dread of uncertainty. Some of the guerrillas had entered the east wing of the house. She heard a babel of jabbering voices, the shuffling of boots and clinking of spurs, the slamming of doors and ransacking of rooms.

Madeline lost faith in her hiding-place. Moreover, she found it impossible to take the chance. The idea of being caught in that dark room by those ruffians filled her with terror. She must get out into the light. Swiftly she rose and went to the window. It was rather more of a door than window, being a large aperture closed by two wooden doors on hinges. The iron hook yielded readily to her grasp, and one door stuck fast, while the other opened a few inches. She looked out upon a green slope covered with flowers and bunches of sage and bushes. Neither man nor horse showed in the narrow field of her vision. She believed she would be safer hidden out there in the shrubbery than in the house. The jump from the window would be easy for her. And with her quick decision came a rush and stir of spirit that warded off her weakness.

She pulled at the door. It did not budge. It had caught at the bottom. Pulling with all her might proved to be in vain. Pausing, with palms hot and bruised, she heard a louder, closer approach of the invaders of her home. Fear, wrath, and impotence contested for supremacy over her and drove her to desperation. She was alone here, and she must rely on herself. And as she strained every muscle to move that obstinate door and heard the quick, harsh voices of men and the sounds of a hurried search she suddenly felt sure that they were hunting for her. She knew it. She did not wonder at it. But she wondered if she were really Madeline Hammond, and if it were possible that brutal men would harm her. Then the tramping of heavy feet on the floor of the adjoining room lent her the last strength of fear. Pushing with hands and shoulders, she moved the door far enough to permit the passage of her body. Then she stepped up on the sill and slipped through the aperture. She saw no one. Lightly she jumped down and ran in among the bushes. But these did not afford her the cover she needed. She stole from one clump to another, finding too late that she had chosen with poor judgment. The position of the bushes had drawn her closer to the front of the house rather than away from it, and just before her were horses, and beyond a group of excited men. With her heart in her throat Madeline crouched down.

A shrill yell, followed by running and mounting guerrillas, roused her hope. They had sighted the cowboys and were in flight. Rapid thumping of boots on the porch told of men hurrying from the house. Several horses dashed past her, not ten feet distant. One rider saw her, for he turned to shout back. This drove Madeline into a panic. Hardly knowing what she did, she began to run away from the house. Her feet seemed leaden. She felt the same horrible powerlessness that sometimes came over her when she dreamed of being pursued. Horses with shouting riders streaked past her in the shrubbery. There was a thunder of hoofs behind her. She turned aside, but the thundering grew nearer. She was being run down.

As Madeline shut her eyes and, staggering, was about to fall, apparently right under pounding hoofs, a rude, powerful hand clapped round her waist, clutched deep and strong, and swung her aloft. She felt a heavy blow when the shoulder of the horse struck her, and then a wrenching of her arm as she was dragged up. A sudden blighting pain made sight and feeling fade from her.

But she did not become unconscious to the extent that she lost the sense of being rapidly borne away. She seemed to hold that for a long time. When her faculties began to return the motion of the horse was no longer violent. For a few moments she could not determine her position. Apparently she was upside down. Then she saw that she was facing the ground, and must be lying across a saddle with her head hanging down. She could not move a hand; she could not tell where her hands were. Then she felt the touch of soft leather. She saw a high-topped Mexican boot, wearing a huge silver spur, and the reeking flank and legs of a horse, and a dusty, narrow trail. Soon a kind of red darkness veiled her eyes, her head swam, and she felt motion and pain only dully.

After what seemed a thousand weary hours someone lifted her from the horse and laid her upon the ground, where gradually, as the blood left her head and she could see, she began to get the right relation of things.

She lay in a sparse grove of firs, and the shadows told of late afternoon. She smelled wood smoke, and she heard the sharp crunch of horses' teeth nipping grass. Voices caused her to turn her face. A group of men stood and sat round a campfire eating like wolves. The looks of her captors made Madeline close her eyes, and the fascination, the fear they roused in her made her open them again. Mostly they were thin-bodied, thin-bearded Mexicans, black and haggard and starved. Whatever they might be, they surely were hunger-stricken and squalid. Not one had a coat. A few had scarfs. Some wore belts in which were scattered cartridges. Only a few had guns, and these were of diverse patterns. Madeline could see no packs, no blankets, and only a few cooking utensils, all battered and blackened. Her eyes fastened upon men she believed were white men; but it was from their features and not their color that she judged. Once she had seen a band of nomad robbers in the Sahara, and somehow was reminded of them by this motley outlaw troop.

They divided attention between the satisfying of ravenous appetites and a vigilant watching down the forest aisles. They expected some one, Madeline thought, and, manifestly, if it were a pursuing posse, they did not show anxiety. She could not understand more than a word here and there that they uttered. Presently, however, the name of Don Carlos revived keen curiosity in her and realization of her situation, and then once more dread possessed her breast.

A low exclamation and a sweep of arm from one of the guerrillas caused the whole band to wheel and concentrate their attention in the opposite direction. They heard something. They saw some one. Grimly hands sought weapons, and then every man stiffened. Madeline saw what hunted men looked like at the moment of discovery, and the sight was terrible. She closed her eyes, sick with what she saw, fearful of the moment when the guns would leap out.

There were muttered curses, a short period of silence followed by whispering, and then a clear voice rang out, "El Capitan!"

A strong shock vibrated through Madeline, and her eyelids swept open. Instantly she associated the name El Capitan with Stewart and experienced a sensation of strange regret. It was not pursuit or rescue she thought of then, but death. These men would kill Stewart. But surely he had not come alone. The lean, dark faces, corded and rigid, told her in what direction to look. She heard the slow, heavy thump of hoofs. Soon into the wide aisle between the trees moved the form of a man, arms flung high over his head. Then Madeline saw the horse, and she recognized Majesty, and she knew it was really Stewart who rode the roan. When doubt was no longer possible she felt a suffocating sense of gladness and fear and wonder.

Many of the guerrillas leaped up with drawn weapons. Still Stewart approached with his hands high, and he rode right into the campfire circle. Then a guerilla, evidently the chief, waved down the threatening men and strode up to Stewart.

He greeted him. There was amaze and pleasure and respect in the greeting. Madeline could tell that, though she did not know what was said. At the moment Stewart appeared to her as cool and careless as if he were dismounting at her porch steps. But when he got down she saw that his face was white. He shook hands with the guerrilla, and then his glittering eyes roved over the men and around the glade until they rested upon Madeline. Without moving from his tracks he seemed to leap, as if a powerful current had shocked him. Madeline tried to smile to assure him she was alive and well; but the intent in his eyes, the power of his controlled spirit telling her of her peril and his, froze the smile on her lips.

With that he faced the chief and spoke rapidly in the Mexican jargon Madeline had always found so difficult to translate. The chief answered, spreading wide his hands, one of which indicated Madeline as she lay there. Stewart drew the fellow a little aside and said something for his ear alone. The chief's hands swept up in a gesture of surprise and acquiescence. Again Stewart spoke swiftly. His hearer then turned to address the band. Madeline caught the words "Don Carlos" and "pesos." There was a brief muttering protest which the chief thundered down. Madeline guessed her release had been given by this guerrilla and bought from the others of the band.

Stewart strode to her side, leading the roan. Majesty reared and snorted when he saw his mistress prostrate. Stewart knelt, still holding the bridle.

"Are you all right?" he asked.

"I think so," she replied, essaying a laugh that was rather a failure. "My feet are tied."

Dark blood blotted out all the white from his face, and lightning shot from his eyes. She felt his hands, like steel tongs, loosening the bonds round her ankles. Without a word he lifted her upright and then upon Majesty. Madeline reeled a little in the saddle, held hard to the pommel with one hand, and tried to lean on Stewart's shoulder with the other.

"Don't give up," he said.

She saw him gaze furtively into the forest on all sides. And it surprised her to see the guerrillas riding away. Putting the two facts together, Madeline formed an idea that neither Stewart nor the others desired to meet with some one evidently due shortly in the glade. Stewart guided the roan off to the right and walked beside Madeline, steadying her in the saddle.

At first Madeline was so weak and dizzy that she could scarcely retain her seat. The dizziness left her presently, and then she made an effort to ride without help. Her weakness, however, and a pain in her wrenched arm made the task laborsome.

Stewart had struck off the trail, if there were one, and was keeping to denser parts of the forest. The sun sank low, and the shafts of gold fell with a long slant among the firs. Majesty's hoofs made no sound on the soft ground, and Stewart strode on without speaking. Neither his hurry nor vigilance relaxed until at least two miles had been covered. Then he held to a straighter course and did not send so many glances into the darkening woods. The level of the forest began to be cut by little hollows, all of which sloped and widened. Presently the soft ground gave place to bare, rock soil. The horse snorted and tossed his head. A sound of splashing water broke the silence. The hollow opened into a wider one through which a little brook murmured its way over the stones. Majesty snorted again and stopped and bent his head.

"He wants a drink," said Madeline. "I'm thirsty, too, and very tired."

Stewart lifted her out of the saddle, and as their hands parted she felt something moist and warm. Blood was running down her arm and into the palm of her hand.

"I'm—bleeding," she said, a little unsteadily. "Oh, I remember. My arm was hurt."

She held it out, the blood making her conscious of her weakness. Stewart's fingers felt so firm and sure. Swiftly he ripped the wet sleeve. Her forearm had been cut or scratched. He washed off the blood.

"Why, Stewart, it's nothing. I was only a little nervous. I guess that's the first time I ever saw my own blood."

He made no reply as he tore her handkerchief into strips and bound her arm. His swift motions and his silence gave her a hint of how he might meet a more serious emergency. She felt safe. And because of that impression, when he lifted his head and she saw that he was pale and shaking, she was surprised. He stood before her folding his scarf, which was still wet, and from which he made no effort to remove the red stains.

"Miss Hammond," he said, hoarsely, "it was a man's hands —a Greaser's finger-nails—that cut your arm. I know who he

127

was. I could have killed him. But I mightn't have got your freedom. You understand? I didn't dare."

Madeline gazed at Stewart, astounded more by his speech than his excessive emotion.

"My dear boy!" she exclaimed. And then she paused. She could not find words.

He was making an apology to her for not killing a man who had laid a rough hand upon her person. He was ashamed and seemed to be in a torture that she would not understand why he had not killed the man. There seemed to be something of passionate scorn in him that he had not been able to avenge her as well as free her.

"Stewart, I understand. You were being *my* kind of cowboy. I thank you."

But she did not understand so much as she implied. She had heard many stories of this man's cool indifference to peril and death. He had always seemed as hard as granite. Why should the sight of a little blood upon her arm pale his cheek and shake his hand and thicken his voice? What was there in his nature to make him implore her to see the only reason he could not kill an outlaw? The answer to the first question was that he loved her. It was beyond her to answer the second. But the secret of it lay in the same strength from which his love sprang—an intensity of feeling which seemed characteristic of these Western men of simple, lonely, elemental lives. All at once over Madeline rushed a tide of realization of how greatly it was possible for such a man as Stewart to love her. The thought came to her in all its singular power. All her Eastern lovers who had the graces that made them her equals in the sight of the world were without the only great essential that a lonely, hard life had given to Stewart. Nature here struck a just balance. Something deep and dim in the future, an unknown voice, called to Madeline and disturbed her. And because it was not a voice to her intelligence she deadened the ears of her warm and throbbing life and decided never to listen.

"Is it safe to rest a little?" she asked. "I am so tired. Perhaps I'll be stronger if I rest."

"We're all right now," he said. "The horse will be better, too. I ran him out. And uphill, at that."

"Where are we?"

"Up in the mountains, ten miles and more from the ranch.

There's a trail just below here. I can get you home by midnight. They'll be some worried down there."

"What happened?"

"Nothing much to any one but you. That's the—the hard luck of it. Florence caught us out on the slope. We were returning from the fire. We were dead beat. But we got to the ranch before any damage was done. We sure had trouble in finding a trace of you. Nick spotted the prints of your heels under the window. And then we knew. I had to fight the boys. If they'd come after you we'd never have gotten you without a fight. We didn't want that. Old Bill came out packing a dozen guns. He was crazy. I had to rope Monty. Honest. I tied him to the porch. Nels and Nick promised to stay and hold him till morning. That was the best I could do. I was sure lucky to come up with the band so soon. I had figured right. I knew that guerrilla chief. He's a bandit in Mexico. It's a business with him. But he fought for Madero, and I was with him a good deal. He may be a Greaser, but he's white."

"How did you effect my release?"

"I offered them money. That's what the rebels all want. They need money. They're a lot of poor, hungry devils."

"I gathered that you offered to pay ransom. How much?"

"Two thousand dollars Mex. I gave my word. I'll have to take the money. I told them when and where I'd meet them."

"Certainly. I'm glad I've got the money." Madeline laughed. "What a strange thing to happen to me! I wonder what dad would say to that? Stewart, I'm afraid he'd say two thousand dollars is more than I'm worth. But tell me. That rebel chieftain did not demand money?"

"No. The money is for his men."

"What did you say to him? I saw you whisper in his ear."

Stewart dropped his head, averting her direct gaze.

"We were comrades before Juarez. One day I dragged him out of a ditch. I reminded him. Then I—I told him something I—I thought—"

"Stewart, I know from the way he looked at me that you spoke of me."

Her companion did not offer a reply to this, and Madeline did not press the point.

"I heard Don Carlos's name several times. That interests me. What have Don Carlos and his *vaqueros* to do with this?"

"That Greaser has all to do with it," replied Stewart, grimly. "He burned his ranch and corrals to keep us from getting them. But he also did it to draw all the boys away from your home. They had a deep plot, all right. I left orders for some one to stay with you. But Al and Stillwell, who're both hot-headed, rode off this morning. Then the guerillas came down."

"Well, what was the idea—the plot—as you call it?"

"To get you," he said, bluntly.

"Me! Stewart, you do not mean my capture—whatever you call it—was anything more than mere accident?"

"I do mean that. But Stillwell and your brother think the guerrillas wanted money and arms, and they just happened to make off with you because you ran under a horse's nose."

"You do not incline to that point of view?"

"I don't. Neither does Nels nor Nick Steele. And *we* know Don Carlos and the Greasers. Look how the *vaqueros* chased Flo for you!"

"What do you think, then?"

"I'd rather not say."

"But, Stewart, I would like to know. If it is about me surely I ought to know," protested Madeline. "What reason have Nels and Nick to suspect Don Carlos of plotting to abduct me?"

"I suppose they've no reason you'd take. Once I heard Nels say he'd seen the Greaser look at you, and if he ever saw him do it again he'd shoot him."

"Why, Stewart, that is ridiculous. To shoot a man for looking at a woman! This is a civilized country."

"Well, maybe it would be ridiculous in a civilized country. There's some things about civilization I don't care for."

"What, for instance?"

"For one thing, I can't stand for the way men let other men treat women."

"But, Stewart, this is strange talk from you, who that night I came—"

She broke off, sorry that she had spoken. His shame was not pleasant to see. Suddenly he lifted his head, and she felt scorched by flaming eyes.

"Suppose I was drunk. Suppose I had met some ordinary girl. Suppose I had really made her marry me. Don't you think I would have stopped being a drunkard and have been good to her?"

"Stewart, I do not know what to think about you," replied Madeline.

Then followed a short silence. Madeline saw the last bright rays of the setting sun glide up over a distant crag. Stewart rebridled the horse and looked at the saddle-girths.

"I got off the trail. About Don Carlos I'll say right out, not what Nels and Nick think, but what *I* know. Don Carlos hoped to make off with you for himself, the same as if you had been a poor peon slave-girl down in Sonora. Maybe he had a deeper plot than my rebel friend told me. Maybe he even went so far as to hope for American troops to chase him. The rebels are trying to stir up the United States. They'd welcome intervention. But, however, that may be, the Greaser meant evil to you, and has meant it ever since he saw you first. That's all."

"Stewart, you have done me and my family a service we can never hope to repay."

"I've done the service. Only don't mention pay to me. But there's one thing I'd like to know, and I find it hard to say. It's prompted, maybe, by what I know you think of me and what I imagine your family and friends would think if they knew. It's not prompted by pride or conceit. And it's this: Such a woman as you should never have come to this God-forsaken country unless she meant to forget herself. But as you *did* come, and as you *were* dragged away by those devils, I want you to know that all your wealth and position and influence —all that power behind you—would never have saved you from hell tonight. Only such a man as Nels or Nick Steele or I could have done that."

Madeline Hammond felt the great leveling force of the truth. Whatever the difference between her and Stewart, or whatever the imagined difference set up by false standards of class and culture, the truth was that here on this wild mountainside she was only a woman and he was simply a man. It was a man that she needed, and if her choice could have been considered in this extremity it would have fallen upon him who had just faced her in quiet, bitter speech. Here was food for thought.

"I reckon we'd better start now," he said, and drew the horse close to a large rock. "Come."

Madeline's will greatly exceeded her strength. For the first time she acknowledged to herself that she had been hurt. Still, she did not feel much pain except when she moved her shoulder. Once in the saddle, where Stewart lifted her, she drooped weakly. The way was rough; every step the horse took hurt her; and the slope of the ground threw her forward on the pommel. Presently, as the slope grew rockier and her discomfort increased, she forgot everything except that she was suffering.

"Here is the trail," said Stewart, at length.

Not far from that point Madeline swayed, and but for Stewart's support would have fallen from the saddle. She heard him swear under his breath.

"Here, this won't do," he said. "Throw your leg over the pommel. The other one—there."

Then, mounting he slipped behind her and lifted and turned her, and then held her with his left arm so that she lay across the saddle and his knees, her head against his shoulder.

As the horse started into a rapid walk Madeline gradually lost all pain and discomfort when she relaxed her muscles. Presently she let herself go and lay inert, greatly to her relief. For a little while she seemed to be half drunk with the gentle swaying of a hammock. Her mind became at once dreamy and active, as if it thoughtfully recorded the slow, soft impressions pouring in from all her senses.

A red glow faded in the west. She could see out over the foothills, where twilight was settling gray on the crests, dark in the hollows. Cedar and piñon trees lined the trail, and there were no more firs. At intervals huge drab-colored rocks loomed over her. The sky was clear and steely. A faint star twinkled. And lastly, close to her, she saw Stewart's face, once more dark and impassive, with the inscrutable eyes fixed on the trail.

His arm, like a band of iron, held her, yet it was flexible and yielded her to the motion of the horse. One instant she felt the brawn, the bone, heavy and powerful; the next the stretch and ripple, the elasticity of muscles. He held her as easily as if she were a child. The roughness of his flannel shirt rubbed her cheek, and beneath that she felt the dampness of the scarf he used to bathe her arm, and deeper still the regular pound of his heart. Against her ear, filling it with strong, vibrant beat, his heart seemed a mighty engine deep within a great cavern. Her head had never before rested on a man's breast, and she had no liking for it there; but she felt more than the physical contact. The position was mysterious and fascinating, and something natural in it made her think of life. Then as the cool wind blew down from the heights, loosening her tumbled hair, she was compelled to see strands of it curl softly into Stewart's face, before his eyes, across his lips. She was unable to reach it with her free hand, and therefore could not refasten it. And when she shut her eyes she felt those loosened strands playing against his cheeks.

In the keener press of such sensations she caught the smell of dust and a faint, wild, sweet tang on the air. There was a low, rustling sigh of wind in the brush along the trail. Suddenly the silence ripped apart to the sharp bark of a coyote, and then, from far away, came a long wail. And then Majesty's metal-rimmed hoof rang on a stone.

These later things lent probability to that ride for Madeline. Otherwise it would have seemed like a dream. Even so it was hard to believe. Again she wondered if this woman who had begun to think and feel so much was Madeline Hammond. Nothing had ever happened to her. And here, playing about her like her hair played about Stewart's face, was adventure, perhaps death, and surely life. She could not believe the evidence of the day's happenings. Would any of her people, her friends, ever believe it? Could she tell it? How impossible to think that a cunning Mexican might have used her to further the interest of a forlorn revolution. She remembered the ghoulish visages of those starved rebels, and marveled at her blessed fortune in escaping them. She was safe, and now self-preservation had some meaning for her. Stewart's arrival in the glade, the courage with which he had faced the outlawed men, grew as real to her now as the iron arm that clasped her. Had it been an instinct which had importuned her to save this man when he lay ill and hopeless in the shack at Chiricahua? In helping him had she hedged round her forces that had just operated to save her life, or if not that, more than life was to her? She believed so.

Madeline opened her eyes after a while and found that night had fallen. The sky was a dark, velvety blue blazing with white stars. The cool wind tugged at her hair, and through waving strands she saw Stewart's profile, bold and sharp against the sky.

133

Then, as her mind succumbed to her bodily fatigue, again her situation became unreal and wild. A heavy languor, like a blanket, began to steal upon her. She wavered and drifted. With the last half-conscious sense of a muffled throb at her ear, a something intangibly sweet, deep-toned, and strange, like a distant calling bell, she fell asleep with her head on Stewart's breast.

12

Friends from the East

Three days after her return to the ranch Madeline could not discover any physical discomfort as a reminder of her adventurous experiences. This surprised her, but not nearly so much as the fact that after a few weeks she found she scarcely remembered the adventures at all. If it had not been for the quiet and persistent guardianship of her cowboys she might almost have forgotten Don Carlos and the raiders. Madeline was assured of the splendid physical fitness to which this ranch life had developed her, and that she was assimilating something of the Western disregard of danger. A hard ride, an accident, a day in the sun and dust, and adventure with outlaws—these might once have been matters of large import, but now for Madeline they were in order with all the rest of her changed life.

There was never a day that something interesting was not brought to her notice. Stillwell, who had ceaselessly reproached himself for riding away the morning Madeline was captured, grew more like an anxious parent than a faithful superintendent. He was never at ease regarding her unless he was near the ranch or had left Stewart there, or else Nels and Nick Steele. Naturally, he trusted more to Stewart than to any one else.

"Miss Majesty, it's sure amazin' strange about Gene," said the old cattleman, as he tramped into Madeline's office.

"What's the matter now?" she inquired.

"Wal, Gene has rustled off into the mountains again."

"Again? I did not know he had gone. I gave him money for that band of guerrillas. Perhaps he went to take it to them."

"No. He took that a day or so after he fetched you back home. Then in about a week he went a second time. An' he packed some stuff with him. Now he's sneaked off, an' Nels, who was down to the lower trail, saw him meet somebody that looked like Padre Marcos. Wal, I went down to the church, and, sure enough, Padre Marcos is gone. What do you think of that, Miss Majesty?"

"Maybe Stewart is getting religious," laughed Madeline. "You told me so once."

Stillwell puffed and wiped his red face.　—

"If you'd heerd him cuss Monty this mawnin' you'd never guess it was religion. Monty an' Nels hev been givin' Gene a lot of trouble lately. They're both sore an' in fightin' mood ever since Don Carlos hed you kidnapped. Sure they're goin' to break soon, an' then we'll hev a couple of wild Texas steers ridin' the range. I've a heap to worry me."

"Let Stewart take his mysterious trips into the mountains. Here, Stillwell, I have news for you that may give you reason for worry. I have letters from home. And my sister, with a party of friends, is coming out to visit me. They are society folk, and one of them is an English lord."

"Wal, Miss Majesty, I reckon we'll all be glad to see them," said Stillwell. "Onless they pack you off back East."

"That isn't likely," replied Madeline, thoughtfully. "I must go back some time, though. Well, let me read you a few extracts from my mail."

Madeline took up her sister's letter with a strange sensation of how easily sight of a crested monogram and scent of delicately perfumed paper could recall the brilliant life she had given up. She scanned the pages of beautiful handwriting. Helen's letter was in turn gay and brilliant and lazy, just as she was herself; but Madeline detected more of curiosity in it than of real longing to see the sister and brother in the Far West. Much of what Helen wrote was enthusiastic anticipation of the fun she expected to have with bashful cowboys. Helen seldom wrote letters, and she never read anything, not even popular novels of the day. She was as absolutely ignorant of the West as the Englishman, who, she said, expected to hunt buffalo and fight Indians. Moreover, there was a satiric note in

135

the letter that Madeline did not like, and which roused her spirit. Manifestly, Helen was reveling in the prospect of new sensation.

When she finished reading aloud a few paragraphs the old cattleman snorted and his face grew redder.

"Did your sister write that?" he asked.

"Yes."

"Wal, I—I beg pawdin, Miss Majesty. But it doesn't seem like you. Does she think we're a lot of wild men from Borneo?"

"Evidently she does. I rather think she is in for a surprise. Now, Stillwell, you are clever and you can see the situation. I want my guests to enjoy their stay here, but I do not want that to be at the expense of the feelings of all of us, or even any one. Helen will bring a lively crowd. They'll crave excitement —the unusual. Let us see that they are not disappointed. You take the boys into your confidence. Tell them what to expect, and tell them how to meet it. I shall help you in that. I want the boys to be on dress parade when they are off duty. I want them to be on their most elegant behavior. I do not care what they do, what measures they take to protect themselves, what tricks they contrive, so long as they do not overstep the limit of kindness and courtesy. I want them to play their parts seriously, naturally, as if they had lived no other way. My guests expect to have fun. Let us meet them with fun. Now what do you say?"

Stillwell rose, his great bulk towering, his huge face beaming.

"Wal, I say it's the most amazin' fine idee I ever heerd in my life."

"Indeed, I am glad you like it," went on Madeline. "Come to me again, Stillwell, after you have spoken to the boys. But, now that I have suggested it, I am a little afraid. You know what cowboy fun is. Perhaps—"

"Don't you go back on that idee," interrupted Stillwell. He was assuring and bland, but his hurry to convince Madeline betrayed him. "Leave the boys to me. Why, don't they all swear by you, same as the Mexicans do to the Virgin? They won't disgrace you, Miss Majesty. They'll be simply immense. It'll beat any show you ever seen."

"I believe it will," replied Madeline. She was still doubtful of her plan, but the enthusiasm of the old cattleman was infectious and irresistible. "Very well, we will consider it settled. My guests will arrive on May ninth. Meanwhile let us get Her Majesty's Rancho in shape for this invasion."

On the afternoon of the ninth of May, perhaps half an hour after Madeline had received a telephone message from Link Stevens announcing the arrival of her guests at El Cajon, Florence called her out upon the porch. Stillwell was there with his face wrinkled by his wonderful smile and his eagle eyes riveted upon the distant valley. Far away, perhaps twenty miles, a thin streak of white dust rose from the valley floor and slanted skyward.

"Look!" said Florence, excitedly.

"What is that?" asked Madeline.

"Link Stevens and the automobile!"

"Oh no! Why, it's only a few minutes since he telephoned saying the party had just arrived."

"Take a look with the glasses," said Florence.

One glance through the powerful binoculars convinced Madeline that Florence was right. And another glance at Stillwell told her that he was speechless with delight. She remembered a little conversation she had had with Link Stevens a short while previous.

"Stevens, I hope the car is in good shape," she had said.

"Now, Miss Hammond, she's as right as the best-trained hoss I ever rode," he had replied.

"The valley road is perfect," she had gone on, musingly. "I never saw such a beautiful road, even in France. No fences, no ditches, no rocks, no vehicles. Just a lonely road on the desert."

"Shore, it's lonely," Stevens had answered, with slowly brightening eyes. "An' safe, Miss Hammond."

"My sister used to like fast riding. If I remember correctly, all of my guests were a little afflicted with the speed mania. It is a common disease with New Yorkers. I hope, Stevens, that you will not give them reason to think we are altogether steeped in the slow, dreamy *mañana* languor of the Southwest."

Link doubtfully eyed her, and then his bronze face changed its dark aspect and seemed to shine.

"Beggin' your pardon, Miss Hammond, thet's shore tall talk fer Link Stevens to savvy. You mean—as long as I drive careful an' safe I can run away from my dust, so to say, an' get here in somethin' less than the Greaser's tomorrow?"

Madeline had laughed her assent. And now, as she watched the thin streak of dust, at that distance moving with snail pace, she reproached herself. She trusted Stevens; she had never known so skillful, daring, and iron-nerved a driver as he was. If she had been in the car herself she would have had no anxiety. But, imagining what Stevens would do on forty miles and more of that desert road, Madeline suffered a prick of conscience.

"Oh, Stillwell!" she exclaimed. "I am afraid I will go back on my wonderful idea. What made me do it?"

"Your sister wanted the *real thing*, didn't she? Said they all wanted it. Wal, I reckon they've begun gettin' it," replied Stillwell.

That statement from the cattleman allayed Madeline's pangs of conscience. She understood just what she felt, though she could not have put it in words. She was hungry for a sight of well-remembered faces; she longed to hear the soft laughter and gay repartee of old friends; she was eager for gossipy first hand news of her old world. Nevertheless, something in her sister's letter, in messages from the others who were coming, had touched Madeline's pride. In one sense the expected guests were hostile, inasmuch as they were scornful and curious about the West that had claimed her. She imagined what they would expect in a Western ranch. They would surely get the real thing, too, as Stillwell said; and in that certainty was satisfaction for a small grain of something within Madeline which approached resentment. She wistfully wondered, however, if her sister or friends would come to see the West even a little as she saw it. That, perhaps, would be hoping too much. She resolved once and for all to do her best to give them the sensation their senses craved, and equally to show them the sweetness and beauty and wholesomeness and strength of life in the Southwest.

"Wal, as Nels says, I wouldn't be in that there ottomobile right now for a million pesos," remarked Stillwell.

"Why? Is Stevens driving fast?"

"Good Lord! Fast? Miss Majesty, there hain't ever been anythin' except a streak of lightnin' run so fast in this country. I'll bet Link for once is in heaven. I can jest see him now, the grim, crooked-legged little devil, hunchin' down over that wheel as if it was a hoss's neck."

"I told him not to let the ride be hot or dusty," remarked Madeline.

"Haw, haw!" roared Stillwell. "Wal, I'll be goin'. I reckon I'd like to be hyar when Link drives up, but I want to be with the boys down by the bunks. It'll be some fun to see Nels, an' Monty when Link comes flyin' along."

"I wish Al had stayed to meet them," said Madeline.

Her brother had rather hurried a shipment of cattle to California: and it was Madeline's supposition that he had welcomed the opportunity to absent himself from the ranch.

"I am sorry he wouldn't stay," replied Florence. "But Al's all business now. And he's doing finely. It's just as well, perhaps."

"Surely. That was my pride speaking. I would like to have all my family and all my old friends see what a man Al has become. Well, Link Stevens is running like the wind. The car will be here before we know it. Florence, we've only a few moments to dress. But first I want to order many and various and exceedingly cold refreshments for that approaching party."

Less than a half-hour later Madeline went again to the porch and found Florence there.

"Oh, you look just lovely!" exclaimed Florence, impulsively, as she gazed wide-eyed up at Madeline. "And somehow so different!"

Madeline smiled a little sadly. Perhaps when she had put on that exquisite white gown something had come to her of the manner which befitted the wearing of it. She could not resist the desire to look fair once more in the eyes of these hypercritical friends. The sad smile had been for the days that were gone. For she knew that what society had once been pleased to call her beauty had trebled since it had last been seen in the drawing-room. Madeline wore no jewels, but at her waist she had pinned two great crimson roses. Against the dead white they had the life and fire and redness of the desert.

"Link's hit the old round-up trail," said Florence, "and oh, isn't he riding that car!"

With Florence, as with most of the cowboys, the car was never driven, but ridden.

A white spot with a long trail of dust showed low down in

the valley. It was now headed almost straight for the ranch. Madeline watched it owing larger moment by moment, and her pleasurable emotion grew accordingly. Then the rapid beat of a horse's hoofs caused her to turn.

Stewart was riding in on his black horse. He had been absent on an important mission, and his duty had taken him to the international boundary line. His presence home long before he was expected was particularly gratifying to Madeline, for it meant that his mission had been brought to a successful issue. Once more. for the hundredth time, the man's reliability struck Madeline. He was a doer of things. The black horse halted wearily without the usual pound of hoofs on the gravel, and the dusty rider dismounted wearily. Both horse and rider showed the heat and dust and wind of many miles.

Madeline advanced to the porch steps. And Stewart, after taking a parcel of papers from a saddlebag, turned toward her.

"Stewart, you are the best of couriers," she said. "I am pleased."

Dust streamed from his sombrero as he doffed it. His dark face seemed to rise as he straightened weary shoulders.

"Here are the reports, Miss Hammond," he replied.

As he looked up to see her standing there, dressed to receive her Eastern guests. he checked his advance with a violent action which recalled to Madeline the one he had made on the night she had met him, when she disclosed her identity. It was not fear nor embarrassment nor awkwardness. And it was only momentary. Yet, slight as had been his pause, Madeline received from it an impression of some strong halting force. A man struck by a bullet might have had an instant jerk of muscular control such as convulsed Stewart. In that instant, as her keen gaze searched his dust-caked face, she met the full, free look of his eyes. Her own did not fall, though she felt a warmth steal to her cheeks. Madeline very seldom blushed. And now, conscious of her sudden color, a genuine blush flamed on her face. It was irritating because it was incomprehensible. She received the papers from Stewart and thanked him. He bowed, then led the black down the path toward the corrals.

"When Stewart looks like that he's been riding," said Florence. "But when his horse looks like that he's sure been burning the wind."

140

Madeline watched the weary horse and rider limp down the path. What had made her thoughtful? Mostly it was something new or sudden or inexplicable that stirred her mind to quick analysis. In this instance the thing that had struck Madeline was Stewart's glance. He had looked at her, and the old burning, inscrutable fire, the darkness, had left his eyes. Suddenly they had been beautiful. The look had not been one of surprise or admiration; nor had it been one of love. She was familiar, too familiar with all three. It had not been a gaze of passion, for there was nothing beautiful in that. Madeline pondered. And presently she realized that Stewart's eyes had expressed a strange joy of pride. That expression Madeline had never before encountered in the look of any man. Probably its strangeness had made her notice it and accounted for her blushing. The longer she lived among these outdoor men the more they surprised her. Particularly, how incomprehensible was this cowboy Stewart! Why should he have pride or joy at sight of her?

Florence's exclamation made Madeline once more attend to the approaching automobile. It was on the slope now, some miles down the gradual slant. Two yellow funnel-shaped clouds of dust seemed to shoot out from behind the car and roll aloft to join the column that stretched down the valley.

"I wonder what riding a mile a minute would be like," said Florence. "I'll sure make Link take me. Oh, but look at him come!"

The giant car resembled a white demon, and but for the dust would have appeared to be sailing in the air. Its motion was steadily forward, holding to the road as if on rails. And its velocity was astounding. Long, gray veils, like pennants, streamed in the wind. A low rushing sound became perceptible, and it grew louder, became a roar. The car shot like an arrow past the alfalfa field by the bunk-houses, where the cowboys waved and cheered. The horses and burros in the corrals began to snort and tramp and race in fright. At the base of the long slope of the foothill Link cut the speed more than half. Yet the car roared up, rolling the dust, flying capes and veils and ulsters, and crashed and cracked to a halt in the yard before the porch.

Madeline descried a gray, disheveled mass of humanity packed inside the car. Besides the driver there were seven occupants, and for the moment they appeared to be coming to life, moving and exclaiming under the veils and wraps and dust shields.

Link Stevens stepped out and, removing helmet and goggles, coolly looked at his watch.

"An hour an' a quarter, Miss Hammond," he said. "It's sixty-three miles by the valley road, an' you know there's a couple of bad hills. I reckon we made fair time, considerin' you wanted me to drive slow an' safe."

From the mass of dusty-veiled humanity in the car came low exclamations and plaintive feminine wails.

Madeline stepped to the front of the porch. Then the deep voices of men and softer voices of women united in one glad outburst, as much a thanksgiving as a greeting. "MAJESTY!"

Helen Hammond was three years younger than Madeline, and a slender, pretty girl. She did not resemble her sister, except in whiteness and fineness of skin, being more of a brown-eyed, brown-haired type. Having recovered her breath soon after Madeline took her to her room, she began to talk.

"Majesty, old girl. I'm here; but you can bet I would never have gotten here if I had known about that ride from the railroad. You never wrote that you had a car. I thought this was out West—stage-coach, and all that sort of thing. Such a tremendous car! And the road! And that terrible little man with the leather trousers! What kind of a chauffeur is he?"

"He's a cowboy. He was crippled by falling under his horse, so I had him instructed to run the car. He can drive, don't you think?"

"Drive? Good gracious! He scared us to death, except Castleton. Nothing could scare that cold-blooded little Englishman. I am crazy yet. Do you know, Majesty, I was delighted when I saw the car. Then your cowboy driver met us at the platform. What a queer-looking individual! He had a big pistol strapped to those leather trousers. That made me nervous. When he piled us all in with our grips, he put me in the seat beside him whether I liked it or not. I was fool enough to tell him I loved to travel fast. What do you think he said? Well, he eyed me in a rather cool and speculative way and said, with a smile 'Miss, I reckon anything you love an' want bad will be coming to you out here!' I didn't know whether it was delightful candor or impudence. Then he said to all of us: 'Shore you had better wrap up in the veils an' dusters. It's a long, slow, hot, dusty ride to the ranch, an' Miss Hammond's order was to drive safe.' He got our baggage checks and gave them to a man with a huge wagon and a four-horse team. Then he cranked the car, jumped in, wrapped his arms round the wheel, and sank down low in his seat. There was a crack, a jerk, a kind of flash around us, and that dirty little town was somewhere on the map behind. For about five minutes I had a lovely time. Then the wind began to tear me to pieces. I couldn't hear anything but the rush of wind and roar of the car. I could see only straight ahead. What a road! I never saw a road in my life till to-day. Miles and miles and miles ahead, with not even a post or a tree. That big car seemed to leap at the miles. It hummed and sang. I was fascinated, then terrified. We went so fast I couldn't catch my breath. The wind went through me, and I expected to be disrobed by it any minute. I was afraid I couldn't hold any clothes on. Presently all I could see was a flashing gray wall with a white line in the middle. Then my eyes blurred. My face burned. My ears grew full of a hundred thousand howling devils. I was about ready to die when the car stopped. I looked and looked, and when I could see, there you stood!"

"Helen, I thought you were fond of speeding," said Madeline, with a laugh.

"I was. But I assure you I never before was in a fast car; I never saw a road; I never met a driver."

"Perhaps I may have a few surprises for you out here in the wild and woolly West."

Helen's dark eyes showed a sister's memory of possibilities.

"You've started well," she said. "I am simply stunned. I expected to find you old and dowdy. Majesty, you're the handsomest thing I ever laid eyes on. You're so splendid and strong, and your skin is like white gold. What's happened to you? What's changed you? This beautiful room, those glorious roses out there, the cool, dark sweetness of this wonderful house! I know you, Majesty, and, though you never wrote it, I believe you have made a home out here. That's the most stunning surprise of all. Come, confess. I know I've always been selfish and not much of a sister; but if you are happy out here I am glad. You were not happy at home. Tell me about yourself and about Alfred. Then I shall give you all the messages and news from the East."

It afforded Madeline exceeding pleasure to have from one

and all of her guests varied encomiums of her beautiful home, and a real and warm interest in what promised to be a delightful and memorable visit.

Of them all Castleton was the only one who failed to show surprise. He greeted her precisely as he had when he had last seen her in London. Madeline, rather to her astonishment, found meeting him again pleasurable. She discovered she liked this imperturbable Englishman. Manifestly her capacity for liking any one had immeasurably enlarged. Quite unexpectedly her old girlish love for her younger sister sprang into life, and with it interest in these half-forgotten friends, and a warm regard for Edith Wayne, a chum of college days.

Helen's party was smaller than Madeline had expected it to be. Helen had been careful to select a company of good friends, all of whom were well known to Madeline. Edith Wayne was a patrician brunette, a serious, soft-voiced woman, sweet and kindly, despite a rather bitter experience that had left her worldly wise. Mrs. Carrollton Beck, a plain, lively person, had chaperoned the party. The fourth and last of the feminine contingent was Miss Dorothy Coombs—Dot, as they called her—a young woman of attractive blond prettiness.

For a man Castleton was of very small stature. He had a pink-and-white complexion, a small golden mustache, and his heavy eyelids, always drooping, made him look dull. His attire, cut to what appeared to be an exaggerated English style, attracted attention to his diminutive size. He was immaculate and fastidious. Robert Weede was a rather large florid young man, remarkable only for his good nature. Counting Boyd Harvey, a handsome, pale-faced fellow, with the careless smile of the man for whom life had been easy and pleasant, the party was complete.

Dinner was a happy hour, especially for the Mexican women who served it and who could not fail to note its success. The mingling of low voices and laughter, the old, gay, superficial talk, the graciousness of a class which lived for the pleasure of things and to make time pass pleasurably for others—all took Madeline far back into the past. She did not care to return to it, but she saw that it was well she had not wholly cut herself off from her people and friends.

When the party adjourned to the porch the heat had markedly decreased and the red sun was sinking over the red desert. An absence of spoken praise, a gradually deepening silence, attested to the impression on the visitors of that noble sunset. Just as the last curve of red rim vanished beyond the Sierra Madres and the golden lightning began to flare brighter Helen broke the silence with an exclamation.

"It wants only life. Ah, there's a horse climbing the hill! See, he's up! He has a rider!"

Madeline knew before she looked the identity of the man riding up the mesa. But she did not know until that moment how the habit of watching for him at this hour had grown upon her. He rode along the rim of the mesa and out to the point, where, against the golden background, horse and rider stood silhouetted in bold relief.

"What's he doing there? Who is he?" inquired the curious Helen.

"That is Stewart, my right-hand man," replied Madeline. "Every day when he is at the ranch he rides up there at sunset. I think he likes the ride and the scene; but he goes to take a look at the cattle in the valley."

"Is he a cowboy?" asked Helen.

"Indeed yes!" replied Madeline, with a little laugh. "You will think so when Stillwell gets hold of you and begins to talk."

Madeline found it necessary to explain who Stillwell was, and what he thought of Stewart, and, while she was about it, of her own accord she added a few details of Stewart's fame.

"El Capitan. How interesting!" mused Helen. "What does he look like?"

"He is superb."

Florence handed the field-glass to Helen and bade her look.

"Oh, thank you!" said Helen, as she complied. "There. I see him. Indeed, he is superb. What a magnificent horse! How still he stands! Why, he seems carved in stone."

"Let me look?" said Dorothy Coombs, eagerly.

Helen gave her the glass.

"You can look, Dot, but that's all. He's mine. I saw him first."

Whereupon Madeline's feminine guests held a spirited contest over the field-glass, and three of them made gay, bantering boasts not to consider Helen's self-asserted rights. Madeline laughed with the others while she watched the dark figure of Stewart and his black outline against the sky. There came over her a thought not by any means new or strange—she wondered what was in Stewart's mind as he stood there in the solitude and faced the desert and the darkening west. Some day she meant to ask him. Presently he turned the horse and rode down into the shadow creeping up the mesa.

"Majesty, have you planned any fun, any excitement for us?" asked Helen. She was restless, nervous, and did not seem to be able to sit still a moment.

"You will think so when I get through with you," replied Madeline.

"What, for instance?" inquired Helen and Dot and Mrs. Beck, in unison. Edith Wayne smiled her interest.

"Well, I am not counting rides and climbs and golf; but these are necessary to train you for trips over into Arizona. I want to show you the desert and the Aravaipa Cañon. We have to go on horseback and pack our outfit. If any of you are alive after those trips and want more we shall go up into the mountains. I should like very much to know what you each want particularly."

"I'll tell you," replied Helen, promptly. "Dot will be the same out here as she was in the East. She wants to look bashfully down at her hand—a hand imprisoned in another, by the way—and listen to a man talk poetry about her eyes. If cowboys don't make love that way Dot's visit will be a failure. Now Elsie Beck wants solely to be revenged upon us for dragging her out here. She wants some dreadful thing to happen to us. I don't know what's in Edith's head, but it isn't fun. Bobby wants to be near Elsie, and no more. Boyd wants what he has always wanted—the only thing he ever wanted that he didn't get. Castleton has a horrible bloodthirsty desire to kill something."

"I declare now, I want to ride and camp out, also," protested Castleton.

"As for myself," went on Helen, "I want—Oh, if I only knew what it is that I want! Well, I know I want to be outdoors, to get into the open, to feel sun and wind, to burn some color into my white face. I want some flesh and blood and life. I am tired out. Beyond all that I don't know very well. I'll try to keep Dot from attaching all the cowboys to her train."

"What a diversity of wants!" said Madeline.

"Above all, Majesty, we want something to happen," concluded Helen, with passionate finality.

146

"My dear sister, maybe you will have your wish fulfilled," replied Madeline. soberly. "Edith, Helen has made me curious about your especial yearning."

"Majesty, it is only that I wanted to be with you for a while," replied this old friend.

There was in the wistful reply, accompanied by a dark and eloquent glance of eyes, what told Madeline of Edith's understanding, of her sympathy, and perhaps a betrayal of her own unquiet soul. It saddened Madeline. How many women might there not be who had the longing to break down the bars of their cage, but had not the spirit.

13

Cowboy Golf

In the whirl of the succeeding days it was a mooted question whether Madeline's guests or her cowboys or herself got the keenest enjoyment out of the flying time. Considering the sameness of the cowboy's ordinary life, she was inclined to think they made the most of the present. Stillwell and Stewart, however, had found the situation trying. The work of the ranch had to go on, and some of it got sadly neglected. Stillwell could not resist the ladies any more than he could resist the fun in the extraordinary goings-on of the cowboys. Stewart alone kept the business of cattle-raising from a serious setback. Early and late he was in the saddle, driving the lazy Mexicans whom he had hired to relieve the cowboys.

One morning in June, Madeline was sitting on the porch with her merry friends when Stillwell appeared on the corral path. He had not come to consult Madeline for several days—an omission so unusual as to be remarked.

"Here comes Bill—in trouble," laughed Florence.

Indeed, he bore some faint resemblance to a thundercloud as he approached the porch; but the greetings he got from Madeline's party, especially from Helen and Dorothy, chased away the blackness from his face and brought the wonderful wrinkling smile.

"Miss Majesty, sure I'm a sad demoralized old cattleman," he said, presently. "An' I'm in need of a heap of help."

"What's wrong now?" asked Madeline, with her encouraging smile.

"Wal, it's so amazin' strange what cowboys will do. I just am about to give up. Why do you think of that? We've changed the shifts, shortened hours, let one an' another off duty, hired Greasers, an', in fact, done everythin' that could be thought of. But this vacation idee growed worse. When Stewart set his foot down, then the boys begin to get sick. Never in my born days as a cattleman have I heerd of so many diseases. An' you ought to see how lame an' crippled an' weak many of the boys have got all of a sudden. The idee of a cowboy comin' to me with a sore finger an' askin' to be let off for a day! There's Booly. Now I've knowed a hoss to fall all over him, an' onct he rolled down a cañon. Never bothered him at all. He's got a blister on his heel, a ridin' blister, an' he says it's goin' to blood-poisonin' if he doesn't rest. There's Jim Bell. He's developed what he says is spinal mengalootis, or some such like. There's Frankie Slade. He swore he had scarlet fever because his face burnt so red, I guess, an' when I hollered that scarlet fever was contagious an' he must be put away somewhere, he up an' says he guessed it wasn't that. But he was sure awful sick an' needed to loaf around an' be amused. Why, even Nels doesn't want to work these days. If it wasn't for Stewart, who's had Greasers with the cattle, I don't know what I'd do."

"Why all this sudden illness and idleness?" asked Madeline.

"Wal, you see, the truth is every blamed cowboy on the range except Stewart thinks it's his bounden duty to entertain the ladies."

"I think that is just fine!" exclaimed Dorothy Coombs; and she joined in the general laugh.

"Stewart, then, doesn't care to help entertain us?" inquired Helen, in curious interest.

"Wal, Miss Helen, Stewart is sure different from the other cowboys," replied Stillwell. "Yet he used to be like them. There never was a cowboy fuller of the devil than Gene. But he's changed. He's foreman here, an' that must be it. All the responsibility rests on him. He sure has no time for amusin' the ladies."

"I imagine that is our loss," said Edith Wayne, in her earnest way. "I admire him."

"Stillwell, you need not be so distressed with what is only gallantry in the boys, even if it does make a temporary confusion in the work," said Madeline.

"Miss Majesty, all I said is not the half, nor the quarter, nor nuthin' of what's troublin' me," answered he, sadly.

"Very well; unburden yourself."

"Wal, the cowboys, exceptin' Gene, have gone plumb batty, jest plain crazy over this heah game of gol-lof."

A merry peal of mirth greeted Stillwell's solemn assertion.

"Oh, Stillwell, you are in fun," replied Madeline.

"I hope to die if I'm not in daid earnest," declared the cattleman. "It's an amazin' strange fact. Ask Flo. She'll tell you. She knows cowboys, an' how if they ever start on somethin' they ride it as they ride a hoss."

Florence being appealed to, and evidently feeling all eyes upon her, modestly replied that Stillwell had scarcely misstated the situation.

"Cowboys play like they work or fight," she added. "They give their whole souls to it. They are great big simple boys."

"Indeed they are," said Madeline. "Oh, I'm glad if they like the game of golf. They have so little play."

"Wal, somethin's got to be did if we're to go on raisin' cattle at Her Majesty's Rancho," replied Stillwell. He appeared both deliberate and resigned.

Madeline remembered that despite Stillwell's simplicity he was as deep as any of his cowboys, and there was absolutely no gagging him where possibilities of fun were concerned. Madeline fancied that his exaggerated talk about the cowboys' sudden craze for golf was in line with certain other remarkable tales that had lately emanated from him. Some very strange things had occurred of late, and it was impossible to tell whether or not they were accidents, mere coincidences, or deep-laid, skilfully worked-out designs of the fun-loving cowboys. Certainly there had been great fun, and at the expense of her guests, particularly Castleton. So Madeline was at a loss to know what to think about Stillwell's latest elaboration. From mere force of habit she sympathized with him and found difficulty in doubting his apparent sincerity.

149

"To go back a ways," went on Stillwell, as Madeline looked up expectantly, "you recollect what pride the boys took in fixin' up that gol-lof course out on the mesa? Wal, they worked on that job, an' though I never seen any other course, I'll gamble yours can't be beat. The boys was sure curious about that game. You recollect also how they all wanted to see you an' your brother play, an' be caddies for you? Wal, whenever you'd quit they'd go to work tryin' to play the game. Monty Price, he was the leadin' spirit. Old as I am, Miss Majesty, an' used as I am to cowboy excentrikities, I nearly dropped daid when I heered that little hobble-footed, burned-up Montana cow-puncher say there wasn't any game too swell for him, an' gol-lof was just his speed. Serious as a preacher, mind you, he was. An' he was always practisin'. When Stewart gave him charge of the course an' the club-house an' all them funny sticks, why, Monty was tickled to death. You see, Monty is sensitive that he ain't much good any more for cowboy work. He was glad to have a job that he didn't feel he was hangin' to by kindness. Wal, he practised the game, an' he read the books in the club-house, an' he got the boys to doin' the same. That wasn't very hard, I reckon. They played early an' late an' in the moonlight. For a while Monty was coach, an' the boys stood it. But pretty soon Frankie Slade got puffed on his game, an' he had to have it out with Monty. Wal, Monty beat him bad. Then one after another the boys tackled Monty. He beat them all. After that they split up an' begin to play matches, two on a side. For a spell this worked fine. But cowboys can't never be satisfied long onless they win all the time. Monty an' Link Stevens, both cripples, you might say, joined forces an' elected to beat all comers. Wal, they did, an' that's the trouble. Long an' patient the other cowboys tried to beat them two game legs, an' hevn't done it. Mebbe if Monty an' Link was perfectly sound in their legs like the other cowboys there wouldn't hev been such a holler. But no sound cowboys'll ever stand for a disgrace like that. Why, down at the bunks in the evenin's it's some mortifyin' the way Monty an' Link crow over the rest of the outfit. They've taken on superior airs. You couldn't reach up to Monty with a trimmed spruce pole. An' Link—wal, he's just amazin' scornful.

" 'It's a swell game, ain't it?' says Link, powerful sarcastic. 'Wal, what's hurtin' you low-down common cowmen? You keep harpin' on Monty's game leg an' on my game leg. If we hed good legs we'd beat you all the wuss. It's brains that wins in gol-lof. Brains an' airstoocratik blood, which of the same you fellers sure hev little.'

"An' then Monty he blows smoke powerful careless an' superior, an' he says:

" 'Sure it's a swell game. You cow-headed gents think beef an' brawn ought to hev the call over skill an' gray matter. You'll all hev to back up an' get down. Go out an' learn the game. You don't know a baffy from a Chinee sandwich. All you can do is waggle with a club an' fozzle the ball.'

"Whenever Monty gets to usin' them queer names the boys go round kind of dotty. Monty an' Link hev got the books an' directions of the game, an' they won't let the other boys see them. They show the rules, but that's all. An' of course, every game ends in a row almost before it's started. The boys are all turrible in earnest about this gol-lof. An' I wants to say, for the good of ranchin', not to mention a possible fight, that Monty an' Link hev got to be beat. There'll be no peace round this ranch till that's done."

Madeline's guests were much amused. As for herself, in spite of her scarcely considered doubt, Stillwell's tale of woe occasioned her anxiety. However, she could hardly control her mirth.

"What in the world can *I* do?"

"Wal, I reckon I couldn't say. I only come to you for advice. It seems that a queer kind of game has locoed my cowboys, an' for the time bein' ranchin' is at a standstill. Sounds ridiculous, I know, but cowboys are as strange as wild cattle. All I'm sure of is that the conceit has got to be taken out of Monty an' Link. Onct, just onct, will square it, an' then we can resoome our work."

"Stillwell, listen," said Madeline, brightly. "We'll arrange a match game, a foursome, between Monty and Link and your best picked team. Castleton, who is an expert golfer, will umpire. My sister, and friends, and I will take turns as caddies for your team. That will be fair, considering yours is the weaker. Caddies may coach, and perhaps expert advice is all that is necessary for your team to defeat Monty's."

"A grand idee," declared Stillwell, with instant decision. "When can we have this match game?"

151

"Why, to-day—this afternoon. We'll all ride out to the links."

"Wal, I reckon I'll be some indebted to you, Miss Majesty, an' all your guests," replied Stillwell, warmly. He rose with sombrero in hand, and a twinkle in his eye again prompted Madeline to wonder. "An' now I'll be goin' to fix up for the game of cowboy gol-lof. *Adios.*"

The idea was as enthusiastically received by Madeline's guests as it had been by Stillwell. They were highly amused and speculative to the point of taking sides and making wagers on their choice. Moreover, this situation so frankly revealed by Stillwell had completed their deep mystification. They were now absolutely nonplussed by the singular character of American cowboys. Madeline was pleased to note how seriously they had taken the cattleman's story. She had a little throb of wild expectancy that made her both fear and delight in the afternoon's prospect.

The June days had set in warm; in fact, hot during the noon hours; and this had inculcated in her insatiable visitors a tendency to profit by the experience of those used to the Southwest. They indulged in the restful siesta during the heated term of the day.

Madeline was awakened by Majesty's well-known whistle and pounding on the gravel. Then she heard the other horses. When she went out she found her party assembled in gala golf attire, and with spirits to match their costumes. Castleton, especially, appeared resplendent in a golf coat that beggared description. Madeline had faint misgivings when she reflected on what Monty and Nels and Nick might do under the influence of that blazing garment.

"Oh, Majesty," cried Helen, as Madeline went up to her horse, "Don't make him kneel! Try that flying mount. We all want to see it. It's so stunning."

"But that way, too, I must have him kneel," said Madeline. "or I can't reach the stirrup. He's so tremendously high."

Madeline had to yield to the laughing insistence of her friends, and after all of them except Florence were up she made Majesty go down on one knee. Then she stood on his left side, facing back, and took a good firm grip on the bridle and pommel and his mane. After she had slipped the toe of her boot firmly into the stirrup she called to Majesty. He jumped and swung her up into the saddle.

152

"Now just to see how it ought to be done watch Florence," said Madeline.

The Western girl was at her best in riding-habit and with her horse. It was beautiful to see the ease and grace with which she accomplished the cowboys' flying mount. Then she led the party down the slope and across the flat to climb the mesa.

Madeline never saw a group of her cowboys without looking them over, almost unconsciously, for her foreman, Gene Stewart. This afternoon, as usual, he was not present. However, she now had a sense—of which she was wholly conscious—that she was both disappointed and irritated. He had really not been attentive to her guests, and he, of all her cowboys, was the one of whom they wanted most to see something. Helen, particularly, had asked to have him attend the match. But Stewart was with the cattle. Madeline thought of his faithfulness, and was ashamed of her momentary lapse into that old imperious habit of desiring things irrespective of reason.

Stewart, however, immediately slipped out of her mind as she surveyed the group of cowboys on the links. By actual count there were sixteen, not including Stillwell. And the same number of splendid horses, all shiny and clean, grazed on the rim in the care of Mexican lads. The cowboys were on dress parade, looking very different in Madeline's eyes, at least, from the way cowboys usually appeared. But they were real and natural to her guests; and they were so picturesque that they might have been stage cowboys instead of real ones. Sombreros with silver buckles and horsehair bands were in evidence; and bright silk scarfs, embroidered vests, fringed and ornamented chaps, huge swinging guns, and clinking silver spurs lent a festive appearance.

Madeline and her party were at once eagerly surrounded by the cowboys, and she found it difficult to repress a smile. If these cowboys were still remarkable to her, what must they be to her guests?

"Wal, you-all raced over, I seen," said Stillwell, taking Madeline's bridle. "Get down—get down. We're sure amazin' glad an' proud. An' Miss Majesty, I'm offering to beg pawdin for the way the boys are packing guns. Mebbe it ain't polite. But it's Stewart's orders."

153

"Stewart's orders!" echoed Madeline. Her friends were suddenly silent.

"I reckon he won't take no chances on the boys being surprised sudden by raiders. An there's raiders operatin' in from the Guadalupes. That's all. Nothin' to worry over. I was just explainin'."

Madeline, with several of her party, expressed relief, but Helen showed excitement and then disappointment.

"Oh, I want something to happen!" she cried.

Sixteen pairs of keen cowboy eyes fastened intently upon her pretty, petulant face; and Madeline divined, if Helen did not, that the desired consummation was not far off.

"So do I," said Dot Coombs. "It would be perfectly lovely to have a real adventure."

The gaze of the sixteen cowboys shifted and sought the demure face of this other discontented girl. Madeline laughed, and Stillwell wore his strange, moving smile.

"Wal, I reckon you ladies sure won't have to go home unhappy," he said. "Why, as boss of this heah outfit I'd feel myself disgraced forever if you didn't have your wish. Just wait. An' now, ladies, the matter on hand may not be amusin' or excitin' to you; but to this heah cowboy outfit it's powerful important. An' all the help you can give us will sure be thankfully received. Take a look across the links. Do you-all see them two apologies for human bein's prancin' like a couple of hobbled broncs? Wal, you're gazin' at Monty Price an' Link Stevens, who have of a sudden got too swell to associate with their old bunkies. They're practisin' for the toornament. They don't want my boys to see how they handle them crooked clubs."

"Have you picked your teams?" inquired Madeline.

Stillwell mopped his red face with an immense bandana, and showed something of confusion and perplexity.

"I've sixteen boys, an' they all want to play," he replied. "Pickin' the team ain't goin' to be an easy job. Mebbe it won't be healthy, either. There's Nels and Nick. They just stated cheerful-like that if they didn't play we won't have any game at all. Nick never tried before, an' Nels, all he wants is a crack at Monty with one of them crooked clubs."

"I suggest you let all your boys drive from the tee and choose the two who drive the farthest," said Madeline.

Stillwell's perplexed face lighted up.

"Wal, that's a plump good idee. The boys'll stand for that."

Wherewith he broke up the admiring circle of cowboys round the ladies.

"Grap a rope—I mean a club—all you cow-punchers, an' march over hyar an' take a swipe at this little white bean."

The cowboys obeyed with alacrity. There was considerable difficulty over the choice of clubs and who should try first. The latter question had to be adjusted by lot. However, after Frankie Slade made several ineffectual attempts to hit the ball from the teeing-ground, at last to send it only a few yards, the other players were not so eager to follow. Stillwell had to push Booly forward, and Booly executed a most miserable shot and retired to the laughing comments of his comrades. The efforts of several succeeding cowboys attested to the extreme difficulty of making a good drive.

"Wal, Nick, it's your turn," said Stillwell.

"Bill, I ain't so all-fired particular about playin'," replied Nick.

"Why? You was roarin' about it a little while ago. Afraid to show how bad you'll play?"

"Nope, jest plain consideration for my feller cow-punchers," answered Nick, with spirit. "I'm appreciatin' how bad they play, an' I'm not mean enough to show them up."

"Wal, you've got to show me," said Stillwell. "I know you never seen a gol-lof stick in your life. What's more, I'll bet you can't hit that little ball square—not in a dozen cracks at it."

"Bill, I'm also too much of a gent to take your money. But you know I'm from Missouri. Gimme a club."

Nick's angry confidence seemed to evaporate as one after another he took up and handled the clubs. It was plain that he had never before wielded one. But, also, it was plain that he was not the kind of a man to give in. Finally he selected a driver, looked doubtfully at the small knob, and then stepped into position on the teeing-ground.

Nick Steele stood six feet four inches in height. He had the rider's wiry slenderness, yet he was broad of shoulder. His arms were long. Manifestly he was an exceedingly powerful man. He swung the driver aloft and whirled it down with a tremendous swing. Crack! The white ball disappeared, and from where it had been rose a tiny cloud of dust.

Madeline's quick sight caught the ball as it lined somewhat

to the right. It was shooting low and level with the speed of a bullet. It went up and up in swift, beautiful flight, then lost its speed and began to sail, to curve, to drop; and it fell out of sight beyond the rim of the mesa. Madeline had never seen a drive that approached this one. It was magnificent, beyond belief except for actual evidence of her own eyes.

The yelling of the cowboys probably brought Nick Steele out of the astounding spell with which he beheld his shot. Then Nick, suddenly alive to the situation, recovered from his trance and, resting nonchalantly upon his club, he surveyed Stillwell and the boys. After their first surprised outburst they were dumb.

"You-all seen thet?" Nick grandly waved his hand. "Thought I was joshin', didn't you? Why, I used to go to St. Louis an' Kansas City to play this here game. There was some talk of the golf clubs takin' me down East to play the champions. But I never cared fer the game. Too easy fer me! Them fellers back in Missouri were a lot of cheap dubs, anyhow, always kickin' because whenever I hit a ball hard I *always lost it*. Why, I hed to hit thet ball off the mesa to show you. I sure wouldn't be seen playin' on your team."

With that Nick sauntered away toward the horses. Stillwell appeared crushed. And not a scornful word was hurled after Nick, which fact proved the nature of his victory. Then Nels strode into the limelight. As far as it was possible for this iron-faced cowboy to be so, he was bland and suave. He remarked to Stillwell and the other cowboys that sometimes it was painful for them to judge of the gifts of superior cowboys such as belonged to Nick and himself. He picked up the club Nick had used and called for a new ball. Stillwell carefully built up a little mound of sand and, placing the ball upon it, squared away to watch. He looked grim and expectant.

Nels was not so large a man as Nick, and did not look so formidable as he waved his club at the gaping cowboys. Still he was lithe, tough, strong. Briskly, with a debonair manner, he stepped up and then delivered a mighty swing at the ball. He missed. The power and momentum of his swing flung him off his feet, and he actually turned upside down and spun round on his head. The cowboys howled. Stillwell's stentorian laugh rolled across the mesa. Madeline and her guests found it impossible to restrain their mirth. And when Nels got up he cast a reproachful glance at Madeline. His feelings were hurt.

His second attempt, not by any means so violent, resulted in as clean a miss as the first, and brought jeers from the cowboys. Nels's red face flamed redder. Angrily he swung again. The mound of sand spread over the teeing-ground and the exasperating little ball rolled a few inches. This time he had to build up the sand mound and replace the ball himself. Stillwell stood scornfully by, and the boys addressed remarks to Nels.

"Take off them blinders," said one.

"Nels, your eyes are shore bad," said another.

"You don't hit where you look."

"Nels, your left eye has sprung a limp."

"Why, you doggoned old fule, you cain't hit thet bawl."

Nels essayed again, only to meet ignominious failure. Then carefully he gathered himself together, gaged distance, balanced the club, swung cautiously. And the head of the club made a beautiful curve round the ball.

"Shore it's jest thet crooked club," he declared.

He changed clubs and made another signal failure. Rage suddenly possessing him, he began to swing wildly. Always, it appeared, the illusive little ball was not where he aimed. Stillwell hunched his huge bulk, leaned hands on knees, and roared his riotous mirth. The cowboys leaped up and down in glee.

"You cain't hit thet bawl," sang out one of the noisiest.

A few more whirling, desperate lunges on the part of Nels, all as futile as if the ball had been thin air, finally brought to the dogged cowboy a realization that golf was beyond him.

Stillwell bawled: "Oh, haw, haw, haw! Nels, you're—too old—eyes no good!"

Nels slammed down the club, and when he straightened up with the red leaving his face, then the real pride and fire of the man showed. Deliberately he stepped off ten paces and turned toward the little mound upon which rested the ball. His arm shot down, elbow crooked, hand like a claw.

"Aw, Nels, this is fun!" yelled Stillwell.

But swift as a gleam of light Nels flashed his gun, and the report came with the action. Chips flew from the mound. Nels had hit it without raising the dust. Then he dropped the gun back in its sheath and faced the cowboys.

"Mebbe my eyes ain't so orful bad," he said, coolly, and started to walk off."

"But look ah-heah, Nels," yelled Stillwell, "we come out to play gol-lof! We can't let you knock the ball around with your gun. What'd you want to get mad for? It's only fun. Now you an' Nick hang round heah an' be sociable. We ain't depreciatin' your company none, nor your usefulness on occasions. An' if you just hain't got inborn politeness sufficient to do the gallant before the ladies, why, remember Stewart's orders."

"Stewart's orders?" queried Nels, coming to a sudden halt.

"That's what I said," replied Stillwell, with asperity. "His orders. Are you forgettin' orders? Wal, you're a fine cowboy. You an' Nick an' Monty, 'specially, are to obey orders."

Nels took off his sombrero and scratched his head. "Bill, I reckon I'm forgetful. But I was mad. I'd 'a' remembered pretty soon, an' mebbe my manners."

"Sure you would," replied Stillwell. "Wal, now, we don't seem to be proceedin' much with my gol-lof team. Next ambitious player step up."

In Ambrose, who showed some skill in driving, Stillwell found one of his team. The succeeding players, however, were so poor and so evenly matched that the earnest Stillwell was in despair. He lost his temper just as speedily as Nels had. Finally Ed Linton's wife appeared riding up with Ambrose's wife, and perhaps this helped, for Ed suddenly disclosed ability that made Stillwell single him out.

"Let me coach you a little," said Bill.

"Sure, if you like," replied Ed. "But I know more about this game than you do."

"Wal, then let's see you hit a ball straight. Seems to me you got good all-fired quick. It's amazin' strange." Here Bill looked around to discover the two young wives modestly casting eyes of admiration upon their husbands. "Haw, haw! It ain't so darned strange. Mebbe that'll help some. Now, Ed, stand up and don't sling your club as if you was ropin' a steer. Come round easy-like an' hit straight."

Ed made several attempts which, although better than those of his predecessors, were rather discouraging to the exacting coach. Presently, after a particularly atrocious shot, Stillwell strode in distress here and there, and finally stopped a dozen paces or more in front of the teeing-ground. Ed, who for a cowboy was somewhat phlegmatic, calmly made ready for another attempt.

"Fore!" he called.

Stillwell stared.

"*Fore!*" yelled Ed.

"Why're you hollerin' that way at me?" demanded Bill.

"I mean for you to lope off the horizon. Get back from in front."

"Oh, that was one of them durned crazy words Monty is always hollerin'. Wal, I reckon I'm safe enough hyar. You couldn't hit me in a million years."

"Bill, ooze away," urged Ed.

"Didn't I say you couldn't hit me? What am I coachin' you for? It's because you hit crooked, ain't it? Wal, go ahaid an' break your back."

Ed Linton was a short, heavy man, and his stocky build gave evidence of considerable strength. His former strokes had not been made at the expense of exertion, but now he got ready for a supreme effort. A sudden silence clamped down upon the exuberant cowboys. It was one of those fateful moments when the air was charged with disaster. As Ed swung the club it fairly whistled.

Crack! Instantly came a thump. But no one saw the ball until it dropped from Stillwell's shrinking body. His big hands went spasmodically to the place that hurt, and a terrible groan rumbled from him.

Then the cowboys broke into a frenzy of mirth that seemed to find adequate expression only in dancing and rolling accompaniment of their howls. Stillwell recovered his dignity as soon as he caught his breath, and he advanced with a rueful face.

"Wal, boys, it's on Bill," he said. "I'm a livin' proof of the pig-headedness of mankind. Ed, you win. You're captain of the team. You hit straight, an' if I hadn't been obstructin' the general atmosphere that ball would sure have gone clear to the Chiricahuas."

Then making a megaphone of his huge hands, he yelled a loud blast of defiance at Monty and Link.

"Hey, you swell gol-lofers! We're waitin'. Come on if you ain't scared."

Instantly Monty and Link quit practising, and like two emperors came stalking across the links.

"Guess my bluff didn't work much," said Stillwell. Then he turned to Madeline and her friends. "Sure I hope, Miss Majesty, that you-all won't weaken an' go over to the enemy.

159

Monty is some eloquent, an', besides, he has a way of gettin' people to agree with him. He'll be plumb wild when he heahs what he an' Link are up against. But it's a square deal, because he wouldn't help us or lend the book that shows how to play. An', besides, it's policy for us to beat him. Now, if you'll elect who's to be caddies an' umpire I'll be powerful obliged."

Madeline's friends were hugely amused over the prospective match; but, except for Dorothy and Castleton, they disclaimed any ambition for active participation. Accordingly, Madeline appointed Castleton to judge the play, Dorothy to act as caddie for Ed Linton, and she herself to be caddie for Ambrose. While Stillwell beamingly announced this momentous news to his team and supporters Monty and Link were striding up.

Both were diminutive in size, bow-legged, lame in one foot, and altogether unprepossessing. Link was young, and Monty's years, more than twice Link's, had left their mark. But it would have been impossible to tell Monty's age. As Stillwell said, Monty was burned to the color and hardness of a cinder. He never minded the heat, and always wore heavy sheepskin chaps with the wool outside. This made him look broader than he was long. Link, partial to leather, had, since he became Madeline's chauffeur, taken to leather altogether. He carried no weapon, but Monty wore a huge gun-sheath and gun. Link smoked a cigarette and looked coolly impudent. Monty was dark-faced, swaggering, for all the world like a barbarian chief.

"That Monty makes my flesh creep," said Helen, low-voiced. "Really, Mr. Stillwell, is he so bad—desperate—as I've heard? Did he ever kill anybody?"

"Sure. 'Most as many as Nels," replied Stillwell, cheerfully.

"Oh! And is that nice Mr. Nels a desperado, too! I wouldn't have thought so. He's so kind and old-fashioned and soft-voiced."

"Nels is sure an example of the dooplicity of men, Miss Helen. Don't you listen to his soft voice. He's really as bad as a side-winder rattlesnake."

At this juncture Monty and Link reached the teeing-ground and Stillwell went out to meet them. The other cowboys pressed forward to surround the trio. Madeline heard Stillwell's voice, and evidently he was explaining that his team was to have skilled advice during the play. Suddenly there came from the center of the group a loud, angry roar that broke off as suddenly. Then followed excited voices all mingled together. Presently Monty appeared, breaking away from restraining hands, and he strode toward Madeline.

Monty Price was a type of cowboy who had never been known to speak to a woman unless he was first addressed, and then he answered in blunt, awkward shyness. Upon this great occasion, however, it appeared that he meant to protest or plead with Madeline, for he showed stress of emotion. Madeline had never gotten acquainted with Monty. She was a little in awe, if not in fear, of him, and now she found it imperative for her to keep in mind that more than any other of the wild fellows on her ranch this one should be dealt with as if he were a big boy.

Monty removed his sombrero—something he had never done before—and the single instant when it was off was long enough to show his head entirely bald. This was one of the hallmarks of that terrible Montana prairie fire through which he had fought to save the life of a child. Madeline did not forget it, and all at once she wanted to take Monty's side. Remembering Stillwell's wisdom, however, she forebore yielding to sentiment, and called upon her wits.

"Miss—Miss Hammond," began Monty, stammering, "I'm extendin' admirin' greetin's to you an' your friends. Link an' me are right down proud to play the match game with you watchin'. But Bill says you're goin' to caddie for his team an' coach 'em on the fine points. An' I want to ask, all respectful, if thet's fair an' square?"

"Monty, that is for you to say," replied Madeline. "It was my suggestion. But if you object in the least, of course we shall withdraw. It seems fair to me, because you have learned the game; you are expert, and I understand the other boys have no chance with you. Then you have coached Link. I think it would be sportsman-like of you to accept the handicap."

"Aw, a handicap! Thet was what Bill was drivin' at. Why didn't he say so? Every time Bill comes to a word thet's pie to us old golfers he jest stumbles. Miss Majesty, you've made it all clear as print. An' I may say with becomin' modesty thet you wasn't mistaken none about me bein' sportsmanlike. Me an' Link was born thet way. An' we accept the handicap. Lackin' thet handicap, I reckon Link an' me would have no

161

ambish to play our most be-ootiful game. An' thankin' you, Miss Majesty, an' all your friends, I want to add thet if Bill's outfit couldn't beat us before, they've got a swell chanct now, with you ladies a-watchin' me an' Link."

Monty had seemed to expand with pride as he delivered this speech, and at the end he bowed low and turned away. He joined the group round Stillwell. Once more there was animated discussion and argument and expostulation. One of the cowboys came for Castleton and led him away to exploit upon ground rules.

It seemed to Madeline that the game never would begin. She strolled on the rim of the mesa, arm in arm with Edith Wayne, and while Edith talked she looked out over the gray valley leading to the rugged black mountains and the vast red wastes. In the foreground on the gray slope she saw cattle in movement and cowboys riding to and fro. She thought of Stewart. Then Boyd Harvey came for them, saying all details had been arranged. Stillwell met them halfway, and this cool, dry, old cattleman, whose face and manner scarcely changed at the announcement of a cattle-raid, now showed extreme agitation.

"Wal, Miss Majesty, we've gone an' made a foozle right at the start," he said dejectedly.

"A foozle? But the game has not yet begun," replied Madeline.

"A bad start, I mean. It's amazin' bad, an' we're licked already."

"What in the world is wrong?"

She wanted to laugh, but Stillwell's distress restrained her.

"Wal, it's this way. That darn Monty is as cute an' slick as a fox. After he got done declaimin' about the handicap he an' Link was so happy to take, he got Castleton over hyar an' drove us all dotty with his crazy gol-lof names. Then he borrowed Castleton's gol-lof coat. I reckon borrowed is some kind word. He just about took that blazin' coat off the Englishman. Though I ain't sayin but that Castleton was agreeable when he tumbled to Monty's meanin'. Which was nothing more'n to break Ambrose's heart. That coat dazzles Ambrose. You know how vain Ambrose is. Why, he'd die to get to wear that Englishman's gol-lof coat. An' Monty forestalled him. It's plumb pitiful to see the look in Ambrose's eyes. He won't be able to play much. Then what do you think? Monty

162

fixed Ed Linton, all right. Usually Ed is easygoin' an cool. But now he's on the rampage. Wal, mebbe it's news to you to learn that Ed's wife is powerful, turrible jealous of him. Ed was somethin' of a devil with the wimmen. Monty goes over an' tells Beulah—that's Ed's wife—that Ed is goin' to have for caddie the lovely Miss Dorothy with the goo-goo eyes. I reckon this was some disrespectful, but with all doo respect to Miss Dorothy she has a pair of unbridled eyes. Mebbe it's just natural for her to look at a feller like that. Oh, it's all right; I'm not sayin' anythin'! I know it's all proper an' regular for girls back East to use their eyes. But out hyar it's bound to result disastrous. All the boys talk about among themselves is Miss Dot's eyes, an' all they brag about is which feller is the luckiest. Anyway, sure Ed's wife knows it. An' Monty up an' told her that it was fine for her to come out an' see how swell Ed was prancin' round under the light of Miss Dot's brown eyes. Beulah calls over Ed, figgertively speakin', ropes him for a minnit. Ed comes back huggin' a grouch as big as a hill. Oh, it was funny! He was goin' to punch Monty's haid off. An' Monty stands there an' laughs. Says Monty, sarcastic as alkali water: 'Ed, we-all knowed you was a heap married man, but you're some locoed to give yourself away.' That settled Ed. He's touchy about the way Beulah henpecks him. He lost his spirit. An' now he couldn't play marbles, let alone gol-lof. Nope, Monty was too smart. An' I reckon he was right about brains bein' what wins."

The game began. At first Madeline and Dorothy essayed to direct the endeavors of their respective players. But all they said and did only made their team play the worse. At the third hole they were far behind and hopelessly bewildered. What with Monty's borrowed coat, with its dazzling effect upon Ambrose, and Link's oft-repeated allusion to Ed's matrimonial state, and Stillwell's vociferated disgust, and the clamoring good intention and pursuit of the ladies, Ambrose and Ed wore through all manner of strange play until it became ridiculous.

"Hey, Link," came Monty's voice booming over the links, "our esteemed rivals are playin' shinny."

Madeline and Dorothy gave up, presently, when the game became a rout, and they sat down with their followers to watch the fun. Whether by hook or crook, Ed and Ambrose forged ahead to come close upon Monty and Link. Castleton

163

disappeared in a mass of gesticulating, shouting cowboys. When the compact mass disintegrated Castleton came forth rather hurriedly, it appeared, to stalk back toward his hostess and friends.

"Look!" exclaimed Helen, in delight. "Castleton is actually excited. Whatever did they do to him? Oh, this is immense!"

Castleton was excited, indeed, and also somewhat disheveled.

"By Jove! that was a rum go," he said, as he came up. "Never saw such blooming golf! I resigned my office as umpire."

Only upon considerable pressure did he reveal the reason.

"It was like this, don't you know. They were all together over there, watching each other. Monty Price's ball dropped into a hazard, and he moved it to improve the lie. By Jove! they've all been doing that. But over there the game was waxing hot. Stillwell and his cowboys saw Monty move the ball, and there was a row. They appealed to me. I corrected the play, showed the rules. Monty agreed he was in the wrong. However, when it came to moving his ball back to its former lie in the hazard there was more blooming trouble. Monty placed the ball to suit him, and then he transfixed me with an evil eye.

" 'Dook,' he said. I wish the bloody cowboy would not call me that. 'Dook, mebbe this game ain't as important as international politics or some other things relatin' but there's some health an' peace dependin' on it. Savvy? For some space our opponents have been dead to honor an' sportsmanlike conduct. I calculate the game depends on our next drive. I'm placin' my ball as near to where it was as human eyesight could. You seen where it was same as I seen it. You're the umpire, an', Dook, I take you as a honorable man. Moreover, never in my born days has my word been doubted without sorrow. So I'm askin' you, wasn't my ball layin' just about here?'

"The bloody little desperado smiled cheerfully, and he dropped his right hand down to the butt of his gun. By Jove, he did! Then I had to tell a blooming lie!"

Castleton even caught the tone of Monty's voice, but it was plain that he had not the least conception that Monty had been fooling. Madeline and her friends divined it, however; and, there being no need of reserve, they let loose the fountains of mirth.

14

Bandits

When Madeline and her party recovered composure they sat up to watch the finish of the match. It came with spectacular suddenness. A sharp yell pealed out, and all the cowboys turned attentively in its direction. A big black horse had surmounted the rim of the mesa and was just breaking into a run. His rider yelled sharply to the cowboys. They wheeled to dash toward their grazing horses.

"That's Stewart. There is something wrong," said Madeline, in alarm.

Castleton stared. The other men exclaimed uneasily. The women sought Madeline's face with anxious eyes.

The black got into his stride and bore swiftly down upon them.

"Oh, look at that horse run!" cried Helen. "Look at that fellow ride!"

Helen was not alone in her admiration, for Madeline divided her emotions between growing alarm of some danger menacing and a thrill and quickening of pulse-beat that tingled over her whenever she saw Stewart in violent action. No action of his was any longer insignificant, but violent action meant so much. It might mean anything. For one moment she remembered Stillwell and all his talk about fun, and plots, and tricks to amuse her guests. Then she discountenanced the thought. Stewart might lend himself to a little fun, but he cared too much for a horse to run him at that speed unless there was imperious need. That alone sufficed to answer Madeline's questioning curiosity. And her alarm mounted to fear not so much for herself as for her guests. But what danger could there be? She could think of nothing except the guerrillas.

Whatever threatened, it would be met and checked by this man Stewart, who was thundering up on his fleet horse; and as he neared her, so that she could see the dark gleam of face and eyes, she had a strange feeling of trust in her dependence upon him.

The big black was so close to Madeline and her friends that when Stewart pulled him the dust and sand kicked up by his pounding hoofs flew in their faces.

"Oh, Stewart, what is it?" cried Madeline.

"Guess I scared you, Miss Hammond," he replied. "But I'm pressed for time. There's a gang of bandits hiding on the ranch, most likely in a deserted hut. They held up a train near Agua Prieta. Pat Hawe is with the posse that's trailing them, and you know Pat has no use for us. I'm afraid it wouldn't be pleasant for you or your guests to meet either the posse or the bandits."

"I fancy not," said Madeline, considerably relieved. "We'll hurry back to the house."

They exchanged no more speech at the moment, and Madeline's guests were silent. Perhaps Stewart's actions and looks belied his calm words. His piercing eyes roved round the rim of the mesa, and his face was as hard and stern as chiseled bronze.

Monty and Nick came galloping up, each leading several horses by the bridles. Nels appeared behind them with Majesty, and he was having trouble with the roan. Madeline observed that all the other cowboys had disappeared.

One sharp word from Stewart calmed Madeline's horse; the other horses, however, were frightened and not inclined to stand. The men mounted without trouble, and likewise Madeline and Florence. But Edith Wayne and Mrs. Beck, being nervous and almost helpless, were with difficulty gotten into the saddle.

"Beg pardon, but I'm pressed for time," said Stewart, coolly, as with iron arm he forced Dorothy's horse almost to its knees. Dorothy, who was active and plucky, climbed astride; and when Stewart loosened his hold on bit and mane the horse doubled up and began to buck. Dorothy screamed as she shot into the air. Stewart, as quick as the horse, leaped forward and caught Dorothy in his arms. She had slipped head downward, and, had he not caught her, would have had a serious fall. Stewart, handling her as if she were a child,

166

turned her right side up to set her upon her feet. Dorothy evidently thought only of the spectacle she presented, and made startled motions to readjust her riding-habit. It was no time to laugh, though Madeline felt as if she wanted to. Besides, it was impossible to be anything but sober with Stewart in violent mood. For he had jumped at Dorothy's stubborn mount. All cowboys were masters of horses. It was wonderful to see him conquer the vicious animal. He was cruel, perhaps, yet it was from necessity. When, presently, he led the horse back to Dorothy she mounted without further trouble. Meanwhile, Nels and Nick had lifted Helen into her saddle.

"We'll take the side trail," said Stewart, shortly, as he swung upon the big black. Then he led the way, and the other cowboys trotted in the rear.

It was only a short distance to the rim of the mesa, and when Madeline saw the steep trail, narrow and choked with weathered stone, she felt that her guests would certainly flinch.

"That's a jolly bad course," observed Castleton.

The women appeared to be speechless.

Stewart checked his horse at the deep cut where the trail started down.

"Boys, drop over, and go slow," he said, dismounting. "Flo, you follow. Now, ladies, let your horses loose and hold on. Lean forward and hang to the pommel. It looks bad. But the horses are used to such trails."

Helen followed closely after Florence; Mrs. Beck went next, and then Edith Wayne. Dorothy's horse balked.

"I'm not so—so frightened," said Dorothy. "If only he would behave!"

She began to urge him into the trail, making him rear, when Stewart grasped the bit and jerked the horse down.

"Put your foot in my stirrup," said Stewart. "We can't waste time."

He lifted her upon his horse and started him down over the rim.

"Go on, Miss Hammond. I'll have to lead this nag down. It'll save time."

Then Madeline attended to the business of getting down herself. It was a loose trail. The weathered slopes seemed to slide under the feet of the horses. Dust clouds formed; rocks rolled and rattled down; cactus spikes tore at horse and rider.

167

Mrs. Beck broke into laughter, and there was a note in it that suggested hysteria. Once or twice Dorothy murmured plaintively. Half the time Madeline could not distinguish those ahead through the yellow dust. It was dry and made her cough. The horses snorted. She heard Stewart close behind, starting little avalanches that kept rolling on Majesty's fetlocks. She feared his legs might be cut or bruised, for some of the stones cracked by and went rattling down the slope. At length the clouds of dust thinned and Madeline saw the others before her ride out upon a level. Soon she was down, and Stewart also.

Here there was a delay, occasioned by Stewart changing Dorothy from his horse to her own. This struck Madeline as being singular, and made her thoughtful. In fact, the alert, quiet manner of all the cowboys was not reassuring. As they resumed the ride it was noticeable that Nels and Nick were far in advance, Monty stayed far in the rear, and Stewart rode with the party. Madeline heard Boyd Harvey ask Stewart if lawlessness such as he mentioned was not unusual. Stewart replied that, except for occasional deeds of outlawry such as might break out in any isolated section of the country, there had been peace and quiet along the border for years. It was the Mexican revolution that had revived wild times, with all the attendant raids and holdups and gun-packing. Madeline knew that they were really being escorted home under armed guard.

When they rounded the head of the mesa, bringing into view the ranch-house and the valley, Madeline saw dust or smoke hovering over a hut upon the outskirts of the Mexican quarters. As the sun had set and the light was fading, she could not distinguish which it was. Then Stewart set a fast pace for the house. In a few minutes the party was in the yard, ready and willing to dismount.

Stillwell appeared, ostensibly cheerful, too cheerful to deceive Madeline. She noted also that a number of armed cowboys were walking with their horses just below the house.

"Wal, you-all had a nice little run," Stillwell said, speaking generally. "I reckon there wasn't much need of it. Pat Hawe thinks he's got some outlaws corralled on the ranch. Nothin' at all to be fussed up about. Stewart's that particular he won't have you meetin' with any rowdies."

Many and fervent were the expressions of relief from Madeline's feminine guests as they dismounted and went into the house. Madeline lingered behind to speak with Stillwell and Stewart.

"Now, Stillwell, out with it," she said, briefly.

The cattleman stared, and then he laughed, evidently pleased with her keenness.

"Wal, Miss Majesty, there's goin' to be a fight somewhere, an' Stewart wanted to get you-all in before it come off. He says the valley's overrun by *vaqueros* an' guerrillas an' robbers, an' Lord knows what else."

He stamped off the porch, his huge spurs rattling, and started down the path toward the waiting men.

Stewart stood in his familiar attentive position, erect, silent, with a hand on pommel and bridle.

"Stewart, you are exceedingly thoughtful of my interests," she said, wanting to thank him, and not readily finding words. "I would not know what to do without you. Is there danger?"

"I'm not sure. But I want to be on the safe side."

She hesitated. It was no longer easy for her to talk to him, and she did not know why.

"May I know the special orders you gave Nels and Nick and Monty?" she asked.

"Who said I gave those boys special orders?"

"I heard Stillwell tell them so."

"Of course I'll tell you if you insist. Buy why should you worry over something that'll likely never happen?"

"I insist, Stewart," she replied, quietly.

"My orders were that at least one of them must be on guard near you day and night—never to be out of hearing of your voice."

"I thought as much. But why Nels or Monty or Nick? That seems rather hard on them. For that matter, why put any one to keep guard over me? Do you not trust any other of my cowboys?"

"I'd trust their honesty, but not their ability."

"Ability? Of what nature?"

"With guns."

"Stewart!" she exclaimed.

"Miss Hammond, you have been having such a good time entertaining your guests that you forget. I'm glad of that. I wish you had not questioned me."

"Forget what?"

"Don Carlos and his guerrillas."

"Indeed I have not forgotten. Stewart, you still think Don Carlos tried to make off with me—may try it again?"

"I don't think. I know."

"And besides all your other duties you have shared the watch with these three cowboys?"

"Yes."

"It has been going on without my knowledge?"

"Yes."

"Since when?"

"Since I brought you down from the mountains last month."

"How long is it to continue?"

"That's hard to say. Till the revolution is over, anyhow."

She mused a moment, looking away to the west, where the great void was filling with red haze. She believed implicitly in him, and the menace hovering near her fell like a shadow upon her present happiness.

"What must I do?" she asked.

"I think you ought to send your friends back East and go with them, until this guerilla war is over."

"Why, Stewart, they would be brokenhearted, and so would I."

He had no reply for that.

"If I do not take your advice it will be the first time since I have come to look to you for so much," she went on. "Cannot you suggest something else? My friends are having such a splendid visit. Helen is getting well. Oh, I should be sorry to see them go before they want to."

"We might take them up into the mountains and camp out for a while," he said, presently. "I know a wild place up among the crags. It's a hard climb, but worth the work. I never saw a more beautiful spot. Fine water, and it will be cool. Pretty soon it'll be too hot here for your party to go out-of-doors."

"You mean to hide me away among the crags and clouds?" replied Madeline, with a laugh.

"Well, it'd amount to that. Your friends need not know. Perhaps in a few weeks this spell of trouble on the border will be over till fall."

"You say it's a hard climb up to this place?"

170

"It surely is. Your friends will get the real thing if they make that trip."

"That suits me. Helen especially wants something to happen. And they are all crazy for excitement."

"They'd get it up there. Bad trails, cañons to head, steep climbs, windstorms, thunder and lightning, rain, mountain lions and wildcats."

"Very well, I am decided. Stewart, of course you will take charge? I don't believe I—Stewart, isn't there something more you could tell me—why, you think, why you know my own personal liberty is in peril?"

"Yes. But do not ask me what it is. If I hadn't been a rebel soldier I would never have known."

"If you had not been a rebel soldier, where would Madeline Hammond be now?" she asked, earnestly.

He made no reply.

"Stewart," she continued, with warm impulse, "you once mentioned a debt you owed me—" And seeing his dark face pale, she wavered, then went on. "It is paid."

"No, no," he answered, huskily.

"Yes. I will not have it otherwise."

"No. That never can be paid."

Madeline held out her hand.

"It is paid, I tell you," she repeated.

Suddenly he drew back from the outstretched white hand that seemed to fascinate him.

"I'd kill a man to touch your hand. But I won't touch it on the terms you offer."

His unexpected passion disconcerted her.

"Stewart, no man ever before refused to shake hands with me, for any reason. It—it is scarcely flattering," she said, with a little laugh. "Why won't you? Because you think I offer it as mistress to servant—rancher to cowboy?"

"No."

"Then why? The debt you owed me is paid. I cancel it. So why not shake hands upon it, as men do?"

"I won't. That's all."

"I fear you are ungracious, whatever your reason," she replied. "Still, I may offer it again some day. Good night."

He said good night and turned. Madeline wonderingly watched him go down the path with his hand on the black horse's neck.

She went in to rest a little before dressing for dinner, and, being fatigued from the day's riding and excitement, she fell asleep. When she awoke it was twilight. She wondered why her Mexican maid had not come to her, and she rang the bell. The maid did not put in an appearance, nor was there any answer to the ring. The house seemed unusually quiet. It was a brooding silence, which presently broke to the sound of footsteps on the porch. Madeline recognized Stillwell's tread, though it appeared to be light for him. Then she heard him call softly in at the open door of her office. The suggestion of caution in his voice suited the strangeness of his walk. With a boding sense of trouble she hurried through the rooms. He was standing outside her office door.

"Stillwell!" she exclaimed.

"Anybody with you?" he asked, in a low tone.

"No."

"Please come out on the porch," he added.

She complied, and, once out, was enabled to see him. His grave face, paler than she had ever beheld it, caused her to stretch an appealing hand toward him. Stillwell intercepted it and held it in his own.

"Miss Majesty, I'm amazin' sorry to tell worrisome news." He spoke almost in a whisper, cautiously looked about him, and seemed both hurried and mysterious. "If you'd heerd Stewart cuss you'd sure know how we hate to hev to tell you this. But it can't be avoided. The fact is we're in a bad fix. If your guests ain't scared out of their skins it'll be owin' to your nerve an' how you carry out Stewart's orders."

"You can rely upon me," replied Madeline, firmly, though she trembled.

"Wal, what we're up against is this: that gang of bandits Pat Hawe was chasin'—they're hidin' in the house!"

"In the house?" echoed Madeline, aghast.

"Miss Majesty, it's the amazing truth, and shamed indeed am I to admit it. Stewart—why, he's wild with rage to think it could hev happened. You see, it couldn't hev happened if I hedn't sloped the boys off to the gol-lof-links, an' if Stewart hedn't rid out on the mesa after us. It's my fault. I've hed too much femininity around fer my old haid. Gene cussed me—he cussed me sure scandalous. But now we've got to face it—to figger."

"Do you mean that a gang of hunted outlaws—bandits—

172

have actually taken refuge somewhere in my house?" demanded Madeline.

"I sure do. Seems powerful strange to me why you didn't find somethin' was wrong, seein' all your servants hev sloped."

"Gone? Ah, I missed my maid! I wondered why no lights were lit. Where did my servants go?"

"Down to the Mexican quarters, an' scared half to death. Now listen. When Stewart left you an hour or so ago he follered me direct to where me an' the boys was tryin' to keep Pat Hawe from tearin' the ranch to pieces. At that we was helpin' Pat all we could to find them bandits. But when Stewart got there he made a difference. Pat was nasty before, but seein' Stewart made him wuss. I reckon Gene to Pat is the same as red to a Greaser bull. Anyway, when the sheriff set fire to an old adobe hut Stewart called him an' called him hard. Pat Hawe hed six fellers with him, an' from all appearances bandit-huntin' was some *fiesta*. There was a row, an' it looked bad fer a little. But Gene was cool, an' he controlled the boys. Then Pat an' his tough de-pooties went into what was only a farce. I reckon Pat could hev kept on foolin' me an' the boys, but as soon as Stewart showed up on the scene—wal, either Pat got to blunderin' or else we-all shed our blinders. Anyway, the facts stood plain. Pat Hawe wasn't lookin' hard fer any bandits; he wasn't daid set huntin' anythin', unless it was trouble fer Stewart. Finally, when Pat's men made fer our storehouse, where we keep ammunition, grub, liquors, an' sich, then Gene called a halt. An' he ordered Pat Hawe off the ranch. It was hyar Hawe an' Stewart locked horns. An' hyar the truth come out. There was a gang of bandits hid somewheres, an' at fust Pat Hawe hed been powerful active an' earnest in his huntin'. But sudden-like he'd fetched a pecooliar change of heart. He had been some flustered with Stewart's eyes a-pryin' into his moves, an' then, mebbe to hide somethin' mebbe jest nat'rul, he got mad. He hollered law. He pulled down off the shelf his old stock grudge on Stewart, accusin' him over again of that Greaser murder last fall. Stewart made him look like a fool—showed him up as bein' scared of the bandits or hevin' some reason fer slopin' off the trail. Anyway, the row started all right, an' but fer Nels it might hev amounted to a fight. In the thick of it, one of them de-pooties lost his head an' went fer his gun. Nels throwed his gun an' crippled the feller's arm. Monty jumped then an' throwed two

173

forty-fives, an' fer a second or so it looked ticklish. But the bandit-hunters crawled, an' then lit out."

Stillwell paused in the rapid delivery of his narrative; he still retained Madeline's hand, as if by that he might comfort her.

"After Pat left we put our haids together," began the old cattleman, with a long respiration. "We rounded up a lad who hed seen a dozen or so fellers—he wouldn't say they was Greasers—breakin' through the shrubbery to the back of the house. That was while Stewart was ridin' out to the mesa. Then this lad seen your servants all runnin' down the hill toward the village. Now, heah's the way Gene figgers. There sure was some deviltry down along the railroad, an' Pat Hawe trailed bandits up to the ranch. He hunts hard an' then all to onct he quits. Stewart says Pat Hawe wasn't scared, but he discovered signs or somethin', or got wind in some strange way that there was in the gang of bandits some fellers he didn't want to ketch. *Sabe?* Then Gene, quicker 'n a flash, springs his plan on me. He'd go down to Padre Marcos an' hev him help to find out all possible from your Mexican servants. I was to hurry up hyar an' tell you—give you orders, Miss Majesty. Ain't that amazin' strange? Wal, you're to assemble all your guests in the kitchen. Make a grand bluff an' pretend, as your help has left, that it'll be great fun fer your guests to cook dinner. The kitchen is the safest room in the house. While you're joshin' your party along, makin' a kind of picnic out of it, I'll place cowboys in the long corridor, an' also outside in the corner where the kitchen joins on to the main house. It's pretty sure the bandits think no one's wise to where they're hid. Stewart says they're in that end room where the alfalfa is, an' they'll slope in the night. Of course, with me an' the boys watchin', you-all will be safe to go to bed. An' we're to rouse your guests early before daylight, to hit the trail up into the mountains. Tell them to pack outfits before goin' to bed. Say as your servants hev sloped, you might as well go campin' with the cowboys. That's all. If we hev any luck your friends'll never know they've been sittin' on a powder-mine."

"Stillwell, do you advise that trip up into the mountains?" asked Madeline.

"I reckon I do, considerin' everythin'. Now, Miss Majesty, I've used up a lot of time explainin'. You'll sure keep your nerve?"

174

"Yes," Madeline replied, and was surprised at herself.

"Better tell Florence. She'll be a power of comfort to you. I'm goin' now to fetch up the boys."

Instead of returning to her room Madeline went through the office into the long corridor. It was almost as dark as night. She fancied she saw a slow-gliding figure darker than the surrounding gloom; and she entered upon the fulfilment of her part of the plan in something like trepidation. Her footsteps were noiseless. Finding the door to the kitchen, and going in, she struck lights. Upon passing out again she made certain she discerned a dark shape, now motionless, crouching along the wall. But she mistrusted her vivid imagination. It took all her boldness to enable her unconcernedly and naturally to strike the corridor light. Then she went on through her own rooms and thence into the patio.

Her guests laughingly and gladly entered into the spirit of the occasion. Madeline fancied her deceit must have been perfect, seeing that it deceived even Florence. They trooped merrily into the kitchen. Madeline, delaying at the door, took a sharp but unobtrusive glance down the great, barnlike hall. She saw nothing but blank dark space. Suddenly from one side, not a rod distant, protruded a pale, gleaming face breaking the even blackness. Instantly it flashed back out of sight. Yet that time was long enough for Madeline to see a pair of glittering eyes, and to recognize them as Don Carlos's.

Without betraying either hurry or alarm, she closed the door. It had a heavy bolt which she slowly, noiselessly shot. Then the cold amaze that had all but stunned her into inaction throbbed into wrath. How dared that Mexican steal into her home! What did he mean? Was he one of the bandits supposed to be hidden in her house? She was thinking herself into greater anger and excitement, and probably would have betrayed herself had not Florence, who had evidently seen her bolt the door and now read her thoughts, come toward her with a bright, intent, questioning look. Madeline caught herself in time.

Thereupon she gave each of her guests a duty to perform. Leading Florence into the pantry, she unburdened herself of the secret in one brief whisper. Florence's reply was to point out of the little open window, passing which was a file of stealthily moving cowboys. Then Madeline lost both anger and fear, retaining only the glow of excitement.

Madeline could be gay, and she initiated the abandonment of dignity by calling Castleton into the pantry, and, while interesting him in some pretext or other, imprinting the outlines of her flour-covered hands upon the back of his black coat. Castleton innocently returned to the kitchen to be greeted with a roar. That surprising act of the hostess set the pace, and there followed a merry noisy time. Everybody helped. The miscellaneous collection of dishes so confusingly contrived made up a dinner which they all heartily enjoyed. Madeline enjoyed it herself, even with the feeling of a sword hanging suspended over her.

The hour was late when she rose from the table and told her guests to go to their rooms, don their riding-clothes, pack what they needed for the long and adventurous camping trip that she hoped would be the climax of their Western experience, and to snatch a little sleep before the cowboys roused them for the early start.

Madeline went immediately to her room, and was getting out her camping apparel when a knock interrupted her. She thought Florence had come to help her pack. But this knock was upon the door opening out in the porch. It was repeated.

"Who's there?" she questioned.

"Stewart," came the reply.

She opened the door. He stood on the threshold. Beyond him, indistinct in the gloom, were several cowboys.

"May I speak to you?" he asked.

"Certainly." She hesitated a moment, then asked him in and closed the door. "Is—is everything all right?"

"No. These bandits stick to cover pretty close. They must have found out we're on the watch. But I'm sure we'll get you and your friends away before anything starts. I wanted to tell you that I've talked with your servants. They were just scared. They'll come back tomorrow, soon as Bill gets rid of this gang. You need not worry about them or your property."

"Do you have any idea who is hiding in the house?"

"I was worried some at first. Pat Hawe acted queer. I imagined he'd discovered he was trailing bandits who might turn out to be his smuggling guerrilla cronies. But talking with your servants, finding a bunch of horses hidden down in the mesquite behind the pond—several things have changed my mind. My idea is that a cowardly handful of riffraff outcasts from the border have hidden in your house, more by accident than design. We'll let them go—get rid of them without even a shot. If I didn't think so—well, I'd be considerably worried. It would make a different state of affairs."

"Stewart, you are wrong," she said.

He started, but his reply did not follow swiftly. The expression of his eyes altered. Presently he spoke:

"How so?"

"I saw one of these bandits. I distinctly recognized him."

One long step brought him close to her.

"Who was he?" demanded Stewart.

"Don Carlos."

He muttered low and deep, then said, "Are you sure?"

"Absolutely. I saw his figure twice in the hall, then his face in the light. I could never mistake his eyes."

"Did he know you saw him?"

"I am not positive, but I think so. Oh, he must have known! I was standing full in the light. I had entered the door, then purposely stepped out. His face showed from around a corner, and swiftly flashed out of sight."

Madeline was tremblingly conscious that Stewart underwent a transformation. She saw as well as felt the leaping passion that changed him.

"Call your friends—get them in here!" he ordered, tersely, and wheeled toward the door.

"Stewart, wait!" she said.

He turned. His white face, his burning eyes, his presence now charged with definite, fearful meaning, influenced her strangely, weakened her.

"What will you do?" she asked.

"That needn't concern you. Get your party in here. Bar the windows and lock the doors. You'll be safe."

"Stewart! Tell me what you intend to do."

"I won't tell you," he replied, and turned away again.

"But I will know," she said. With a hand on his arm she detained him. She saw how he halted—felt the shock in him as she touched him. "Oh, I do know. You mean to fight!"

"Well, Miss Hammond, isn't it about time?" he asked. Evidently he overcame a violent passion for instant action. There was weariness, dignity, even reproof in his question. "The fact of that Mexican's presence here in your house ought to prove to you the nature of the case. These *vaqueros*, these guerrillas, have found out you won't stand for any fighting on the part of

177

your men. Don Carlos is a sneak, a coward, yet he's not afraid to hide in your own house. He has learned you won't let your cowboys hurt anybody. He's taking advantage of it. He'll rob, burn, and make off with you. He'll murder, too, if it falls his way. These Greasers use knives in the dark. So I ask —isn't it about time we stop him?"

"Stewart, I forbid you to fight, unless in self-defense. I forbid you."

"What I mean to do is self-defense. Haven't I tried to explain to you that just now we've wild times along this stretch of border? Must I tell you again that Don Carlos is hand in glove with the revolution? The rebels are crazy to stir up the United States. You are a woman of prominence. Don Carlos would make off with you. If he got you, what little matter to cross the border with you! Well, where would the hue and cry go? Through the troops along the border! To New York! To Washington! Why, it would mean that the rebels are working for—United States intervention. In other words, war!"

"Oh, surely you exaggerate!" she cried.

"Maybe so. But I'm beginning to see the Don's game. And, Miss Hammond, I— It's awful for me to think what you'd suffer if Don Carlos got you over the line. I know these low-caste Mexicans. I've been among the peons—the slaves."

"Stewart, don't let Don Carlos get me," replied Madeline, in sweet directness.

She saw him shake, saw his throat swell as he swallowed hard, saw the hard fierceness return to his face.

"I won't. That's why I'm going after him."

"But I forbade you to start a fight deliberately."

"Then I'll go ahead and start one without your permission," he replied shortly, and again he wheeled.

This time when Madeline caught his arm she held to it, even after he stopped.

"No," she said, imperiously.

He shook off her hand and strode forward.

"Please don't go!" she called, beseechingly. But he kept on. "Stewart!"

She ran ahead of him, intercepted him, faced him with her back against the door. He swept out a long arm as if to brush her aside. But it wavered and fell. Haggard, troubled, with working face, he stood before her.

"It's for your sake," he expostulated.

"If it is for my sake, then do what pleases me."

"These guerrillas will knife somebody. They'll burn the house. They'll make off with you. They'll do something bad unless we stop them."

"Let us risk all that," she importuned.

"But it's a terrible risk, and it oughtn't be run," he exclaimed, passionately. "I know best here. Stillwell upholds me. Let me out, Miss Hammond. I'm going to take the boys and go after these guerrillas."

"No!"

"Good Heavens!" exclaimed Stewart. "Why not let me go? It's the thing to do. I'm sorry to distress you and your guests. Why not put an end to Don Carlos's badgering? Is it because you're afraid a rumpus will spoil your friends' visit?"

"It isn't—not this time."

"Then it's the idea of a little shooting at these Greasers?"

"No."

"You're sick to think of a little Greaser blood staining the halls of your home?"

"No!"

"Well, then, why keep me from doing what I know is best?"

"Stewart, I—I—I—" she faltered, in growing agitation. "I'm frightened—confused. All this is too—too much for me. I'm not a coward. If you *have* to fight you'll see I'm not a coward. But your way seems so reckless—that hall is so dark—the guerrillas would shoot from behind doors. You're so wild, so daring, you'd rush right into peril. Is that necessary? I think—I mean—I don't know just why I feel so—so about you doing it. But I believe it's because I'm afraid you—you might be hurt."

"You're afraid I—*I* might be hurt?" he echoed, wonderingly, the hard whiteness of his face warming, flushing, glowing.

"Yes."

The single word, with all it might mean, with all it might not mean, softened him as if by magic, made him gentle, amazed, shy as a boy, stifling under a torrent of emotions.

Madeline thought she had persuaded him—worked her will with him. Then another of his startlingly sudden moves told her that she had reckoned too quickly. This move was to put her firmly aside so he could pass; and Madeline, seeing he would not hesitate to lift her out of the way, surrendered the door. He turned on the threshold. His face was still working,

179

but the flame-pointed gleam of his eyes indicated the return of that cowboy ruthlessness.

"I'm going to drive Don Carlos and his gang out of the house," declared Stewart. "I think I may promise you to do it without a fight. But if it takes a fight, off he goes!"

15

The Mountain Trail

As Stewart departed from one door Florence knocked upon another; and Madeline, far shaken out of her usual serenity, admitted the cool Western girl with more than gladness. Just to have her near helped Madeline to get back her balance. She was conscious of Florence's sharp scrutiny, then of a sweet, deliberate change of manner. Florence might have been burning with curiosity to know more about the bandits hidden in the house, the plans of the cowboys, the reason for Madeline's suppressed emotion; but instead of asking Madeline questions she introduced the important subject of what to take on the camping trip. For an hour they discussed the need of this and that article, selected those things most needful, and then packed them in Madeline's dufflebags.

That done, they decided to lie down, fully dressed as they were in riding-costume, and sleep, or at least rest, the little remaining time left before the call to saddle. Madeline turned out the light and, peeping through her window, saw dark forms standing sentinel-like in the gloom. This fidelity to her swelled her heart, while the need of it presaged that fearful something which, since Stewart's passionate appeal to her, haunted her as inevitable.

Madeline did not expect to sleep, yet she did sleep, and it seemed to have been only a moment until Florence called her. She followed Florence outside. It was the dark hour before dawn. She could discern saddled horses being held by cowboys. There was an air of hurry and mystery about the departure. Helen, who came tiptoeing out with Madeline's other

180

guests, whispered that it was like an escape. She was delighted. The others were amused. To Madeline it was indeed an escape.

In the darkness Madeline could not see how many escorts her party was to have. She heard low voices, the champing of bits and thumping of hoofs, and she recognized Stewart when he led up Majesty for her to mount. Then came a pattering of soft feet and the whining of dogs. Cold noses touched her hands, and she saw the long, gray, shaggy shapes of her pack of Russian wolfhounds. That Stewart meant to let them go with her was indicative of how he studied her pleasure. She loved to be out with the hounds and her horse.

Stewart led Majesty out into the darkness past a line of mounted horses.

"Guess we're ready," he said. "I'll make the count." He went back along the line, and on the return Madeline heard him say several times, "Now, everybody ride close to the horse in front, and keep quiet till daylight." Then the snorting and pounding of the big black horse in front of her told Madeline that Stewart had mounted.

"All right, we're off," he called.

Madeline lifted Majesty's bridle and let the roan go. There was a crack and crunch of gravel, fire struck from stone, a low whinny, a snort, and then steady, short, clip-clop of iron hoofs on hard ground. Madeline could just discern Stewart and his black outlined in shadowy gray before her. Yet they were almost within touching distance. Once or twice one of the huge stag-hounds leaped up at her and whined joyously. A thick belt of darkness lay low, and seemed to thin out above to a gray fog, through which a few wan stars showed. It was altogether an unusual departure from the ranch; and Madeline, always susceptible even to ordinary incident that promised well, now found herself thrillingly sensitive to the soft beat of hoofs, the feel of cool, moist air, the dim sight of Stewart's dark figure. The caution, the early start before dawn, the enforced silence—these lent the occasion all that was needed to make it stirring.

Majesty plunged into a gully, where sand and rough going made Madeline stop romancing to attend to riding. In the darkness Stewart was not so easy to keep close to even on smooth trails, and now she had to be watchfully attentive to do it. Then followed a long march through dragging sand.

Meantime the blackness gradually changed to gray. At length Majesty climbed out of the wash, and once more his iron shoes rang on stone. He began to climb. The figure of Stewart and his horse loomed more distinctly in Madeline's sight. Bending over, she tried to see the trail, but could not. She wondered how Stewart could follow a trail in the dark. His eyes must be as piercing as they sometimes looked. Over her shoulder Madeline could not see the horse behind her, but she heard him.

As Majesty climbed steadily Madeline saw the gray darkness grow opaque, change and lighten, lose its substance, and yield the grotesque shapes of yucca and ocotillo. Dawn was about to break. Madeline imagined she was facing east, still she saw no brightening of sky. All at once, to her surprise, Stewart and his powerful horse stood clear in her sight. She saw the characteristic rock and cactus and brush that covered the foothills. The trail was old and seldom used, and it zig-zagged and turned and twisted. Looking back, she saw the short, squat figure of Monty Price humped over his saddle. Monty's face was hidden under his sombrero. Behind him rode Dorothy Coombs, and next loomed up the lofty form of Nick Steele. Madeline and the members of her party were riding between cowboy escorts.

Bright daylight came, and Madeline saw the trail was leading up through foothills. It led in a roundabout way through shallow gullies full of stone and brush washed down by floods. At every turn now Madeline expected to come upon water and the waiting pack-train. But time passed, and miles of climbing, and no water or horses were met. Expectation in Madeline gave place to desire; she was hungry.

Presently Stewart's horse went splashing into a shallow pool. Beyond that damp places in the sand showed here and there, and again more water in rocky pockets. Stewart kept on. It was eight o'clock by Madeline's watch when, upon turning into a wide hollow, she saw horses grazing on spare grass, a great pile of canvas-covered bundles, and a fire round which cowboys and two Mexican women were busy.

Madeline sat her horse and reviewed her followers as they rode up single file. Her guests were in merry mood, and they all talked at once.

"Breakfast—and rustle," called out Stewart, without ceremony.

"No need to tell me to rustle," said Helen. "I am simply ravenous. This air makes me hungry."

For that matter, Madeline observed Helen did not show any marked contrast to the others. The hurry order, however, did not interfere with the meal being somewhat in the nature of a picnic. While they ate and talked and laughed, the cowboys were packing horses and burros and throwing the diamond-hitch, a procedure so interesting to Castleton that he got up with coffee cup in hand and tramped from one place to another.

"Heard of that diamond-hitch-up," he observed to a cowboy. "Bally nice little job!"

As soon as the pack-train was in readiness Stewart started it off in the lead to break trail. A heavy growth of shrub interspersed with rock and cactus covered the slopes; and now all the trail appeared to be uphill. It was not a question of comfort for Madeline and her party, for comfort was impossible; it was a matter of making the travel possible for them. Florence wore corduroy breeches and high-top boots, and the advantage of this masculine garb was at once in evidence. The riding-habits of the other ladies suffered considerably from the sharp spikes. It took Madeline's watchfulness to save her horse's legs, to pick the best bits of open ground, to make cutoffs from the trail, and to protect herself from outreaching thorny branches, so that the time sped by without her knowing it. The pack-train forged ahead, and the trailing couples grew farther apart. At noon they got out of the foothills to face the real ascent of the mountains. The sun beat down hot. There was little breeze, and the dust rose thick and hung in a pall. The view was restricted, and what scenery lay open to the eye was dreary and drab, a barren monotony of slow-mounting slopes ridged by rocky canons.

Once Stewart waited for Madeline, and as she came up he said:

"We're going to have a storm."

"That will be a relief. It's so hot and dusty," replied Madeline.

"Shall I call a halt and make camp?"

"Here? Oh no! What do you think best?"

"Well, if we have a good healthy thunderstorm it will be something new for your friends. I think we'd be wise to keep on the go. There's no place to make a good camp. The wind would blow us off this slope if the rain didn't wash us off. It'll take all-day travel to reach a good campsite, and I don't promise that. We're making slow time. If it rains, let it rain. The pack outfit is well covered. We will have to get wet."

"Surely," replied Madeline; and she smiled at his inference. She knew what a storm was in that country, and her guests had yet to experience one. "If it rains, let it rain."

Stewart rode on, and Madeline followed. Up the slope toiled and nodded the pack animals, the little burros going easily where the horses labored. Their packs, like the humps of camels, bobbed from side to side. Stones rattled down; the heat waves wavered black; the dust puffed up and sailed. The sky was a pale blue, like heated steel, except where dark clouds peeped over the mountain crests. A heavy, sultry atmosphere made breathing difficult. Down the slope the trailing party stretched out in twos and threes, and it was easy to distinguish the weary riders.

Half a mile farther up Madeline could see over the foothills to the north and west and a little south, and she forgot the heat and weariness and discomfort for her guests in wide, unlimited prospects of sun-scorched earth. She marked the gray valley and the black mountains and the wide, red gateway of the desert, and the dim, shadowy peaks, blue as the sky they pierced. She was sorry when the bleak, gnarled cedar trees shut off her view.

Then there came a respite from the steep climb, and the way led in a winding course through a matted, storm-wrenched forest of stunted trees. Even up to this elevation the desert reached with its gaunt hand. The clouds overspreading the sky, hiding the sun, made a welcome change. The pack-train rested, and Stewart and Madeline waited for the party to come up. Here he briefly explained to her that Don Carlos and his bandits had left the ranch some time in the night. Thunder rumbled in the distance, and a faint wind rustled the scant foliage of the cedars. The air grew oppressive; the horses panted.

"Sure it'll be a hummer," said Stewart. "The first storm almost always is bad. I can feel it in the air."

The air, indeed, seemed to be charged with a heavy force that was waiting to be liberated.

One by one the couples mounted to the cedar forest, and the feminine contingent declaimed eloquently for rest. But

184

there was to be no permanent rest until night and then that depended upon reaching the crags. The pack-train wagged onward, and Stewart fell in behind. The storm-center gathered slowly around the peaks; low rumble and bowl of thunder increased in frequence; slowly the light shaded as smoky clouds rolled up; the air grew sultrier, and the exasperating breeze puffed a few times and then failed.

An hour later the party had climbed high and was rounding the side of a great bare ridge that long had hidden the crags. The last burro of the pack-train plodded over the ridge out of Madeline's sight. She looked backward down the slope, amused to see her guests change wearily from side to side in their saddles. Far below lay the cedar flat and the foothills. Far to the west the sky was still clear, with shafts of sunlight shooting down from behind the encroaching clouds.

Stewart reached the summit of the ridge and, though only a few rods ahead, he waved to her, sweeping his hand round to what he saw beyond. It was an impressive gesture, and Madeline, never having climbed as high as this, anticipated much.

Majesty surmounted the last few steps and, snorting, halted beside Stewart's black. To Madeline the scene was as if the world had changed. The ridge was a mountain-top. It dropped before her into a black, stone-ridged, shrub-patched, many-cañoned gulf. Eastward, beyond the gulf, round, bare mountain-heads loomed up. Upward, on the right, led giant steps of cliff and bench and weathered slope to the fir-bordered and pine-fringed crags standing dark and bare against the stormy sky. Massed inky clouds were piling across the peaks, obscuring the highest ones. A fork of white lightning flashed, and, like the booming of an avalanche, thunder followed.

That bold world of broken rock under the slow mustering of storm-clouds was a grim, awe-inspiring spectacle. It had beauty of the sublime and majestic kind. The fierce desert had reached up to meet the magnetic heights where heat and wind and frost and lightning and flood contended in everlasting strife. And before their onslaught this mighty upflung world of rugged stone was crumbling, splitting, and wearing to ruin.

Madeline glanced at Stewart. He had forgotten her presence. Immovable as stone, he sat his horse, dark-faced, dark-eyed, and, like an Indian unconscious of thought, he watched and watched. To see him thus, to divine the strange affinity between the soul of this man, become primitive, and the savage environment that had developed him, were powerful helps to Madeline Hammond in her strange desire to understand his nature.

A cracking of iron-shod hoofs behind her broke the spell. Monty had reached the summit.

"Gene, what it won't all be doin' in a minnut Moses hisself couldn't tell," observed Monty.

Then Dorothy climbed to his side and looked.

"Oh, isn't it just perfectly lovely!" she exclaimed. "But I wish it wouldn't storm. We'll all get wet."

Once more Stewart faced the ascent, keeping to the slow heave of the ridge as it rose southward toward the looming spires of rock. Soon he was off smooth ground, and Madeline, some rods behind him, looked back with concern at her friends. Here the real toil, the real climb began, and a mountain storm was about to burst in all its fury.

The slope that Stewart entered upon was a magnificent monument to the ruined crags above. It was a southerly slope, and therefore semi-arid, covered with cercocarpus and yucca and some shrub that Madeline believed was manzanita. Every foot of the trail seemed to slide under Majesty. What hard ground there was could not be traveled upon, owing to the spiny covering or masses of shattered rocks. Gullies lined the slope.

Then the sky grew blacker; the slow-gathering clouds appeared to be suddenly agitated; they piled and rolled and mushroomed and obscured the crags. The air moved heavily and seemed to be laden with sulphurous smoke, and sharp lightning flashes began to play. A distant roar of wind could be heard between the peals of thunder.

Stewart waited for Madeline under the lee of a shelving cliff, where the cowboys had halted the pack-train. Majesty was sensitive to the flashes of lightning. Madeline patted his neck and softly called to him. The weary burros nodded; the Mexican women covered their heads with their mantles. Stewart untied the slicker at the back of Madeline's saddle and helped her on with it. Then he put on his own. The other cowboys followed suit. Presently Madeline saw Monty and Dorothy rounding the cliff, and hoped the others would come soon.

A blue-white, knotted rope of lightning burned down out of the clouds, and instantly a thunderclap crashed, seeming to shake the foundations of the earth. Then it rolled, as if banging from cloud to cloud, and boomed along the peaks, and reverberated from deep to low, at last to rumble away into silence. Madeline felt the electricity in Majesty's mane, and it seemed to tingle through her nerves. The air had a weird, bright cast. The ponderous clouds swallowed more and more of the eastern domes. This moment of the breaking of the storm, with the strange growing roar of wind, like a moaning monster, was pregnant with a heart-disturbing emotion for Madeline Hammond. Glorious it was to be free, healthy, out in the open, under the shadow of the mountain and cloud, in the teeth of the wind and rain and storm.

Another dazzling blue blaze showed the bold mountainside and the storm-driven clouds. In the flare of light Madeline saw Stewart's face.

"Are you afraid?" she asked.

"Yes," he replied, simply.

Then the thunderbolt racked the heavens, and as it boomed away in lessening power Madeline reflected with surprise upon Stewart's answer. Something in his face had made her ask him what she considered a foolish question. His reply amazed her. She loved a storm. Why should he fear it—he, with whom she could not associate fear?

"How strange! Have you been out in many storms?"

A smile that was only a gleam flitted over his dark face.

"In hundreds of them. By day, with the cattle stampeding. At night, alone on the mountain, with the pines crashing and the rocks rolling—in flood on the desert."

"It's not only the lightning, then?" she asked.

"No. All the storm."

Madeline felt that henceforth she would have less faith in what she had imagined was her love of the elements. What little she knew! If this iron-nerved man feared a storm, then there was something about a storm to fear.

And suddenly, as the ground quaked under her horse's feet, and all the sky grew black and crisscrossed by flaming streaks, and between thunderous reports there was a strange hollow roar sweeping down upon her, she realized how small was her knowledge and experience of the mighty force of nature. Then, with perversity of character of which she was wholly conscious, she was humble, submissive, reverent, and fearful even while she gloried in the grandeur of the dark, cloud-shadowed crags and cañons, the stupendous strife of sound, the wonderful driving lances of white fire.

With blacker gloom and deafening roar came the torrent of rain. It was a cloudburst. It was like solid water tumbling down. For long Madeline sat her horse, head bent to the pelting rain. When its force lessened and she heard Stewart call for all to follow, she looked up to see that he was starting once more. She shot a glimpse at Dorothy and as quickly glanced away. Dorothy, who would not wear a hat suitable for inclement weather, nor one of the horrid yellow, sticky slickers, was a drenched and disheveled spectacle. Madeline did not trust herself to look at the other girls. It was enough to hear their lament. So she turned her horse into Stewart's trail.

Rain fell steadily. The fury of the storm, however, had passed, and the roll of thunder diminished in volume. The air had wonderfully cleared and was growing cool. Madeline began to feel uncomfortably cold and wet. Stewart was climbing faster than formerly, and she noted that Monty kept at her heels, pressing her on. Time had been lost, and the campsite was a long way off. The stag-hounds began to lag and get footsore. The sharp rocks of the trail were cruel to their feet. Then, as Madeline began to tire, she noticed less and less around her. The ascent grew rougher and steeper—slow toil for panting horses. The thinning rain grew colder, and sometimes a stronger whip of wind lashed stingingly in Madeline's face. Her horse climbed and climbed, and brush and sharp corners of stone everlastingly pulled and tore at her wet garments. A gray gloom settled down around her. Night was approaching. Majesty heaved upward with a snort, the wet saddle creaked, and an even motion told Madeline she was on level ground. She looked up to see looming crags and spires, like huge pipe-organs, dark at the base and growing light upward. The rain had ceased, but the branches of fir trees and juniper were water-soaked arms reaching out for her. Through an opening between crags Madeline caught a momentary glimpse of the west. Red sunshafts shone through the murky, broken clouds. The sun had set.

Stewart's horse was on a jog-trot now, and Madeline left the trail more to Majesty than to her own choosing. The shadows deepened, and the crags grew gloomy and spectral. A cool wind moaned through the dark trees. Coyotes, scenting the hounds, kept apace of them, and barked and howled off in the gloom. But the tired hounds did not appear to notice.

As black night began to envelop her surroundings, Madeline marked that the fir trees had given place to pine forest. Suddenly a pin-point of light pierced the ebony blackness. Like a solitary star in dark sky it twinkled and blinked. She lost sight of it—found it again. It grew larger. Black tree-trunks crossed her line of vision. The light was a fire. She heard a cowboy song and the wild chorus of a pack of coyotes. Drops of rain on the branches of trees glittered in the rays of the fire. Stewart's tall figure, with sombrero slouched down, was now and then outlined against a growing circle of light. And by the aid of that light she saw him turn every moment or so to look back, probably to assure himself that she was close behind.

With a prospect of fire and warmth, and food and rest, Madeline's enthusiasm revived. What a climb! There was promise in this wild ride and lonely trail and hidden craggy height, not only in the adventure her friends yearned for, but in some nameless joy and spirit for herself.

16

The Crags

Glad indeed was Madeline to be lifted off her horse beside a roaring fire—to see steaming pots upon redhot coals. Except about her shoulders, which had been protected by the slicker, she was wringing wet. The Mexican women came quickly to help her change in a tent near by; but Madeline preferred for the moment to warm her numb feet and hands and to watch the spectacle of her arriving friends.

Dorothy plumped off her saddle into the arms of several waiting cowboys. She could scarcely walk. Far removed in appearance was she from her usual stylish self. Her face was hidden by a limp and lopsided hat. From under the disheveled brim came a plaintive moan: "O-h-h! what a-an a-awful ride!" Mrs. Beck was in worse condition; she had to be taken off her horse. "I'm paralyzed—I'm a wreck. Bobby, get a rollerchair." Bobby was solicitous and willing, but there were no rollerchairs. Florence dismounted easily, and but for her mass of hair, wet and tumbling, would have been taken for a handsome cowboy. Edith Wayne had stood the physical strain of the ride better than Dorothy; however, as her mount was rather small, she had been more at the mercy of cactus and brush. Her habit hung in tatters. Helen had preserved a remnant of style, as well as of pride, and perhaps a little strength. But her face was white, her eyes were big, and she limped. "Majesty!" she exclaimed. "What did you want to do to us? Kill us outright or make us homesick?" Of all of them, however, Ambrose's wife, Christine, the little French maid, had suffered the most in that long ride. She was unaccustomed to horses. Ambrose had to carry her into the big tent. Florence persuaded Madeline to leave the fire, and when they went in with the others Dorothy was wailing because her wet boots would not come off, Mrs. Beck was weeping and trying to direct a Mexican woman to unfasten her bedraggled dress, and there was general pandemonium.

"Warm clothes—hot drinks and grub—warm blankets," rang out Stewart's sharp order.

Then, with Florence helping the Mexican women, it was not long until Madeline and the feminine side of the party were comfortable, except for the weariness and aches that only rest and sleep could alleviate.

Neither fatigue nor pains, however, nor the strangeness of being packed sardine-like under canvas, nor the howls of coyotes, kept Madeline's guests from stretching out with long, grateful sighs, and one by one dropping into deep slumber. Madeline whispered a little to Florence, and laughed with her once or twice, and then the light flickering on the canvas faded and her eyelids closed. Darkness and roar of camp life, low voices of men, thump of horses' hoofs, coyote serenade, the sense of warmth and sweet rest—all drifted away.

When she awakened shadows of swaying branches moved on the sunlit canvas above her. She heard the ringing strokes of an ax, but no other sound from outside. Slow, regular breathing attested to the deep slumbers of her tent comrades.

She observed presently that Florence was missing from the number. Madeline rose and peeped out between the flaps.

An exquisitely beautiful scene surprised and enthralled her gaze. She saw a level space, green with long grass, bright with flowers, dotted with groves of graceful firs and pines and spruces, reaching to superb crags, rosy and golden in the sunlight. Eager to get out where she could enjoy an unrestricted view, she searched for her pack, found it in a corner, and then hurriedly and quietly dressed.

Her favorite stag-hounds, Russ and Tartar, were asleep before the door, where they had been chained. She awakened them and loosened them, thinking the while that it must have been Stewart who had chained them near her. Close at hand also was a cowboy's bed rolled up in a tarpaulin.

The cool air, fragrant with pine and spruce and some subtle nameless tang, sweet and tonic, made Madeline stand erect and breathe slowly and deeply. It was like drinking of a magic draught. She felt it in her blood, that it quickened its flow. Turning to look in the other direction, beyond the tent, she saw the remnants of last night's temporary camp, and farther on a grove of beautiful pines from which came the sharp ring of the ax. Wider gaze took in a wonderful park, not only surrounded by lofty crags, but full of crags of lesser height, many lifting their heads from dark-green groves of trees. The morning sun, not yet above the eastern elevations, sent its rosy and golden shafts in between the towering rocks, to tip the pines.

Madeline, with the hounds beside her, walked through the nearest grove. The ground was soft and springy and brown with pine needles. Then she saw that a clump of trees had prevented her from seeing the most striking part of this natural park. The cowboys had selected a campsite where they would have the morning sun and afternoon shade. Several tents and flies were already up; there was a huge lean-to made of spruce boughs; cowboys were busy round several campfires; piles of packs lay covered with tarpaulins, and beds were rolled up under the trees. This space was a kind of rolling meadow, with isolated trees here and there, and other trees in aisles and circles; and it mounted up in low, grassy banks to great towers of stone five hundred feet high. Other crags rose behind these. From under a mossy cliff, huge and green and cool, bubbled a full, clear spring. Wild flowers fringed its banks. Out in the meadow the horses were knee-deep in grass that waved in the morning breeze.

Florence espied Madeline under the trees and came running. She was like a young girl, with life and color and joy. She wore a flannel blouse, corduroy skirt, and moccasins. And her hair was fastened under a band like an Indian's.

"Castleton's gone with a gun, for hours, it seems," said Florence. "Gene just went to hunt him up. The other gentlemen are still asleep. I imagine they sure will sleep up heah in this air."

Then, businesslike, Florence fell to questioning Madeline about details of camp arrangement which Stewart, and Florence herself, could hardly see to without suggestion.

Before any of Madeline's sleepy guests awakened the camp was completed. Madeline and Florence had a tent under a pine tree, but they did not intend to sleep in it except during stormy weather. They spread a tarpaulin, made their bed on it, and elected to sleep under the light of the stars. After that, taking the hounds with them, they explored. To Madeline's surprise, the park was not a little half-mile nook nestling among the crags, but extended farther than they cared to walk, and was rather a series of parks. They were no more than small valleys between gray-toothed peaks. As the day advanced the charm of the place grew upon Madeline. Even at noon, with the sun beating down, there was comfortable warmth rather than heat. It was the kind of warmth that Madeline liked to feel in the spring. And the sweet, thin, rare atmosphere began to affect her strangely. She breathed deeply of it until she felt lightheaded, as if her body lacked substance and might drift away like a thistledown. All at once she grew uncomfortably sleepy. A dreamy languor possessed her, and, lying under a pine with her head against Florence, she went to sleep. When she opened her eyes the shadows of the crags stretched from the west, and between them streamed a red-gold light. It was hazy, smoky sunshine losing its fire. The afternoon had far advanced. Madeline sat up. Florence was lazily reading. The two Mexican women were at work under the fly where the big stone fireplace had been erected. No one else was in sight.

Florence, upon being questioned, informed Madeline that incident about camp had been delightfully absent. Castleton had returned and was profoundly sleeping with the other men.

Presently a chorus of merry calls attracted Madeline's attention, and she turned to see Helen limping along with Dorothy, and Mrs. Beck and Edith supporting each other. They were all rested, but lame, and delighted with the place, and as hungry as bears awakened from a winter's sleep. Madeline forthwith escorted them round the camp, and through the many aisles between the trees, and to the mossy, pine-matted nooks under the crags.

Then they had dinner, sitting on the ground after the manner of Indians; and it was a dinner that lacked merriment only because everybody was too busily appeasing appetite.

Later Stewart led them across a neck of the park, up a rather steep climb between towering crags, to take them out upon a grassy promontory that faced the great open west—a vast, ridged, streaked, and reddened sweep of earth rolling on, as it seemed, to the golden sunset end of the world. Castleton said it was a jolly fine view; Dorothy voiced her usual languid enthusiasm; Helen was on fire with pleasure and wonder; Mrs. Beck appealed to Bobby to see how he liked it before she ventured, and she then reiterated his praise; and Edith Wayne, like Madeline and Florence, was silent. Boyd was politely interested; he was the kind of man who appeared to care for things as other people cared for them.

Madeline watched the slow transformation of the changing west, with its haze of desert dust, through which mountain and cloud and sun slowly darkened. She watched until her eyes ached, and scarcely had a thought of what she was watching. When her eyes shifted to encounter the tall form of Stewart standing motionless on the rim, her mind became active again. As usual, he stood apart from the others, and now he seemed aloof and unconscious. He made a dark, powerful figure, and he fitted that wild promontory.

She experienced a strange, annoying surprise when she discovered both Helen and Dorothy watching Stewart with peculiar interest. Edith, too, was alive to the splendid picture the cowboy made. But when Edith smiled and whispered in her ear, "It's so good to look at a man like that," Madeline again felt the surprise, only this time the accompaniment was a vague pleasure rather than annoyance. Helen and Dorothy were flirts, one deliberate and skilled, the other unconscious and natural. Edith Wayne, occasionally—and Madeline reflected that the occasions were infrequent—admired a man sincerely. Just here Madeline might have fallen into a somewhat revealing state of mind if it had not been for the fact that she believed Stewart was only an object of deep interest to her, not as a man, but as a part of this wild and wonderful West which was claiming her. So she did not inquire of herself why Helen's coquetry and Dorothy's languishing allurement annoyed her, or why Edith's eloquent smile and words had pleased her. She got as far, however, as to think scornfully how Helen and Dorothy would welcome and meet a flirtation with this cowboy and then go back home and forget him as utterly as if he had never existed. She wondered, too, with a curious twist of feeling that was almost eagerness, how the cowboy would meet their advances. Obviously the situation was unfair to him; and if by some strange accident he escaped unscathed by Dorothy's beautiful eyes he would never be able to withstand Helen's subtle and fascinating and imperious personality.

They returned to camp in the cool of the evening and made merry round a blazing campfire. But Madeline's guests soon succumbed to the persistent and irresistible desire to sleep.

Then Madeline went to bed with Florence under the pine tree. Russ lay upon one side and Tartar upon the other. The cool night breeze swept over her, fanning her face, waving her hair. It was not strong enough to make any sound through the branches, but it stirred a faint, silken rustle in the long grass. The coyotes began their weird bark and howl. Russ raised his head to growl at their impudence.

Madeline faced upward, and it seemed to her that under those wonderful white stars she would never be able to go to sleep. They blinked down through the black-barred, delicate crisscross of pine foliage, and they looked so big and so close. Then she gazed away to open space, where an expanse of sky glittered with stars, and the longer she gazed the larger they grew and the more she saw.

It was her belief that she had come to love all the physical things from which sensations of beauty and mystery and strength poured into her responsive mind; but best of all she loved these Western stars, for they were to have something to do with her life, were somehow to influence her destiny.

For a few days the prevailing features of camp life for Madeline's guests were sleep and rest. Dorothy Coombs slept through twenty-four hours, and then was so difficult to awaken that for a while her friends were alarmed. Helen almost fell asleep while eating and talking. The men were more visibly affected by the mountain air than the women. Castleton, however, would not succumb to the strange drowsiness while he had a chance to prowl around with a gun.

This languorous spell disappeared presently, and then the days were full of life and action. Mrs. Beck and Bobby and Boyd, however, did not go in for anything very strenuous. Edith Wayne, too, preferred to walk through the groves or sit upon the grassy promontory. It was Helen and Dorothy who wanted to explore the crags and cañons, and when they could not get the others to accompany them they went alone, giving the cowboy guides many a long climb.

Necessarily, of course, Madeline and her guests were now thrown much in company with the cowboys. And the party grew to be like one big family. Her friends not only adapted themselves admirably to the situation, but came to revel in it. As for Madeline, she saw that outside of a certain proclivity of the cowboys to be gallant and on dress-parade and alive to possibilities of fun and excitement, they were not greatly different from what they were at all times. If there were a leveling process here it was made by her friends coming down to meet the Westerners. Besides, any class of people would tend to grow natural in such circumstances and environment.

Madeline found the situation one of keen and double interest for her. If before she had cared to study her cowboys, particularly Stewart, now, with the contrasts afforded by her guests, she felt by turns she was amused and mystified and perplexed and saddened, and then again subtly pleased.

Monty, once he had overcome his shyness, became a source of delight to Madeline, and, for that matter, to everybody. Monty had suddenly discovered that he was a success among the ladies. Either he was exalted to heroic heights by this knowledge or he made it appear so. Dorothy had been his undoing, and in justice to her Madeline believed her innocent. Dorothy thought Monty hideous to look at, and, accordingly, if he had been a hero a hundred times and had saved a hundred poor little babies' lives, he could not have interested her. Monty followed her around, reminding her, she told Madeline, of a little adoring dog one moment and the next of a huge, devouring gorilla.

Nels and Nick stalked at Helen's heels like grenadiers on duty, and if she as much as dropped her glove they almost came to blows to see who should pick it up.

In a way Castleton was the best feature of the camping party. He was such an absurd-looking little man, and his abilities were at such tremendous odds with what might have been expected of him from his looks. He could ride, tramp, climb, shoot. He liked to help around the camp, and the cowboys could not keep him from it. He had an insatiable desire to do things that were new to him. The cowboys played innumerable tricks upon him, not one of which he ever discovered. He was serious, slow in speech and action, and absolutely imperturbable. If imperturbablity could ever be good humor, then he was always good-humored. Presently the cowboys began to understand him, and then to like him. When they liked a man it meant something. Madeline had been sorry more than once to see how little the cowboys chose to speak to Boyd Harvey. With Castleton, however, they actually became friends. They did not know it, and certainly such a thing never occurred to him; all the same, it was a fact. And it grew solely out of the truth that the Englishman was manly in the only way cowboys could have interpreted manliness. When, after innumerable attempts, he succeeded in throwing the diamond-hitch on a pack-horse the cowboys began to respect him. Castleton needed only one more accomplishment to claim their hearts, and he kept trying that—to ride a bucking bronco. One of the cowboys had a bronco that they called Devil. Every day for a week Devil threw the Englishman all over the park, ruined his clothes, bruised him, and finally kicked him. Then the cowboys solicitously tried to make Castleton give up; and this was remarkable enough, for the spectacle of an English lord on a bucking bronco was one that any Westerner would have ridden a thousand miles to see. Whenever Devil threw Castleton the cowboys went into spasms. But Castleton did not know the meaning of the word fail, and there came a day when Devil could not throw him. Then it was a singular sight to see the men line up to shake hands with the cool Englishman. Even Stewart, who had watched from the background, came forward with a warm and pleasant smile on his dark face. When Castleton went to his tent there was much characteristic cowboy talk, and this time vastly different from the former persiflage.

"By Gawd!" ejaculated Monty Price, who seemed to be the most amazed and elated of them all. "Thet's the fust Englishman I ever seen! He's orful deceivin' to look at, but I know now why England rules the wurrld. Jest take a peek at thet bronco. His spirit is broke. Rid by a leetle English dook no bigger'n a grasshopper! Fellers, if it hain't dawned on you yit, let Monty Price give you a hunch. There's no flies on Castleton. An' I'll bet a million steers to a rawhide rope thet next he'll be throwin' a gun as good as Nels."

It was a distinct pleasure for Madeline to realize that she liked Castleton all the better for the traits brought out so forcibly by his association with the cowboys. On the other hand, she liked the cowboys better for something in them that contact with Easterners brought out. This was especially true in Stewart's case. She had been wholly wrong when she had imagined he would fall an easy victim to Dorothy's eyes and Helen's lures. He was kind, helpful, courteous, and watchful. But he had no sentiment. He did not see Dorothy's charms or feel Helen's fascination. And their efforts to captivate him were now so obvious that Mrs. Beck taunted them, and Edith smiled knowingly, and Bobby and Boyd made playful remarks. All of which cut Helen's pride and hurt Dorothy's vanity. They essayed open conquest of Stewart.

So it came about that Madeline unconsciously admitted the cowboy to a place in her mind never occupied by any other. The instant it occurred to her why he was proof against the wiles of the other women she drove that amazing and strangely disturbing thought from her. Nevertheless, as she was human, she could not help thinking and being pleased and enjoying a little the discomfiture of the two coquettes.

Moreover, from this thought of Stewart, and the watchfulness growing out of it, she discovered more about him. He was not happy; he often paced up and down the grove at night; he absented himself from camp sometimes during the afternoon when Nels and Nick and Monty were there; he was always watching the trails, as if he expected to see someone come riding up. He alone of the cowboys did not indulge in the fun and talk around the campfire. He remained preoccupied and sad, and was always looking into distance. Madeline had a strange sense of his guardianship over her; and, remembering Don Carlos, she imagined he worried a good deal over his charge, and, indeed, over the safety of all the party.

But if he did worry about possible visits from wandering guerrillas, why did he absent himself from camp? Suddenly into Madeline's inquisitive mind flashed a remembrance of the dark-eyed Mexican girl, Bonita, who had never been heard of since that night she rode Stewart's big horse out of El Cajon. The remembrance of her brought an idea. Perhaps Stewart had a rendezvous in the mountains, and these lonely trips of his were to meet Bonita. With the idea hot blood flamed into Madeline's cheeks. Then she was amazed at her own feelings —amazed because her swiftest succeeding thought was to deny the idea—amazed that its conception had fired her cheek with shame. Then her old self, the one aloof from this red-blooded new self, gained control over her emotions.

But Madeline found that newborn self a creature of strange power to return and govern at any moment. She found it fighting loyally for what intelligence and wisdom told her was only her romantic conception of a cowboy. She reasoned: If Stewart were the kind of man her feminine skepticism wanted to make him, he would not have been so blind to the coquettish advances of Helen and Dorothy. He had once been—she did not want to recall what he had once been. But he had been uplifted. Madeline Hammond declared that. She was swayed by a strong, beating pride, and her instinctive woman's faith told her that he could not stoop to such dishonor. She reproached herself for having momentarily thought of it.

One afternoon a huge storm cloud swooped out of the sky and enveloped the crags. It obscured the westering sun and laid a mantle of darkness over the park. Madeline was uneasy because several of her party, including Helen and Dorothy, had ridden off with the cowboys that afternoon and had not returned. Florence assured her that even if they did not get back before the storm broke there was no reason for apprehension. Nevertheless, Madeline sent for Stewart and asked him to go or send some one in search of them.

Perhaps half an hour later Madeline heard the welcome pattering of hoofs on the trail. The big tent was brightly lighted by several lanterns. Edith and Florence were with her. It was so black outside that Madeline could not see a rod before her face. The wind was moaning in the trees, and big drops of rain were pelting upon the canvas.

Presently, just inside the door, the horses halted, and there was a sharp bustle of sound, such as would naturally result from a hurried dismounting and confusion in the dark. Mrs. Beck came running into the tent out of breath and radiant because they had beaten the storm. Helen entered next, and a little later came Dorothy, but long enough to make her entrance more noticeable. The instant Madeline saw Dorothy's blazing eyes she knew something unusual had happened. Whatever it was might have escaped comment had not Helen caught sight of Dorothy.

"Heavens, Dot, but you're handsome occasionally!" remarked Helen. "When you get some life in your face and eyes!"

Dorothy turned her face away from the others, and perhaps it was only accident that she looked into a mirror hanging on the tent wall. Swiftly she put her hand up to feel a wide welt on her cheek. Dorothy had been assiduously careful of her soft, white skin, and here was an ugly mark marring its beauty.

"Look at that!" she cried, in distress. "My complexion's ruined!"

"How did you get such a splotch?" inquired Helen, going closer.

"I've been kissed!" exclaimed Dorothy, dramatically.

"What?" queried Helen, more curiously, while the others laughed.

"I've been kissed—hugged and kissed by one of those shameless cowboys! It was so pitch-dark outside I couldn't see a thing. And so noisy I couldn't hear. But somebody was trying to help me off my horse. My foot caught in the stirrup, and away I went—right into somebody's arms. Then he did it, the wretch! He hugged and kissed me in a most awful bearish manner. I couldn't budge a finger. I'm simply boiling with rage!"

When the outburst of mirth subsided Dorothy turned her big, dilated eyes upon Florence.

"Do these cowboys really take advantage of a girl when she's helpless and in the dark?"

"Of course they do," replied Florence, with her frank smile.

"Dot, what in the world could you expect?" asked Helen. "Haven't you been dying to be kissed?"

"No."

199

"Well, you acted like it, then. I never before saw you in a rage over being kissed."

"I—I wouldn't care so much if the brute hadn't scoured the skin off my face. He had whiskers as sharp and stiff as sandpaper. And when I jerked away he rubbed my cheek with them."

This revelation as to the cause of her outraged dignity almost prostrated her friends with glee.

"Dot, I agree with you; it's one thing to be kissed, and quite another to have your beauty spoiled," replied Helen, presently. "Who was this particular savage?"

"I don't know!" burst out Dorothy. "If I did I'd—I'd—"

Her eyes expressed the direful punishment she could not speak.

"Honestly now, Dot, haven't you the least idea who did it?" questioned Helen.

"I hope—I think it was Stewart," replied Dorothy.

"Ah! Dot, your hope is father to the thought. My dear, I'm sorry to riddle your little romance. Stewart did not—could not have been the offender or hero."

"How do you know he couldn't?" demanded Dorothy, flushing.

"Because he was clean-shaven today at noon, before we rode out. I remember perfectly how nice and smooth and brown his face looked."

"Oh, do you? Well, if your memory for faces is so good, maybe you can tell me which one of these cowboys wasn't clean-shaven."

"Merely a matter of elimination," replied Helen, merrily. "It was not Nick; it was not Nels; it was not Frankie. There was only one other cowboy with us, and he had a short, stubby growth of black beard, much like that cactus we passed on the trail."

"Oh, I was afraid of it," moaned Dorothy. "I *knew* he was going to do it. That horrible little smiling demon, Monty Price!"

A favorite lounging spot of Madeline's was a shaded niche under the lee of crags facing the east. Here the outlook was entirely different from that on the western side. It was not red and white and glaring, nor so changeable that it taxed attention. This eastern view was one of the mountains and valleys, where to be sure, there were arid patches; but the restful green of pine and fir was there, and the cool gray of crags. Bold and rugged indeed were these mountain features, yet they were companionably close, not immeasurably distant and unattainable like the desert. Here in the shade of afternoon Madeline and Edith would often lounge under a low-branched tree. Seldom they talked much, for it was afternoon and dreamy with the strange spell of this mountain fastness. There was smoky haze in the valleys, a fleecy cloud resting over the peaks, a sailing eagle in the blue sky, silence that was the unbroken silence of the wild heights, and a soft wind laden with incense of pine.

One afternoon, however, Edith appeared prone to talk seriously.

"Majesty, I must go home soon. I cannot stay out here forever. Are you going back with me?"

"Well, maybe," replied Madeline, thoughtfully. "I have considered it. I shall have to visit home some time. But this summer mother and father are going to Europe."

"See here, Majesty Hammond, do you intend to spend the rest of your life in this wilderness?" asked Edith, bluntly.

Madeline was silent.

"Oh, it is glorious! Don't misunderstand me, dear," went on Edith earnestly, as she laid her hand on Madeline's. "This trip has been a revelation to me. I did not tell you, Majesty, that I was ill when I arrived. Now I'm well. So well! Look at Helen, too. Why, she was a ghost when we got here. Now she is brown and strong and beautiful. If it were for nothing else than this wonderful gift of health I would love the West. But I have come to love it for other things—even spiritual things. Majesty, I have been studying you. I see and feel what this life has made of you. When I came I wondered at your strength, your virility, your serenity, your happiness. And I was stunned. I wondered at the causes of your change. Now I know. You were sick of idleness, sick of uselessness, if not society—sick of the horrible noises and smells and contacts one can no longer escape in the cities. I am sick of all that, too, and I could tell you many women of our kind who suffer in a like manner. You have done what many of us want to do, but have not the courage. You have left it. I am not blind to the splendid difference you have made in your life. I think I would have discovered, even if your brother had not told me, what good you have done to the Mexicans and cattlemen of your range. Then you have work to do. That is much the secret of your happiness, is it not? Tell me. Tell me something of what it means to you?"

"Work, of course, has much to do with any one's happiness," replied Madeline. "No one can be happy who has no work. As regards myself—for the rest I can hardly tell you. I have never tried to put it in words. Frankly, I believe, if I had not had money that I could not have found such contentment here. That is not in any sense a judgment against the West. But if I had been poor I could not have bought and maintained my ranch. Stillwell tells me there are many larger ranches than mine, but none just like it. Then I am almost paying my expenses out of my business. Think of that! My income, instead of being wasted, is mostly saved. I think—I hope I am useful. I have been of some little good to the Mexicans—eased the hardships of a few cowboys. For the rest, I think my life is a kind of dream. Of course my ranch and range are real, my cowboys are typical. If I were to tell you how I feel about them it would simply be a story of how Madeline Hammond sees the West. They are true to the West. It is I who am strange, and what I feel for them may be strange, too. Edith, hold to your own impressions."

"But, Majesty, my impressions have changed. At first I did not like the wind, the dust, the sun, the endless open stretches. But now I do like them. Where once I saw only terrible wastes of barren ground now I see beauty and something noble. Then, at first, your cowboys struck me as dirty, rough, loud, crude, savage—all that was primitive. I did not want them near me. I imagined them callous, hard men, their only joy a carouse with their kind. But I was wrong. I have changed. The dirt was only dust, and this desert dust is clean. They are still rough, loud, crude and savage in my eyes, but with a difference. They are natural men. They are little children. Monty Price is one of nature's noblemen. The hard thing is to discover it. All his hideous person, all his actions and speech, are masks of his real nature. Nels is a joy, a simple, sweet, kindly, quiet man whom some woman should have loved. What would love have meant to him! He told me that no woman ever loved him except his mother, and he lost her when he was ten. Every man ought to be loved—especially a man as Nels. Somehow his gun record does not impress me. I

202

never could believe he killed a man. Then take your foreman, Stewart. He is a cowboy, his work and life the same as the others. But he has education and most of the graces we are in the habit of saying make a gentleman. Stewart is a strange fellow, just like this strange country. He's a man, Majesty, and I admire him. So, you see, my impressions are developing with my stay out here."

"Edith, I am so glad you told me that," replied Madeline, warmly.

"I like the country, and I like the men," went on Edith. "One reason I want to go home soon is because I am discontented enough at home now, without falling in love with the West. For, of course, Majesty, I would. I *could* not live out here. And that brings me to my point. Admitting all the beauty and charm and wholesomeness and good of this wonderful country, still it is no place for *you*, Madeline Hammond. You have your position, your wealth, your name, your family. You must marry. You must have children. You must not give up all that for a quixotic life in a wilderness."

"I am convinced, Edith, that I shall live here all the rest of my life."

"Oh, Majesty! I hate to preach this way. But I promised your mother I would talk to you. And the truth is I hate—I *hate* what I'm saying. I envy you your courage and wisdom. I know you have refused to marry Boyd Harvey. I could see that in his face. I believe you will refuse Castleton. Whom will you marry? What chance is there for a woman of your position to marry out here? What in the world will become of you?"

"*Quien sabe?*" replied Madeline, with a smile that was almost sad.

Not so many hours after this conversation with Edith Madeline sat with Boyd Harvey upon the grass promontory overlooking the west, and she listened once again to his suave courtship.

Suddenly she turned to him and said, "Boyd, if I married you would you be willing—glad to spend the rest of your life here in the West?"

"Majesty!" he exclaimed. There was amaze in the voice usually so even and well modulated—amaze in the handsome face usually so indifferent. Her question had startled him. She saw him look down the iron-gray cliffs, over the barren slopes and cedared ridges, beyond the cactus-covered foothills to the grim and ghastly desert. Just then, with its red veils of sunlit dust clouds, its illimitable waste of ruined and upheaved earth, it was a sinister spectacle.

"No," he replied, with a tinge of shame in his cheek.

Madeline said no more, nor did he speak. She was spared the pain of refusing him, and she imagined he would never ask her again. There was both relief and regret in the conviction. Humiliated lovers seldom made good friends.

It was impossible not to like Boyd Harvey. The thought of that, and why she could not marry him, concentrated her never-satisfied mind upon the man. She looked at him, and she thought of him.

He was handsome, young, rich, well born, pleasant, cultivated—he was all that made a gentleman of his class. If he had any vices she had not heard of them. She knew he had no thirst for drink or craze for gambling. He was considered a very desirable and eligible young man. Madeline admitted all this.

Then she thought of things that were perhaps exclusively her own strange ideas. Boyd Harvey's white skin did not tan even in this southwestern sun and wind. His hands were whiter than her own, and as soft. They were really beautiful, and she remembered what care he took of them. They were a proof that he never worked. His frame was tall, graceful, elegant. It did not bear evidence of ruggedness. He had never indulged in a sport more strenuous than yachting. He hated effort and activity. He rode horseback very little, disliked any but moderate motoring, spent much time in Newport and Europe, never walked when he could help it, and had no ambition unless it were to pass the days pleasantly. If he ever had any sons they would be like him, only a generation more toward the inevitable extinction of his race.

Madeline returned to camp in just the mood to make a sharp, deciding contrast. It happened—fatefully, perhaps—that the first man she saw was Stewart. He had just ridden into camp, and as she came up he explained that he had gone down to the ranch for the important mail about which she had expressed anxiety.

"Down and back in one day!" she exclaimed.

"Yes," he replied. "It wasn't so bad."

"But why did you not send one of the boys, and let him make the regular two-day trip?"

"You were worried about your mail," he answered, briefly, as he delivered it. Then he bent to examine the fetlocks of his weary horse.

It was midsummer now, Madeline reflected, and exceedingly hot and dusty on the lower trail. Stewart had ridden down the mountain and back again in twelve hours. Probably no horse in the outfit, except his big black or Majesty, could have stood that trip. And his horse showed the effects of a grueling day. He was caked with dust and lame and weary.

Stewart looked as if he had spared the horse his weight on many a mile of that rough ascent. His boots were evidence of it. His heavy flannel shirt, wet through with perspiration, adhered closely to his shoulders and arms, so that every ripple of muscle plainly showed. His face was black, except round the temples and forehead, where it was bright red. Drops of sweat, running off his blackened hands dripped to the ground. He got up from examining the lame foot, and then threw off the saddle. The black horse snorted and lunged for the watering-pool. Stewart let him drink a little, then with iron arms dragged him away. In this action the man's lithe, powerful form impressed Madeline with a wonderful sense of muscular force. His brawny wrist was bare; his big, strong hand, first clutching the horse's mane, then patting his neck, had a bruised knuckle, and one finger was bound up. That hand expressed as much gentleness and thoughtfulness for the horse as it had strength to drag him back from too much drinking at a dangerous moment.

Stewart was a combination of fire, strength, and action. These attributes seemed to cling about him. There was something vital and compelling in his presence. Worn and spent and drawn as he was from the long ride, he thrilled Madeline with his potential youth and unused vitality and promise of things to be, red-blooded deeds, both of flesh and spirit. In him she saw the strength of his forefathers unimpaired. The life in him was marvelously significant. The dust, the dirt, the sweat, the soiled clothes, the bruised and bandaged hand, the brawn and bone—these had not been despised by the knights of ancient days nor by modern women whose eyes shed soft light upon coarse and bloody toilers.

Madeline Hammond compared the man of the East with the man of the West; and that comparison was the last parting regret for her old standards.

 END

17

◆

The Lost Mine of the Padres

In the cool, starry evenings the campers sat around a blazing fire and told and listened to stories thrillingly fitted to the dark crags and the wild solitude.

Monty Price had come to shine brilliantly as a storyteller. He was an atrocious liar, but this fact would not have been evident to his enthralled listeners if his cowboy comrades, in base jealousy, had not betrayed him. The truth about his remarkable fabrications, however, had not become known to Castleton, solely because of the Englishman's obtuseness. And there was another thing much stranger than this and quite as amusing. Dorothy Coombs knew Monty was a liar; but she was so fascinated by the glittering, basilisk eyes he riveted upon her, so taken in by his horrible tales of blood, that despite her knowledge she could not help believing them.

Manifestly Monty was very proud of his suddenly acquired gift. Formerly he had hardly been known to open his lips in the presence of strangers. Monty had developed more than one singular and hitherto unknown trait since his supremacy at golf had revealed his possibilities. He was as sober and vain and pompous about his capacity for lying as about anything else. Some of the cowboys were jealous of him because he held the attention and, apparently, the admiration of the ladies; and Nels was jealous, not because Monty made himself out to be a wonderful gunman, but because Monty could tell a story. Nels really had been the hero of a hundred fights; he had never been known to talk about them, but Dorothy's eyes and Helen's smile had somehow upset his modesty. Whenever Monty would begin to talk Nels would growl and knock his pipe on a log, and make it appear he could not stay and listen, though he never really left the charmed circle of the campfire. Wild horses could not have dragged him away.

One evening at twilight, as Madeline was leaving her tent, she encountered Monty. Evidently, he had waylaid her. With the most mysterious of signs and whispers he led her a little aside.

"Miss Hammond, I'm makin' bold to ask a favor of you," he said.

Madeline smiled her willingness.

"Tonight, when they've all shot off their chins an' it's quiet-like, I want you to ask me, jest this way, 'Monty, seein' as you've hed more adventures than all them cowpunchers put together, tell us about the most turrible time you ever hed.' Will you ask me, Miss Hammond, jest kinda sincere like?"

"Certainly I will, Monty," she replied.

His dark, seared face had no more warmth than a piece of cold, volcanic rock, which it resembled. Madeline appreciated how monstrous Dorothy found this burned and distorted visage, how deformed the little man looked to a woman of refined sensibilities. It was difficult for Madeline to look into his face. But she saw behind the blackened mask. And now she saw in Monty's deep eyes a spirit of pure fun.

So, true to her word, Madeline remembered at an opportune moment, when conversation had hushed and only the long, dismal wail of coyotes broke the silence, to turn toward the little cowboy.

"Monty," she said, and paused for effect—"Monty, seeing that you have had more adventures than all the cowboys together, tell us about the most terrible time you ever had."

Monty appeared startled at the question that fastened all eyes upon him. He waved a deprecatory hand.

"Aw, Miss Hammond, thankin' you all modest-like fer the compliment, I'll hev to refuse," replied Monty, laboring in distress. "It's too harrowin' fer tender-hearted gurls to listen to."

"Go on!" cried everybody except the cowboys. Nels began to nod his head as if he, as well as Monty, understood human nature. Dorothy hugged her knees with a kind of shudder. Monty had fastened the hypnotic eyes upon her. Castleton ceased smoking, adjusted his eyeglass, and prepared to listen in great earnestness.

Monty changed his seat to one where the light from the

blazing logs fell upon his face; and he appeared plunged into melancholy and profound thought.

"Now I tax myself, I can't jest decide which was the orfulest time I ever hed," he said, reflectively.

Here Nels blew forth an immense cloud of smoke, as if he desired to hide himself from sight. Monty pondered, and then when the smoke rolled away he turned to Nels.

"See hyar, old pard, me an' you seen somethin' of each other in the Panhandle, more'n thirty years ago—"

"Which we didn't," interrupted Nels, bluntly. "Shore you cain't make me out an ole man."

"Mebbe it wasn't so darn long. Anyhow, Nels, you recollect them three hoss-thieves I hung all on one cottonwood-tree, an' likewise thet boo-tiful blond gurl I rescooed from a band of cutthroats who murdered her paw, old Bill Warren, the buffalo-hunter? Now, which of them two scraps was the turriblest, in your idee?"

"Monty, my memory's shore bad," replied the unimpeachable Nels.

"Tell us about the beautiful blonde," cried at least three of the ladies. Dorothy, who had suffered from nightmare because of a former story of hanging men on trees, had voicelessly appealed to Monty to spare her more of that.

"All right, we'll hev the blond gurl," said Monty, settling back, "though I ain't thinkin' her story is most turrible of the two, an' it'll rake over tender affections long slumberin' in my breast."

As he paused there came a sharp, rapping sound. This appeared to be Nels knocking the ashes out of his pipe on a stump—a true indication of the passing of content from that jealous cowboy.

"It was down in the Panhandle, 'way over in the west end of thet Comanche huntin'-ground, an' all the redskins an' outlaws in thet country were hidin' in the river-bottoms, an' chasin' some of the last buffalo herds thet hed wintered in there. I was a young buck them days, an' purty much of a desperado, I'm thinkin'. Though of all the seventeen notches on my gun —an' each notch meant a man killed face to face—there was only one thet I was ashamed of. Thet one was fer an express messenger who I hit on the head most unprofessional like, jest because he wouldn't hand over a leetle package. I hed the kind

208

of a reputashun thet made all the fellers in saloons smile an' buy drinks.

"Well, I dropped into a place named Taylor's Bend, an' was peaceful standin' to the bar when three cowpunchers come in, an', bein' with my back turned, they didn't recognize me an' got playful. I didn't stop drinkin', an' I didn't turn square round; but when I stopped shootin' under my arm the saloon-keeper hed to go over to the sawmill an' fetch a heap of saw-dust to cover up what was left of them three cow-punchers, after they was hauled out. You see I was rough them days, an' would shoot ears off an' noses off an' hands off; when in later days I'd jest kill a man, quick, same as Wild Bill.

"News drifts into town thet night thet a gang of cutthroats hed murdered ole Bill Warren an' carried off his gurl. I gathers up a few good gunmen, an' we rid out an' down the river-bottom, to an ole log cabin, where the outlaws hed a ronde-voo. We rid up boldlike, an' made a hell of a racket. Then the gang began to throw lead from the cabin, an' we all hunted cover. Fightin' went on all night. In the mornin' all my outfit was killed but two, an' they was shot up bad. We fought all day without eatin' or drinkin', except some whiskey I hed, an' at night I was on the job by my lonesome.

"Bein' bunged up some myself, I laid off an' went down to the river to wash the blood off, tie up my wounds, an' drink a leetle. While I was down there along comes one of the cutthroats with a bucket. Instead of gettin' water he got lead, an' as he was about to croak he tells me a whole bunch of out-laws was headin' in there, doo tomorrer. An' if I wanted to rescoo the gurl I hed to be hurryin'. There was five fellers left in the cabin.

"I went back to the thicket where I hed left my hoss, an' loaded up with two more guns an' another belt, an' busted a fresh box of shells. If I recollect proper, I got some cigarettes, too. Well, I mozied back to the cabin. It was a boo-ti-ful moonshiny night, an' I wondered if ole Bill's gurl was as purty as I'd heerd. The grass growed long round the cabin, an' I crawled up to the door without startin' anythin'. Then I fig-gered. There was only one door in thet cabin, an' it was black dark inside. I jest grabbed open the door an' slipped in quick. It worked all right. They heerd me, but hedn't been quick enough to ketch me in the light of the door. Of course there was some shots, but I ducked too quick, an' changed my position.

"Ladies an' gentlemen, thet there was some dool by night. An' I wasn't often in the place where they shot. I was most wonderful patient, an' jest waited until one of them darned ruffians would get so nervous he'd hev to hunt me up. When mornin' come there they was all piled up on the floor, all shot to pieces. I found the gurl. Purty! Say, she was boo-tiful. We went down to the river, where she begun to bathe my wounds. I'd collected a dozen more or so, an' the sight of tears in her lovely eyes, an' my blood a-stainin' of her little hands, jest nat'rally weakened a trembly spell in my heart, I seen she was took the same way, an' thet settled it.

"We was comin' up from the river, an' I hed just straddled my hoss, with the gurl behind, when we run right into thet cutthroat gang thet was doo about then. Bein' some handicapped, I couldn't drop more 'n one gunround of them, an' then I hed to slope. The whole gang follered me, an' some miles out chased me over a ridge right into a big herd of buffalo. Before I knowed what was what thet herd broke into a stampede with me in the middle. Purty soon the buffalo closed in tight. I knowed I was in some peril then. But the gurl trusted me somethin' pitiful. I seen again thet she hed fell in love with me. I could tell from the way she hugged me an' yelled. Before long I was some put to it to keep my hoss on his feet. Far as I could see was dusty, black, bobbin', shaggy humps. A huge cloud of dust went along over our heads. The roar of tramplin' hoofs was turrible. My hoss weakened, went down, an' was carried along a leetle while I slipped off with the gurl on to the backs of the buffalo.

"Ladies, I ain't denyin' that then Monty Price was some scairt. Fust time in my life! But the trustin' face of thet bootiful girl, as she lay in my arms an' hugged me an' yelled, made my spirit leap like a shootin' star. I just began to jump from buffalo to buffalo. I must hev jumped a mile of them bobbin' backs before I come to open places. An' here's where I performed the greatest stunts of my life. I hed on my big spurs, an' I jest sit down an' rid an' spurred till thet pertickler buffalo I was on got near another, an' then I'd flop over. Thusly I got to the edge of the herd, tumbled off'n the last one, an' rescooed the gurl.

"Well, as my memory takes me back, thet was a most affectin' walk home to the little town where she lived. But she wasn't troo to me, an' married another feller. I was too much a sport to kill him. But thet low-down trick rankled in my breast. Gurls is strange. I've never stopped wonderin' how any gurl who has been hugged an' kissed by one man could marry another. But matoor experience teaches me thet sich is the case."

The cowboys roared; Helen and Mrs. Beck and Edith laughed till they cried; Madeline found repression absolutely impossible; Dorothy sat hugging her knees, her horror at the story no greater than at Monty's unmistakable reference to her and to the fickleness of women; and Castleton for the first time appeared to be moved out of his imperturbability, though not in any sense by humor. Indeed, when he came to notice it, he was dumfounded by the mirth.

"By Jove! you Americans are an extraordinary people," he said. "I don't see anything blooming funny in Mr. Price's story of his adventure. By Jove! That was a bally warm occasion. Mr. Price, when you speak of being frightened for the only time in your life, I appreciate what you mean. I have experienced that. I was frightened once."

"Dook, I wouldn't hev thought it of you," replied Monty. "I'm sure tolerable curious to hear about it."

Madeline and her friends dared not break the spell, for fear that the Englishman might hold to his usual modest reticence. He had explored in Brazil, seen service in the Boer War, hunted in India and Africa—matters of experience of which he never spoke. Upon this occasion, however, evidently taking Monty's recital word for word as literal truth, and excited by it into a Homeric mood, he might tell a story. The cowboys almost fell upon their knees in their importunity. There was a suppressed eagerness in their solicitations, a hint of something that meant more than desire, great as it was, to hear a story told by an English lord. Madeline divined instantly that the cowboys had suddenly fancied that Castleton was not the dense and easily fooled person they had made such game of; that he had played his part well; that he was having fun at their expense; that he meant to tell a story, a lie which would simply dwarf Monty's. Nels's keen, bright expectation suggested how he would welcome the joke turned upon Monty. The slow closing of Monty's cavernous smile, the gradual

211

sinking of his proud bearing, the doubt with which he began to regard Castleton—these were proofs of his fears.

"I have faced charging tigers and elephants in India, and charging rhinos and lions in Africa," began Castleton, his quick and fluent speech so different from the drawl of his ordinary conversation; "but I never was frightened but once. It will not do to hunt those wild beasts if you are easily balled up. This adventure I have in mind happened in British East Africa, in Uganda. I was out with safari, and we were in a native district much infested by man-eating lions. Perhaps I may as well state that man-eaters are very different from ordinary lions. They are always matured beasts, and sometimes—indeed, mostly—are old. They become man-eaters most likely by accident or necessity. When old they find it more difficult to make a kill, being slower, probably, and with poorer teeth. Driven by hunger, they stalk and kill a native, and once having tasted human blood, they want no other. They become absolutely fearless and terrible in their attacks.

"The natives of this village near where we camped were in a terrorized state owing to depredations of two or more man-eaters. The night of our arrival a lion leaped a stockade fence, seized a native from among others sitting round a fire, and leaped out again, carrying the screaming fellow away into the darkness. I determined to kill these lions, and made a permanent camp in the village for that purpose. By day I sent beaters into the brush and rocks of the river valley, and by night I watched. Every night the lions visited us, but I did not see one. I discovered that when they roared around the camp they were not so liable to attack as when they were silent. It was indeed remarkable how silently they could stalk a man. They could creep through a thicket so dense you would not believe a rabbit could get through, and do it without the slightest sound. Then, when ready to charge, they did so with terrible onslaught and roar. They leaped right into a circle of fires, tore down huts, even dragged natives from the low trees. There was no way to tell at which point they would make an attack.

"After ten days or more of this I was worn out by loss of sleep. And one night, when tired out with watching I fell asleep. My gun-bearer was alone in the tent with me. A terrible roar awakened me, then an unearthly scream pierced right into my ears. I always slept with my rifle in my hands, and, grasping it, I tried to rise. But I could not for the reason that a lion was standing over me. Then I lay still. The screams of my gun-bearer told me that the lion had him. I was fond of this fellow and wanted to save him. I thought it best, however, not to move while the lion stood over me. Suddenly he stepped, and I felt poor Luki's feet dragging across me. He screamed, 'Save me, master!' And instinctively I grasped at him and caught his foot. The lion walked out of the tent dragging me as I held to Luki's foot. The night was bright moonlight. I could see the lion distinctly. He was a huge, black-maned brute, and he held Luki by the shoulder. The poor lad kept screaming frightfully. The man-eater must have dragged me forty yards before he became aware of a double incumbrance to his progress. Then he halted and turned. By Jove! he made a devilish fierce object with his shaggy, massive head, his green-fire eyes, and his huge jaws holding Luki. I let go of Luki's foot and bethought myself of the gun. But as I lay there on my side, before attempting to rise, I made a horrible discovery. I did not have my rifle at all. I had Luki's iron spear, which he always had near him. My rifle had slipped out of the hollow of my arm, and when the lion awakened me, in my confusion I picked up Luki's spear instead. The bloody brute dropped Luki and uttered a roar that shook the ground. It was then I felt frightened. For an instant I was almost paralyzed. The lion meant to charge, and in one spring he could reach me. Under circumstances like those a man can think many things in a little time. I knew to try to run would be fatal. I remembered how strangely lions had been known to act upon occasion. One had been frightened by an umbrella; one had been frightened by a blast from a cow-horn; another had been frightened by a native who in running from one lion ran right at the other which he had not seen. Accordingly, I wondered if I could frighten the lion that meant to leap at me. Acting upon wild impulse, I prodded him in the hind quarters with the spear. Ladies and gentlemen, I am a blooming idiot if that lion did not cower like a whipped dog, put his tail down, and begin to slink away. Quick to see my chance, I jumped up yelling, and made after him, prodding him again. He let out a bellow such as you could imagine would come from an outraged king of beasts. I prodded again, and then he loped off. I found Luki not badly hurt. In fact he got well. But I've never forgotten that scare."

When Castleton finished his narrative there was a trenchant silence. All eyes were upon Monty. He looked beaten, disgraced, a disgusted man. Yet there shone from his face a wonderful admiration for Castleton.

"Dook, you win!" he said; and, dropping his head, he left the camp-fire circle with the manner of a deposed emperor.

Then the cowboys exploded. The quiet, serene, low-voiced Nels yelled like a madman and he stood upon his head. All the other cowboys went through marvelous contortions. Mere noise was insufficient to relieve their joy at what they considered the fall and humiliation of the tyrant Monty.

The Englishman stood there and watched them in amused consternation. They baffled his understanding. Plain it was to Madeline and her friends that Castleton had told the simple truth. But never on the earth, or anywhere else, could Nels and his comrades have been persuaded that Castleton had not lied deliberately to humble their great exponent of Ananias.

Everybody seemed reluctant to break the campfire spell. The logs had burned out to a great heap of opal and gold and red coals, in the heart of which quivered a glow alluring to the spirit of dreams. As the blaze subsided the shadows of the pines encroached darker and darker upon the circle of fading light. A cool wind fanned the embers, whipped up flakes of white ashes, and moaned through the trees. The wild yelps of coyotes were dying in the distance, and the sky was a wonderful dark-blue dome spangled with white stars.

"What a perfect night!" said Madeline. "This is a night to understand the dream, the mystery, the wonder of the Southwest. Florence, for long you have promised to tell us the story of the lost mine of the padres. It will give us all pleasure, make us understand something of the thrall in which this land held the Spaniards who discovered it so many years ago. It will be especially interesting now, because this mountain hides somewhere under its crags the treasures of the lost mine of the padres."

"In the sixteenth century," Florence began, in her soft, slow voice so suited to the nature of the legend, "a poor young padre of New Spain was shepherding his goats upon a hill when the Virgin appeared before him. He prostrated himself at her feet, and when he looked up she was gone. But upon the maguey plant near where she had stood there were golden ashes of a strange and wonderful substance. He took the incident as a good omen and went again to the hilltop. Under the maguey had sprung up slender stalks of white, bearing delicate gold flowers, and as these flowers waved in the wind a fine golden dust, as fine as powdered ashes, blew away toward the north. Padre Juan was mystified, but believed that great fortune attended upon him and his poor people. So he went again and again to the hilltop in hope that the Virgin would appear to him.

"One morning, as the sun rose gloriously, he looked across the windy hill toward the waving grass and golden flowers under the maguey, and he saw the Virgin beckoning to him. Again he fell upon his knees; but she lifted him and gave him of the golden flowers, and bade him leave his home and people to follow where these blowing golden lands led. There he would find gold—pure gold—wonderful fortune to bring back to his poor people to build a church for them, and a city.

"Padre Juan took the flowers and left his home, promising to return, and he traveled northward over the hot and dusty desert, through the mountain passes, to a new country where fierce and warlike Indians menaced his life. He was gentle and good, and of a persuasive speech. Moreover, he was young and handsome of person. The Indians were Apaches, and among them he became a missionary, while always he was searching for the flowers of gold. He heard of gold lying in pebbles upon the mountain slopes, but he never found any. A few of the Apaches he converted; the most of them, however, were prone to be hostile to him and his religion. But Padre Juan prayed and worked on.

"There came a time when the old Apache chief, imagining the padre had designs upon his influence with the tribe, sought to put him to death by fire. The chief's daughter, a beautiful, dark-eyed maiden, secretly loved Juan and believed in his mission, and she interceded for his life and saved him. Juan fell in love with her. One day she came to him wearing golden flowers in her dark hair, and as the wind blew the flowers a golden dust blew upon it. Juan asked her where to find such flowers, and she told him that upon a certain day she would take him to the mountain to look for them. And upon the day she led up to the mountain-top from which they could see beautiful valleys and great trees and cool waters. There, at the top of a wonderful slope that looked down upon the world, she showed Juan the flowers. And Juan found gold in such abundance that he thought he would go out of his mind. Dust of gold! Grains of gold! Pebbles of gold! Rocks of gold! He was rich beyond all dreams. He remembered the Virgin and her words. He must return to his people and build their church, and the great city that would bear his name.

"But Juan tarried. Always he was going *mañana*. He loved the dark-eyed Apache girl so well that he could not leave her. He hated himself for his infidelity to his Virgin, to his people. He was weak and false, a sinner, but he could not go, and he gave himself up to the love of the Indian maiden.

"The old Apache chief discovered the secret love of his daughter and the padre. And, fierce in his anger, he took her up into the mountains and burned her alive and cast her ashes upon the wind. He did not kill Padre Juan. He was too wise, and perhaps too cruel, for he saw the strength of Juan's love. Besides, many of his tribe had learned much from the Spaniard.

"Padre Juan fell into despair. He had no desire to live. He faded and wasted away. But before he died he went to the old Indians who had burned the maiden, and he begged them, when he was dead, to burn his body and to cast his ashes to the wind from that wonderful slope, where they would blow away to mingle forever with those of his Indian sweetheart.

"The Indians promised, and when Padre Juan died they burned his body and took his ashes to the mountain heights and cast them to the wind, where they drifted and fell to mix with the ashes of the Indian girl he had loved.

"Years passed. More padres traveled across the desert to the home of the Apaches, and they heard the story of Juan. Among their number was a padre who in his youth had been one of Juan's people. He set forth to find Juan's grave where he believed he would also find the gold. And he came back with pebbles of gold and flowers that shed a golden dust, and he told a wonderful story. He had climbed and climbed into the mountains, and he had come to a wonderful slope under the crags. That slope was yellow with golden flowers. When he touched them golden ashes drifted from them and blew down among the rocks. There the padre found dust of gold, grains of gold, pebbles of gold, rocks of gold.

"Then all the padres went into the mountains. But the discoverer of the mine lost his way. They searched and searched until they were old and gray, but never found the wonderful slope and flowers that marked the grave and the mine of Padre Juan.

"In the succeeding years the story was handed down from father to son. But of the many who hunted for the lost mine of the padres there was never a Mexican or an Apache. For the Apache the mountain slopes were haunted by the spirit of an Indian maiden who had been false to her tribe and forever accursed. For the Mexican the mountain slopes were haunted by the spirit of the false padre who rolled stones upon the heads of those adventurers who sought to find his grave and his accursed gold."

18

Bonita

Florence's story of the lost mine fired Madeline's guests with the fever for gold-hunting. But after they had tried it a few times and the glamour of the thing wore off they gave up and remained in camp. Having exhausted all the resources of the mountain, such that had interest for them, they settled quietly down for a rest, which Madeline knew would soon end in a desire for civilized comforts. They were almost tired of roughing it. Helen's discontent manifested itself in her remark, "I guess nothing is going to happen, after all."

Madeline awaited their pleasure in regard to the breaking of camp; and meanwhile, as none of them cared for more exertion, she took her walks without them, sometimes accompanied by one of the cowboys, always by the stag-hounds. These walks furnished her exceeding pleasure. And, now that the cowboys would talk to her without reserve, she grew fonder of listening to their simple stories. The more she knew of them the more she doubted the wisdom of shut-in lives. Companionship with Nels and most of the cowboys was in its effect like that of the rugged pines and crags and the untainted wind. Humor, their predominant trait when a person grew to know them, saved Madeline from finding their hardness trying. They were dreamers, as all men who lived lonely lives in the wilds were dreamers.

The cowboys all had secrets. Madeline learned some of them. She marveled most at the strange way in which they hid emotions, except of violence of mirth and temper so easily aroused. It was all the more remarkable in view of the fact that they felt intensely over little things to which men of the world were blind and dead. Madeline had to believe that a hard and perilous life in a barren and wild country developed great principles in men. Living close to earth, under the cold, bleak peaks, on the dust-veiled desert, men grew like the nature that developed them—hard, fierce, terrible, perhaps, but big—big with elemental force.

But one day, while out walking alone, before she realized it she had gone a long way down a dim trail winding among the rocks. It was the middle of a summer afternoon, and all about her were shadows of the crags crossing the sunlit patches. The quiet was undisturbed. She went on and not blind to the fact that she was perhaps going too far from camp, but risking it because she was sure of her way back, and enjoying the wild, craggy recesses that were new to her. Finally she came out upon a bank that broke abruptly into a beautiful little glade. Here she sat down to rest before undertaking the return trip.

Suddenly Russ, the keener of the stag-hounds, raised his head and growled. Madeline feared he might have scented a mountain-lion or wildcat. She quieted him and carefully looked around. To each side was an irregular line of massive blocks of stone that had weathered from the crags. The little glade was open and grassy, with here a pine tree, there a boulder. The outlet seemed to go down into a wilderness of cañons and ridges. Looking in this direction, Madeline saw the slight, dark figure of a woman coming stealthily along under the pines. Madeline was amazed, then a little frightened, for that stealthy walk from tree to tree was suggestive of secrecy, if nothing worse.

Presently the woman was joined by a tall man who carried a package, which he gave to her. They came on up the glade and appeared to be talking earnestly. In another moment Madeline recognized Stewart. She had no greater feeling of surprise than had at first been hers. But for the next moment she scarcely thought at all—merely watched the couple approaching. In a flash came back her former curiosity as to Stewart's strange absences from camp, and then with the return of her doubt of him the recognition of the woman. The small, dark head, the brown face, the big eyes—Madeline now saw distinctly—belonged to the Mexican girl Bonita. Stewart had met her there. This was the secret of his lonely trips, taken ever since he had come to work for Madeline. This secluded glade was a rendezvous. He had her hidden there.

Quietly Madeline arose, with a gesture to the dogs, and went back along the trail toward camp. Succeeding her surprise was a feeling of sorrow that Stewart's regeneration had not been complete. Sorrow gave place to insufferable distrust that while she had been romancing about this cowboy, dreaming of her good influence over him, he had been merely base. Somehow it stung her. Stewart had been nothing to her, she thought, yet she had been proud of him. She tried to resolve the thing, to be fair to him, when every instinctive tendency was to expel him, and all pertaining to him, from her thoughts. And her effort at sympathy, at extenuation, failed utterly before her pride. Exerting her will power, she dismissed Stewart from her mind.

Madeline did not think of him again till late that afternoon, when, as she was leaving her tent to join several of her guests, Stewart appeared suddenly in her path.

"Miss Hammond, I saw your tracks down the trail," he began, eagerly, but his tone was easy and natural. "I'm thinking—well, maybe you sure got the idea—"

"I do not wish for an explanation," interrupted Madeline.

Stewart gave a slight start. His manner had a semblance of the old, cool audacity. As he looked down at her it subtly changed.

What effrontery, Madeline thought, to face her before her guests with an explanation of his conduct! Suddenly she felt an inward flash of fire that was pain, so strange, so incomprehensible, that her mind whirled. Then anger possessed her, not at Stewart, but at herself, that anything could rouse in her a raw emotion. She stood there, outwardly cold, serene, with level, haughty eyes upon Stewart; but inwardly she was burning with rage and shame.

"I'm sure not going to have you think—" He began passionately, but he broke off, and a slow, dull crimson blotted over the healthy red-brown of his neck and cheeks.

"What you do or think, Stewart, is no concern of mine."

"Miss—Miss Hammond! You don't believe—" faltered Stewart.

The crimson receded from his face, leaving it pale. His eyes were appealing. They had a kind of timid look that struck Madeline even in her anger. There was something boyish about him then. He took a step forward and reached out with his hand open-palmed in a gesture that was humble, yet held a certain dignity.

"But listen. Never mind now what you—you think about me. There's a good reason—"

"I have no wish to hear your reason."

"But you ought to," he persisted.

"Sir!"

Stewart underwent another swift change. He started violently. A dark tide shaded his face and a glitter leaped to his eyes. He took two long strides—loomed over her.

"I'm not thinking about myself," he thundered. "Will you listen?"

"No," she replied; and there was freezing hauteur in her voice. With a slight gesture of dismissal, unmistakable in its finality, she turned her back upon him. Then she joined her guests.

Stewart stood perfectly motionless. Then slowly he began to lift his right hand in which he held his sombrero. He swept it up and up, high over his head. His tall form towered. With fierce suddenness he flung his sombrero down. He leaped at his black horse and dragged him to where his saddle lay. With one pitch he tossed the saddle upon the horse's back. His strong hands flashed at girths and straps. Every action was swift, decisive, fierce. Bounding for his bridle, which hung over a bush, he ran against a cowboy who awkwardly tried to avoid the onslaught.

"Get out of my way!" he yelled.

Then with the same savage haste he adjusted the bridle on his horse.

"Mebbe you better hold on a minnit, Gene, old feller," said Monty Price.

"Monty, do you want me to brain you?" said Stewart, with the short, hard ring in his voice.

"Now, considerin' the high class of my brains, I oughter be real careful to keep 'em," replied Monty. "You can betcher life, Gene, I ain't goin' to git in front of you. But I jest says— Listen!"

Stewart raised his dark face. Everybody listened. And everybody heard the rapid beat of a horse's hoofs. The sun had set, but the park was light. Nels appeared down the trail, and his horse was running. In another moment he was in the circle, pulling his bay back to a sliding halt. He leaped off abreast of Stewart.

Madeline saw and felt a difference in Nel's presence.

"What's up, Gene?" he queried, sharply.

"I'm leaving camp," replied Stewart, thickly. His black horse began to stamp as Stewart grasped bridle and mane and kicked the stirrup round.

Nel's long arm shot out, and his hand fell upon Stewart, holding him down.

"Shore I'm sorry," said Nels, slowly. "Then you was goin' to hit the trail?"

"I am going to. Let go, Nels."

"Shore you ain't goin', Gene?"

"Let go, damn you!" cried Stewart, as he wrestled free.

"What's wrong?" asked Nels, lifting his hand again.

"Man! Don't touch me!"

Nels stepped back instantly. He seemed to become aware of Stewart's white, wild passion. Again Stewart moved to mount.

"Nels, don't make me forget we've been friends," he said.

"Shore I ain't fergettin'," replied Nels. "An' I resign my job right here an' now!"

His strange speech checked the mounting cowboy. Stewart stepped down from the stirrup. Then their hard faces were still and cold while their eyes locked glances.

Madeline was as much startled by Nels's speech as Stewart. Quick to note a change in these men, she now sensed one that was unfathomable.

"Resign?" questioned Stewart.

"Shore. What'd you think I'd do under circumstances such as has come up?"

"But see here, Nels, I won't stand for it."

"You're not my boss no more, an' I ain't beholdin' to Miss Hammond, neither. I'm my own boss, an' I'll do as I please. *Sabe,* señor?"

Nels's words were at variance with the meaning in his face.

"Gene, you sent me on a little scout down in the mountains, didn't you?" he continued.

"Yes, I did," replied Stewart, with a new sharpness in his voice.

"Wal, shore you was so good an' right in your figgerin', as opposed to mine, that I'm sick with admirin' of you. If you hedn't sent me—wal, I'm reckonin' something might hev happened. As it is we're shore up against a hell of a proposition!"

How significant was the effect of his words upon all the cowboys! Stewart made a fierce and violent motion, terrible where his other motions had been but passionate. Monty leaped straight up into the air in a singular action as suggestive of surprise as it was of wild acceptance of menace. Like a stalking giant Nick Steele strode over to Nels and Stewart. The other cowboys rose silently, without a word.

Madeline and her guests, in a little group, watched and listened, unable to divine what all this strange talk and action meant.

"Hold on, Nels, they don't need to hear it," said Stewart, hoarsely, as he waved a hand toward Madeline's silent group.

"Wal, I'm sorry, but I reckon they'd as well know fust as last. Mebbe thet yearnin' wish of Miss Helen's fer somethin' to happen will come true. Shore I—"

"Cut out the joshin'," rang out Monty's strident voice.

It had as decided an effect as any preceding words or action. Perhaps it was the last thing needed to transform these men, doing unaccustomed duty as escorts of beautiful women, to their natural state as men of the wild.

"Tell us what's what," said Stewart, cool and grim.

"Don Carlos an' his guerrillas are campin' on the trails thet lead up here. They've got them trails blocked. By to-morrer they'd hed us corralled. Mebbe they meant to surprise us. He's got a lot of Greasers an' outlaws. They're well armed. Now what do they mean? You-all can figger it out to suit yourselves. Mebbe the Don wants to pay a sociable call on our ladies. Mebbe his gang is some hungry, as usual. Mebbe they want to steal a few hosses, or anythin' they can lay hands on. Mebbe they mean wuss, too. Now my idee is this, an' mebbe it's wrong. I long since separated from love with Greasers. Thet black-faced Don Carlos has got a deep game. Thet two-bit of a revolution is hevin' hard times. The rebels want American intervention. They'd stretch any point to make trouble. We're only ten miles from the border. Suppose them guerrillas got our crowd across thet border? The U.S. cavalry would foller. You-all know what thet'd mean. Mebbe Don Carlos's mind works thet way. Mebbe it don't. I reckon we'll know soon. An' now, Stewart, whatever the Don's game is, shore you're the man to outfigger him. Mebbe it's just as well you're good an' mad about somethin'. An' I resign my job because I want to feel unbeholdin' to anybody. Shore it struck me long since thet the old days hed come back fer a little spell, an' there I was trailin' a promise not to hurt any Greaser."

19

Don Carlos

Stewart took Nels, Monty and Nick Steele aside out of earshot, and they evidently entered upon an earnest colloquy. Presently the other cowboys were called. They all talked more or less, but the deep voice of Stewart predominated over the others. Then the consultation broke up, and the cowboys scattered.

"Rustle, you Indians!" ordered Stewart.

The ensuing scene of action was not reassuring to Madeline and her friends. They were quiet, awaiting someone to tell them what to do. At the offset the cowboys appeared to have forgotten Madeline. Some of them ran off into the woods, others into the open, grassy places, where they rounded up the horses and burros. Several cowboys spread tarpaulins upon the ground and began to select and roll small packs, evidently for hurried travel. Nels mounted his horse to ride down the trail. Monty and Nick Steele went off into the grove, leading their horses. Stewart climbed up a steep jumble of stone between two sections of low, cracked cliff back of the camp.

Castleton offered to help the packers, and was curtly told he would be in the way. Madeline's friends all importuned her: Was there real danger? Were the guerrillas coming? Would a start be made at once for the ranch? Why had the cowboys suddenly become so different? Madeline answered as best she could; but her replies were only conjecture, and modified to allay the fears of her guests. Helen was in a white glow of excitement.

Soon cowboys appeared riding barebacked horses, driving in others and the burros. Some of these horses were taken away and evidently hidden in deep recesses between the crags. The string of burros were packed and sent off down the trail in charge of a cowboy. Nick Steel and Monty returned. Then Stewart appeared, clambering down the break between the cliffs.

His next move was to order all the baggage belonging to Madeline and her guests taken up the cliff. This was strenuous toil, requiring the need of lassoes to haul up the effects.

"Get ready to climb," said Stewart, turning to Madeline's party.

"Where?" asked Helen.

He waved his hand at the ascent to be made. Exclamations of dismay followed his gesture.

"Mr. Stewart, is there danger?" asked Dorothy; and her voice trembled.

This was the question Madeline had upon her lips to ask Stewart, but she could not speak it.

"No, there's no danger," replied Stewart, "but we're taking precautions we all agreed on as best."

Dorothy whispered that she believed Stewart lied. Castleton asked another question, and then Harvey followed suit. Mrs. Beck made a timid query.

"Please keep quiet and do as you're told," said Stewart, bluntly.

At this juncture, when the last of the baggage was being hauled up the cliff, Monty approached Madeline and removed his sombrero. His black face seemed the same, yet this was a vastly changed Monty.

"Miss Hammond, I'm givin' notice I resign my job," he said.

"Monty! What do you mean? What does Nels mean now, when danger threatens?"

"We jest quit. Thet's all," replied Monty, tersely. He was

224

stern and somber; he could not stand still; his eyes roved everywhere.

Castleton jumped up from the log where he had been sitting, and his face was very red.

"Mr. Price, does all this blooming fuss mean we are to be robbed or attacked or abducted by a lot of ragamuffin guerillas?"

"You've called the bet."

Dorothy turned a very pale face toward Monty.

"Mr. Price, you wouldn't—you couldn't desert us now? You and Mr. Nels—"

"Desert you?" asked Monty, blankly.

"Yes, desert us. Leave us when we may need you so much, with something dreadful coming."

Monty uttered a short, hard laugh as he bent a strange look upon the girl.

"Me an' Nels is purty much scared, an' we're goin' to slope. Miss Dorothy, bein' as we've rustled round so much, it sorta hurts us to see nice young girls dragged off by the hair."

Dorothy uttered a little cry and then became hysterical. Castleton for once was fully aroused.

"By Gad! You and your partner are a couple of blooming cowards. Where now is that courage you boasted of?"

Monty's dark face expressed extreme sarcasm.

"Dook, in my time I've seen some bright fellers, but you take the cake. It's most marvelous how bright you are. Figger'n' me an' Nels so correct. Say, Dook, if you don't git rustled off to Mexico an' roped to a cactus bush you'll hev a swell story fer your English chums. Bah Jove! You'll tell 'em how you seen two old-time gunmen run like scared jackrabbits from a lot of Greasers. Like hell you will! Unless you lie like the time you told about proddin' the lion. That there story allus—"

"Monty, shut up!" yelled Stewart, as he came hurriedly up. Then Monty slouched away, cursing to himself.

Madeline and Helen, assisted by Castleton, worked over Dorothy, and with some difficulty quieted her. Stewart passed several times without noticing them, and Monty, who had been so ridiculously eager to pay every little attention to Dorothy, did not see her at all. Rude it seemed; in Monty's case more than that. Madeline hardly knew what to make of it.

Stewart directed cowboys to go to the head of the open place in the cliff and let down lassoes. Then, with little waste of words, he urged the women toward this rough ladder of stones.

"We want to hide you," he said, when they demurred. "If the geurrillas come we'll tell them you've all gone down to the ranch. If we have to fight you'll be safe up there."

Helen stepped boldly forward and let Stewart put the loop of a lasso round her and tighten it. He waved his hand to the cowboys above.

"Just walk up, now," he directed Helen.

It proved to the watchers to be an easy, safe, and rapid means of scaling the steep passage. The men climbed up without assistance. Mrs. Beck, as usual, had hysteria; she half walked and was half dragged up. Stewart supported Dorothy with one arm, while with the other he held to the lasso. Ambrose had to carry Christine. The Mexican women required no assistance. Edith Wayne and Madeline climbed last; and once up, Madeline saw a narrow bench, thick with shrubs, and overshadowed by huge, leaning crags. There were holes in the rock, and dark fissures leading back. It was a rough, wild place. Tarpaulins and bedding were then hauled up, and food and water. The cowboys spread comfortable beds in several of the caves, and told Madeline and her friends to be as quiet as possible, not to make a light, and to sleep dressed, ready for travel at a moment's notice.

After the cowboys had gone down it was not a cheerful group left there in the darkening twilight. Castleton prevailed upon them to eat.

"This is simply great," whispered Helen.

"Oh, it's awful!" moaned Dorothy. "It's your fault, Helen. You prayed for something to happen."

"I believe it's a horrid trick those cowboys are playing," said Mrs. Beck.

Madeline assured her friends that no trick was being played upon them, and that she deplored the discomfort and distress, but felt no real alarm. She was more inclined to evasive kindness here than to sincerity, for she had a decided uneasiness. The swift change in the manner and looks of her cowboys had been a shock to her. The last glance she had of Stewart's face, then stern, almost sad, and haggard with worry, remained to augment her foreboding.

226

Darkness appeared to drop swiftly down; the coyotes began their haunting, mournful howls; the stars showed and grew brighter; the wind moaned through the tips of the pines. Castleton was restless. He walked to and fro before the overhanging shelf of rock, where his companions sat lamenting, and presently he went out to the ledge of the bench. The cowboys below had built a fire, and the light from it rose in a huge, fan-shaped glow. Castleton's little figure stood out black against this light. Curious and anxious also, Madeline joined him and peered down from the cliff. The distance was short, and occasionally she could distinguish a word spoken by the cowboys. They were unconcernedly cooking and eating. She marked the absence of Stewart, and mentioned it to Castleton. Silently Castleton pointed almost straight down, and there in the gloom stood Stewart, with the two stag-hounds at his feet.

Presently Nick Steele silenced the campfire circle by raising a warning hand. The cowboys bent their heads, listening. Madeline listened with all her might. She heard one of the hounds whine, then the faint beat of a horse's hoofs. Nick spoke again and turned to his supper, and the other men seemed to slacken in attention. The beat of hoofs grew louder, entered the grove, then the circle of light. The rider was Nels. He dismounted, and the sound of his low voice just reached Madeline.

"Gene, it's Nels. Somethin' doin'," Madeline heard one of the cowboys call, softly.

"Send him over," replied Stewart.

Nels stalked away from the fire.

"See here, Nels, the boys are all right, but I don't want them to know everything about this mix-up," said Stewart, as Nels came up. "Did you find the girl?"

Madeline guessed that Stewart referred to the Mexican girl Bonita.

"No. But I met"—Madeline did not catch the name— "an' he was wild. He was with a forest ranger. An' they said Pat Hawe had trailed her an' was takin' her down under arrest."

Stewart muttered deep under his breath, evidently cursing.

"Wonder why he didn't come on up here?" he queried, presently. "He can see a trail."

"Wal, Gene, Pat knowed you was here all right, fer thet ranger said Pat hed wind of the guerrillas, an' Pat said if Don

227

Carlos didn't kill you—which he hoped he'd do—then it'd be time enough to put you in jail when you come down."

"He's dead set to arrest me, Nels."

"An' he'll do it, like the old lady who kept tavern out West. Gene, the reason thet red-faced coyote didn't trail you up here is because he's scared. He allus was scared of you. But I reckon he's shore scared to death of me an' Monty."

"Well, we'll take Pat in his turn. The thing now is, when will that Greaser stalk us, and what'll we do when he comes?"

"My boy, there's only one way to handle a Greaser. I shore told you thet. He means rough toward us. He'll come smilin' up, all soci'ble like, insinuatin' an' sweeter'n a woman. But he's treacherous; he's wuss than an Indian. An', Gene, we know for a positive fact how his gang hev been operatin' between these hills an Agua Prieta. They're no nervy gang of outlaws like we used to hev. But they're plumb bad. They've raided and murdered through the San Luis Pass an' Gualalupe Cañon. They've murdered women, an' wuss than thet, both north an' south of Agua Prieta. Mebbe the U.S. cavalry don't know it, an' the good old States; but we, *you* an' *me* an' *Monty* an' *Nick*, *we* know it. We know jest about what thet rebel war down there amounts to. It's guerilla war, an' shore some harvest-time fer a lot of cheap thieves an' outcasts."

"Oh, you're right, Nels. I'm not disputing that," replied Stewart. "If it wasn't for Miss Hammond and the other women, I'd rather enjoy seeing you and Monty open up on that bunch. I'm thinking I'd be glad to meet Don Carlos. But Miss Hammond! Why, Nels, such a woman as she is would *never* recover from the sight of real gunplay, let alone any stunts with a rope. These Eastern women are different. I'm not belittling our Western women. It's in the blood. Miss Hammond is—is—"

"Shore she is," interrupted Nels; "but she's got a damn sight more spunk than you think she has, Gene Stewart. I'm no thick-skulled cow. I'd hate somethin' powerful to hev Miss Hammond see any rough work, let alone me an' Monty startin' somethin'. An' me an' Monty'll stick to you, Gene, as long as seems reasonable. Mind, ole feller, beggin' your pardon, you're shore stuck on Miss Hammond, an' over-tender not to hurt her feelin's or make her sick by lettin' some blood. We're in bad here, an' mebbe we'll hev to fight. *Sabe*, señor? Wal, if we do you can jest gamble thet Miss Hammond'll be game. An' I'll bet you a million pesos thet if you got goin' onct, an' she seen you as I've seen you—wal, I know what she'd think of you. This old world ain't changed much. Some women may be white-skinned an' soft-eyed an' sweet-voiced an' high-souled, but they all like to see a man! Gene, here's your game. Let Don Carlos come along. Be civil. If he an' his gang are hungry, feed 'em. Take even a little overbearin' Greaser talk. Be blind if he wants his gang to steal somethin'. Let him think the women hev mosied down to the ranch. But if he says you're lyin'—if he as much as looks around to see the women—jest jump him same as you jumped Pat Hawe. Me an' Monty'll hang back fer thet, an' if your strong bluff don't go through, if the Don's gang even *thinks* of flashin' guns, then we'll open up. An' all I got to say is if them Greasers stand fer real gun-play they'll be the fust I ever seen."

"Nels, there are white men in that gang," said Stewart.

"Shore. But me an' Monty'll be thinkin' of thet. If they start anythin' it'll hev to be shore quick."

"All right, Nels, old friend, and thanks," replied Stewart.

Nels returned to the campfire, and Stewart resumed his silent guard.

Madeline led Castleton away from the brink of the wall.

"By Jove! Cowboys are blooming strange folk!" he exclaimed. "They are not what they pretend to be."

"Indeed, you are right," replied Madeline. "I cannot understand them. Come, let us tell the others that Nels and Monty were only talking and do not intend to leave us. Dorothy, at least, will be less frightened if she knows."

Dorothy was somewhat comforted. The others, however, complained of the cowboys' singular behavior. More than once the idea was advanced that an elaborate trick had been concocted. Upon general discussion this idea gained ground. Madeline did not combat it, because she saw it tended to a less perturbed condition of mind among her guests. Castleton for once proved that he was not absolutely obtuse, and helped along the idea.

They sat talking in low voices until a late hour. The incident now began to take on the nature of Helen's long-yearned-for adventure. Some of the party even grew merry in a subdued way. Then, gradually, one by one they tired and went to bed. Helen vowed she could not sleep in a place where there were bats and crawling things. Madeline fancied, how-ever, that they all went to sleep while she lay wide-eyed, star-ing up at the black bulge of overhanging rock and beyond the starry sky.

To keep from thinking of Stewart and the burning anger he had caused her to feel for herself, Madeline tried to keep her mind on other things. But thought of him recurred, and each time there was a hot commotion in her breast hard to stifle. Intelligent reasoning seemed out of her power. In the daylight it had been possible for her to be oblivious to Stewart's deceit after the moment of its realization. At night, however, in the strange silence and hovering shadows of gloom, with the speaking stars seeming to call to her, with the moan of the wind in the pines, and the melancholy mourn of coyotes in the distance, she was not able to govern her thought and emo-tion. The day was practical, cold; the night was strange and tense. In the darkness she had fancies wholly unknown to her in the bright light of the sun. She battled with a haunting thought. She had inadvertently heard Nel's conversation with Stewart; she had listened, hoping to hear some good news or to hear the worst; she had learned both, and, moreoever, en-lightenment on one point of Stewart's complex motives. He wished to spare her any sight that might offend, frighten, or disgust her. Yet this Stewart, who showed a fineness of feeling that might have been wanting even in Boyd Harvey, main-tained a secret rendezvous with that pretty, abandoned Bo-nita. Here always the hot shame, like a live, stinging, internal fire, abruptly ended Madeline's thought. It was intolerable, and it was the more so because she could neither control nor understand it. The hours wore on, and at length, as the stars began to pale and there was no sound whatever, she fell asleep.

She was called out of her slumber. Day had broken bright and cool. The sun was still below the eastern crags. Ambrose, with several other cowboys, had brought up buckets of springwater, and hot coffee and cakes. Madeline's party ap-peared to be none the worse for the night's experience. In-deed, the meager breakfast might have been as merrily par-taken of as it was hungrily had not Ambrose enjoined silence.

"They're expectin' company down below," he said.

This information and the summary manner in which the cowboys soon led the party higher up among the ruined shelves of rock caused a recurrence of anxiety. Madeline insisted on not going beyond a projection of cliff from which she could see directly down into the camp. As the vantage point was one affording concealment, Ambrose consented, but he placed the frightened Christine near Madeline and remained there himself.

"Ambrose, do you really think the guerrillas will come?" asked Madeline.

"Sure. We know. Nels just rode in and said they were on their way up. Miss Hammond, can I trust you? You won't let out a squeal if there's a fight down there? Stewart told me to hide you out of sight or keep you from lookin'."

"I promise not to make any noise," replied Madeline.

Madeline arranged her coat so that she could lie upon it, and settled down to wait developments. There came a slight rattling of stones in the rear. She turned to see Helen sliding down a bank with a perplexed and troubled cowboy. Helen came stooping low to where Madeline lay and said: "I am going to see what happens, if I die in the attempt! I can stand it if you can." She was pale and big-eyed. Ambrose promptly swore at the cowboy who let her get away from him. "Take a half hitch on her yourself an' see where you end up," replied the fellow, and disappeared in the jumble of rocks. Ambrose, finding words useless, sternly and heroically prepared to carry Helen back to the others. He laid hold of her. In a fury, with eyes blazing, Helen whispered:

"Let go of me! Majesty, what does this fool mean?"

Madeline laughed. She knew Helen, and had marked the whisper when ordinarily Helen would have spoken imperiously, and not low. Madeline explained to her the exigency of the situation. "I might run, but I'll never scream," said Helen. With that Ambrose had to be content to let her stay. However, he found her a place somewhat farther back from Madeline's position, where he said there was less danger of her being seen. Then he sternly bound her to silence, tarried a moment to comfort Christine, and returned to where Madeline lay concealed. He had been there scarcely a moment when he whispered:

"I hear hosses. The guerrillas are comin'."

Madeline's hiding place was well protected from possible discovery from below. She could peep over a kind of parapet, through an opening in the tips of the pines that reached up to

231

the cliff, and obtain a commanding view of the camp circle and its immediate surroundings. She could not, however, see far either to right or left of the camp, owing to the obstructing foliage. Presently the sound of horses' hoofs quickened the beat of her pulse and caused her to turn a keener gaze upon the cowboys below.

Although she had some inkling of the course Stewart and his men were to pursue, she was not by any means prepared for the indifference she saw. Frank was asleep, or pretended to be. Three cowboys were lazily and unconcernedly attending to campfire duties such as baking biscuits, watching the ovens, and washing tins and pots. The elaborate set of aluminum plates, cups, etc., together with the other camp fixtures that had done service for Madeline's party, had disappeared. Nick Steele sat with his back to a log, smoking his pipe. Another cowboy had just brought the horses closer into camp, where they stood waiting to be saddled. Nels appeared to be fussing over a pack. Stewart was rolling a cigarette. Monty had apparently nothing to do for the present except whistle, which he was doing much more loudly than melodiously. The whole ensemble gave an impression of careless indifference.

The sound of horses' hoofs grew louder and slowed its beat. One of the cowboys pointed down the trail, toward which several of his comrades turned their heads for a moment, then went on with their occupations.

Presently a shaggy, dusty horse bearing a lean, ragged, dark rider rode into camp and halted. Another followed, and another. Horses with Mexican riders came in single file and stopped behind the leader.

The cowboys looked up and the guerillas looked down.

"*Buenos dias,* señor," ceremoniously said the foremost guerilla.

By straining her ears Madeline heard that voice, and she recognized it as belonging to Don Carlos. His graceful bow to Stewart was also familiar. Otherwise she would never have recognized the former elegant *vaquero* in this uncouth, roughly dressed Mexican.

Stewart answered the greeting in Spanish, and, waving his hand toward the campfire, added in English. "Get down and eat."

The guerrillas were anything but slow in complying. They crowded to the fire, then spread in a little circle and squatted upon the ground, laying their weapons beside them. In appearance they tallied with the band of guerrillas that had carried Madeline up in the foothills, only this band was larger and better armed. The men, moreover, were just as hungry and as wild and beggarly. The cowboys were not cordial in their reception of this visit, but they were hospitable. The law of the desert had always been to give food and drink to wayfaring men, whether lost or hunted or hunting.

"There's twenty-three in that outfit," whispered Ambrose, "includin' four white men. Pretty rummy outfit."

"They appear to be friendly enough," whispered Madeline.

"Things down there ain't what they seem," replied Ambrose.

"Ambrose, tell me—explain to me. This is my opportunity. As long as you will let me watch them, please let me know the —real thing."

"Sure. But recollect, Miss Hammond, that Gene'll give it to me good if he ever knows I let you look and told you what's what. Well, decent-like Gene is seein' them poor devils get a square meal. They're only a lot of calf-thieves in this country. Across the border they're bandits, some of them, the others just riffraff outlaws. That rebel bluff doesn't go down with us. I'd have to see first before I'd believe them Greasers would fight. They're a lot of hard-ridin' thieves, and they'd steal a fellow's blanket or tobacco. Gene thinks they're after you ladies—to carry you off. But Gene— Oh, Gene's some high-falutin' in his ideas lately. Most of us boys think the guerrillas are out to rob—that's all."

Whatever might have been the secret motive of Don Carlos and his men, they did not allow it to interfere with a hearty appreciation of a generous amount of food. Plainly, each individual ate all that he was able to eat at the time. They jabbered like a flock of parrots; some were even merry, in a kind of wild way. Then, as each and every one began to roll and smoke the inevitable cigarette of the Mexican there was a subtle change in manner. They smoked and looked about the camp, off into the wood, up at the crags, and back at the leisurely cowboys. They had the air of men waiting for something.

"Señor," began Don Carlos, addressing Stewart. As he spoke he swept his sombrero to indicate the camp circle.

Madeline could not distinguish his words but his gesture

plainly indicated a question in regard to the rest of the camping party. Stewart's reply and the wave of his hand down the trail meant that his party had gone home. Stewart turned to some task, and the guerrilla leader quietly smoked. He looked cunning and thoughtful. His men gradually began to manifest a restlessness, noticeable in the absence of former languor and slow puffing of cigarette smoke. Presently a big boned man with a bullet head and blistered red face of evil coarseness got up and threw away his cigarette. He was an American.

"Hey, cull," he called in loud voice, "ain't ye going' to cough up a drink?"

"My boys don't carry liquor on the trail," replied Stewart. He turned now to face the guerrillas.

"Haw, haw! I heerd over in Rodeo that ye was gittin' to be shore some fer temperance," said this fellow. "I hate to drink water, but I guess I've gotter do it."

He went to the spring, sprawled down to drink, and all of a sudden he thrust his arm down in the water to bring forth a basket. The cowboys in the hurry of packing had neglected to remove this basket; and it contained bottles of wine and liquors for Madeline's guests. They had been submerged in the spring to keep them cold. The guerrilla fumbled with the lid, opened it, and then got up, uttering a loud roar of delight.

Stewart made an almost imperceptible motion, as if to leap forward; but he checked the impulse, and after a quick glance at Nels he said to the guerrilla:

"Guess my party forgot that. You're welcome to it."

Like bees the guerrillas swarmed around the lucky finder of the bottles. There was a babel of voices. The drink did not last long, and it served only to liberate the spirit of restlessness. The several white outlaws began to prowl around the camp; some of the Mexicans did likewise; others waited, showing by their ill-concealed expectancy the nature of their thoughts.

It was the demeanor of Stewart and his comrades that puzzled Madeline. Apparently they felt no anxiety or even particular interest. Don Carlos, who had been covertly watching them, now made his scrutiny open, even aggressive. He looked from Stewart to Nels and Monty, and then to the other cowboys. While some of his men prowled around the others watched him, and the waiting attitude had taken on something sinister. The guerilla leader seemed undecided, but not in any sense puzzled. When he turned his cunning face upon Nels and Monty he had the manner of a man in whom decision was lacking.

In her growing excitement Madeline had not clearly heard Ambrose's low whispers and she made an effort to distract some of her attention from those below to the cowboy crouching beside her.

The quality, the note of Ambrose's whisper had changed. It had a slight sibilant sound.

"Don't be mad if sudden-like I clap my hands over your eyes, Miss Hammond," he was saying. "Somethin's brewin' below. I never seen Gene so cool. That's a dangerous sign in him. And look, see how the boys are workin' together! Oh, it's slow and accident-like, but I know it's sure not accident. That foxy Greaser knows, too. But maybe his men don't. If they are wise they haven't sense enough to care. The Don, though —he's worried. He's not payin' so much attention to Gene, either. It's Nels and Monty he's watchin'. And well he need do it! There, Nick and Frank have settled down on that log with Booly. They don't seem to be packin' guns. But look how heavy their vests hang. A gun in each side! Those boys can pull a gun and flop over that log quicker than you can think. Do you notice how Nels and Monty and Gene are square between them guerrillas and the trail up here? It doesn't seem on purpose, but it *is*. Look at Nels and Monty. How quiet they are confabbin' together, payin' no attention to the guerrillas, I see Monty look at Gene, then I see Nels look at Gene. Well, it's up to Gene. And they're goin' to back him. I reckon, Miss Hammond, there'd be dead Greasers round that camp long ago if Nels and Monty were foot-loose. They're beholdin' to Gene. That's plain. And Lord! how it tickles me to watch them! Both packin' two forty-fives, butts swingin' clear. There's twenty-four shots in them four guns. And there's twenty-three guerrillas. If Nels and Monty ever throw guns at that close range, why, before you'd know what was up there'd be a pile of Greasers. There! Stewart said something to the Don. I wonder what. I'll gamble it was something to get the Don's outfit all close together. Sure! Greasers have no sense. But them white guerrillas, they're lookin' some dubious. Whatever's comin' off will come soon, you can bet. I wish I was down there. But maybe it won't come to a scrap. Stewart's set on avoidin' that. He's a wonderful chap to get his way. Lord, though, I'd like to see him go after that overbearin' Greaser! See! the Don can't stand prosperity. All this strange behavior of cowboys is beyond his pulque-soaked brains. Then he's a Greaser. If Gene doesn't knock him on the head presently he'll begin to get over his scare, even of Nels and Monty. But Gene'll pick out the right time. And I'm gettin' nervous. I want somethin' to start. Never saw Nels in but one fight, then he just shot a Greaser's arm off for tryin' to draw on him. But I've heard all about him. And Monty! Monty's the real old-fashioned gun-man. Why, none of them stories, them lies he told to entertain the Englishman, was a marker to what Monty has done. What I don't understand is how Monty keeps so quiet and easy and peaceful-like. That's not his way, with such an outfit lookin' for trouble. O-ha! Now for the grand bluff. Looks like no fight at all!"

The guerrilla leader had ceased his restless steps and glances and turned to Stewart with something of bold resolution in his aspect.

"*Gracias,* señor," he said. "*Adios.*" He swept his sombrero in the direction of the trail leading down the mountain to the ranch: and as he completed the gesture a smile, crafty and jeering, crossed his swarthy face.

Ambrose whispered so low that Madeline scarcely heard him. "If the Greaser goes that way he'll find our horses and get wise to the trick. Oh, he's wise now! But I'll gamble he never even starts on that trail."

Neither hurriedly nor guardedly Stewart rose out of his leaning posture and took a couple of long strides toward Don Carlos.

"Go back the way you came," he fairly yelled; and his voice had the ring of a bugle.

Ambrose nudged Madeline; his whisper was tense and rapid: "Don't miss nothin'. Gene's called him. Whatever's comin' off will be here quick as lightnin'. See! I guess maybe that Greaser don't savvy good U.S. lingo. Look at that dirty yaller face turn green. Put one eye on Nels and Monty! That's great—just to see 'em. Just as quiet and easy. But oh, the difference! Bent and stiff—that means every muscle is like a rawhide riata. They're watchin' with eyes that can see the workin's of them Greasers' minds. Now there ain't a hoss-hair between them Greasers and hell!"

Don Carlos gave Stewart one long malignant stare; then he

threw back his head, swept up the sombrero, and his evil smile showed gleaming teeth.

"Señor—" he began.

With a magnificent bound Stewart was upon him. The guerilla's cry was throttled in his throat. A fierce wrestling ensued, too swift to see clearly; then heavy, sodden blows, and Don Carlos was beaten to the ground. Stewart leaped back. Then, crouching with his hands on the butts of guns at his hips he yelled, he thundered at the guerrillas. He had been quicker than a panther and now his voice was so terrible that it curdled Madeline's blood, and the menace of deadly violence in his crouching position made her shut her eyes. But she had to open them. In that single instant Nels and Monty had leaped to Stewart's side. Both were bent down, with hands on the butts of guns at their hips. Nels's piercing yell seemed to divide Monty's roar of rage. Then they ceased, and echoes clapped from the crags. The silence of those three men crouching like tigers about to leap was more menacing than the nerve-racking yells.

Then the guerrillas wavered and broke and ran for their horses. Don Carlos rolled over, rose, and staggered away, to be helped upon his mount. He looked back, his pale and bloody face that of a thwarted demon. The whole band got into action and were gone in a moment.

"I knew it," declared Ambrose. "Never seen a Greaser who could face gun-play. That was some warm. And Monty Price never flashed a gun! He'll never get over that. I reckon, Miss Hammond, we're some lucky to avoid trouble. Gene has his way, as you seen. We'll be makin' tracks for the ranch in about two shakes."

"Why?" whispered Madeline, breathlessly. She became conscious that she was weak and shaken.

"Because the guerrillas sure will get their nerve back and come sneakin' on our trail or try to head us off by ambushin'," replied Ambrose. "That's their way. Otherwise three cowboys couldn't bluff a whole gang like that. Gene knows the nature of Greasers. They're white-livered. But I reckon we're in more danger now than before, unless we get a good start down the mountain. There! Gene's callin'. Come! Hurry!"

Helen had slipped down from her vantage point, and therefore had not seen the last act in that little campfire drama. It

237

seemed, however, that her desire for excitement was satisfied, for her face was pale and she trembled when she asked if the guerrillas were gone.

"I didn't see the finish, but those horrible yells were enough for me."

Ambrose hurried the three women over the rough rocks, down the cliff. The cowboys below were saddling horses in haste. Evidently all the horses had been brought out of hiding. Swiftly, with regard only for life and limb, Madeline, Helen, and Christine were lowered by lassoes and half carried down to the level. By the time they were safely down the other members of the party appeared on the cliff above. They were in excellent spirits, appearing to treat the matter as a huge joke.

Ambrose put Christine on a horse and rode away through the pines; Frankie Slade did likewise with Helen. Stewart led Madeline's horse up to her, helped her to mount, and spoke one stern word, "Wait!" Then as fast as one of the women reached the level she was put upon a horse and taken away by a cowboy escort. Few words were spoken. Haste seemed to be the great essential. The horses were urged, and once in the trail, spurred and led into a swift trot. One cowboy drove up four pack-horses, and these were hurriedly loaded with the party's baggage. Castleton and his companions mounted, and galloped off to catch the others in the lead. This left Madeline behind with Stewart and Nels and Monty.

"They're goin' to switch off at the holler thet heads near the trail a few miles down," Nels was saying, as he tightened his saddle-girth. "Thet holler heads into a big cañon. Once in thet, it'll be every man fer hisself. I reckon there won't be anythin' wuss than a rough ride."

Nels smiled reassuringly at Madeline, but he did not speak to her. Monty took her canteen and filled it at the spring and hung it over the pommel of her saddle. He put a couple of biscuits in the saddle-bag.

"Don't fergit to take a drink an' a bite as you're ridin' along," he said. "An' don't worry, Miss Majesty. Stewart'll be with you, an' me an' Nels hanging on the back-trail."

His somber and sullen face did not change in its strange intensity, but the look in his eyes Madeline felt she would never forget. Left alone with these three men, now stripped of all pretense, she realized how fortune had favored her and what

238

peril still hung in the balance. Stewart swung astride his big black, spurred him, and whistled. At the whistle Majesty jumped, and with swift canter followed Stewart. Madeline looked back to see Nels already up and Monty handing him a rifle. Then the pines hid her view.

Once in the trail, Stewart's horse broke into a gallop. Majesty changed her gait and kept at the black's heels. Stewart called back a warning. The low, wide-spreading branches of trees might brush Madeline out of the saddle. Fast riding through the forest along a crooked, obstructed trail called forth all her alertness. Likewise the stirring of her blood, always susceptible to the spirit and motion of a ride, let alone one of peril, now began to throb and burn away the worry, the dread, the coldness that had weighted her down.

Before long Stewart wheeled at right angles off the trail and entered a hollow between two low bluffs. Madeline saw tracks in the open patches of ground. Here Stewart's horse took to a brisk walk. The hollow deepened, narrowed, became rocky, full of logs and brush. Madeline exerted all her keenness, and needed it, to keep close to Stewart. She did not think of him nor her own safety, but of keeping Majesty close in the tracks of the black, of eluding sharp spikes in the dead brush, of avoiding the treacherous loose stones.

At last Madeline was brought to a dead halt by Stewart and his horse blocking the trail. Looking up, she saw they were at the head of a cañon that yawned beneath and widened its gray-walled, green-patched slopes down to a black forest of fir. The drab monotony of the foothills made contrast below the forest, and away in the distance, rosy and smoky, lay the desert. Retracting her gaze, Madeline saw pack-horses cross an open space a mile below, and she thought she saw the staghounds. Stewart's dark eyes searched the slopes high up along the craggy escarpments. Then he put the black to the descent.

If there had been a trail by the leading cowboys, Stewart did not follow it. He led off to the right, zigzagging an intricate course through the roughest ground Madeline had ever ridden over. He crashed through cedars, threaded a tortuous way among boulders, made his horse slide down slanting banks of soft earth, picked a slow and cautious progress across weathered slopes of loose rock. Madeline followed, finding in this ride a tax on strength and judgment. On an ordinary horse she never could have kept in Stewart's trail. It

239

was dust and heat, a parching throat, that caused Madeline to think of time; and she was amazed to see the sun sloping to the west. Stewart never stopped; he never looked back; he never spoke. He must have heard the horse close behind him. Madeline remembered Monty's advice about drinking and eating as she rode along. The worst of that rough travel came at the bottom of the cañon. Dead cedars and brush and logs were easy to pass compared with the miles, it seemed, of loose boulders. The horses slipped and stumbled. Stewart proceed here with exceeding care. At last, when the cañon opened into a level forest of firs, the sun was setting red in the west.

Stewart quickened the gait of his horse. After a mile or so of easy travel the ground again began to fall decidedly, sloping in numerous ridges, with draws between. Soon night shadowed the deep gullies. Madeline was refreshed by the cooling of the air.

Stewart traveled slowly now. The barks of coyotes seemed to startle him. Often he stopped to listen. And during one of those intervals the silence was broken by sharp rifle shots. Madeline could not tell whether they were near or far, to right or left, behind or before. Evidently Stewart was both alarmed and baffled. He dismounted. He went cautiously forward to listen. Madeline fancied she heard a cry, low and far away. It was only that of a coyote, she convinced herself, yet it was so wailing, so human, that she shuddered. Stewart came back. He slipped the bridles of both horses, and he led them. Every few paces he stopped to listen. He changed his direction several times, and the last time he got among rough, rocky ridges. The iron shoes of the horses cracked on the rocks. That sound must have penetrated far into the forest. It perturbed Stewart, for he searched for softer ground. Meanwhile the shadows merged into darkness. The stars shone. The wind rose. Madeline believed hours passed.

Stewart halted again. In the gloom Madeline discerned a log cabin and beyond it spear-pointed dark trees piercing the skyline. She could just make out Stewart's tall form as he leaned against his horse. Either he was listening or debating what to do—perhaps both. Presently he went inside the cabin. Madeline heard the scratching of a match; she saw a faint light. The cabin appeared to be deserted. Probably it was one of the many habitations belonging to prospectors and foresters who lived in the mountains. Stewart came out again. He walked around the horses, out into the gloom, then back to Madeline. For a long moment he stood as still as a statue and listened. Then she heard him mutter, "If we have to start quick I can ride bareback." With that he took the saddle and blanket off his horse and carried them into the cabin.

"Get off," he said, in a low voice, as he stepped out of the door.

He helped her down and led her inside where again he struck a match. Madeline caught a glimpse of a rude fireplace and rough-hewn logs. Stewart's blanket and saddle lay on the hard-packed earthen floor.

"Rest a little," he said. "I'm going into the woods a piece to listen. Gone only a minute or so."

Madeline had to feel round in the dark to locate the saddle and blanket. When she lay down it was with a grateful sense of ease and relief. As her body rested, however, her mind became the old thronging maze for sensation and thought. All day she had attended to the alert business of helping her horse. Now, what had already happened, the night, the silence, the proximity of Stewart and his strange, stern caution, the possible happenings to her friends—all claimed their due share of her feeling. She went over them all with lightning swiftness of thought. She believed, and she was sure Stewart believed, that her friends, owing to their quicker start down the mountain, had not been headed off in their travel by any of the things which had delayed Stewart. This conviction lifted the suddenly returning dread from her breast; and as for herself, somehow she had no fear. But she could not sleep; she did not try to.

Stewart's soft steps sounded outside. His dark form loomed in the door. As he sat down Madeline heard the thump of a gun that he laid beside him on the sill; then the thump of another as he put that down, too. The sounds thrilled her. Stewart's wide shoulders filled the door; his finely shaped head and strong, stern profile showed clearly in outline against the sky; the wind waved his hair. He turned his ear to that wind and listened. Motionless he sat for what to her seemed hours.

Then the stirring memory of the day's adventure, the feeling of the beauty of the night, and a strange, deep-seated, sweetly vague consciousness of happiness portending, were all burned out in hot, pressing pain at the remembrance of

Stewart's disgrace in her eyes. Something had changed within her so that what had been anger at herself was sorrow for him. He was such a splendid man. She could not feel the same; she knew her debt to him, yet she could not thank him, could not speak to him. She fought an unintelligible bitterness.

Then she rested with closed eyes, and time seemed neither short nor long. When Stewart called her she opened her eyes to see the gray of dawn. She rose and stepped outside. The horses whinnied. In a moment she was in the saddle, aware of cramped muscles and a weariness of limbs. Stewart led off at a sharp trot into the fir forest. They came to a trail into which he turned. The horses traveled steadily; the descent grew less steep; the firs thinned out; the gray gloom brightened.

When Madeline rode out of the firs the sun had risen and the foothills rolled beneath her; and at their edge, where the gray of valley began, she saw a dark patch that she knew was the ranch-house.

20

The Sheriff of El Cajon

About the middle of the forenoon of that day Madeline reached the ranch. Her guests had all arrived there late the night before, and wanted only her presence and the assurance of her well-being to consider the last of the camping trip a rare adventure. Likewise, they voted it the cowboys' masterpiece of a trick. Madeline's delay, they averred, had been only a clever coup to give a final effect. She did not correct their impression, nor think it needful to state that she had been escorted home by only one cowboy.

Her guests reported an arduous ride down the mountain, with only one incident to lend excitement. On the descent they had fallen in with Sheriff Hawe and several of his deputies, who were considerably under the influence of drink and very greatly enraged by the escape of the Mexican girl Bonita. Hawe had used insulting language to the ladies and, according to Ambrose, would have inconvenienced the party on some pretext or other if he had not been sharply silenced by the cowboys.

Madeline's guests were two days in recovering from the hard ride. On the third day they leisurely began to prepare for departure. This period was doubly trying for Madeline. She had her own physical need of rest, and, moreover, had to face a mental conflict that could scarcely be postponed further. Her sister and friends were kindly and earnestly persistent in their entreaties that she go back East with them. She desired to go. It was not going that mattered: it was how and when and under what circumstances she was to return that roused in her disturbing emotion. Before she went East she wanted to have fixed in her mind her future relation to the ranch and the West. When the crucial hour arrived she found that the West had not claimed her yet. These old friends had warmed cold ties.

It turned out, however, that there need be no hurry about making the decision. Madeline would have welcomed any excuse to procrastinate; but, as it happened, a letter from Alfred made her departure out of the question for the present. He wrote that his trip to California had been very profitable, that he had a proposition for Madeline from a large cattle company, and, particularly, that he wanted to marry Florence soon after his arrival home and would bring a minister from Douglas for that purpose.

Madeline went so far, however, as to promise Helen and her friends that she would go East soon, at the very latest by Thanksgiving. With that promise they were reluctantly content to say goodby to the ranch and to her. At the last moment there seemed a great likelihood of a hitch in plans for the first stage of that homeward journey. All of Madeline's guests held up their hands, Western fashion, when Link Stevens appeared with the big white car. Link protested innocently, solemnly, that he would drive slowly and safely; but it was necessary for Madeline to guarantee Link's word and to accompany them before they would enter the car. At the station good-bys were spoken and repeated, and Madeline's promise was exacted for the hundredth time.

Dorothy Coombs's last words were: "Give my love to Monty Price. Tell him I'm—I'm *glad* he kissed me!"

Helen's eyes had a sweet, grave, yet mocking light as she said:

"Majesty, bring Stewart with you when you come. He'll be the rage."

Madeline treated the remark with the same merry lightness with which it was received by the others; but after the train had pulled out and she was on her way home she remembered Helen's words and looks with something almost amounting to a shock. Any mention of Stewart, any thought of him, displeased her.

"What did Helen mean?" mused Madeline. And she pondered. That mocking light in Helen's eyes had been simply an ironical glint, a cynical gleam from that wordly experience so suspicious and tolerant in its wisdom. The sweet gravity of Helen's look had been a deeper and more subtle thing. Madeline wanted to understand it, to divine in it a new relation between Helen and herself, something fine and sisterly that might lead to love. The thought, however, revolving around a strange suggestion of Stewart, was poisoned at its inception, and she dismissed it.

Upon the drive in to the ranch, as she was passing the lower lake, she saw Stewart walking listlessly along the shore. When he became aware of the approach of the car he suddenly awakened from his aimless sauntering and disappeared quickly in the shade of the shrubbery. This was not by any means the first time Madeline had seen him avoid a possible meeting with her. Somehow the act had pained her, though affording her a relief. She did not want to meet him face to face.

It was annoying for her to guess that Stillwell had something to say in Stewart's defense. The old cattleman was evidently distressed. Several times he had tried to open a conversation with Madeline relating to Stewart; she had evaded him until the last time, when his persistence had brought a cold and final refusal to hear another word about the foreman. Stillwell had been crushed.

As days passed Stewart remained at the ranch without his old faithfulness to his work. Madeline was not moved to a kinder frame of mind to see him wandering dejectedly around. It hurt her, and because it hurt her she grew all the harder. Then she could not help hearing snatches of conversation which strengthened her suspicions that Stewart was losing his grip on himself, that he would soon take the downward course again. Verification of her own suspicion made it a belief, and belief brought about a sharp conflict between her generosity and some feeling that she could not name. It was not a question of justice or mercy or sympathy. If a single word could have saved Stewart from sinking his splendid manhood into the brute she had recoiled from at Chiricahua, she would not have spoken it. She could not restore him to his former place in her regard; she really did not want him at the ranch at all. Once, considering in wonder her knowledge of men, she interrogated herself to see just why she could not overlook Stewart's transgression. She never wanted to speak to him again, or see him, or think of him. In some way, through her interest in Stewart, she had come to feel for herself an inexplicable thing close to scorn.

A telegram from Douglas, heralding the coming of Alfred and a minister, put an end to Madeline's brooding, and she shared something of Florence Kingsley's excitement. The cowboys were as eager and gossipy as girls. It was arranged to have the wedding ceremony performed in Madeline's great hall-chamber, and the dinner in the cool, flower-scented patio.

Alfred and his minister arrived at the ranch in the big white car. They appeared considerably windblown. In fact, the minister was breathless, almost sightless, and certainly hatless. Alfred, used as he was to wind and speed, remarked that he did not wonder at Nels's aversion to riding a fleeting cannon ball. The imperturbable Link took off his cap and goggles and, consulting his watch, made his usual apologetic report to Madeline, deploring the fact that a teamster and a few stray cattle on the road had held him down to the *mañana* time of only a mile a minute.

Arrangements for the wedding brought Alfred's delighted approval. When he had learned all Florence and Madeline would tell him he expressed a desire to have the cowboys attend; and then he went on to talk about California, where he was going to take Florence on a short trip. He was curiously interested to find out all about Madeline's guests and what had happened to them. His keen glance at Madeline grew softer as she talked.

"I breathe again," he said, and laughed. "I was afraid. Well, I must have missed some sport. I can just fancy what Monty and Nels did to that Englishman. So you went up to the crags. That's a wild place. I'm not surprised at guerrillas falling in with you up there. The crags were a famous rendezvous for Apaches—it's near the border—almost inaccessible—good water and grass. I wonder what the U.S. cavalry would think if they knew these guerrillas crossed the border right under their noses. Well, it's practically impossible to patrol some of that border-line. It's desert, mountain, and cañon, exceedingly wild and broken. I'm sorry to say that there seems to be more trouble in sight with these guerrillas than at any time heretofore. Orozco, the rebel leader, has failed to withstand Madero's army. The Federals are occupying Chihuahua now, and are driving the rebels north. Orozco has broken up his army into guerrilla bands. They are moving north and west, intending to carry on guerrilla warfare in Sonora. I can't say just how this will affect us here. But we're too close to the border for comfort. These guerrillas are night-riding hawks; they can cross the border, raid us here, and get back the same night. Fighting, I imagine, will not be restricted to northern Mexico. With the revolution a failure the guerrillas will be more numerous, bolder, and hungrier. Unfortunately, we happen to be favorably situated for them down here in this wilderness corner of the state."

On the following day Alfred and Florence were married. Florence's sister and several friends from El Cajon were present, besides Madeline, Stillwell, and his men. It was Alfred's express wish that Stewart attend the ceremony. Madeline was amused when she noticed the painfully suppressed excitement of the cowboys. For them a wedding must have been an unusual and impressive event. She began to have a better understanding of the nature of it when they cast off restraint and pressed forward to kiss the bride. In all her life Madeline had never seen a bride kissed so much and so heartily, nor one so flushed and disheveled and happy. This indeed was a joyful occasion. There was nothing of the "effete East" about Alfred Hammond; he might have been a Westerner all his days. When Madeline managed to get through the press of cowboys to offer her congratulations, Alfred gave her a bear hug and a kiss. This appeared to fascinate the cowboys. With shining eyes and faces aglow, with smiling, boyish boldness, they made a rush at Madeline. For one instant her heart leaped to her throat. They looked as if they could most shamelessly kiss and maul her. That little, ugly-faced, soft-eyed, rude, tenderhearted ruffian, Monty Price, was in the lead. He resembled a dragon actuated by sentiment. All at once Madeline's instinctive antagonism to being touched by strange hands or lips battled with a real, warm, and fun-loving desire to let the cowboys work their will with her. But she saw Stewart hanging at the back of the crowd, and something—some fierce, dark expression of pain—amazed her, while it froze her desire to be kind. Then she did not know what change must have come to her face and bearing; but she saw Monty fall back sheepishly and the other cowboys draw aside to let her lead the way into the patio.

The dinner began quietly enough with the cowboys divided between embarrassment and voracious appetites that they evidently feared to indulge. Wine, however, loosened their tongues, and when Stillwell got up to make the speech everybody seemed to expect of him they greeted him with a roar.

Stillwell was now one huge, mountainous smile. He was so happy that he appeared on the verge of tears. He rambled on ecstatically till he came to raise his glass.

"An' now girls an' boys, let's all drink to the bride and groom; to their sincere an' lastin' love; to their happiness an' prosperity; to their good health an' long life. Let's drink to the unitin' of the East with the West. No man full of red blood an' real breath of life could resist a Western girl an' a good hoss an' God's free hand—that open country out there. So we claim Al Hammond, an' may we be true to him. An', friends, I think it fittin' that we drink to his sister an' to our hopes. Heah's to the lady we hope to make *our* Majesty! Heah's to the man who'll come ridin' out of the west, a fine, big-hearted man with a fast hoss an' a strong rope, an' may he win an' hold her! Come, friends, drink."

A heavy pound of horses' hoofs and a yell outside arrested Stillwell's voice and halted his hand in midair.

The patio became as silent as an unoccupied room.

Through the open doors and windows of Madeline's chamber burst the sounds of horses stamping to a halt, then harsh speech of men, and a low cry of a woman in pain.

Rapid steps crossed the porch, entered Madeline's room. Nels appeared in the doorway. Madeline was surprised to see that he had not been at the dinner table. She was disturbed at sight of his face.

"Stewart, you're wanted outdoors," called Nels, bluntly. "Monty, you slope out here with me. You, Nick, an' Stillwell

—I reckon the rest of you had better shut the doors an' stay inside."

Nels disappeared. Quick as a cat Monty glided out. Madeline heard his soft, swift steps pass from her room into her office. He had left his guns there. Madeline trembled. She saw Stewart get up quietly and without any change of expression on his dark, sad face leave the patio. Nick Steele followed him. Stillwell dropped his wine-glass. As it broke, shivering the silence, his huge smile vanished. His face set into the old cragginess and the red slowly thickened into black. Stillwell went out and closed the door behind him.

Then there was a blank silence. The enjoyment of the moment had been rudely disrupted. Madeline glanced down the lines of brown faces to see the pleasure fade into the old familiar hardness.

"What's wrong?" asked Alfred, rather stupidly. The change of mood had been too rapid for him. Suddenly he awakened, thoroughly aroused at the interruption. "I'm going to see who's butted in here to spoil our dinner," he said, and strode out.

He returned before any one at the table had spoken or moved, and now the dull red of anger mottled his forehead.

"It's the sheriff of El Cajon!" he exclaimed, contemptuously. "Pat Hawe with some of his tough deputies come to arrest Gene Stewart. They've got that poor little Mexican girl out there tied on a horse. Confound that sheriff!"

Madeline calmly rose from the table, eluding Florence's entreating hand, and started for the door. The cowboys jumped up. Alfred barred her progress.

"Alfred, I am going out," she said.

"No, I guess not," he replied. "That's no place for you."

"I am going." She looked straight at him.

"Madeline! Why, what is it? You look— Dear, there's pretty sure to be trouble outside. Maybe there'll be a fight. You can do nothing. You must not go."

"Perhaps, I can prevent trouble," she replied.

As she left the patio she was aware that Alfred, with Florence at his side and the cowboys behind, were starting to follow her. When she got out of her room up on the porch she heard several men in loud, angry discussion. Then, at sight of Bonita helplessly and cruelly bound upon a horse, pale and disheveled and suffering, Madeline experienced the thrill that

248

sight or mention of this girl always gave her. It yielded to a hot pang in her breast—that live pain which so shamed her. But almost instantly, as a second glance showed an agony in Bonita's face, her bruised arms where the rope bit deep into the flesh, her little brown hands stained with blood, Madeline was overcome by pity for the unfortunate girl and a woman's righteous passion at such barbarous treatment of one of her own sex.

The man holding the bridle of the horse on which Bonita had been bound was at once recognized by Madeline as the big-bodied, bullet-headed guerrilla who had found the basket of wine in the spring at camp. Redder of face, blacker of beard, coarser of aspect, evidently under the influence of liquor, he was as fierce-looking as a gorilla and as repulsive. Besides him there were three other men present, all mounted on weary horses. The one in the foreground, gaunt, sharp-featured, red-eyed, with a pointed beard, she recognized as the sheriff of El Cajon.

Madeline hesitated, then stopped in the middle of the porch. Alfred, Florence, and several others followed her out; the rest of the cowboys and guests crowded the windows and doors. Stillwell saw Madeline and, throwing up his hands, roared to be heard. This quieted the gesticulating, quarreling men.

"Wal now, Pat Hawe, what's drivin' you like a locoed steer on the rampage?" demanded Stillwell.

"Keep in the traces, Bill," replied Hawe. "You savvy what I come fer. I've been bidin' my time. But I'm ready now. I'm hyar to arrest a criminal."

The huge frame of the old cattleman jerked as if he had been stabbed. His face turned purple.

"What criminal?" he shouted, hoarsely.

The sheriff flicked his quirt against his dirty boot, and he twisted his thin lips into a leer. The situation was agreeable to him.

"Why, Bill, I knowed you hed a no-good outfit ridin' this range; but I wasn't wise thet you hed more 'n one criminal."

"Cut that talk! Which cowboy are you wantin' to arrest?"

Hawe's manner altered.

"Gene Stewart," he replied, curtly.

"On what charge?"

"Fer killin' a Greaser one night last fall."

"So you're still harpin' on that? Pat, you're on the wrong trail. You can't lay that killin' onto Stewart. The thing's ancient by now. But if you insist on bringin' him to court, let the arrest go today—we're hevin' some fiesta hyar—an' I'll fetch Gene in to El Cajon."

"Nope. I reckon I'll take him when I got the chance, before he slopes."

"I'm givin' you my word," thundered Stillwell.

"I reckon I don't hev to take your word, Bill, or anybody else's."

Stillwell's great bulk quivered with his rage, yet he made a successful effort to control it.

"See hyar, Pat Hawe, I know what's reasonable. Law is law. But in this country there always has been an' is now a safe an' sane way to proceed with the law. Mebbe you've forgot that. The law as invested in one man in a wild country is liable, owin' to that man's weaknesses an' onlimited authority, to be disputed even by a decent old cattleman like myself. I'm a-goin' to give you a hunch. Pat, you're not overliked in these parts. You've rid too much with a high hand. Some of your deals hev been shady, an' don't you overlook what I'm sayin'. But you're the sheriff, an' I'm respecting your office. I'm respectin' it this much. If the milk of human decency is so soured in your breast that you can't hev a kind of feelin', then try to avoid the onpleasantness that'll result from any contrary move on your part today. Do you get that hunch?"

"Stillwell, you're threatenin' an officer," replied Hawe, angrily.

"Will you hit the trail quick out of hyar?" queried Stillwell, in strained voice. "I guarantee Stewart's appearance in El Cajon any day you say."

"No. I come to arrest him, an' I'm goin' to."

"So that's your game!" shouted Stillwell. "We-all are glad to get you straight, Pat. Now listen, you cheap, red-eyed coyote of a sheriff! You don't care how many enemies you make. You know you'll never get office again in this county. What do you care now? It's amazin' strange how earnest you are to hunt down the man who killed that particular Greaser. I reckon there's been some dozen or more killing's of Greasers in the last year. Why don't you take to trailin' some of them killin's? I'll tell you why. You're afraid to go near the border. An' your hate of Gene Stewart makes you want to hound him

250

an' put him where he's never been yet—in jail. You want to spite his friends. Wal, listen, you lean-jawed, skunk-bitten coyote! Go ahead an' try to arrest him!"

Stillwell took one mighty stride off the porch. His last words had been cold. His rage appeared to have been transferred to Hawe. The sheriff had begun to stutter and shake a lanky red hand at the cattleman when Stewart stepped out.

"Here, you fellows, give me a chance to say a word."

As Stewart appeared the Mexican girl suddenly seemed vitalized out of her stupor. She strained at her bonds, as if to lift her hands beseechingly. A flush animated her haggard face, and her big dark eyes lighted.

"Señor Gene!" she moaned. "Help me! I so seek. They beat me, rope me, 'mos keel me. Oh, help me, Señor Gene!"

"Shut up, er I'll gag you," said the man who held Bonita's horse.

"Muzzle her, Sneed, if she blabs again," called Hawe.

Madeline felt something tense and strained working in the short silence. Was it only a phase of her thrilling excitement? Her swift glance showed the faces of Nels and Monty and Nick to be brooding, cold, watchful. She wondered why Stewart did not look toward Bonita. He too, was now darkfaced, cool, quiet, with something ominous about him.

"Hawe, I'll submit to arrest without any fuss," he said, slowly, "if you'll take the ropes off that girl."

"Nope," replied the sheriff. "She got away from me onct. She's hawg-tied now, an' she'll stay hawg-tied."

Madeline thought she saw Stewart give a slight start. But an unaccountable dimness came over her eyes, at brief intervals obscuring her keen sight. Vaguely she was conscious of a clogged and beating tumult in her breast.

"All right, let's hurry out of here," said Stewart. "You've made annoyance enough. Ride down to the corral with me. I'll get my horse and go with you."

"Hold on!" yelled Hawe, as Stewart turned away. "Not so fast. Who's doin' this? You don't come no El Capitan stunts on me. You'll ride one of my packhorses, an' you'll go in irons."

"You want to handcuff me?" queried Stewart, with sudden swift start of passion.

"Want to? Haw, haw! Nope, Stewart, thet's jest my way with hoss-thieves, raiders, Greasers, murderers, an' sich. See hyar, you Sneed, git off an' put the irons on this man."

251

The guerrilla called Sneed slid off his horse and began to fumble in his saddle-bags.

"You see, Bill," went on Hawe, "I swore in a new depooty fer this particular job. Sneed is some handy. He rounded up thet little Mexican cat fer me."

Stillwell did not hear the sheriff; he was gazing at Stewart in a kind of imploring amaze.

"Gene, you ain't goin' to stand fer them handcuffs?" he pleaded.

"Yes," replied the cowboy. "Bill, old friend, I'm an outsider here. There's no call for Miss Hammond and—and her brother and Florence to be worried further about me. Their happy day has already been spoiled on my account. I want to get out quick."

"Wal, you might be too damn considerate of Miss Hammond's sensitive feelin's." There was now no trace of the courteous, kindly old rancher. He looked harder than stone. "How about my feelin's? I want to know if you're goin' to let this sneakin' coyote, this last gasp of the old rum-guzzlin' frontier sheriffs, put you in irons an' hawg-tie you an' drive you off to jail?"

"Yes," replied Stewart, steadily.

"Wal, by Gawd! *You, Gene Stewart!* What's come over you? Why, man, go in the house, an' I'll 'tend to this feller. Then tomorrow you can ride in an' give yourself up like a gentleman."

"No. I'll go. Thanks, Bill, for the way you and the boys would stick to me. Hurry, Hawe, before my mind *changes*."

His voice broke at the last, betraying the wonderful control he had kept over his passions. As he ceased speaking he seemed suddenly to become spiritless. He dropped his head.

Madeline saw in him then a semblance to the hopeless, shamed Stewart of earlier days. The vague riot in her breast leaped into conscious fury—a woman's passionate repudiation of Stewart's broken spirit. It was not that she would have him be a lawbreaker; it was that she could not bear to see him deny his manhood. Once she had entreated him to become her kind of a cowboy—a man in whom reason tempered passion. She had let him see how painful and shocking any violence was to her. And the idea had obsessed him, softened him had grown like a stultifying lichen upon his will, had shorn him of a wild, bold spirit she now strangely longed to

252

see him feel. When the man Sneed came forward, jingling the iron fetters, Madeline's blood turned to fire. She would have forgiven Stewart then for lapsing into the kind of cowboy it had been her blind and sickly sentiment to abhor. This was a man's West—a man's game. What right had a woman reared in a softer mold to use her beauty and her influence to change a man who was bold and free and strong? At that moment, with her blood hot and racing, she would have gloried in the violence which she had so deplored; she would have welcomed the action that had characterized Stewart's treatment of Don Carlos; she had in her the sudden dawning temper of a woman who had been assimilating the life and nature around her and who would not have turned her eyes away from a harsh and bloody deed.

But Stewart held forth his hands to be manacled. Then Madeline heard her own voice burst out in a ringing, imperious *"Wait!"*

In the time it took her to make the few steps to the edge of the porch, facing the men, she not only felt her anger and justice and pride summoning forces to her command, but there was something else calling—a deep, passionate, mysterious thing not born of the moment.

Sneed dropped the manacles. Stewart's face took on a chalky whiteness. Hawe, in a slow, stupid embarrassment beyond his control, removed his sombrero in a respect that seemed wrenched from him.

"Mr. Hawe, I can prove to you that Stewart was not concerned in any way whatever with the crime for which you want to arrest him."

The sheriff's stare underwent a blinking change. He had been thrown completely off his balance. Astonishment slowly merged into discomfiture.

"It was absolutely impossible for Stewart to have been connected with that assault," went on Madeline, swiftly, "for he was with me in the waiting room of the station at the moment the assault was made outside. I assure you I have a distinct and vivid recollection. The door was open. I heard the voices of quarreling men. They grew louder. The language was Spanish. Evidently these men had left the dance hall opposite and were approaching the station. I heard a woman's voice mingling with the others. It, too, was Spanish, and I could not understand. But the tone was beseeching. Then I heard footsteps on the gravel. I know Stewart heard them. I could see from his face that something dreadful was about to happen. Just outside the door then there were hoarse, furious voices, a scuffle, a muffled shot, a woman's cry, the thud of a falling body, and rapid footsteps of a man running away. Next, the girl Bonita staggered into the door. She was white, trembling, terror-stricken. She recognized Stewart, appealed to him. Stewart supported her and endeavored to calm her. He was excited. He asked her if Danny Mains had been shot, or if he had done the shooting. The girl said no. She told Stewart that she had danced a little, flirted a little with *vaqueros,* and they had quarreled over her. Then Stewart took her outside and put her upon his horse. I saw the girl ride that horse down the street to disappear in the darkness."

While Madeline spoke another change appeared to be working in the man Hawe. He was not long disconcerted, but his discomfiture wore to a sullen fury, and his sharp features fixed in an expression of craft.

"Thet's mighty interestin', Miss Hammond, 'most as interestin' as a storybook," he said. "Now, since you're so obliging a witness, I'd sure like to put a question or two. What time did you arrive at El Cajon thet night?"

"It was after eleven o'clock," replied Madeline.

"Nobody there to meet you?"

"No."

"The station agent an' operator both gone?"

"Yes."

"Wal, how soon did this feller Stewart show up?" Hawe continued, with a wry smile.

"Very soon after my arrival. I think—perhaps fifteen minutes, possibly a little more."

"Some dark an' lonesome around thet station, wasn't it?"

"Indeed yes."

"An' what time was the Greaser shot?" queried Hawe, with his little eyes gleaming like coals.

"Probably close to half past one. It was two o'clock when I looked at my watch at Florence Kingsley's house. Directly after Stewart sent Bonita away he took me to Miss Kingsley's. So, allowing for that walk and a few minutes' conversation with her, I can pretty definitely say the shooting took place at about half past one."

Stillwell heaved his big frame a step closer to the sheriff.

"What're you drivin' at?" he roared, his face black again.

"Evidence," snapped Hawe.

Madeline marveled at this interruption; and as Stewart irresistibly drew her glance she saw him gray-faced as ashes, shaking, utterly unnerved.

"I thank you, Miss Hammond," he said, huskily. "But you needn't answer any more of Hawe's questions. He's—he's— It's not necessary. I'll go with him now, under arrest. Bonita will corroborate your testimony in court, and that will save me from this—this man's spite."

Madeline, looking at Stewart, seeing a humility she at first took for cowardice, suddenly divined that it was not fear for himself which made him dread further disclosures of that night, but fear for her—fear of shame she might suffer through him.

Pat Hawe cocked his head to one side, like a vulture about to strike with his beak, and cunningly eyed Madeline.

"Considered as testimony, what you've said is sure important an' conclusive. But I'm calculatin' thet the court will want to hev explained *why* you stayed from eleven-thirty till one-thirty in thet waitin'-room alone with Stewart."

His deliberate speech met with what Madeline imagined a remarkable reception from Stewart, who gave a tigerish start; from Stillwell, whose big hands tore at the neck of his shirt, as if he was choking; from Alfred, who now strode hotly forward, to be stopped by the cold and silent Nels; from Monty Price, who uttered a violent *"Aw!"* which was both a hiss and a roar.

In the rush of her thought Madeline could not interpret the meaning of these things which seemed so strange at that moment. But they were portentous. Even as she was forming a reply to Hawe's speech she felt a chill creep over her.

"Stewart detained me in the waiting room," she said, clear-voiced as a bell. "But we were not alone—all the time."

For a moment the only sound following her words was a gasp from Stewart. Hawe's face became transformed with a hideous amaze and joy.

"Detained?" he whispered, craning his lean and corded neck. "How's thet?"

"Stewart was drunk. He—"

With a sudden passionate gesture of despair Stewart appealed to her:

255

"Oh, Miss Hammond, don't! *don't!* Don't! . . ."

Then he seemed to sink down, head lowered upon his breast, in utter shame. Stillwell's great hand swept to the bowed shoulder, and he turned to Madeline.

"Miss Majesty, I reckon you'd be wise to tell all," said the old cattleman, gravely. "There ain't one of us who could misunderstand any motive or act of yours. Mebbe a stroke of lightnin' might clear this murky air. Whatever Gene Stewart did that onlucky night—you tell it."

Madeline's dignity and self-possession had been disturbed by Stewart's importunity. She broke into swift, disconnected speech:

"He came into the station—a few minutes after I got there. I asked—to be shown to a hotel. He said there wasn't any that would accommodate married women. He grasped my hand—looked for a wedding-ring. Then I saw he was—he was intoxicated. He told me he would go for a hotel porter. But he came back with a padre—Padre Marcos. The poor priest was —terribly frightened. So was I. Stewart had turned into a devil. He fired his gun at the padre's feet. He pushed me into a bench. Again he shot—right before my face. I—I nearly fainted. But I heard him cursing the padre—heard the padre praying or chanting—I didn't know what. Stewart tried to make me say things in Spanish. All at once he asked my name. Then I told him. He jerked at my veil. I took it off. Then he threw his gun down—pushed the padre out of the door. That was just before the *vaqueros* approached with Bonita. Padre Marcos must have seen them—must have heard them. After that Stewart grew quickly sober. He was mortified—distressed—stricken with shame. He told me he had been drinking at a wedding—I remember, it was Ed Linton's wedding. Then he explained—the boys were always gambling—he wagered he would marry the first girl who arrived at El Cajon. I happened to be the first one. He tried to force me to marry him. The rest—relating to the assault on the *vaquero*—I have already told you."

Madeline ended out of breath and panting, with her hands pressed upon her heaving bosom. Revelation of that secret liberated emotion; those hurried outspoken words had made her throb and tremble and burn. Strangely then she thought of Alfred and his wrath. But he stood motionless, as if dazed. Stillwell was trying to bolster up the crushed Stewart.

Hawe rolled his eyes and threw back his head.

"Ho, ho, ho! Ho, ho, ho! Say, Sneed, you didn't miss any of it, did ye? Haw, haw! Best I ever heerd in all my born days. Ho, ho!"

Then he ceased laughing, and with glinting gaze upon Madeline, insolent and vicious and savage, he began to drawl:

"Wal now, my lady, I reckon your story, if it tallies with Bonita's an' Padre Marcos's, will clear Gene Stewart in the eyes of the court." Here he grew slower, more biting, sharper and harder of face. "But you needn't expect Pat Hawe or the court to swaller thet part of your story—*about bein' detained unwillin'!*"

Madeline had not time to grasp the sense of his last words. Stewart had convulsively sprung upward, white as chalk. As he leaped at Hawe, Stillwell interposed his huge bulk and wrapped his arms around Stewart. There was a brief, whirling, wrestling struggle. Stewart appeared to be besting the old cattleman.

"Help, boys, help!" yelled Stillwell. "I can't hold him. Hurry, or there's goin' to be blood spilled!"

Nick Steele and several cowboys leaped to Stillwell's assistance. Stewart, getting free, tossed one aside and then another. They closed in on him. For an instant a furious straining wrestle of powerful bodies made rasp and shock and blow. Once Stewart heaved them from him. But they plunged back upon him—conquered him.

"Gene! Why, Gene!" panted the old cattleman. "Sure you're locoed—to act this way. Cool down! Cool down! Why boy, it's all right. Jest stand still—give us a chance to talk to you. It's only ole Bill, you know—your ole pal who's tried to be a daddy to you. He's only wantin' you to hev sense—to be cool—to wait."

"Let me go! Let me go!" cried Stewart; and the poignancy of that cry pierced Madeline's heart. "Let me go, Bill, if you're my friend. I saved your life once—over in the desert. You swore you'd never forget. Boys, make him let me go! Oh, I don't care what Hawe's said or done to me! It was that about *her!* Are you all a lot of Greasers? How can you stand it? Damn you for a lot of cowards! There's a limit, I tell you." Then his voice broke, fell to a whisper. "Bill, dear old Bill, let me go. *I'll kill him! You know I'll kill him!*"

"Gene, I know you'd kill him if you hed an even break,"

..plied Stillwell, soothingly. "But, Gene, why, you ain't even packin' a gun! An' there's Pat lookin' nasty, with his hand nervous-like. He seen you hed no gun. He'd jump at the chance to plug you now, an' then holler about opposition to the law. Cool down, son; it'll all come right."

Suddenly Madeline was transfixed by a terrible sound. Her startled glance shifted from the anxious group round Stewart to see that Monty Price had leaped off the porch. He crouched down with his hands below his hips, where the big guns swung. From his distorted lips issued that sound which was combined roar and bellow and Indian war-whoop, and, more than all, a horrible warning cry. He resembled a hunchback about to make the leap of a demon. He was quivering, vibrating. His eyes, black and hot, were fastened with most piercing intentness upon Hawe and Sneed.

"Git back, Bill, git back!" he roared. "Git 'em back!"

With one lunge Stillwell shoved Stewart and Nick and the other cowboys up on the porch. Then he crowded Madeline and Alfred and Florence to the wall, tried to force them farther. His motions were rapid and stern. But failing to get them through door and windows, he planted his wide person between the women and danger. Madeline grasped his arm, held on, and peered fearfully from behind his broad shoulder.

"You, Hawe! You, Sneed!" called Monty, in that same wild voice. "Don't you move a finger er an eyelash!"

Madeline's faculties nerved to keen, thrilling divination. She grasped the relation between Monty's terrible cry and the strange hunched posture he had assumed. Stillwell's haste and silence, too, were pregnant of catastrophe.

"Nels, git in this!" yelled Monty; and all the time he never shifted his intent gaze as much as a hair's-breadth from Hawe and his deputy. "Nels, chase away them two fellers hangin' back there. Chase 'em quick!"

These men, the two deputies who had remained in the background with the pack-horses, did not wait for Nels. They spurred their mounts, wheeled, and galloped away.

"Now, Nels, cut the gurl loose," ordered Monty.

Nels ran forward, jerked the halter out of Sneed's hand, and pulled Bonita's horse in close to the porch. As he slit the rope which bound her she fell into his arms.

"Hawe, git down!" went on Monty. "Face front an' stiff."

The sheriff swung his leg, and, never moving his hands, with his face now a deathly, sickening white, he slid to the ground.

"Line up there beside your guerrilla pard. There! You two make a damn fine pictoor, a damn fine team of pizened coyote an' a cross between a wild mule an' a Greaser. Now listen!"

Monty made a long pause, in which his breathing was plainly audible.

Madeline's eyes were riveted upon Monty. Her mind, swift as lightning, had gathered the subtleties in action and word succeeding his domination of the men. Violence, terrible violence, the thing she had felt, the thing she had feared, the thing she had sought to eliminate from among her cowboys, was, after many months, about to be enacted before her eyes. It had come at last. She had softened Stillwell, she had influenced Nels, she had changed Stewart; but this little black-faced, terrible Monty Price now rose, as it were, out of his past wild years, and no power on earth or in heaven could stay his hand. It was the hard life of wild men in wild country that was about to strike this blow at her. She did not shudder; she did not wish to blot out from sight this little man, terrible in his mood of wild justice. She suffered a flash of horror that Monty, blind and dead to her authority, cold as steel toward her presence, understood the deeps of a woman's soul. For in this moment of strife, of insult to her, of torture to the man she had uplifted and then broken, the passion of her reached deep toward primitive hate. With eyes slowly hazing red, she watched Monty Price; she listened with thrumming ears; she waited, slowly sagging against Stillwell.

"Hawe, if you an' your dirty pard hev loved the sound of human voice, then listen an' listen hard," said Monty. "Fer I've been goin' contrary to my ole style jest to hev a talk with you. You all but got away on your nerve, didn't you? 'Cause why? You roll in here like a mad steer an' flash your badge an' talk mean, then almost bluff away with it. You heerd all about Miss Hammond's cowboy outfit stoppin' drinkin' and cussin' an' packin' guns. They've took on religion an' decent livin', an' sure they'll be easy to hobble an' drive to jail. Hawe, listen. There was a good an' noble an' be-ootiful woman come out of the East somewhere, an' she brought a lot of sunshine an' happiness an' new idees into the tough lives of cowboys. I reckon it's beyond you to know what she come to mean to

259

them. Wal, I'll tell you. They-all went clean out of their heads. They-all got soft an' easy an' sweet-tempered. They got so they couldn't kill a coyote, a crippled calf in a mud-hole. They took to books, an' writin' home to mother an' sister, an' to savin' money, an' to gittin' married. Onct they was only a lot of poor cowboys, an' then sudden like they was human bein's, livin' in a big world that hed somethin' sweet even fer them. Even fer me—an ole, worn-out, hobble-legged, burned-up cowman like me! Do you git thet? An' you, Mister Hawe, you come along, not satisfied with ropin' an' beatin', an' Gaw knows what else, of thet friendless little Bonita; you come along an' face the lady we fellers honor an' love an' reverence, an' you—you—*Hell's fire!*"

With whistling breath, foaming at the mouth, Monty Price crouched lower, hands at his hips, and he edged inch by inch farther out from the porch, closer to Hawe and Sneed. Madeline saw them only in the blurred fringe of her sight. They resembled specters. She heard the shrill whistle of a horse and recognized Majesty calling her from the corral.

"That's all!" roared Monty, in a voice now strangling. Lower and lower he bent, a terrible figure of ferocity. "Now, both you armed officers of the law, come on! Flash your guns! Throw 'em, an' be quick! Monty Price is done! There'll be daylight through you both before you fan a hammer! But I'm givin' you a chanst to sting me. You holler law, an' my way is the ole law."

His breath came quicker, his voice grew hoarser, and he crouched lower. All his body except his rigid arms quivered with a wonderful muscular convulsion.

"Dogs! Skunks! Buzzards! Flash them guns, er I'll flash mine! *Aha!*"

To Madeline it seemed the three stiff, crouching men leaped into instant and united action. She saw streaks of fire —streaks of smoke. Then a crushing volley deafened her. It ceased as quickly. Smoke veiled the scene. Slowly it drifted away to disclose three fallen men, one of whom, Monty, leaned on his left hand, a smoking gun in his right. Then with a terrible smile, he slid back and stretched out.

21

Unbridled

In waking and sleeping hours Madeline Hammond could not release herself from thralling memory of that tragedy. She was haunted by Monty Price's terrible smile. Only in action of some kind could she escape; and to that end she worked, she walked and rode. She even overcame a strong feeling, which she feared was unreasonable disgust, for the Mexican girl Bonita, who lay ill at the ranch, bruised and feverish, in need of skillful nursing.

Madeline felt there was something inscrutable changing her soul. That strife—the struggle to decide her destiny for East or West—held still further aloof. She was never spiritually alone. There was a step on her trail. Indoors she was oppressed. She required the open—the light and wind, the sight of endless slope, the sounds of corral and pond and field, physical things, natural things.

One afternoon she rode down to the alfalfa fields, round them, and back up to the spillway of the lower lake, where a group of mesquite trees, owing to the water that seeped through the sand to their roots, had taken on bloom and beauty of renewed life. Under these trees there was shade enough to make a pleasant place to linger. Madeline dismounted, desiring to rest a little. She liked this quiet, lonely spot. It was really the only secluded nook near the house. If she rode down into the valley or out to the mesa or up on the foothills she could not go alone. Probably now Stillwell or Nels knew her whereabouts. But as she was comparatively hidden here, she imagined a solitude that was not actually hers.

Her horse, Majesty, tossed his head and flung his mane and switched his tail at the flies. He would rather have been cutting the wind down the valley slope. Madeline sat with her back against a tree, and took off her sombrero. The soft breeze, fanning her face, blowing strands of her hair, was refreshingly cool. She heard the slow tramp of cattle going in to drink. That sound ceased, and the grove of mesquites appeared to be lifeless, except for her and her horse. It was, however, only after moments of attention that she found the place was far from being dead. Keen eyes and ears brought reward. Desert quail, as gray as the bare earth, were dusting themselves in a shady spot. A bee, swift as light, hummed by. She saw a horned toad, the color of stone, squatting low, hiding fearfully in the sand within reach of her whip. She extended the point of the whip, and the toad quivered and swelled and hissed. It was instinct with fight. The wind faintly stirred the thin foliage of the mesquites, making a mournful sigh. From far up in the foothills, barely distinguishable, came the scream of an eagle. The bray of a burro brought a brief, discordant break. Then a brown bird darted down from an unseen perch and made a swift, irregular flight after a fluttering winged insect. Madeline heard the sharp snapping of a merciless beak. Indeed, there was more than life in the shade of the mesquites.

Suddenly Majesty picked up his long ears and snorted. Then Madeline heard a slow pad of hoofs. A horse was approaching from the direction of the lake. Madeline had learned to be wary, and, mounting Majesty, she turned him toward the open. A moment later she felt glad of her caution, for, looking back between the trees, she saw Stewart leading a horse into the grove. She would as lief have met a guerrilla as this cowboy.

Majesty had broken into a trot when a shrill whistle rent the air. The horse leaped and, wheeling so swiftly that he nearly unseated Madeline, he charged back straight for the mesquites. Madeline spoke to him, cried angrily at him, pulled with all her strength upon the bridle, but was helplessly unable to stop him. He whistled a piercing blast. Madeline realized then that Stewart, his old master, had called him and that nothing could turn him. She gave up trying, and attended to the urgent need of intercepting mesquite boughs that Majesty thrashed into motion. The horse thumped into an aisle between the trees and, stopping before Stewart, whinnied eagerly.

Madeline, now knowing what to expect, had not time for

any feeling but amaze. A quick glance showed her Stewart in rough garb, dressed for the trail, and leading a wiry horse, saddled and packed. When Stewart, without looking at her, put his arm around Majesty's neck and laid his face against the flowing mane Madeline's heart suddenly began to beat with unwonted quickness. Stewart seemed oblivious to her presence. His eyes were closed. His dark face softened, lost its hardness and fierceness and sadness, and for an instant became beautiful.

Madeline instantly divined what his action meant. He was leaving the ranch; this was his good-by to his horse. How strange, sad, fine was this love between man and beast! A dimness confused Madeline's eyes; she hurriedly brushed it away, and it came back wet and blurring. She averted her face, ashamed of the tears Stewart might see. She was sorry for him. He was going away, and this time, judging from the nature of his farewell to his horse, it was to be forever. Like a stab from a cold blade a pain shot through Madeline's heart. The wonder of it, the incomprehensibility of it, the utter newness and strangeness of this sharp pain that now left behind a dull pang, made her forget Stewart, her surroundings, everything except to search her heart. Maybe here was the secret that had eluded her. She trembled on the brink of something unknown. In some strange way the emotion brought back her girlhood. Her mind revolved swift queries and replies; she was living, feeling, learning; happiness mocked at her from behind a barred door, and the bar of that door seemed to be an inexplicable pain. Then like lightning strokes shot the questions: Why should pain hide her happiness? What was her happiness? What relation had it to this man? Why should she feel strangely about his departure? And the voices within her were silenced, stunned, unanswered.

"I want to talk to you," said Stewart.

Madeline started, turned to him, and now she saw the earlier Stewart, the man who reminded her of their first meeting at El Cajon, of that memorable meeting at Chiricahua.

"I want to ask you something," he went on. "I've been wanting to know something. That's why I've hung on here. You never spoke to me, never noticed me, never gave me a chance to ask you. But now I'm going over—over the border. And I want to know. Why did you refuse to listen to me?"

At his last words that hot shame, tenfold more stifling than

263

when it had before humiliated Madeline, rushed over her, sending the scarlet in a wave to her temples. It seemed that his words made her realize she was actually face to face with him, that somehow a shame she would rather have died than revealed was being liberated. Biting her lips to hold back speech, she jerked on Majesty's bridle, struck him with her whip, spurred him. Stewart's iron arm held the horse. Then Madeline, in a flash of passion, struck at Stewart's face, missed it, struck again, and hit. With one pull, almost drawing her from the saddle, he tore the whip from her hands. It was not that action on his part, or the sudden strong masterfulness of his look, so much as the livid mark on his face where the whip had lashed that quieted, if did not check, her fury.

"That's nothing," he said, with something of his old audacity. "That's nothing to how you've hurt me."

Madeline battled with herself for control. This man would not be denied. Never before had the hardness of his face, the flinty hardness of these desert-bred men, so struck her with its revelation of the unbridled spirit. He looked stern, haggard, bitter. The dark shade was changing to gray—the gray to ash-color of passion. About him now there was only the ghost of that finer, gentler man she had helped to bring into being. The piercing dark eyes he bent upon her burned her, went through her as if he were looking into her soul. Then Madeline's quick sight caught a fleeting doubt, a wistfulness, a surprised and saddened certainty in his eyes, saw it shade and pass away. Her woman's intuition, as keen as her sight, told her Stewart in that moment had sustained a shock of bitter, final truth.

For the third time he repeated his question to her. Madeline did not answer; she could not speak.

"You don't know I love you, do you?" he continued, passionately. "That ever since you stood before me in that hole at Chiricahua I've loved you? You can't see I've been another man, loving you, working for you, living for you? You won't believe I've turned my back on the old wild life, that I've been decent and honorable and happy and useful—*your kind of a cowboy?* You couldn't tell, though I loved you, that I never wanted you to know it, that I never dared to think of you except as my angel, my holy Virgin? What do you know of a man's heart and soul? How could you tell of the love, the salvation of a man who's lived his life in the silence and loneli-

264

ness? Who could teach you the actual truth—that a wild cowboy, faithless to mother and sister, except in memory, riding a
hard, drunken trail straight to hell, had looked into the face,
the eyes of a beautiful woman infinitely beyond him, above
him, and had so loved her that he was saved—that he became
faithful again—that he saw her face in every flower and her
eyes in the blue heaven? Who could tell you, when at night I
stood alone under these Western stars, how deep in my soul I
was glad just to be alive, to be able to do something for you,
to be near you, to stand between you and worry, trouble,
danger, to feel somehow that I was a part, just a little part of
the West you had come to love?"

Madeline was mute. She heard her heart thundering in her
ears.

Stewart leaped at her. His powerful hand closed on her
arm. She trembled. His action presaged the old instinctive violence.

"No; but you think I kept Bonita up in the mountains, that
I went secretly to meet her, that all the while I served you I
was— Oh, I *know* what you think! I know *now*. I never knew
till I made you look at me. Now, say it! *Speak!*"

White-hot, blinded utterly in the fiery grasp of passion,
powerless to stem the rush of a word both shameful and revealing and fatal, Madeline cried:

"Yes!"

He had wrenched that word from her, but he was not subtle enough, not versed in the mystery of woman's motive
enough, to divine the deep significance of her reply.

For him the word had only literal meaning confirming the
dishonor in which she held him. Dropping her arm, he shrank
back, a strange action for the savage and crude man she
judged him to be.

"But that day at Chiricahua you spoke of faith," he burst
out. "You said the greatest thing in the world was faith in
human nature. You said the finest men had been those who
had fallen low and had risen. You said you had faith in me!
You made me have faith in myself!"

His reproach, without bitterness or scorn, was a lash to her
old egoistic belief in her fairness. She had preached a beautiful principle that she had failed to live up to. She understood
his rebuke, she wondered and wavered, but the affront to her
pride had been too great, the tumult within her breast had

been too startlingly fierce; she could not speak, the moment passed, and with it his brief, rugged splendor of simplicity.

"You think I am vile," he said. "You think that about Bonita! And all the time I've been . . . I could make you ashamed —I could tell you—"

His passionate utterance ceased with a snap of his teeth. His lips set in a thin, bitter line. The agitation of his face preceded a convulsive wrestling of his shoulders. All this swift action denoted an inner combat, and it nearly overwhelmed him.

"No, no!" he panted. Was it his answer to some mighty temptation? Then, like a bent sapling released, he sprang erect. "But I'll be the man—the dog—you think me!"

He laid hold of her arm with rude, powerful clutch. One pull drew her sliding half out of the saddle into his arms. She fell with her breast against his, not wholly free of stirrups or horse. And there she hung, utterly powerless. Maddened, writhing, she tore to release herself. All she could accomplish was to twist herself, raise herself high enough to see his face. That almost paralyzed her. Did he mean to kill her? Then he wrapped his arms around her and crushed her tighter, closer to him. She felt the pound of his heart; her own seemed to have frozen. Then he pressed his burning lips to hers. It was a long terrible kiss. She felt him shake.

"Oh, Stewart! I—implore—you—let—me—go!" she whispered.

His white face loomed over hers. She closed her eyes. He rained kisses upon her face, but no more upon her mouth. On her closed eyes, her hair, her cheeks, her neck he pressed swift lips—lips that lost their fire and grew cold. Then he released her, and lifting and righting her in the saddle, he still held her arm to keep her from falling.

For a moment Madeline sat on her horse with shut eyes. She dreaded the light.

"Now you can't say you've never been kissed," Stewart said. His voice seemed a long way off. "But that was coming to you, so be game. Here!"

She felt something hard and cold and metallic thrust into her hand. He made her fingers close over it, hold it. The feel of the thing revived her. She opened her eyes. Stewart had given her his gun. He stood with his broad breast against her knee, and she looked up to see that old mocking smile on his face.

"Go ahead! Throw my gun on me! Be a thoroughbred!"

Madeline did not yet grasp his meaning.

"You can put me down in that quiet place on the hill—beside Monty Price."

Madeline dropped the gun with a shuddering cry of horror. The sense of his words, the memory of Monty, the certainty that she would kill Stewart if she held the gun an instant longer tortured the self-accusing cry from her.

Stewart stooped to pick up the weapon.

"You might have saved me a hell of a lot of trouble," he said, with another flash of the mocking smile. "You're beautiful and sweet and proud, but you're no thoroughbred! *Majesty Hammond, adios!*"

Stewart leaped for the saddle of his horse, and with the flying mount crashed through the mesquites to disappear.

22

The Secret Told

In the shaded seclusion of her room, buried face down deep among the soft cushions on her couch, Madeline Hammond lay prostrate and quivering under the outrage she had suffered.

The afternoon wore away; twilight fell; night came; and then Madeline rose to sit by the window to let the cool wind blow upon her hot face. She passed through hours of unintelligible shame and impotent rage and futile striving to reason away her defilement.

The train of brightening stars seemed to mock her with their unattainable passionless serenity. She had loved them, and now she imagined she hated them and everything connected with this wild, fateful, and abrupt West.

She would go home.

Edith Wayne had been right; the West was no place for

Madeline Hammond. The decision to go home came easily, naturally, she thought, as the result of events. It caused her no mental strife. Indeed, she fancied she felt relief. The great stars, blinking white and cold over the dark crags, looked down upon her, and, as always, after she had watched them for a while they enthralled her. "Under Western stars," she mused, thinking a little scornfully of the romantic destiny they had blazed for her idle sentiment. But they were beautiful; they were speaking; they were mocking; they drew her. "Ah!" she sighed. "It will not be so very easy to leave them, after all."

Madeline closed and darkened the window. She struck a light. It was necessary to tell the anxious servants who knocked that she was well and required nothing. A soft step on the walk outside arrested her. Who was there—Nels or Nick Steele or Stillwell? Who shared the guardianship over her, now that Monty Price was dead and that other—that savage—? It was monstrous and unfathomable that she regretted him.

The light annoyed her. Complete darkness fitted her strange mood. She retired and tried to compose herself to sleep. Sleep for her was not a matter of will. Her cheeks burned so hotly that she rose to bathe them. Cold water would not alleviate this burn, and then, despairing of forgetfulness, she lay down again with a shameful gratitude for the cloak of night. Stewart's kisses were there, scorching her lips, her closed eyes, her swelling neck. They penetrated deeper and deeper into her blood, into her heart, into her soul—the terrible farewell kisses of a passionate, hardened man. Despite his baseness, he had loved her.

Late in the night Madeline fell asleep. In the morning she was pale and languid, but in a mental condition that promised composure.

It was considerably after her regular hour that Madeline repaired to her office. The door was open, and just outside, tipped back in a chair, sat Stillwell.

"Mawnin', Miss Majesty," he said, as he rose to greet her with his usual courtesy. There were signs of trouble in his lined face. Madeline shrank inwardly, fearing his old lamentations about Stewart. Then she saw a dusty, ragged pony in the yard and a little burro drooping under a heavy pack. Both animals bore evidence of long, arduous travel.

"To whom do they belong?" asked Madeline.

"Them critters? Why, Danny Mains," replied Stillwell, with a cough that betrayed embarrassment.

"Danny Mains?" echoed Madeline, wonderingly.

"Wal, I said so."

Stillwell was indeed not himself.

"Is Danny Mains here?" she asked, in sudden curiosity.

The old cattleman nodded gloomily.

"Yep, he's hyar, all right. Sloped in from the hills, an' he hollered to see Bonita. He's locoed, too, about that little blackeyed hussy. Why, he hardly said, 'Howdy, Bill,' before he begun to ask wild an' eager questions. I took him in to see Bonita. He's been there more'n a half-hour now."

Evidently Stillwell's sensitive feelings had been ruffled. Madeline's curiosity changed to blank astonishment, which left her with a thrilling premonition. She caught her breath. A thousand thoughts seemed thronging for clear conception in her mind.

Rapid footsteps with an accompaniment of clinking spurs sounded in the hallway. Then a young man ran out upon the porch. He resembled a cowboy in his lithe build, his garb and action, in the way he wore his gun, but his face, instead of being red, was clear brown tan. His eyes were blue, his hair was light and curly. He was a handsome, frank-faced boy. At sight of Madeline he slammed down his sombrero and, leaping at her, he possessed himself of her hands. His swift violence not only alarmed her, but painfully reminded her of something she wished to forget.

This cowboy bent his head and kissed her hands and wrung them, and when he straightened up he was crying.

"Miss Hammond, she's safe an' almost well, an' what I feared most ain't so, thank God," he cried. "Sure I'll never be able to pay you for all you've done for her. She's told me how she was dragged down here, how Gene tried to save her, how you spoke up for Gene an' her, too, how Monty at the last throwed his guns. Poor Monty! We were good friends, Monty an' I. But it wasn't friendship for me that made Monty stand in there. He would have saved her, anyway. Monty Price was the whitest man I ever knew. There's Nels an' Nick an' Gene, he's been some friend to me; but Monty Price was—he was grand. He never knew, any more than you or Bill, here, or the boys, what Bonita was to me."

Stillwell's kind and heavy hand fell upon the cowboy's shoulder.

"Danny, what's all this queer gab?" he asked. "An' you're takin' some liberty with Miss Hammond, who never seen you before. Sure I'm makin' allowance fer amazin' strange talk. I see you're not drinkin'. Mebbe you're plumb locoed. Come, ease up now an' talk sense."

The cowboy's fine, frank face broke into a smile. He dashed the tears from his eyes. Then he laughed. His laugh had a pleasant, boyish ring—a happy ring.

"Bill, old pal, stand bridle down a minute, will you?" Then he bowed to Madeline. "I beg your pardon, Miss Hammond, for seemin' rudeness. I'm Danny Mains. An' Bonita is my wife. I'm so crazy glad she's safe an' unharmed—so grateful to you that—why, sure it's a wonder I didn't kiss you outright."

"Bonita's your wife!" ejaculated Stillwell.

"Sure. We've been married for months," replied Danny, happily. "Gene Stewart did it. Good old Gene, he's hell on marryin'. I guess maybe I haven't come to pay him up for all he's done for me! You see, I've been in love with Bonita for two years. An' Gene—you know, Bill, what a way Gene has with girls—he was—well, he was tryin' to get Bonita to have me."

Madeline's quick, varying emotions were swallowed up in a boundless gladness. Something dark, deep, heavy, and somber was flooded from her heart. She had a sudden rich sense of gratitude toward this smiling, clean-faced cowboy whose blue eyes flashed through tears.

"Danny Mains!" she said, tremulously and smilingly. "If you are as glad as your news has made me—if you really think I merit such a reward—you *may* kiss me outright."

With a bashful wonder, but with right hearty will, Danny Mains availed himself of this gracious privilege.

Stillwell snorted. The signs of his phenomenal smile were manifest, otherwise Madeline would have thought that snort an indication of furious disapproval.

"Bill, straddle a chair," said Danny. "You've gone back a heap these last few months, frettin' over your bad boys, Danny an' Gene. You'll need support under you while I'm throwin' my yarn. Story of my life, Bill." He placed a chair for Madeline. "Miss Hammond, beggin' your pardon again, I want you to listen, also. You've the face an' eyes of a woman who loves to hear of other people's happiness. Besides, somehow, it's easy for me to talk lookin' at you."

His manner subtly changed then. Possibly it took on a little swagger; certainly he lost the dignity that he had shown under stress of feeling; he was now more like a cowboy about to boast or effect some stunning maneuver. Walking off the porch, he stood before the weary horse and burro.

"Played out!" he exclaimed.

Then with the swift violence so characteristic of men of his class he slipped the pack from the burrow and threw saddle and bridle from the horse.

"There! See 'em! Take a look at the last doggone weight you ever packed! You've been some faithful to Danny Mains. An' Danny Mains pays! Never a saddle again or a strap or a halter or a hobble so long as you live! So long as you live nothin' but grass an' clover, an' cool water in shady places, an' dusty swales to roll in an' rest an' sleep!"

Then he untied the pack and, taking a small, heavy sack from it came back upon the porch. Deliberately he dumped the contents of the sack at Stillwell's feet. Piece after piece of rock thumped upon the floor. The pieces were sharp, ragged, evidently broken from a ledge; the body of them was white in color, with yellow veins and bars and streaks. Stillwell grasped up one rock after another, stared and stuttered, put the rocks to his lips, dug into them with his shaking fingers; then he lay back in his chair, head against the wall, and as he gaped at Danny the old smile began to transform his face.

"Lord, Danny, if you hevn't been an' gone an' struck it rich!"

Danny regarded Stillwell with lofty condescension.

"Some rich," he said. "Now, Bill, what've we got here, say, offhand?"

"Oh, Lord, Danny! I'm afraid to say. Look, Miss Majesty, jest look at the gold. I've lived among prospectors an' goldmines fer thirty years, an' I never seen the beat of this."

"The Lost Mine of the Padres!" cried Danny, in stentorian voice. *"An' it belongs to me!"*

Stillwell made some incoherent sound as he sat up fascinated, quite beside himself.

"Bill, it was some long time ago since you saw me," said Danny. "Fact is, I know how you felt, because Gene kept me posted. I happened to run across Bonita, an' I wasn't goin' to let her ride away alone, when she told me she was in trouble. We hit the trail for the Peloncillos. Bonita had Gene's horse, an' she was to meet him up on the trail. We got to the mountains all right, an' nearly starved for a few days till Gene found us. He had got in trouble himself an' couldn't fetch much with him.

"We made for the crags an' built a cabin. I come down that day Gene sent his horse Majesty to you. Never saw Gene so broken-hearted. Well, after he sloped for the border Bonita an' I were hard put to it to keep alive. But we got along, an' I think it was then she began to care a little for me. Because I was decent. I killed cougars an' went down to Rodeo to get bounties for the skins, an' bought grub an' supplies I needed. Once I went to El Cajon an' run plumb into Gene. He was back from the revolution an' cuttin' up some. But I got away from him after doin' all I could to drag him out of town. A long time after that Gene trailed up to the crags an' found us. Gene had stopped drinkin', he'd changed wonderful, was fine an' dandy. It was then he began to pester the life out of me to make me marry Bonita. I was happy, so was she, an' I was some scared of spoilin' it. Bonita had been a little flirt, an' I was afraid she'd get shy of a halter, so I bucked against Gene. But I was all locoed, as it turned out. Gene would come up occasionally, packin' supplies for us an' always he'd get after me to do the right thing by Bonita. Gene's so dog-gone hard to buck against! I had to give in, an' I asked Bonita to marry me. Well, she wouldn't at first—said she wasn't good enough for me. But I saw the marriage idea was workin' deep, an' I just kept on bein' as decent as I knew how. So it was my wantin' to marry Bonita—my bein' glad to marry her—that made her grow soft an' sweet an' pretty as—as a mountain quail. Gene fetched up Padre Marcos, an' he married us."

Danny paused in his narrative, breathing hard, as if the memory of the incident described had stirred strong and thrilling feeling in him. Stillwell's smile was rapturous. Madeline leaned toward Danny with her eyes shining.

"Miss Hammond, an' you, Bill Stillwell, now listen, for this is strange I've got to tell you. The afternoon Bonita an' I were married, when Gene an' the padre had gone, I was happy one minute an' low-hearted the next. I was miserable because I had a bad name. I couldn't buy even a decent dress for my

272

pretty wife. Bonita heard me an' she was some mysterious. She told me the story of the lost mine of the padres, an' she kissed me an' made joyful over me in the strangest way. I knew marriage went to women's heads, an' I thought even Bonita had a spell.

"Well, she left me for a little, an' when she came back she wore some pretty yellow flowers in her hair. Her eyes were big an' black an' beautiful. She said some queer things about spirits rollin' rocks down the cañon. Then she said she wanted to show me where she always sat an' waited an' watched for me when I was away. She led me around under the crags to a long slope. It was some pretty there—clear an' open, with a long sweep, an' the desert yawnin' deep an' red. There were yellow flowers on that slope, the same kind she had in her hair—*the same kind that Apache girl wore hundreds of years ago when she led the padre to the gold-mine.*

"When I thought of that, an' saw Bonita's eyes, an' then heard the strange crack of rollin' rocks—heard them rattle down an' roll an' grow faint—I was some out of my head. But not for long. Them rocks were rollin' all right, only it was the weatherin' of the cliffs.

"An' there under the crags was a gold pocket.

"Then I was worse than locoed. I went gold-crazy. I worked like seventeen burros. Bill, I dug a lot of gold-bearin' quartz. Bonita watched the trails for me, brought me water. That was how she come to get caught by Pat Hawe an' his guerrillas. Sure! Pat Hawe was so set on doin' Gene dirt that he mixed up with Don Carlos. Bonita will tell you some staggerin' news about that outfit. Just now my story is all gold."

Danny Mains got up and kicked back his chair. Blue lightning gleamed from his eyes as he thrust a hand toward Stillwell.

"Bill, old pal, put her there—give me your hand," he said. "You were always my friend. You had faith in me. Well, Danny Mains owes you, an' he owes Gene Stewart a good deal, an' Danny Mains pays. I want two pardners to help me work my gold-mine. You an' Gene. If there's any ranch hereabouts that takes your fancy I'll buy it. If Miss Hammond ever gets tired of her range an' stock an' home I'll buy them for Gene. If there's any railroad or town round here that she likes I'll buy it. If I see anythin' myself that I like I'll buy it. Go out; find Gene for me. I'm achin' to see him, to tell him.

273

Go fetch him; an' right here in this house, with my wife an' Miss Hammond as witnesses, we'll draw up a pardnership. Go find him, Bill. I want to show him this gold, show him how Danny Mains pays! An' the only bitter drop in my cup today is that I can't ever pay Monty Price."

Madeline's lips tremblingly formed to tell Danny Mains and Stillwell that the cowboy they wanted so much had left the ranch; but the flame of fine loyalty that burned in Danny's eyes, the happiness that made the old cattleman's face at once amazing and beautiful, stiffened her lips. She watched the huge Stillwell and the little cowboy, both talking wildly, as they walked off arm in arm to find Stewart. She imagined something of what Danny's disappointment would be, of the elder man's consternation and grief, when he learned Stewart had left for the border. At this juncture she looked up to see a strange, yet familiar figure approaching. Padre Marcos! Certain it was that Madeline felt herself trembling. What did his presence mean on this day? He had always avoided meeting her whenever possible. He had been exceedingly grateful for all she had done for his people, his church, and himself; but he had never thanked her in person. Perhaps he had come for that purpose now. But Madeline did not believe so.

Mention of Padre Marcos, sight of him, had always occasioned Madeline a little indefinable shock; and now as he stepped to the porch, a shrunken, stooped, and sad-faced man, she was startled.

The padre bowed low to her.

"Señora, will you grant me audience?" he asked, in perfect English, and his voice was low-toned and grave.

"Certainly, Padre Marcos," replied Madeline; and she led him into her office.

"May I beg to close the door?" he asked. "It is a matter of great moment, which you might not care to have any one hear."

Wonderingly Madeline inclined her head. The padre gently closed one door and then the others.

"Señora, I have come to disclose a secret—my own sinfulness in keeping it—and to implore your pardon. Do you remember that night Señor Stewart dragged me before you in the waiting-room at El Cajon?"

"Yes," replied Madeline.

"Señora, since that night you have been Señor Stewart's wife!"

Madeline became as motionless as stone. She seemed to feel nothing, only to hear.

"You are Señor Stewart's wife. I have kept the secret under fear of death. But I could keep it no longer. Señor Stewart may kill me now. Ah, Señora, it is very strange to you. You were so frightened that night, you knew not what happened. Señor Stewart threatened me. He forced you. He made me speak the service. He made you speak the Spanish yes. And I, Señora, knowing the deeds of these sinful cowboys, fearing worse than disgrace to one so beautiful and so good as you, I could not do less than marry you truly. At least you should be his wife. So I married you, truly, in the service of my church."

"My God!" cried Madeline, rising.

"Hear me! I implore you, Señora, hear me out! Do not leave me! Do not look so—so— Ah, Señora, let me speak a word for Señor Stewart. He was drunk that night. He did not know what he was about. In the morning he came to me, made me swear by my cross that I would not reveal the disgrace he had put upon you. If I did he would kill me. Life is nothing to the American *vaquero*, Señora. I promised to respect his command. But I did not tell him you were his wife. He did not dream I had truly married you. He went to fight for the freedom of my country—Señora, he is one splendid soldier—and I brooded over the sin of my secret. If he were killed I need never tell you. But if he lived I knew that I must some day.

"Strange indeed that Señor Stewart and Padre Marcos should both come to this ranch together. The great change your goodness wrought in my beloved people was no greater than the change in Señor Stewart. Señora, I feared you would go away one day, go back to your Eastern home, ignorant of the truth. The time came when I confessed to Stewart—said I must tell you. Señora, the man went mad with joy. I have never seen so supreme a joy. He threatened no more to kill me! That strong, cruel *vaquero* begged me not to tell the secret—never to reveal it. He confessed his love for you—a love something like the desert storm. He swore by all that was once sacred to him, and by my cross and my church, that he would be a good man, that he would be worthy to have you

275

secretly his wife for the little time life left him to worship at your shrine. You needed never to know. So I held my tongue, half pitying him, half fearing him, and praying for some God-sent light.

"Señora, it was a fool's paradise that Stewart lived in. I saw him often. When he took me up into the mountains to have me marry that wayward Bonita and her lover I came to have respect for a man whose ideas about nature and life and God were at a variance with mine. But the man is a worshiper of God in all material things. He is a part of the wind and sun and desert and mountain that have made him. I have never heard more beautiful words than those in which he persuaded Bonita to accept Señor Mains, to forget her old lovers, and henceforth to be happy. He is their friend. I wish I could tell you what that means. It sounds so simple. It *is* really simple. All great things are so. For Señor Stewart it was natural to be loyal to his friend, to have a fine sense of the honor due to a woman who had loved and given, to bring about their marriage, to succor them in their need and loneliness. It was natural for him never to speak of them. It would have been natural for him to give his life in their defense if peril menaced them. Señora, I want you to understand that to me the man has the same stability, the same strength, the same elements which I am in the habit of attributing to the physical life around me in this wild and rugged desert."

Madeline listened as one under a spell. It was only that this soft-voiced, eloquent priest knew how to move the heart, stir the soul; but his defense, his praise of Stewart, if they had been couched in the crude speech of cowboys, would have been a glory to her.

"Señora, I pray you, do not misunderstand my mission. Beyond my confession to you I have only a duty to tell you of the man whose wife you are. But I am a priest and I can read the soul. The ways of God are inscrutable. I am only a humble instrument. You are a noble woman, and Señor Stewart is a man of desert iron forged anew in the crucible of love. *Quien sabe?* Señor Stewart swore he would kill me if I betrayed him. But he will not lift his hand against me. For the man bears you a very great and pure love, and it has changed him. I no longer fear his threat, but I do fear his anger, should he ever know I spoke of his love, of his fool's paradise. I have watched his dark face turned to the sun setting over the desert. I have watched him lift it to the light of the stars. Think, my gracious and noble lady, think what *is* his paradise? To love you above the spirit of the flesh; to know you are his wife, his, never to be another's except by *his* sacrifice; to watch you with a secret glory of joy and pride; to stand, while he might, between you and evil; to find his happiness in service; to wait, with never a dream of telling you, for the hour to come when to leave you free he must go out and get himself shot! Señora, that is beautiful, it is sublime, it is terrible. It has brought me to you with my confession. I repeat, Señora, the ways of God are inscrutable. What is the meaning of your influence upon Señor Stewart? Once he was merely an animal, brutal, unquickened; now he is a man— I have not seen his like! So I beseech you in my humble office as priest, as a lover of mankind, before you send Stewart to his death, to be sure there is here no mysterious dispensation of God. Love, that mighty and blessed and unknown thing, might be at work. Señora, I have heard that somewhere in the rich Eastern cities you are a very great lady. I know you are good and noble. That is all I want to know. To me you are only a woman, the same as Señor Stewart is only a man. So I pray you, Señora, before you let Stewart give you freedom at such cost be sure you do not want his love, lest you cast away something sweet and ennobling which you yourself have created."

23

The Light of Western Stars

Blinded, like a wild creature, Madeline Hammond ran to her room. She felt as if a stroke of lightning had shattered the shadowy substance of the dream she had made of real life. The wonder of Danny Mains's story, the strange regret with which she had realized her injustice to Stewart, the astounding secret as revealed by Padre Marcos—these were forgotten in the sudden consciousness of her own love.

277

Madeline fled as if pursued. With trembling hands she locked the doors, drew the blinds of the windows that opened on the porch, pushed chairs aside so that she could pace the length of her room. She was now alone, and she walked with soft, hurried, uneven steps. She could be herself here; she needed no mask; the long habit of serenely hiding the truth from the world and from herself could be broken. The seclusion of her darkened chamber made possible that betrayal of herself to which she was impelled.

She paused in her swift pacing to and fro. She liberated the thought that knocked at the gates of her mind. With quivering lips she whispered it. Then she spoke aloud:

"I will say it—hear it. I—I love him!"

"I love him!" She repeated the astounding truth, but she doubted her identity.

"Am I still Madeline Hammond? What has happened. Who am I?" She stood where the light from one unclosed window fell upon her image in the mirror. "Who is this woman?"

She expected to see a familiar, dignified person, a quiet, unruffled figure, a tranquil face with dark, proud eyes and calm, proud lips. No, she did not see Madeline Hammond. She did not see any one she knew. Were her eyes, like her heart, playing her false? The figure before her was instinct with pulsating life. The hands she saw, clasped together, pressed deep into a swelling bosom that heaved with each panting breath. The face she saw—white, rapt, strangely glowing, with parted, quivering lips, with great, staring tragic eyes—this could not be Madeline Hammond's face.

Yet as she looked she knew no fancy could really deceive her, that she was only Madeline Hammond come at last to the end of brooding dreams. She swiftly realized the change in her, divined its cause and meaning, accepted it as inevitable, and straightway fell back again into the mood of bewildering amaze.

Calmness was unattainable. The surprise absorbed her. She could not go back to count the innumerable, imperceptible steps of her undoing. Her old power of reflecting, analyzing, even thinking at all, seemed to have vanished in a pulse-stirring sense of one new emotion. She only felt all her instinctive outward action that was a physical relief, all her involuntary inner strife that was maddening, yet unutterably

278

sweet; and they seemed to be just one bewildering effect of surprise.

In a nature like hers, where strength of feeling had long been inhibited as a matter of training, such a transforming surprise as sudden consciousness of passionate love required time for its awakening, time for its sway.

By and by that last enlightening movement came, and Madeline Hammond faced not only the love in her heart, but the thought of the man she loved.

Suddenly, as she raged, something in her—this dauntless new personality—took arms against indictment of Gene Stewart. Her mind whirled about him and his life. She saw him drunk, brutal; she saw him abandoned, lost. Then out of the picture she had of him thus slowly grew one of a different man—weak, sick, changed by shock, growing strong, strangely, spiritually altered, silent, lonely like an eagle, secretive, tireless, faithful, soft as a woman, hard as iron to endure, and at the last noble.

She softened. In a flash her complex mood changed to one wherein she thought of the truth, the beauty, the wonder of Stewart's uplifting. Humbly she trusted that she had helped him to climb. That influence had been the best she had ever exerted. It had wrought magic in her own character. By it she had reached some higher, nobler plane of trust in man. She had received infinitely more than she had given.

Her swiftly flying memory seemed to assort a vast mine of treasures of the past. Of that letter Stewart had written to her brother she saw vivid words. But ah! she had known, and if it had not made any difference then, now it made all in the world. She recalled how her loosened hair had blown across his lips that night he had ridden down from the mountains carrying her in his arms. She recalled the strange joy of pride in Stewart's eyes when he had suddenly come upon her dressed to receive her Eastern guests in the white gown with the red roses at her breast.

Swiftly as they had come these dreamful memories departed. There was to be no rest for her mind. All she had thought and felt seemed only to presage a tumult.

Heedless, desperate, she cast off the remnant of self-control, turned from the old proud, pale, cold, self-contained ghost of herself to face this strange, strong, passionate woman. Then, with hands pressed to her beating heart, with eyes shut, she listened to the ringing trip-hammer voice of circumstance, of truth, of fatality. The whole story was revealed, simple enough in the sum of its complicated details, strange and beautiful in part, remorseless in its proof of great love on Stewart's side, in dreaming blindness on her own, and from the first fatal moment to the last, prophetic of tragedy.

Madeline, like a prisoner in a cell, began to pace to and fro.

"Oh, it is all terrible!" she cried. "I am his wife. His wife! That meeting with him—the marriage—then his fall, his love, his rise, his silence, his pride! And I can never be anything to him. Could I be anything to him? I, Madeline Hammond? But I am his wife, and I love him! His wife! I am the wife of a cowboy! That might be undone. Can my love be undone? Ah, do I want anything undone? He is gone. *Gone!* Could he have meant—I will not, dare not think of that. He will come back. No, he never will come back. Oh, what shall I do?"

For Madeline Hammond the days following that storm of feeling were leaden-footed, endless, hopeless—a long succession of weary hours, sleepless hours, passionate hours, all haunted by a fear slowly growing into torture, a fear that Stewart had crossed the border to invite the bullet which would give her freedom. The day came when she knew this to be true. The spiritual tidings reached her, not subtly as so many divinations had come, but in a clear, vital flash of certainty. Then she suffered. She burned inwardly, and the nature of that deep fire showed through her eyes. She kept to herself, waiting, waiting for her fears to be confirmed.

At times she broke out in wrath at the circumstances she had failed to control, at herself, at Stewart.

"He might have learned from Ambrose!" she exclaimed, sick with a bitterness she knew was not consistent with her pride. She recalled Christine's trenchant exposition of Ambrose's wooing: "He tell me he love me; he kees me; he hug me; he put me on his horse; he ride away with me; he marry me."

Then in the next breath Madeline denied this insistent clamoring of a love that was gradually breaking her spirit. Like a somber shadow remorse followed her, shading blacker. She had been blind to a man's honesty, manliness, uprightness, faith, and striving. She had been dead to love, to nobility that she had herself created. Padre Marcos's grave, wise words returned to haunt her. She fought her bitterness, scorned her intelligence, hated her pride, and weakening, gave up more and more to a yearning, hopeless hope.

She had shunned the light of the stars as she had violently dismissed every hinting suggestive memory of Stewart's kisses. But one night she went deliberately to her window. There they shone. Her stars! Beautiful, passionless as always, but strangely closer, warmer, speaking a kinder language, helpful as they had never been, teaching her now that regret was futile, revealing to her in their one grand, blazing task the supreme duty of life—to be true.

Those shining stars made her yield. She whispered to them that they had claimed her—the West claimed her—Stewart claimed her forever, whether he lived or died. She gave up to her love. And it was as if he was there in person, dark-faced, fire-eyed, violent in his action, crushing her to his breast in that farewell moment, kissing her with one burning kiss of passion, then with cold, terrible lips of renunciation.

"I am your wife!" she whispered to him. In that moment, throbbing, exalted, quivering in her first sweet, tumultuous surrender to love, she would have given her all, her life, to be in his arms again, to meet his lips, to put forever out of his power any thought of wild sacrifice.

And on the morning of the next day, when Madeline went out upon the porch, Stillwell, haggard and stern, with a husky, incoherent word, handed her a message from El Cajon. She read:

El Capitan Stewart captured by rebel soldiers in fight at Agua Prieta yesterday. He was a sharpshooter in the Federal ranks. Sentenced to death Thursday at sunset.

24

The Ride

"STILLWELL!"

Madeline's cry was more than the utterance of a breaking heart. It was full of agony. But also it uttered the shattering of a structure built of false pride, of old beliefs, of bloodless standards, of ignorance of self. It betrayed the final conquest of her doubts, and out of their darkness blazed the unquenchable spirit of a woman who had found herself, her love, her salvation, her duty to a man, and who would not be cheated.

The old cattleman stood mute before her, staring at her white face, at her eyes of flame.

"Stillwell! I am Stewart's wife!"

"My Gawd, Miss Majesty!" he burst out. "I knowed somethin' turrible was wrong. Aw, sure it's a pity—"

"Do you think I'll let him be shot when I know him now, when I'm no longer blind, when I love him?" she asked, with passionate swiftness. "I will save him. This is Wednesday morning. I have thirty-six hours to save his life. Stillwell, send for Link and the car!"

She went into her office. Her mind worked with extraordinary rapidity and clearness. Her plan, born in one lightning-like flash of thought, necessitated the careful wording of telegrams to Washington, to New York, to San Antonio. These were to Senators, Representatives, men high in public and private life, men who would remember her and who would serve her to their utmost. Never before had her position meant anything to her comparable with what it meant now. Never in all her life had money seemed the power that it was then. If she had been poor! A shuddering chill froze the thought at its inception. She dispelled heartbreaking thoughts. She had power. She had wealth. She would set into operation all the unlimited means these gave her—the wires and pulleys and strings underneath the surface of political and international life, the open, free, purchasing value of money or the deep, underground, mysterious, incalculably powerful influence moved by gold. She could save Stewart. She must await results—deadlocked in feeling, strained perhaps almost beyond endurance, because the suspense would be great; but she would allow no possibility of failure to enter her mind.

When she went outside the car was there with Link, helmet in hand, a cool, bright gleam in his eyes, and with Stillwell, losing his haggard misery, beginning to respond to Madeline's spirit.

"Link, drive Stillwell to El Cajon in time for him to catch the El Paso train," she said. "Wait there for his return, and if any message comes from him, telephone it at once to me."

Then she gave Stillwell the telegrams to send from El Cajon and drafts to cash in El Paso. She instructed him to go before the rebel junta, then stationed at Juarez, to explain the situation, to bid them expect communications from Washington officials requesting and advising Stewart's exchange as a prisoner of war, to offer to buy his release from the rebel authorities.

When Stillwell had heard her through his huge, bowed form straightened, a ghost of his old smile just moved his lips. He was no longer young, and hope could not at once drive away stern and grim realities. As he bent over her hand his manner appeared courtly and reverent. But either he was speechless or felt the moment not one for him to break silence.

He climbed to a seat beside Link, who pocketed the watch he had been studying and leaned over the wheel. There was a crack, a muffled sound bursting into a roar, and the big car jerked forward to bound over the edge of the slope, to leap down the long incline, to shoot out upon the level valley floor and disappear in moving dust.

For the first time in days Madeline visited the gardens, the corrals, the lakes, the quarters of the cowboys. Though imagining she was calm, she feared she looked strange to Nels, to Nick, to Frankie Slade, to those boys best known to her. The situation for them must have been one of tormenting pain and bewilderment. They acted as if they wanted to say something to her, but found themselves spellbound. She wondered—did they know she was Stewart's wife? Stillwell had not had time to tell them; besides he would not have mentioned the fact. These cowboys only knew that Stewart was sentenced to be shot; they knew if Madeline had not been angry with him he would not have gone in desperate fighting mood across the border. She spoke of the weather, of the horses and cattle, asked Nels when he was to go on duty, and turned away from the wide, sunlit, adobe-arched porch where the cowboys stood silent and bareheaded. Then one of her subtle impulses checked her.

"Nels, you and Nick need not go on duty today," she said "I may want you. I—I—"

She hesitated, paused, and stood lingering there. Her glance had fallen upon Stewart's big black horse prancing in a nearby corral.

"I have sent Stillwell to El Paso," she went on, in a low voice she failed to hold steady. "He will save Stewart. I have to tell you—I am Stewart's wife!"

She felt the stricken amaze that made these men silent and immovable. With level gaze averted she left them. Returning to the house and her room, she prepared for something—for what? To wait!

Then a great invisible shadow seemed to hover behind her. She essayed many tasks, to fail of attention, to find that her mind held only Stewart and his fortunes. Why had he become a Federal? She reflected that he had won his title, El Capitan, fighting for Madero, the rebel. But Madero was now a Federal, and Stewart was true to him. In crossing the border had Stewart any other motive than the one he had implied to Madeline in his mocking smile and scornful words, "You might have saved me a hell of a lot of trouble!" What trouble? She felt again the cold shock of contact with the gun she had dropped in horror. He meant the trouble of getting himself shot in the only way a man could seek death without cowardice. But had he any other motive? She recalled Don Carlos and his guerrillas. Then the thought leaped up in her mind with gripping power that Stewart meant to hunt Don Carlos, to meet him, to kill him. It would be the deed of a silent, vengeful, implacable man driven by wild justice such as had been the deadly leaven in Monty Price. It was a deed to expect of Nels or Nick Steel—and, aye, of Gene Stewart. Madeline felt regret that Stewart, as he had climbed so high, had not risen above deliberate seeking to kill his enemy, however evil that enemy.

The local newspapers, which came regularly a day late from El Paso and Douglas, had never won any particular interest from Madeline; now, however, she took up any copies she could find and read all the information pertaining to the revolution. Every word seemed vital to her, of moving significant force.

AMERICANS ROBBED BY MEXICAN REBELS

MADERA, STATE OF CHIHUAHUA, MEXICO, July 17 Having looted the Madera Lumber Company's storehouses of $25,000 worth of goods and robbed scores of foreigners of horses and saddles, the rebel command of Gen. Antonio Rojas, comprising a thousand men, started westward today through the state of Sonora for Aguaymas and Pacific coast points.

The troops are headed for Dolores, where a mountain pass leads into the state of Sonora. Their entrance will be opposed by 1,000 Maderista volunteers, who are reported to be waiting the rebel invasion.

The railroad south of Madera is being destroyed and many Americans who were traveling to Chihuahua from Juarez are marooned here.

General Rojas executed five men while here for alleged offenses of a trivial character. Gen. Rosalio y Hernandez, Lieut. Cipriano Amador, and three soldiers were the unfortunates.

WASHINGTON, July 17 Somewhere in Mexico Patrick Dunne, an American citizen, is in prison under sentence of death. This much and no more the State Department learned through Representative Kinkaid of Nebraska. Consular officers in various sections of Mexico have been directed to make every effort to locate Dunne and save his life.

JUAREZ, MEXICO, July 31 General Orozco, chief of the rebels, declared today: "If the United States will throw down the barriers and let us have all the ammunition we can buy, I promise in sixty days to have peace restored in Mexico and a stable government in charge."

CASAS GRANDES, CHIHUAHUA, July 31 Rebel soldiers looted many homes of Mormons near here yesterday. All the Mormon families have fled to El Paso. Although General Salazar had two of his soldiers executed yesterday for robbing Mormons, he has not made any attempt to stop his men looting the unprotected homes of Americans.

Last night's and today's trains carried many Americans from Pearson, Madera, and other localities outside the Mormon settlements. Refugees from Mexico continued to pour into El Paso. About one hundred came last night, the majority of whom were men. Heretofore few men came.

Madeline read on in feverish absorption. It was not a real war, but a starving, robbing, burning, hopeless revolution. Five men executed for alleged offenses of a trivial nature! What chance had, then, a Federal prisoner, an enemy to be feared, an American cowboy in the clutches of those crazed rebels?

Madeline endured patiently, endured for long interminable hours while holding to her hope with indomitable will.

No message came. At sunset she went outdoors, suffering a torment of accumulating suspense. She faced the desert, hoping, praying for strength. The desert did not influence her as did the passionless, unchangeable stars that had soothed her spirit. It was red, mutable, shrouded in shadows, terrible like her mood. A dust-veiled sunset colored the vast, brooding, naked waste of rock and sand. The grim Chiricahua frowned black and sinister. The dim blue domes of the Guadalupes seemed to whisper, to beckon to her. Beyond them somewhere was Stewart, awaiting the end of a few brief hours— hours that to her were boundless, endless, insupportable.

Night fell. But now the white, pitiless stars failed her. Then she sought the seclusion and darkness of her room, there to lie with wide eyes, waiting, waiting. She had always been susceptible to the somber, mystic unrealities of the night, and now her mind slowly revolved round a vague and monstrous gloom. Nevertheless, she was acutely sensitive to outside impressions. She heard the measured tread of a guard, the rustle of wind stirring the window curtain, the remote, mournful wail of a coyote. By and by the dead silence of the night insulated her with leaden oppression. There was silent darkness for so long that when the window casements showed gray she believed it was only fancy and that dawn would never come. She prayed for the sun not to rise, not to begin its short twelve-hour journey toward what might be a fatal setting for Stewart. But the dawn did lighten, swiftly, she thought, remorselessly. Daylight had broken, and this was Thursday!

Sharp ringing of the telephone bell startled her, roused her into action. She ran to answer the call.

"Hello—hello—Miss Majesty!" came the hurried reply. "This's Link talkin'. Messages for you. Favorable, the operator said. I'm to ride out with them. I'll come a-hummin'."

That was all. Madeline heard the bang of the receiver as Stevens threw it down. She passionately wanted to know more, but was immeasurably grateful for so much! Favorable! Then Stillwell had been successful. Her heart leaped. Suddenly she became weak and her hands failed of their accustomed morning deftness. It took her what seemed a thousand years to dress. Breakfast meant nothing to her except that it helped her to pass dragging minutes.

Finally a low hum, mounting swiftly to a roar and ending with a sharp report, announced the arrival of the car. If her feet had kept pace with her heart she would have raced out to meet Link. She saw him, helmet thrown back, watch in hand, and he looked up at her with his cool, bright smile, with his familiar apologetic manner.

"Fifty-three minutes, Miss Majesty," he said, "but I hed to ride round a herd of steers an' bump a couple off the trail."

He gave her a packet of telegrams. Madeline tore them open with shaking fingers, began to read with swift, dim eyes. Some were from Washington, assuring her of every possible service; some were from New York; others written in Spanish were from El Paso, and these she could not wholly translate in a brief glance. Would she never find Stillwell's message. It was the last. It was lengthy. It read:

Bought Stewart's release. Also arranged for his transfer as prisoner of war. Both matters official. He's safe if we can get notice to his captors. Not sure I've reached

them by wire. Afraid to trust it. You go with Link to
Agua Prieta. Take the messages sent you in Spanish.
They will protect you and secure Stewart's freedom.
Take Nels with you. Stop for nothing. Tell Link all—
trust him—let him drive that car.

STILLWELL

The first few lines of Stillwell's message lifted Madeline to
the heights of thanksgiving and happiness. Then, reading on,
she experienced a check, a numb, icy, sickening pang. At the
last line she flung off doubt and dread, and in white, cold passion faced the issue.

"Read," she said, briefly, handing the telegram to Link. He
scanned it and then looked blankly up at her.

"Link, do you know the roads, the trails—the desert between here and Agua Prieta?" she asked.

"Thet's sure my old stampin'-ground. An' I know Sonora,
too."

"We must reach Agua Prieta before sunset—long before,
so if Stewart is in some nearby camp we can get to it in—in
time."

"Miss Majesty, it ain't possible!" he exclaimed. "Stillwell's
crazy to say thet."

"Link, can an automobile be driven from here into northern Mexico?"

"Sure. But it'd take time."

"We must do it in little time," she went on, in swift eagerness. "Otherwise Stewart may be—probably will be—be
shot."

Link Stevens appeared suddenly to grow lax, shriveled, to
lose all his peculiar pert brightness, to weaken and age.

"I'm only a—a cowboy, Miss Majesty." He almost faltered.
It was a singular change in him. "Thet's an awful ride—down
over the border. If by some luck I didn't smash the car I'd
turn your hair gray. You'd never be no good after thet ride!"

"I am Stewart's wife," she answered him, and she looked at
him, not conscious of any motive to persuade or allure, but
just to let him know the greatness of her dependence upon
him.

He started violently—the old action of Stewart, the memorable action of Monty Price. This man was of the same wild
breed.

Then Madeline's words flowed in a torrent. "I am Stewart's wife. I love him; I have been unjust to him; I must save him. Link, I have faith in you. I beseech you to do your best for Stewart's sake—for my sake. I'll risk the ride gladly—bravely. I'll not care where or how you drive. I'd far rather plunge into a cañon—go to my death on the rocks—than not try to save Stewart."

How beautiful the response of this rude cowboy—to realize his absolute unconsciousness of self, to see the haggard shade burn out of his face, the old, cool, devil-may-care spirit return to his eyes, and to feel something wonderful about him then! It was more than will or daring or sacrifice. A blood-tie might have existed between him and Madeline. She sensed again that indefinable brother-like quality, so fine, so almost invisible, which seemed to be an inalienable trait in these wild cowboys.

"Miss Majesty, thet ride figgers impossible, but I'll do it!" he replied. His cool, bright glance thrilled her. "I'll need mebbe half an hour to go over the car an' to pack on what I'll want."

She could not thank him, and her reply was merely a request that he tell Nels and other cowboys off duty to come up to the house. When Link had gone Madeline gave a moment's thought to preparations for the ride. She placed what money she had and the telegrams in a satchel. The gown she had on was thin and white, not suitable for travel, but she would not risk the losing of one moment in changing it. She put on a long coat and wound veils round her head and neck, arranging them in a hood so she could cover her face when necessary. She remembered to take an extra pair of goggles for Nels's use, and then, drawing on her gloves, she went out ready for the ride.

A number of cowboys were waiting. She explained the situation and left them in charge of her home. With that she asked Nels to accompany her down into the desert. He turned white to his lips, and this occasioned Madeline to remember his mortal dread of the car and Link's driving.

"Nels, I'm sorry to ask you," she added. "I know you hate the car. But I need you—may need you, oh! so much."

"Why, Miss Majesty, thet's shore all a mistaken idee of yours about me hatin' the car," he said, in his slow, soft drawl. "I was only jealous of Link; an' the boys, they made

289

thet joke up on me about bein' scared of ridin' fast. Shore I'm powerful proud to go. An' I reckon if you hedn't asked me my feelin's might hev been some hurt. Because if you're goin' down among the Greasers you want me."

His cool, easy speech, his familiar swagger, the smile with which he regarded her did not in the least deceive Madeline. The gray was still in his face. Incomprehensible as it seemed, Nels had a dread, an uncanny fear, and it was of that huge white automobile. But he lied about it. Here again was that strange quality of faithfulness.

Madeline heard the buzz of the car. Link appeared, driving up the slope. He made a short, sliding turn and stopped before the porch. Link had tied two long, heavy planks upon the car, one on each side, and in every available space he had strapped extra tires. A huge cask occupied one back seat, and another seat was full of tools and ropes. There was just room in this rear part of the car for Nels to squeeze in. Link put Madeline in front beside him, then bent over the wheel. Madeline waved her hand at the silent cowboys on the porch. Not an audible good-by was spoken.

The car glided out of the yard, leaped from level to slope, and started swiftly down the road, out into the open valley. Each stronger rush of dry wind in Madeline's face marked the increase of speed. She took one glance at the winding cattle road, smooth, unobstructed, disappearing in the gray of distance. She took another at the leather-garbed, leather-helmeted driver beside her, and then she drew the hood of veils over her face and fastened it round her neck so there was no possibility of its blowing loose.

Harder and stronger pressed the wind till it was like sheeted lead forcing her back in her seat. There was a ceaseless, intense, inconceivably rapid vibration under her; occasionally she felt a long swing, as if she were to be propelled aloft; but no jars disturbed the easy celerity of the car. The buzz, the roar of wheels, of heavy body in flight, increased to a continuous droning hum. The wind became an insupportable body moving toward her, crushing her breast, making the task of breathing most difficult. To Madeline the time seemed to fly with the speed of miles. A moment came when she detected a faint difference in hum and rush and vibration, in the ceaseless sweeping of the invisible weight against her. This difference became marked. Link was reducing speed. Then came swift change of all sensation, and she realized the car had slowed to normal travel.

Madeline removed her hood and goggles. It was a relief to breathe freely, to be able to use her eyes. To her right, not far distant, lay the little town of Chiricahua. Sight of it made her remember Stewart in a way strange to her constant thought of him. To the left inclined the gray valley. The red desert was hidden from view, but the Guadalupe Mountains loomed close in the southwest.

Opposite Chiricahua, where the road forked, Link Stevens headed the car straight south and gradually increased speed. Madeline faced another endless gray incline. It was the San Bernardino Valley. The singing of the car, the stinging of the wind warned her to draw the hood securely down over her face again, and then it was as if she was riding at night. The car lurched ahead, settled into that driving speed which wedged Madeline back as in a vise. Again the moments went by fleet as the miles. Seemingly, there was an acceleration of the car till it reached a certain swiftness—a period of time in which it held that pace, and then a diminishing of all motion and sound which contributed to Madeline's acute sensation. Uncovering her face, she saw Link was passing another village. Could it be Bernardino? She asked Link—repeated the question.

"Sure," he replied, "Eighty miles."

Link did not this time apologize for the work of his machine. Madeline marked the omission with her first thrill of the ride. Leaning over, she glanced at Link's watch, which he had fastened upon the wheel in front of his eyes. A quarter to ten! Link had indeed made short work of the valley miles.

Beyond Bernardino Link sheered off the road and put the car to a long, low-rising slope. Here the valley appeared to run south under the dark brows of the Guadalupes. Link was heading southwest. Madeline observed that the grass began to fail as they climbed the ridge; bare, white, dusty spots appeared; there were patches of mesquite and cactus and scattering areas of broken rock.

She might have been prepared for what she saw from the ridge-top. Beneath them the desert blazed. Seen from afar, it was striking enough, but riding down into its red jaws gave Madeline the first affront to her imperious confidence. All about her ranch had been desert, the valleys were desert; but this was different. Here began the red desert, extending far into Mexico, far across Arizona and California to the Pacific. She saw a bare, hummocky ridge, down which the car was gliding, bounding, swinging, and this long slant seemed to merge into a corrugated world of rock and sand, patched by flats and basins, streaked with cañons and ranges of ragged saw-toothed stone. The distant Sierra Madres were clearer, bluer, less smoky and suggestive of mirage than she had ever seen them. Madeline's sustaining faith upheld her in the face of this appalling obstacle. Then the desert that had rolled its immensity beneath her gradually began to rise, to lose its distant margins, to condense its varying lights and shades, at last to hide its yawning depths and looming heights behind red ridges, which were only little steps, little outposts, little landmarks at its gates.

The bouncing of the huge car, throwing Madeline up, directed her attention and fastened it upon the way Link Stevens was driving and upon the immediate foreground. Then she discovered that he was following an old wagon road. At the foot of that long slope they struck into rougher ground, and here Link took to a cautious zigzag course. The wagon road disappeared and then presently reappeared. But Link did not always hold to it. He made cuts, detours, crosses, and all the time seemed to be getting deeper into a maze of low, red dunes, of flat cañon-beds lined by banks of gravel, of ridges mounting higher. Yet Link Stevens kept on and never turned back. He never headed into a place that he could not pass. Up to this point of travel he had not been compelled to back the car, and Madeline began to realize that it was the cowboy's wonderful judgment of ground that made advance possible. He knew the country; he was never at a loss; after making a choice of direction, he never hesitated.

Then at the bottom of a wide cañon he entered a wash where the wheels just barely turned in dragging sand. The sun beat down white-hot, the dust arose, there was not a breath of wind; and no sound save the slide of a rock now and then down the weathered slopes and the labored chugging of the machine. The snail pace, like the sand at the wheels, began to drag at Madeline's faith. Link gave over the wheel to Madeline, and, leaping out, he called Nels. When they untied the long planks and laid them straight in front for the wheels to pass over Madeline saw how wise had been Link's forethought. With the aid of those planks they worked the car through sand and gravel otherwise impossible to pass.

This cañon widened and opened into space affording an unobstructed view for miles. The desert sloped up in steps, and in the morning light, with the sun bright on the mesas and escarpments, it was gray, drab, stone, slate, yellow, pink, and, dominating all, a dull rust-red. There was level ground ahead, a windswept floor as hard as rock. Link rushed the car over this free distance. Madeline's ears filled with a droning hum like the sound of a monstrous, hungry bee and with a strange, incessant crinkle which she at length guessed to be the spreading of sheets of gravel from under the wheels. The giant car attained such a speed that Madeline could only distinguish the colored landmarks to the fore, and these faded as the wind stung her eyes.

Then Link began the ascent of the first step, a long, sweeping, barren waste with dunes of wonderful violet and heliotrope hues. Here were well-defined marks of an old wagon road lately traversed by cattle. The car climbed steadily, surmounted the height, faced another long bench that had been cleaned smooth by desert winds. The sky was an intense, light, steely blue, hard on the eyes. Madeline veiled her face, and did not uncover it until Link had reduced the racing speed. From the summit of the next ridge she saw more red ruin of desert.

A deep wash crossing the road caused Link Stevens to turn due south. There was a narrow space along the wash just wide enough for the car. Link seemed oblivious to the fact that the outside wheels were perilously close to the edge. Madeline heard the rattle of loosened gravel and earth sliding into the gully. The wash widened and opened out into a sandy flat. Link crossed this and turned up on the opposite side. Rocks impeded the progress of the car, and these had to be rolled out of the way. The shelves of silt, apparently ready to slide with the slightest weight, the little tributary washes, the boulder-strewn stretches of slope, the narrow spaces allowing no more than a foot for the outside wheels, the spear-pointed cactus that had to be avoided—all these obstacles were as nothing to the cowboy driver. He kept on, and when he came to the road again he made up for the lost time by speed.

Another height was reached, and here Madeline fancied that Link had driven the car to the summit of a high pass between two mountain ranges. The western slope of that pass appeared to be exceedingly rough and broken. Below it spread out another gray valley, at the extreme end of which glistened a white spot that Link grimly called Douglas. Part of that white spot was Agua Prieta, the sister town across the line. Madeline looked with eyes that would fain have pierced the intervening distance.

The descent of the pass began under difficulties. Sharp stones and cactus spikes penetrated the front tires, bursting them with ripping reports. It took time to replace them. The planks were called into requisition to cross soft places. A jagged point of projecting rock had to be broken with a sledge. At length a huge stone appeared to hinder any further advance. Madeline caught her breath. There was no room to turn the car. But Link Stevens had no intention of such a thing. He backed the car to a considerable distance, then walked forward. He appeared to be busy around the boulder for a moment and returned down the road on the run. A heavy explosion, a cloud of dust, and a rattle of falling fragments told Madeline that her indomitable driver had cleared a passage with dynamite. He seemed to be prepared for every emergency. Madeline looked to see what effect the discovery of Link carrying dynamite would have upon the silent Nels.

"Shore, now, Miss Majesty, there ain't nothin' goin' to stop Link," said Nels, with a reassuring smile. The significance of the incident had not dawned upon Nels or else he was heedless of it. After all, he was afraid only of the car and Link, and fear was an idiosyncrasy. Madeline began to see her cowboy driver with clearer eyes and his spirit awoke something in her that made danger of no moment. Nels likewise subtly responded, and, though he was gray-faced, tight-lipped, his eyes took on the cool, bright gleam of Link's.

Cactus barred the way, rocks barred the way, gullies barred the way, and these Nels addressed in the grim humor with which he was wont to view tragic things. A mistake on Link's part, a slip of a wheel, a bursting of a tire at a critical moment, an instant of the bad luck which might happen a hundred times on a less perilous ride—any one of these might spell disaster for the car, perhaps death to the occupants. Again and again Link used the planks to cross washes in sand. Sometimes the wheels ran all the length of the planks, sometimes slipped off. Presently Link came to a ditch where water had worn deep into the road. Without hesitation he placed them, measuring distance carefully, and then started across. The danger was in ditching the machine. One of the planks split, sagged a little, but Link made the crossing without a slip.

The road led round under an overhanging cliff and was narrow, rocky, and slightly downhill. Bidding Madeline and Nels walk round this hazardous corner. Link drove the car. Madeline expected to hear it crash down into the cañon, but presently she saw Link waiting to take them aboard again. Then came steeper parts of the road, places that Link could run down if he had space below to control the car, and on the other hand places where the little inclines ended in abrupt ledges upon one side or a declivity upon the other. Here the cowboy, with ropes on the wheels and half-hitches upon the spurs of rock, let the car slide down.

Once at a particularly bad spot Madeline exclaimed involuntarily, "Oh, time is flying!" Link Stevens looked up at her as if he had been reproved for his care. His eyes shone like the glint of steel on ice. Perhaps that utterance of Madeline's was needed to liberate his recklessness to its utmost. Certainly he put the car to seemingly impossible feats. He rimmed gullies, he hurdled rising ground, he leaped little breaks in the even road. He made his machine cling like a goat to steep inclines; he rounded corners with the inside wheels higher than the outside; he crossed weak places. He kept on and on, threading tortuous passages through rockstrewn patches, keeping to the old road where it was clear, abandoning it for open spaces, and always going down.

At length a mile of clean, brown slope, ridged and grooved like a washboard, led gently down to meet the floor of the valley, where the scant grama-grass struggled to give a tinge of gray. The road appeared to become more clearly defined, and could be seen striking straight across the valley.

To Madeline's dismay, that road led down to a deep, narrow wash. It plunged on one side, ascended on the other at a still steeper angle. The crossing would have been laborsome for a horse; for an automobile it was impassable. Link turned the car to the right along the rim and drove as far along the wash as the ground permitted. The gully widened, deepened all the way. Then he took the other direction. When he made his turn Madeline observed that the sun had perceptibly begun its slant westward. It shone in her face, glaring and wrathful. Link drove back to the road, crossed it, and kept on down the line of the wash. It was a deep cut in red earth, worn straight down by swift water in the rainy seasons. It narrowed. In some places it was only five feet wide. Link studied these points and looked up the slope, and seemed to be making deductions. The valley was level now, and there were nothing but little breaks in the rim of the wash. Link drove mile after mile, looking for a place to cross, and there was none. Finally progress to the south was obstructed by impassable gullies where the wash plunged into the head of a cañon. It was necessary to back the car a distance before there was room to turn. Madeline looked at the imperturbable driver. His face revealed no more than the same old hard immutable character. When he reached the narrowest points, which had so interested him he got out of the car and walked from place to place. Once with a little jump he cleared the wash. Then Madeline noted that the farther rim was somewhat lower. In a flash she divined Link's intention. He was hunting a place to jump the car over the crack in the ground.

Soon he found one that seemed to suit him for he tied his red scarf upon a greasewood-bush. Then, returning to the car, he clambered in, and, muttering, broke his long silence; "This ain't no airship but I've outfiggered thet damn wash." He backed up the gentle slope and halted just short of steeper ground. His red scarf waved in the wind. Hunching low over the wheel he started slowly at first then faster and then faster. The great car gave a spring like a huge tiger. The impact of suddenly formed wind almost tore Madeline out of her seat. She felt Nels's powerful hands on her shoulders. She closed her eyes. The jolting headway of the car gave place to a gliding rush. This was broken by a slight jar and then above the hum and roar rose a cowboy yell. Madeline waited with strained nerves for the expected crash. It did not come. Opening her eyes she saw the level valley floor without a break. She had not even noticed the instant when the car had shot over the wash.

A strange breathlessness attacked her and she attributed it to the celerity with which she was being carried along. Pulling the hood down over her face she sank low in the seat. The whir of the car now seemed to be a world-filling sound. Again the feeling of excitement, the poignancy of emotional heights, the ever-present impending sense of catastrophe became held in abeyance to the sheer intensity of physical sensations. There came a time when all her strength seemed to unite in an effort to lift her breast against the terrific force of the wind—to draw air into her flattened lungs. She became partly dazed. The darkness before her eyes was not all occasioned by the blood that pressed like a stone mask on her face. She had a sense that she was floating, sailing, drifting, reeling, even while being borne swiftly as a thunderbolt. Her hands and arms were immovable under the weight of mountains. There was a long, blank period from which she awakened to feel an arm supporting her. Then she rallied. The velocity of the car had been cut to the speed to which she was accustomed. Throwing back the hood, she breathed freely again, recovered fully.

The car was bowling along a wide road upon the outskirts of a city. Madeline asked what place it could be.

"Douglas," replied Link. "An' jest around is Agua Prieta!"

That last name seemed to stun Madeline. She heard no more, and saw little until the car stopped. Nels spoke to some one. Then sight of khaki-clad soldiers quickened Madeline's faculties. She was on the boundary-line between the United States and Mexico, and Agua Prieta, with its white and blue walled houses, its browntiled roofs, lay before her. A soldier, evidently despatched by Nels, returned and said an officer would come at once. Madeline's attention was centered in the foreground, upon the guard over the road, upon the dry, dusty town beyond; but she was aware of noise and people in the rear. A cavalry officer approached the car, stared, and removed his sombrero.

"Can you tell me anything about Stewart, the American cowboy who was captured by rebels a few days ago?" asked Madeline.

"Yes," replied the officer. "There was a skirmish over the line between a company of Federals and a large force of guerrillas and rebels. The Federals were driven west along the line. Stewart is reported to have done reckless fighting and was captured. He got a Mexican sentence. He is known here along the border, and the news of his capture stirred up excitement. We did all we could to get his release. The guerrillas feared to execute him here, and believed he might be aided to escape. So a detachment departed with him for Mezquital."

"He was sentenced to be shot Thursday at sunset—to-night?"

"Yes. It was rumored there was a personal resentment against Stewart. I regret that I can't give you definite information. If you are friends of Stewart's—relatives—I might find—"

"I am his wife," interrupted Madeline. "Will you please read these." She handed him the telegrams. "Advise me—help me, if you can?"

With a wondering glance at her the officer received the telegrams. He read several, and whistled low in amaze. His manner became quick, alert, serious.

"I can't read these written in Spanish, but I know the names signed." Swiftly he ran through the others. "Why, these mean Stewart's release has been authorized. They explain mysterious rumors we have heard here. Greaser treachery! For some strange reason messages from the rebel junta have failed to reach their destination. We heard reports of an exchange for Stewart, but nothing came of it. No one departed for Mezquital with authority. What an outrage! Come, I'll go with you to General Salazar, the rebel chief in command. I know him. Perhaps we can find out something."

Nels made room for the officer. Link sent the car whirring across the line into Mexican territory. Madeline's sensibilities were now exquisitely alive. The white road led into Agua Prieta, a town of colored walls and roofs. Goats and pigs and buzzards scattered before the roar of the machine. Native women wearing black mantles peeped through iron-barred windows. Men wearing huge sombreros, cotton shirts and trousers, bright sashes round their waists, and sandals, stood motionless, watching the car go by. The road ended in an immense plaza, in the center of which was a circular structure that in some measure resembled a corral. It was a bull-ring, where the national sport of bull-fighting was carried on. Just now it appeared to be quarters for a considerable army. Ragged, unkempt rebels were everywhere, and the whole square was littered with tents, packs, wagons, arms. There were horses, mules, burrows, and oxen.

The place was so crowded that Link was compelled to drive slowly up to the entrance to the bull-ring. Madeline caught a glimpse of tents inside, then her view was obstructed by a curious, pressing throng. The cavalry officer leaped from the car, pushed his way into the entrance.

"Link, do you know the road to this Mezquital?" asked Madeline.

"Yes. I've been there."

"How far is it?"

"Aw, not so very far," he mumbled.

"Link! How many miles?" she implored.

"I reckon only a few."

Madeline knew that he lied. She asked him no more, nor looked at him, nor at Nels. How stifling was this crowded, ill-smelling plaza! The sun, red and lowering, had sloped far down in the west, but still burned with furnace heat. A swarm of flies whirled over the car. The shadows of low-sailing buzzards crossed Madeline's sight. Then she saw a row of the huge, uncanny black birds sitting upon the tiled roof of a house. They had neither an air of sleeping nor resting. They were waiting. She fought off a horrible ghastly idea before its full realization. These rebels and guerrillas—what lean, yellow, bearded wretches! They curiously watched Link as he went working over the car. No two were alike, and all were ragged. They had glittering eyes sunk deep in their heads. They were an excited, jabbering, gesticulating mob. Madeline shuddered to think how a frenzy to spill blood could run through these poor revolutionists. If it was liberty they fought for, they did not show the intelligence in their faces. They were like wolves upon a scent. They affronted her, shocked her. She wondered if their officers were men of the same class. What struck her at last and stirred pity in her was the fact that every man of the horde her swift glance roamed over, however dirty and bedraggled he was, wore upon him some ornaments, some tassel or fringe or lace, some ensign, some band, bracelet, badge or belt, some twist of scarf, something that betrayed the vanity which was the poor jewel of their souls. It was in the race.

Suddenly the crowd parted to let the cavalry officer and a rebel of striking presence get to the car.

"Madam, it is as I suspected," said the officer, quickly. "The messages directing Stewart's release never reached Salazar. They were intercepted But even without them we might have secured Stewart's exchange if it had not been for the fact that one of his captors wanted him shot. This guerrilla intercepted the orders, and then was instrumental in taking Stewart to Mezquital. It is exceedingly sad. Why, he should be a free man this instant. I regret—"

"Who did this—this thing?" cried Madeline, cold and sick. "Who is the guerrilla?"

"Señor Don Carlos Martinez. He has been a bandit, a man of influence in Sonora. He is more of a secret agent in the affairs of the revolution than an active participator. But he has seen guerrilla service."

"Don Carlos! Stewart in his power! O God!" Madeline sank down, almost overcome. Then two great hands, powerful, thrilling, clasped her shoulders, and Nels bent over her.

"Miss Majesty, shore we're wastin' time here," he said. His voice, like his hands, was uplifting. She wheeled to him in trembling importunity. How cold, bright, blue the flash of his eyes! They told Madeline she must not weaken. But she could not speak her thought to Nels—could only look at Link.

"It figgers impossible, but I'll do it!" said Link Stevens, in answer to her voiceless query. The cold, grim, wild something about her cowboys blanched Madeline's face, steeled her nerve, called to the depths of her for that last supreme courage of a woman. The spirit of the moment was nature with Link and Nels; with her it must be passion

"Can I get a permit to go into the interior—to Mezquital?" asked Madeline of the officer.

"You are going on? Madam, it's a forlorn hope. Mezquital is a hundred miles away. But there's a chance—the barest chance if your man can drive this car. The Mexicans are either murderous or ceremonious in their executions. The arrangements for Stewart's will be elaborate. But, barring unusual circumstances, it will take place precisely at the hour designated. You need no permit. Your messages are official papers. But to save time, perhaps delay, I suggest you take this Mexican, Señor Montes, with you. He outranks Don Carlos and knows the captain of the Mezquital detachment."

"Ah! Then Don Carlos is not in command of the forces holding Stewart?"

"No."

"I thank you, sir. I shall not forget your kindness," concluded Madeline.

She bowed to Señor Montes, and requested him to enter the car. Nels stowed some of the paraphernalia away, making room in the rear seat. Link bent over the wheel. The start was so sudden, with such crack and roar, that the crowd split in wild disorder. Out of the plaza the car ran, gathering headway; down a street lined by white and blue walls; across a square where rebels were building barricades; along a railroad track full of iron flat-cars that carried mounted pieces of artillery; through the outlying guards, who waved to the officer, Montes.

Madeline bound her glasses tightly over her eyes, and wound veils round the lower part of her face. She was all in a strange glow, she had begun to burn, to throb, to thrill, to expand, and she meant to see all that was possible. The sullen sun, red as fire, hung over the mountain range in the west. How low it had sunk! Before her stretched a narrow, white road, dusty, hard as stone—a highway that had been used for centuries. If it had been wide enough to permit passing a vehicle it would have been a magnificent course for automobiles. But the weeds and the dusty flowers and the mesquite boughs and arms of cactus brushed the car as it sped by.

Faster, faster, faster! That old resistless weight began to press Madeline back; the old incessant bellow of wind filled her ears. Link Stevens hunched low over the wheel. His eyes were hidden under leather helmet and goggles, but the lower part of his face was unprotected. He resembled a demon, so dark and stone-hard and strangely grinning was he. All at once Madeline realized how matchless, how wonderful a driver was this cowboy. She divined that weakening could not have been possible to Link Stevens. He was a cowboy, and he really was riding that car, making it answer to his will, as it had been born in him to master a horse. He had never driven to suit himself, had never reached an all-satisfying speed until now. Beyond that his motive was to save Stewart—to make Madeline happy. Life was nothing to him. That fact gave him the superhuman nerve to face the peril of this ride. Because of his disregard of self he was able to operate the machine, to choose the power, the speed, the guidance, the going with the best judgment and highest efficiency possible. Madeline knew he would get her to Mezquital in time to save Stewart or he would kill her in the attempt.

The white, narrow road flashed out of the foreground, slipped with inconceivable rapidity under the car. When she marked a clump of cactus far ahead it seemed to shoot at her, to speed behind her even the instant she noticed it. Nevertheless, Madeline knew Link was not putting the car to its limit. Swiftly as he was flying, he held something in reserve. But he took the turns of the road as if he knew the way was cleared before him. He trusted to a cowboy's luck. A wagon in one of those curves, a herd of cattle, even a frightened steer, meant a wreck. Madeline never closed her eyes at these fateful moments. If Link could stake himself, the others, and her upon such chance, what could not she stake with her motive? So while the great car hummed and thrummed and darted round the curves on two wheels, and sped on like a bullet, Madeline lived that ride, meant to feel it to the uttermost.

But it was not all swift going. A stretch of softer ground delayed Link, made the car labor and pant and pound and grind through gravel. Moreover, the cactus plants assumed an alarming ability to impede progress. Long, slender arms of the ocotillo encroached upon the road; broad, round leaves did likewise, fluted columns, fallen like timbers in a forest, lay along the narrow margins; the bayonet cactus and the bisnagi leaned threateningly; clusters of maguey, shadowed by the huge, looming saguaro, infringed upon the highway to Mezquital. And every leaf and blade and branch of cactus bore wicked thorns, any one of which would be fatal to a tire.

It came at length, the bursting report. The car lurched, went on like a crippled thing, and halted, obedient to the master hand at the wheel. Swift as Link was in replacing the tire, he lost time. The red sun, more sullen, duskier as it neared the black, bold horizon, appeared to mock Madeline, to eye her in derision.

Link leaped in, and the car sprang ahead. The roadbed changed, the trees changed—all the surroundings changed except the cactus. There were miles of rolling ridges, rough in the hollows, and short rocky bits of road, and washes to cross and a low, sandy swale where mesquites grouped a forest along a trickling inch-deep sheet of water. Green things softened the hard, dry aspect of the desert. There were birds and parrots and deer and wild boars. All these Madeline remarked with clear eyes, with remarkable susceptibility of attention; but what she strained to see, what she yearned for, prayed for, was straight, unobstructed road.

But the road began to wind up; it turned and twisted in tantalizing lazy curves; it was in no hurry to surmount a hill that began to assume proportions of a mountain; it was leisurely, as were all things in Mexico except strife. That was quick, fierce, bloody—it was Spanish.

The descent from that elevation was difficult, extremely hazardous, yet Link Stevens drove fast. At the base of the hill rocks and sand all but halted him for good. Then in taking an abrupt curve a grasping spear ruined another tire. This time the car rasped across the road into the cactus, bursting the second front-wheel tire. Like demons indeed Link and Nels worked. Shuddering, Madeline felt the declining heat of the sun, saw with gloomy eyes the shading of the red light over the desert. She did not look back to see how near the sun was to the horizon. She wanted to ask Nels. Strange as anything on this terrible ride was the absence of speech. As yet no word had been spoken. Madeline wanted to shriek to Link to hurry. But he was more than humanly swift in all his actions. So with mute lips, with the fire in her beginning to chill, with a lifelessness menacing her spirit, she watched, hoped against hope, prayed for a long, straight, smooth road.

Quite suddenly she saw it, seemingly miles of clear, narrow lane disappearing like a thin, white streak in distant green. Perhaps Link Stevens's heart leaped like Madeline's. The huge car with a roar and a jerk seemed to answer Madeline's call, a cry no less poignant because it was silent.

Faster, faster, faster! The roar became a whining hum. Then for Madeline sound ceased to be anything—she could not hear. The wind was now heavy, imponderable, no longer a swift, plastic thing, but solid, like an onrushing wall. It bore down upon Madeline with such resistless weight that she could not move. The green of desert plants along the road merged in two shapeless fences, sliding at her from the distance. Objects ahead began to blur the white road, to grow streaky, like rays of light, the sky to take on more of a reddening haze.

Madeline, realizing her sight was failing her, turned for one more look at Link Stevens. It had come to be his ride almost as much as it was hers. He hunched lower than ever, rigid, strained to the last degree, a terrible, implacable driver. This was his hour, and he was great. If he so much as brushed a flying tire against one of the millions of spikes clutching out, striking out from the cactus, there would be a shock, a splitting wave of air—an end. Madeline thought she saw that Link's bulging cheek and jaw were gray, that his tight-shut lips were white, that the smile was gone. Then he really was human—not a demon. She felt a strange sense of brotherhood. He understood a woman's soul as Monty Price had understood it. Link was the lightning-forged automaton, the driving, relentless, unconquerable instrument of a woman's will. He was a man whose force was directed by a woman's passion. He reached up to her height, felt her love, understood the nature of her agony. These made him heroic. But it was the hard life, the wild years of danger on the desert, the companionship of ruthless men, the elemental, that made possible his physical achievement. Madeline loved his spirit then and gloried in the man.

She had pictured upon her heart, never to be forgotten, this little hunched, deformed figure of Link's hanging with dauntless, with deathless grip over the wheel, his gray face like a marble mask.

That waas Madeline's last clear sensation upon the ride. Blinded, dazed, she succumbed to the demands upon her strength. She reeled, fell back, only vaguely aware of a helping hand. Confusion seized her senses. All about her was a dark chaos through which she was rushing, rushing, rushing under the wrathful red eye of a setting sun. Then, as there was no more sound or sight for her, she felt there was no color. But the rush never slackened—a rush through opaque, limitless space. For moments, hours, ages she was propelled with the velocity of a shooting-star. The earth seemed a huge automobile. And it sped with her down an endless white track through the universe. Looming, ghostly, spectral forms of cacti plants, large as pine trees, stabbed her with giant spikes. She became an unstable being in a shapeless, colorless, soundless cosmos of unrelated things, but always rushing, even to meet the darkness that haunted her and never reached her.

But at an end of infinite time that rush ceased. Madeline lost the queer feeling of being disembodied by a frightfully swift careening through boundless distance. She distinguished voices, low at first, apparently far away. Then she opened her eyes to blurred but conscious sight.

The car had come to a stop. Link was lying face down over the wheel. Nels was rubbing her hands, calling to her. She saw a house with clean whitewashed wall and brown-tiled roof. Beyond, over a dark mountain range, peeped the last red curve, the last beautiful ray of the setting sun.

25

At the End of the Road

Madeline saw that the car was surrounded by armed Mexicans. They presented a contrast to the others she had seen that day; she wondered a little at their silence, at their respectful front.

Suddenly a sharp order opened up the ranks next to the house. Señor Montes appeared in the break, coming swiftly. His dark face wore a smile; his manner was courteous, important, authoritative.

"Señora, it is not too late!"

He spoke her language with an accent strange to her, so that it seemed to hinder understanding.

"Señora, you got here in time," he went on. "El Capitan Stewart will be free."

"Free!" she whispered.

She rose, reeling.

"Come," replied Montes, taking her arm. "*Perdóneme*, Señora."

Without his assistance she would have fallen wholly upon Nels who supported her on the other side. They helped her alight from the car. For a moment the white walls, the hazy red sky, the dark figures of the rebels, whirled before Madeline's eyes. She took a few steps, swaying between her escorts; then the confusion of her sight and mind passed away. It was as if she quickened with a thousand vivifying currents, as if she could see and hear and feel everything in the world, as if nothing could be overlooked, forgotten, neglected.

She turned back, remembering Link. He was lurching from the car, helmet and goggles thrust back, the gray shade from his face, the cool, bright gleam of his eyes disappearing for something warmer.

Señor Montes led Madeline and her cowboys through a hall to a patio, and on through a large room with flooring of rough, bare boards that rattled, into a smaller room full of armed quiet rebels facing an open window.

Madeline scanned the faces of these men, expecting to see Don Carlos. But he was not present. A soldier addressed her in Spanish too swiftly uttered, too voluble for her to translate. But, like Señor Montes, he was gracious and, despite his ragged garb and uncouth appearance, he bore the unmistakable stamp of authority.

Montes directed Madeline's attention to a man by the window. A loose scarf of vivid red hung from his hand.

"Señora, they were waiting for the sun to set when we arrived," said Montes. "The signal was about to be given for Señor Stewart's walk to death."

"Stewart's walk!" echoed Madeline.

"Ah, Señora, let me tell you his sentence—the sentence I have had the honor and happiness to revoke for you."

Stewart had been court-martialed and sentenced according to a Mexican custom observed in cases of brave soldiers to whom honorable and fitting executions were due. His hour had been set for Thursday when the sun had sunk. Upon signal he was to be liberated and was free to walk out into the road, to take any direction he pleased. He knew his sentence; knew that death awaited him, that every possible avenue of escape was blocked by men with rifles ready. But he had not the slightest idea at what moment or from what direction the bullets were to come.

"Señora, we have sent messages to every squad of waiting soldiers—an order that El Capitan is not to be shot. He is ignorant of his release. I shall give the signal for his freedom."

Montes was ceremonious, gallant, emotional. Madeline saw his pride, and divined that the situation was one which brought out the vanity, the ostentation, as well as the cruelty of his race. He would keep her in an agony of suspense, let Stewart start upon that terrible walk in ignorance of his freedom. It was the motive of a Spaniard. Suddenly Madeline had a horrible quaking fear that Montes lied, that he meant her to be a witness of Stewart's execution. But no, the man was honest; he was only barbarous. He would satisfy certain instincts of his nature—sentiment, romance, cruelty—by starting Stewart upon that walk, by watching Stewart's actions in the face of seeming death, by seeing Madeline's agony of doubt, fear, pity, love. Almost Madeline felt that she could not endure the situation. She was weak and tottering.

"Señora! Ah, it will be one beautiful thing!" Montes caught the scarf from the rebel's hand. He was glowing, passionate; his eyes had a strange, soft, cold flash; his voice was low, intense. He was living something splendid to him. "I'll wave the scarf, Señora. That will be the signal. It will be just down at the other end of the road. Señor Stewart's jailer will see the signal, take off Stewart's irons, release him, open the door for his walk. Stewart will be free. But he will not know. He will expect death. As he is a brave man, he will face it. He will walk this way. Every step of that walk he will expect to be shot from some unknown quarter. But he will not be afraid. Señora, I have seen El Capitan fighting in the field. What is death to him? Ah, will it not be magnificent to see him come forth—to walk down? Señora, you will see what a man he is. All the way he will expect cold, swift death. Here at this end of the road he will meet his beautiful lady!"

"Is there no—no possibility of a mistake?" faltered Madeline.

"None. My order included unloading of rifles."

"Don Carlos?"

"He is in irons and must answer to General Salazar," replied Montes.

Madeline looked down the deserted road. How strange to see the last ruddy glow of the sun over the brow of the mountain range! The thought of that sunset had been torture for her. Yet it had passed, and now the afterlights were luminous, beautiful, prophetic.

With a heart stricken by both joy and agony, she saw Montes wave the scarf.

Then she waited. No change manifested itself down the length of that lonely road. There was absolute silence in the room behind her. How terribly, infinitely long seemed the waiting! Never in all her future life would she forget the quaint pink, blue, and white walled houses with their colored roofs. That dusty bare road resembled one of the uncovered streets of Pompeii with its look of centuries of solitude.

Suddenly a door opened and a tall man stepped out.

307

Madeline recognized Stewart. She had to place both hands on the window-sill for support, while a storm of emotions swayed her. Like a retreating wave it rushed away. Stewart lived. He was free. He had stepped out into the light. She had saved him. Life changed for her in that instant of realization and became sweet, full, strange.

Stewart shook hands with some one in the doorway. Then he looked up and down the road. The door closed behind him. Leisurely he rolled a cigarette, stood close to the wall while he scratched a match. Even at that distance Madeline's keen eyes caught the small flame, the first little puff of smoke.

Stewart then took to the middle of the road and leisurely began his walk.

To Madeline he appeared natural, walked as unconcernedly as if he were strolling for pleasure; but the absence of any living thing, the silence, the red haze, the surcharged atmosphere —these were all unnatural. From time to time Stewart stopped to turn face forward toward houses and corners. Only silence greeted these significant moves of his. Once he halted to roll and light another cigarette. After that his step quickened.

Madeline watched him, with pride, love, pain, glory combating for a mastery over her. This walk of his seemingly took longer than all her hours of awakening, of strife, of remorse, longer than the ride to find him. She felt that it would be impossible for her to wait till he reached the end of the road. Yet in the hurry and riot of her feelings she had fleeting panics. What could she say to him? How meet him? Well she remembered the tall, powerful form now growing close enough to distinguish its dress. Stewart's face was yet only a dark gleam. Soon she would see it—long before he could know she was there. She wanted to run to meet him. Nevertheless, she stood rooted to her covert behind the window, living that terrible walk with him to the uttermost thought of home, sister, mother, sweetheart, wife, life itself—every thought that could come to a man stalking to meet his executioners. With all that tumult in her mind and heart Madeline still fell prey to the incomprehensible variations of emotion possible to a woman. Every step Stewart took thrilled her. She had some strange subtle intuition that he was not unhappy, and that he believed beyond shadow of doubt that he was walking to his death. His steps dragged a little, though they had begun to be swift. The old, hard, physical, wild nerve of the cowboy was perhaps in conflict with spiritual growth of the finer man, realizing too late that life ought not to be sacrificed.

Then the dark gleam that was his face took shape, grew sharper and clearer. He was stalking now, and there was a suggestion of impatience in his stride. It took these hidden Mexicans a long time to kill him! At a point in the middle of the road, even with the corner of a house and opposite to Madeline's position, Stewart halted stockstill. He presented a fair mark to his executioners, and he stood there motionless a full moment.

Only silence greeted him. Plain it was to Madeline, and she thought to all who had eyes to see, that to Stewart, since for some reason he had been spared all along his walk, this was the moment when he ought to be mercifully shot. But as no shots came a rugged dignity left him for a reckless scorn manifest in the way he strolled across to the corner of the house, rolled yet another cigarette, and, presenting a broad breast to the window, smoked and waited.

That wait was almost unendurable for Madeline. Perhaps it was only a moment, several moments at the longest, but the time seemed a year. Stewart's face was scornful, hard. Did he suspect treachery on the part of his captors, that they meant to play with him as a cat with a mouse, to murder him at leisure? Madeline was sure she caught the old, inscrutable, mocking smile fleeting across his lips. He held that position for what must have been a reasonable time to his mind, then with a laugh and a shrug he threw the cigarette into the road. He shook his head as if at the incomprehensible motives of men who could have no fair reasons now for delay.

He made a sudden violent action that was more than a straightening of his powerful frame. It was the old instinctive violence. Then he faced north. Madeline read his thought, knew he was thinking of her, calling her a last silent farewell. He would serve her to his last breath, leave her free. Keep his secret. That picture of him, dark-browed, fire-eyed, strangely sad and strong, sank indelibly into Madeline's heart of hearts.

The next instant he was striding forward, to force by bold and scornful presence a speedy fulfillment of his sentence.

Madeline stepped into the door, crossed the threshold. Stewart staggered as if indeed the bullets he expected had pierced him in mortal wound. His dark face turned white.

OLD MASTER OF THE OLD WEST
MAX BRAND

Thundering action that never quits—Max Brand
lets you have it just the way you want it.
For the very best in Western entertainment, get
these Max Brand titles, available from
Pocket Books:

- _____ 82890 BELLS OF SAN FILIPO $1.75
- _____ 82893 DANGER TRAIL $1.75
- _____ 82887 FIGHTING FOUR $1.75
- _____ 82894 HUNTED RIDERS $1.75
- _____ 82888 LONGHORN FEUD $1.75
- _____ 82885 LONG, LONG TRAIL $1.75
- _____ 82891 OUTLAW OF BUFFALO FLAT $1.75
- _____ 82886 RAWHIDE JUSTICE $1.75
- _____ 82892 REWARD $1.75
- _____ 82889 SEVEN TRAILS $1.75
- _____ 81751 SHOTGUN LAW $1.75
- _____ 83416 THE OUTLAW $1.75